POKÉMON™ ADVENTURES

GOLD & SILVER

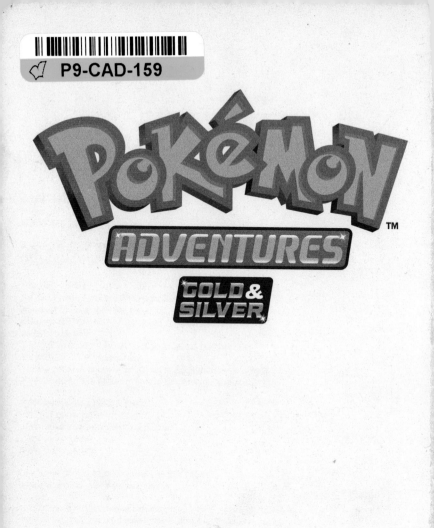

Pokémon ADVENTURES
Volume 11
VIZ Kids Edition

Story by **HIDENORI KUSAKA**
Art by **SATOSHI YAMAMOTO**

© 2011 Pokémon.
©1995-2011 Nintendo/Creatures Inc./GAME FREAK inc.
TM and ® and character names are trademarks of Nintendo.
© 1997 Hidenori KUSAKA and Satoshi YAMAMOTO/Shogakukan
All rights reserved.
Original Japanese edition "POCKET MONSTER SPECIAL"
published by SHOGAKUKAN Inc.
English translation rights in the United States of America, Canada,
the United Kingdom and Ireland arranged with SHOGAKUKAN.

English Adaptation/Gerard Jones
Translation/HC Language Solutions
Touch-up & Lettering/Annaliese Christman
Design/Sam Elzway
Editor/Annette Roman

Printed in the U.S.A.

Published by VIZ Media, LLC
P.O. Box 77010
San Francisco, CA 94107

10 9 8 7 6 5 4 3
First printing, February 2011
Third printing, October 2013

Pokémon™ Adventures

Gold & Silver

11
Volume Eleven

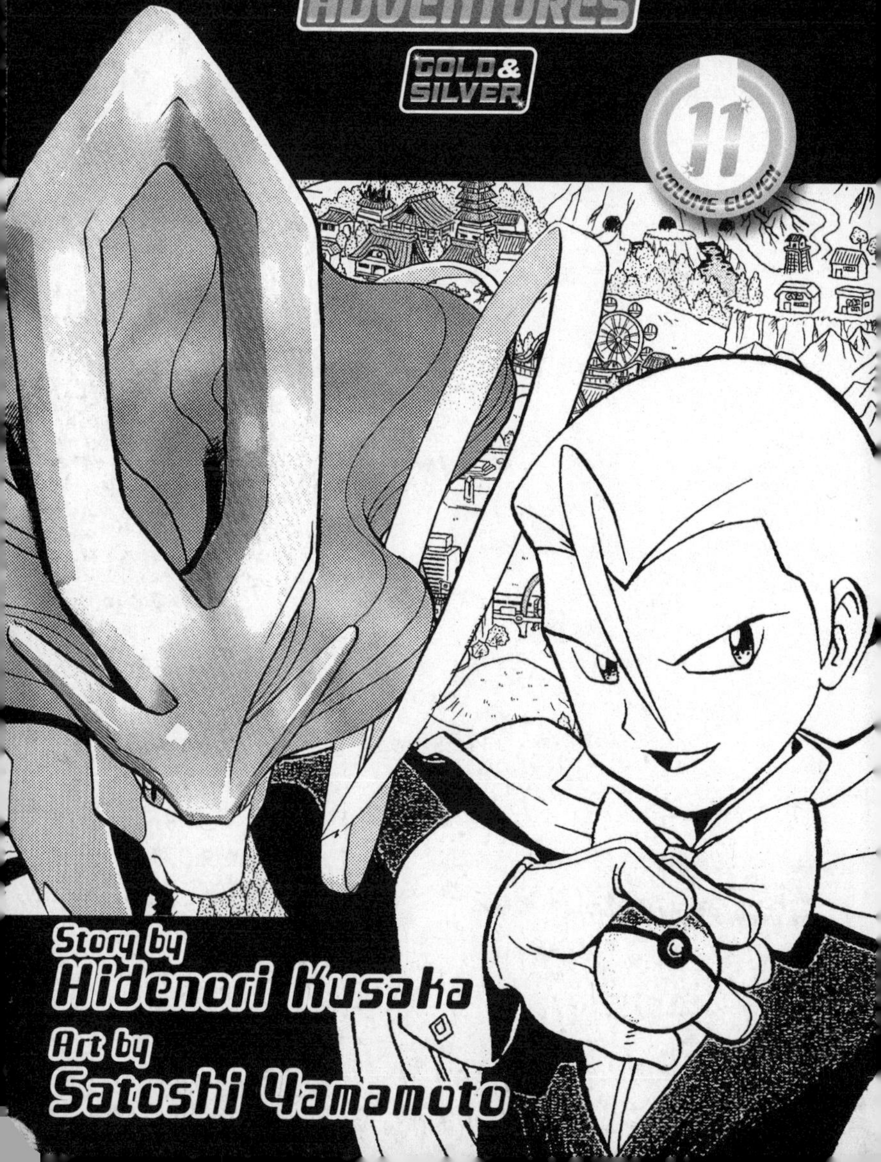

Story by
Hidenori Kusaka
Art by
Satoshi Yamamoto

CHARACTERS THUS FAR

Crystal

A Capture Specialist hired by Prof. Oak to fill out his new Pokédex. Most people call her by her nickname Crys.

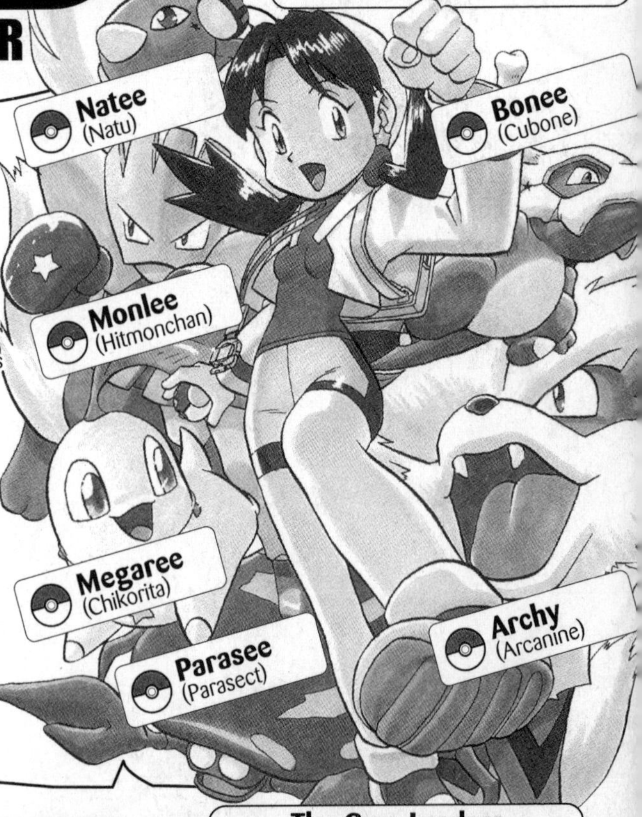
Natee
(Natu)
Bonee
(Cubone)
Monlee
(Hitmonchan)
Megaree
(Chikorita)
Archy
(Arcanine)
Parasee
(Parasect)

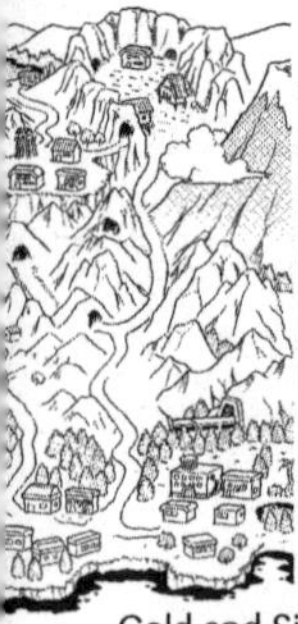

The remnants of Team Rocket prepare for their resurgence under the leadership of the mysterious Masked Man.

Gold and Silver, the new Pokédex owners, confront him, but are overpowered. And now they've both gone missing!

The Gym Leaders

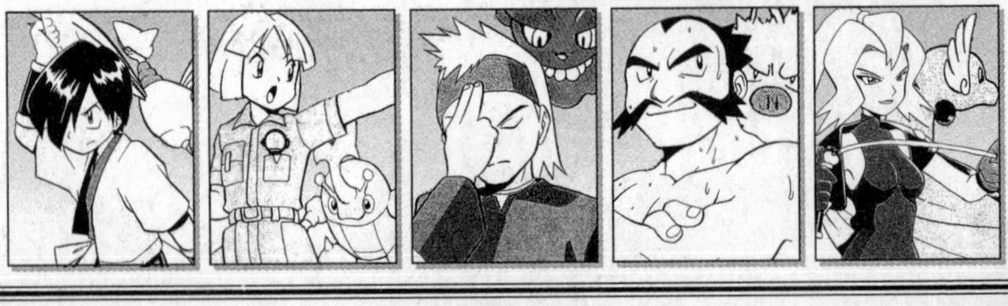

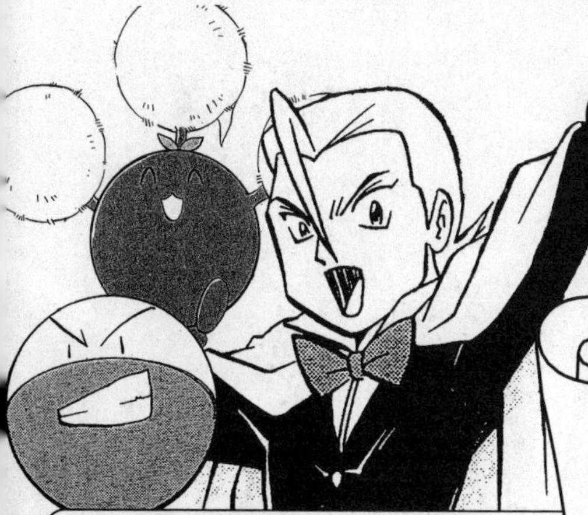

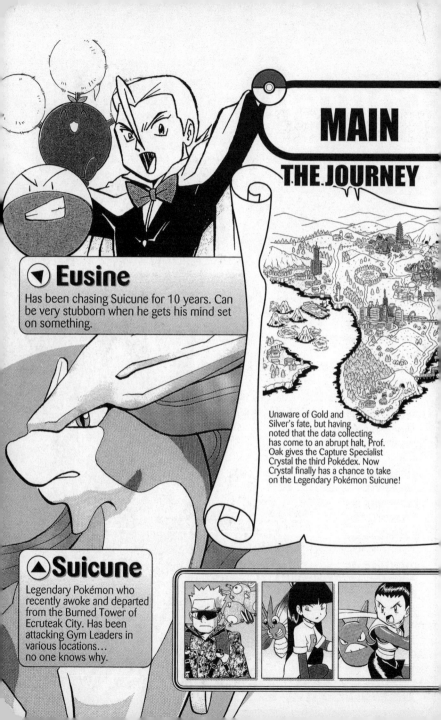

▼ Eusine

Has been chasing Suicune for 10 years. Can be very stubborn when he gets his mind set on something.

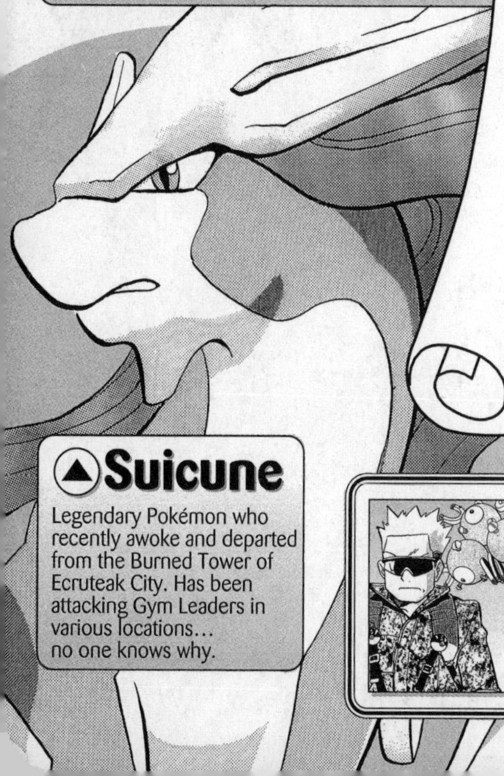

▲ Suicune

Legendary Pokémon who recently awoke and departed from the Burned Tower of Ecruteak City. Has been attacking Gym Leaders in various locations... no one knows why.

MAIN

THE JOURNEY

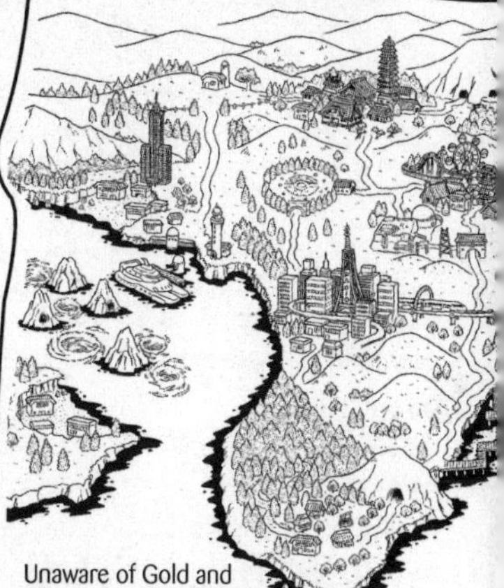

Unaware of Gold and Silver's fate, but having noted that the data collecting has come to an abrupt halt, Prof. Oak gives the Capture Specialist Crystal the third Pokédex. Now Crystal finally has a chance to take on the Legendary Pokémon Suicune!

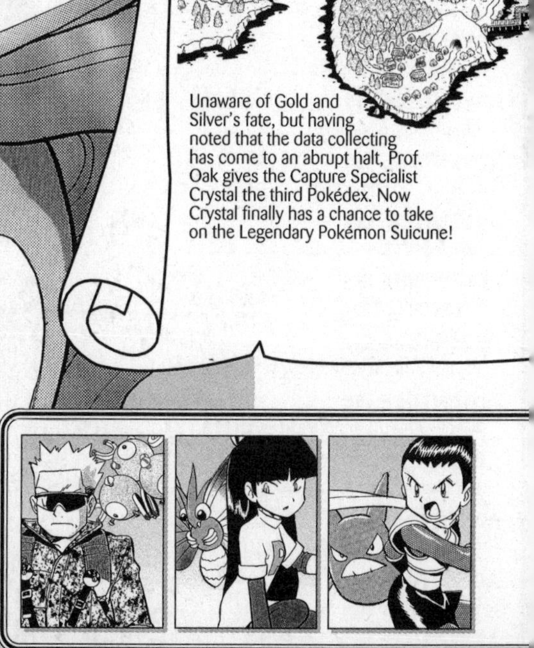

CONTENTS

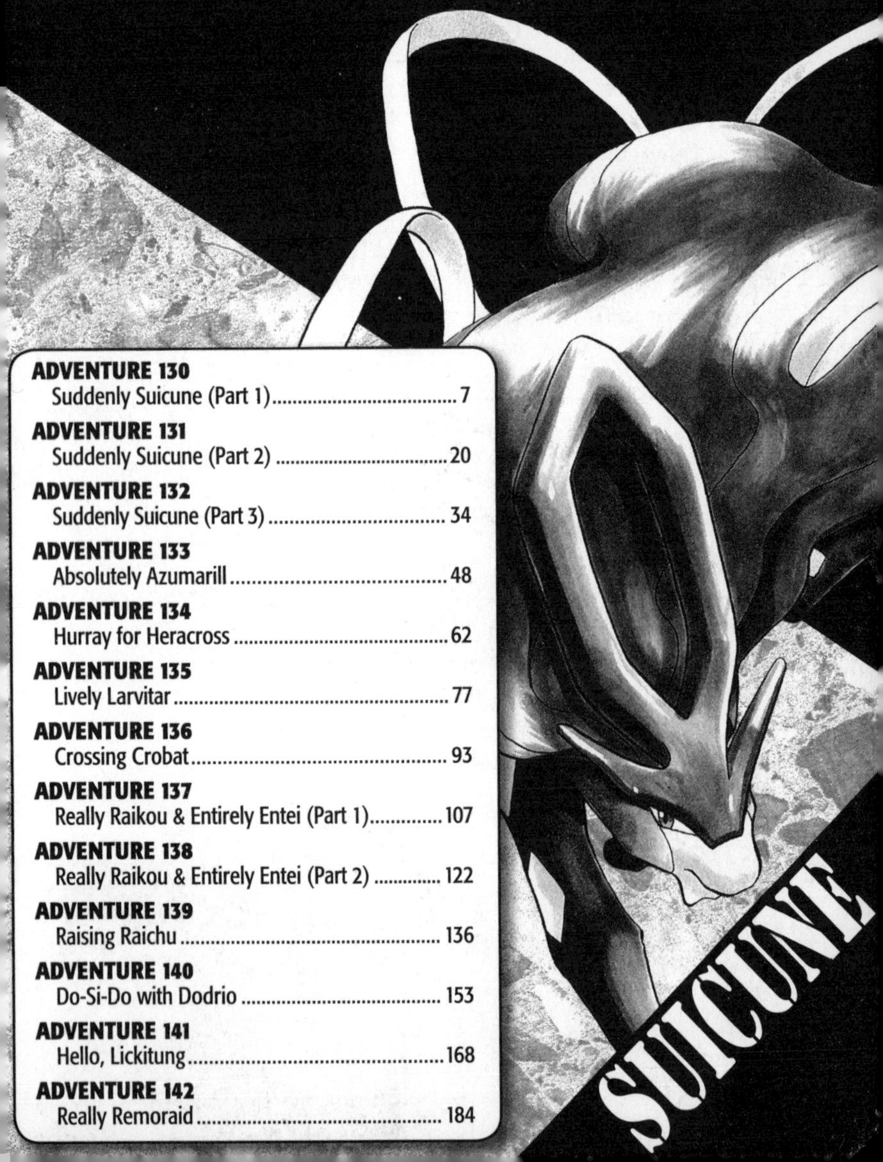
SUICUNE

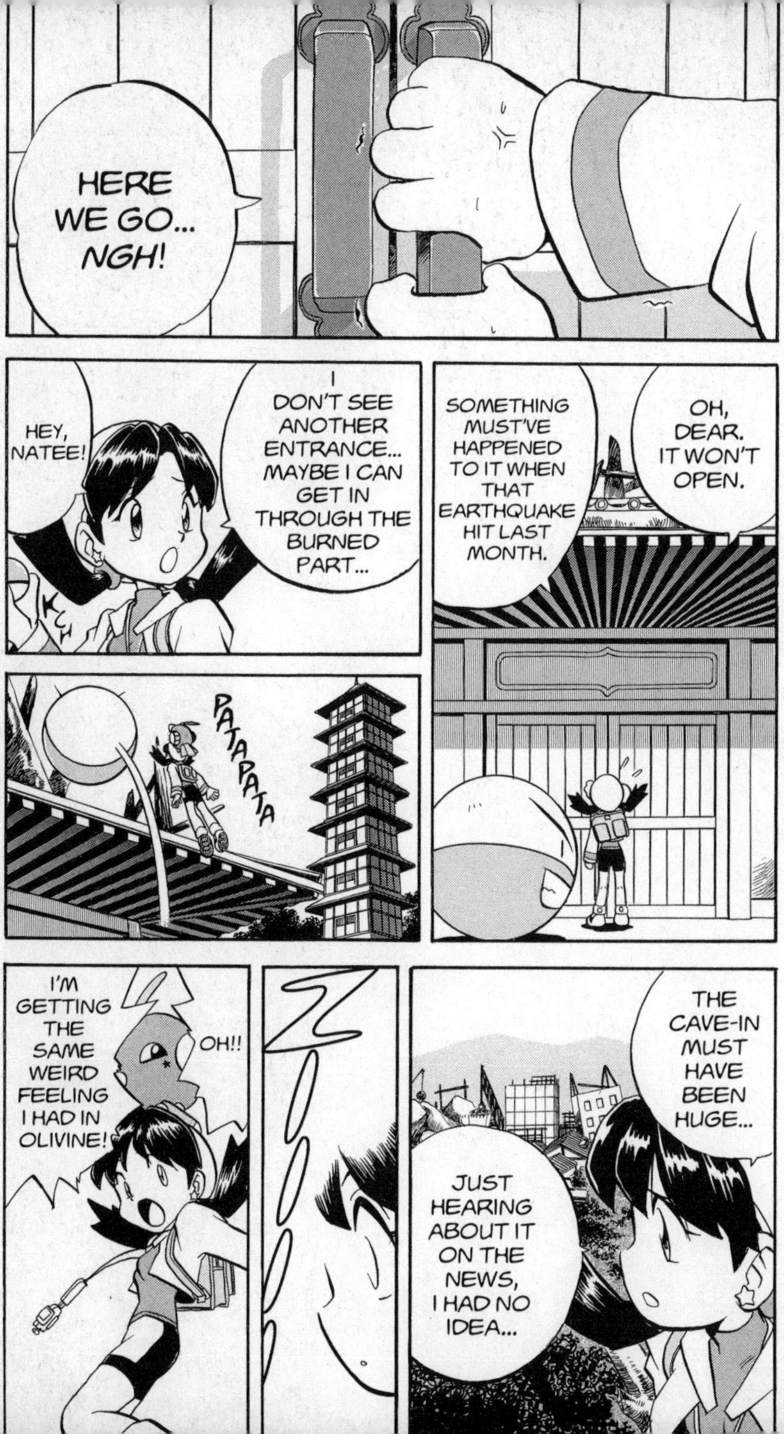
HERE WE GO... NGH!
OH, DEAR. IT WON'T OPEN.
SOMETHING MUST'VE HAPPENED TO IT WHEN THAT EARTHQUAKE HIT LAST MONTH.
I DON'T SEE ANOTHER ENTRANCE... MAYBE I CAN GET IN THROUGH THE BURNED PART...
HEY, NATEE!
PATAPATA
THE CAVE-IN MUST HAVE BEEN HUGE...
JUST HEARING ABOUT IT ON THE NEWS, I HAD NO IDEA...
OH!!
I'M GETTING THE SAME WEIRD FEELING I HAD IN OLIVINE!

130 Suddenly Suicune (Part 1)

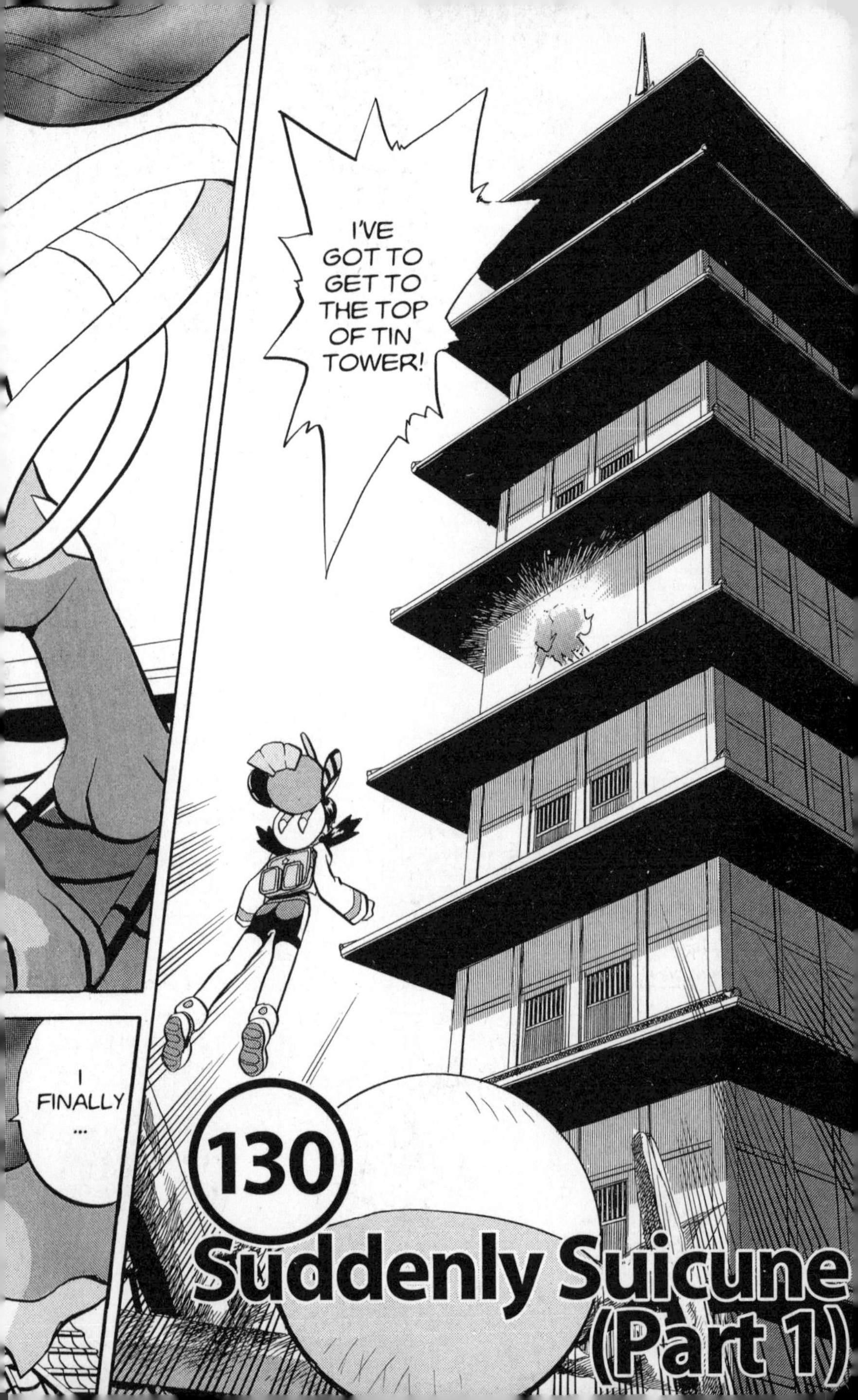
I'VE GOT TO GET TO THE TOP OF TIN TOWER!
I FINALLY ...

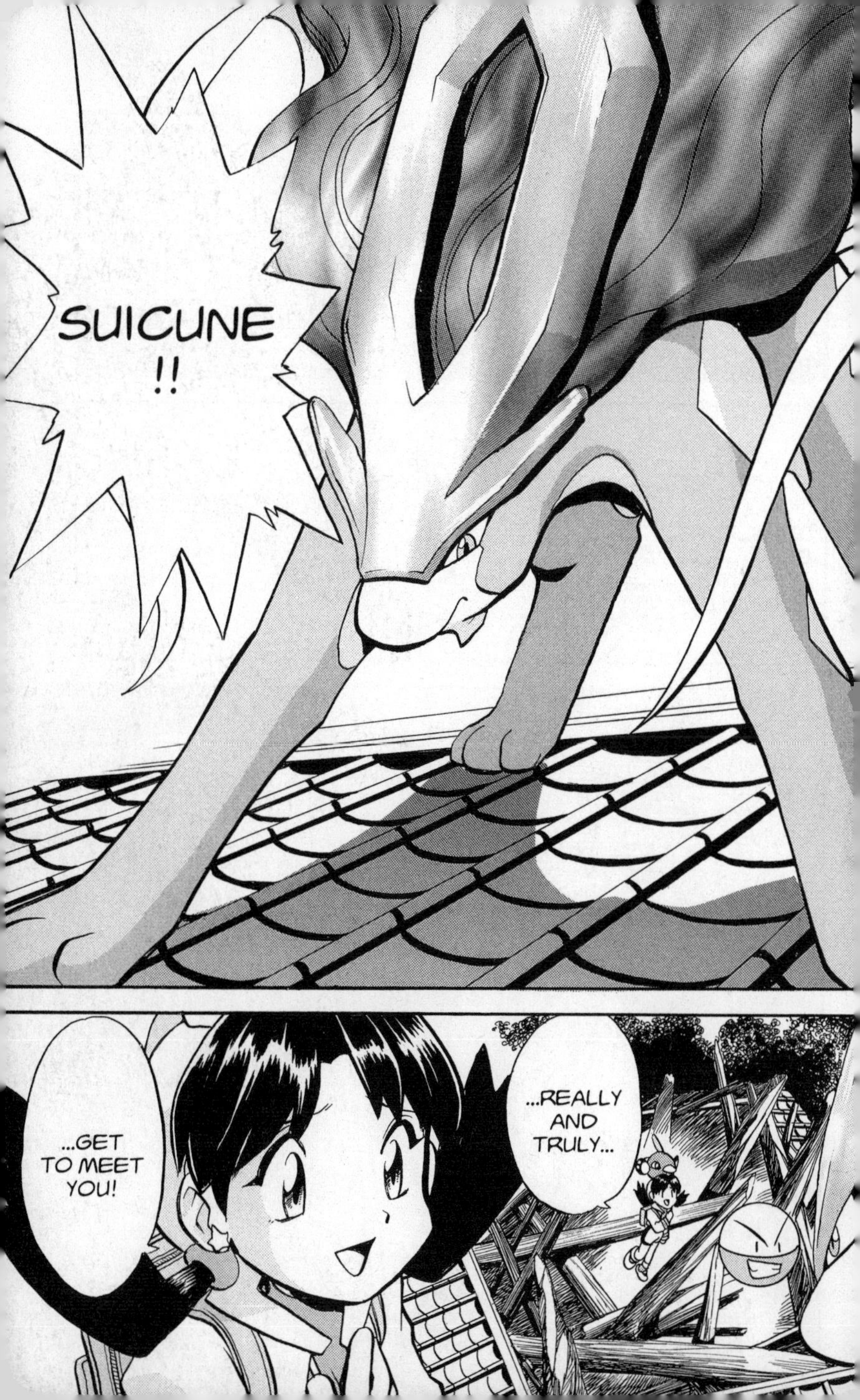
SUICUNE !!
...REALLY AND TRULY...
...GET TO MEET YOU!

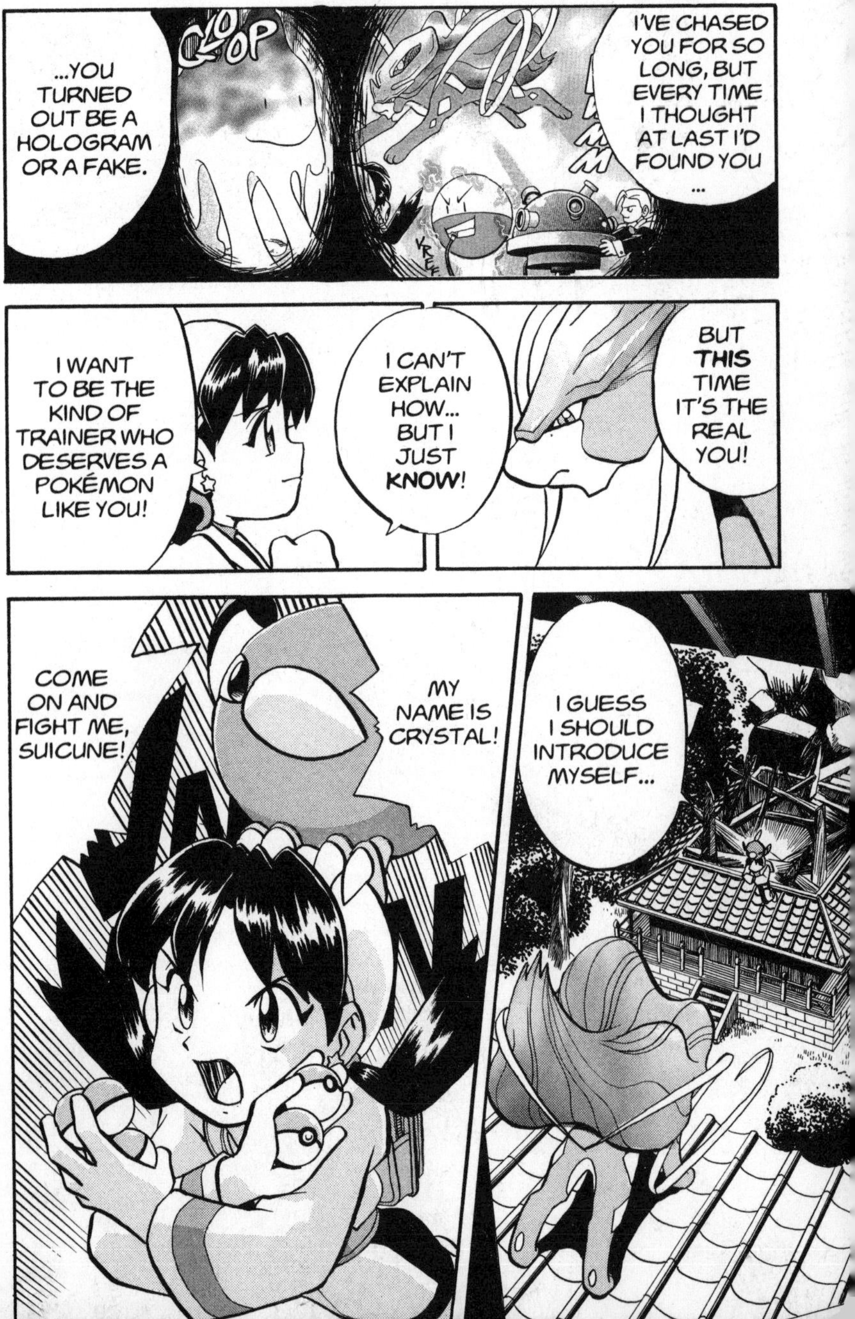
I'VE CHASED YOU FOR SO LONG, BUT EVERY TIME I THOUGHT AT LAST I'D FOUND YOU ...
...YOU TURNED OUT BE A HOLOGRAM OR A FAKE.
BUT **THIS** TIME IT'S THE REAL YOU!
I CAN'T EXPLAIN HOW... BUT I JUST **KNOW**!
I WANT TO BE THE KIND OF TRAINER WHO DESERVES A POKÉMON LIKE YOU!
I GUESS I SHOULD INTRODUCE MYSELF...
MY NAME IS CRYSTAL!
COME ON AND FIGHT ME, SUICUNE!

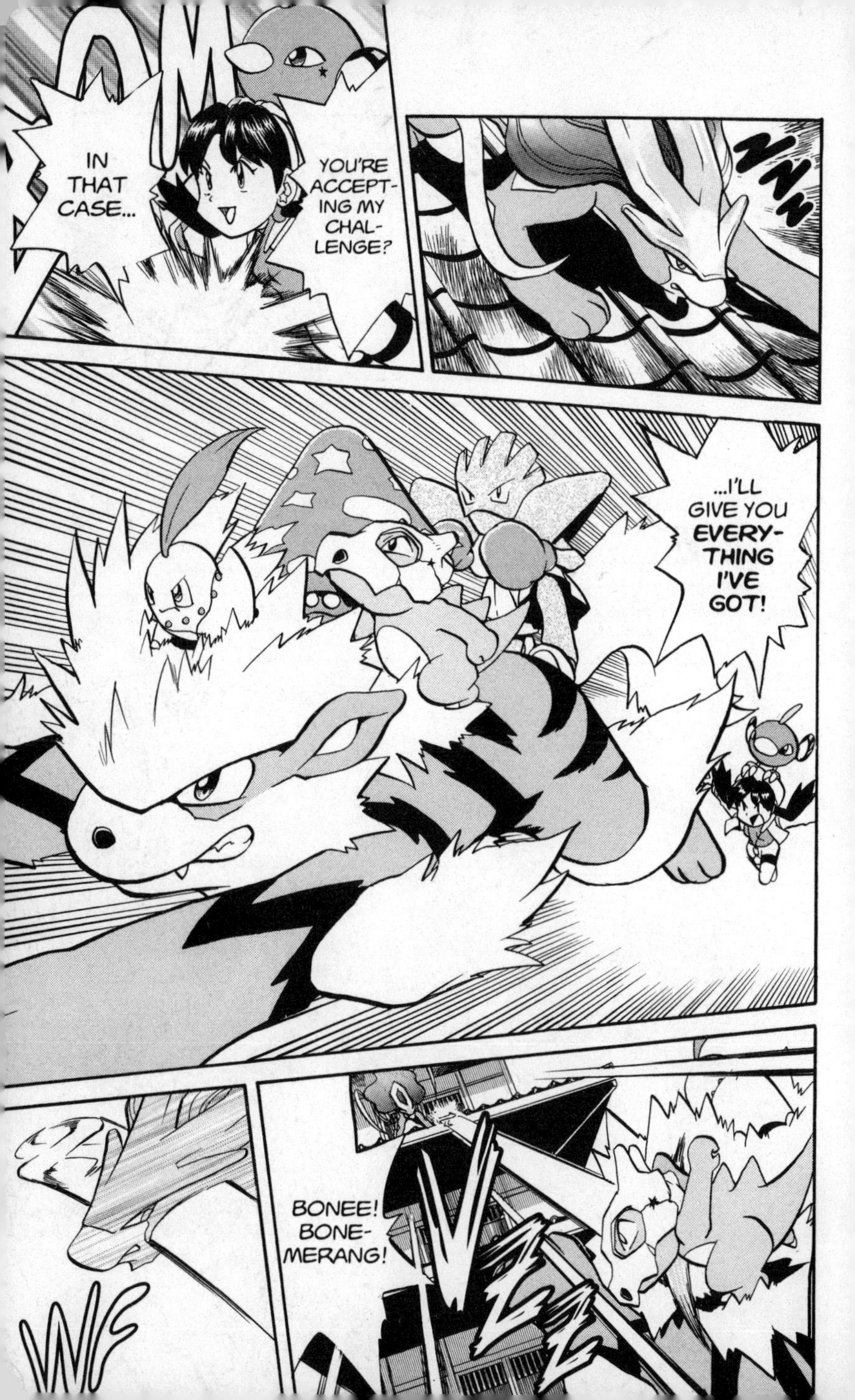
YOU'RE ACCEPT-ING MY CHAL-LENGE?
IN THAT CASE...
...I'LL GIVE YOU EVERY-THING I'VE GOT!
BONEE! BONE-MERANG!

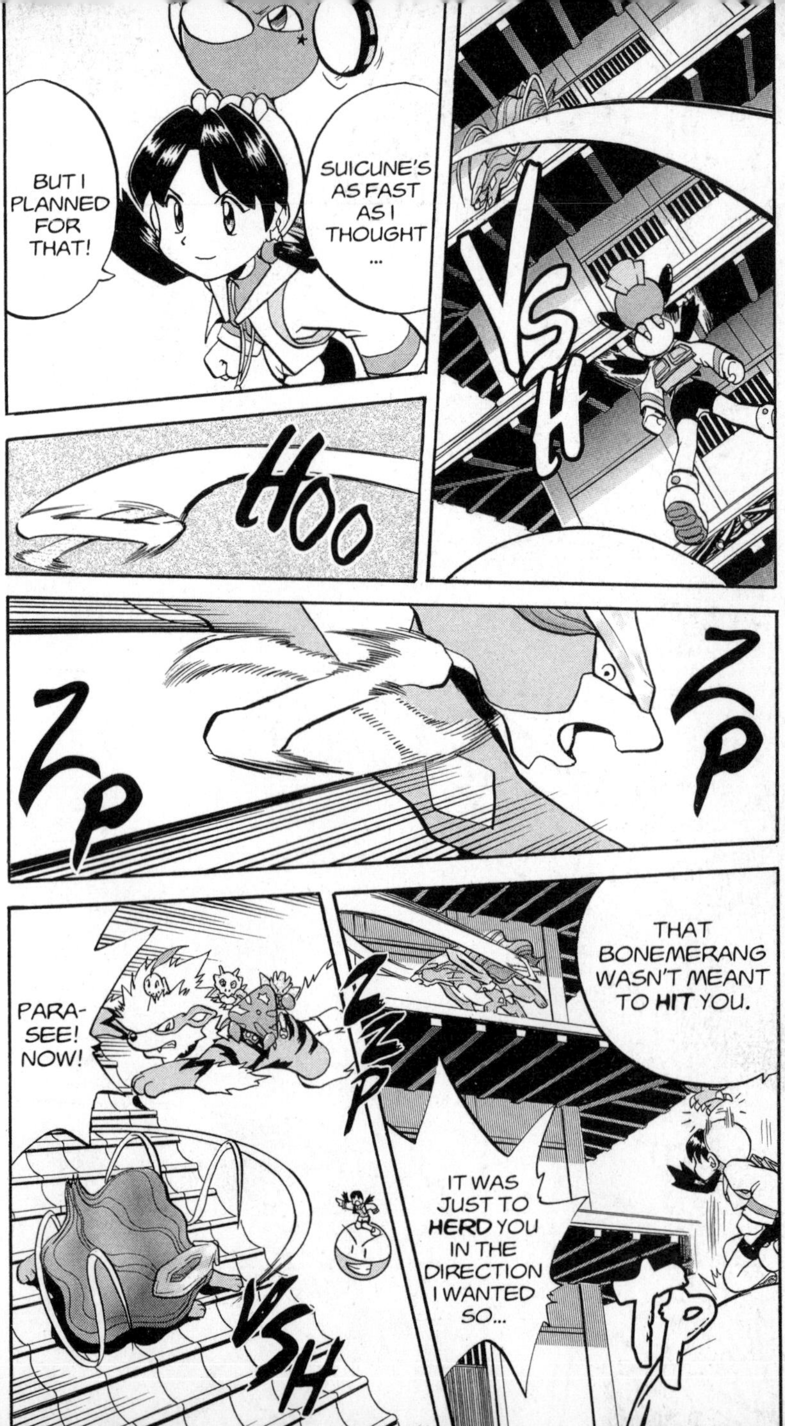
VSH
SUICUNE'S AS FAST AS I THOUGHT ...
BUT I PLANNED FOR THAT!
HOO
ZP
ZP
THAT BONEMERANG WASN'T MEANT TO **HIT** YOU.
IT WAS JUST TO **HERD** YOU IN THE DIRECTION I WANTED SO...
TP
PARA-SEE! NOW!
VSH

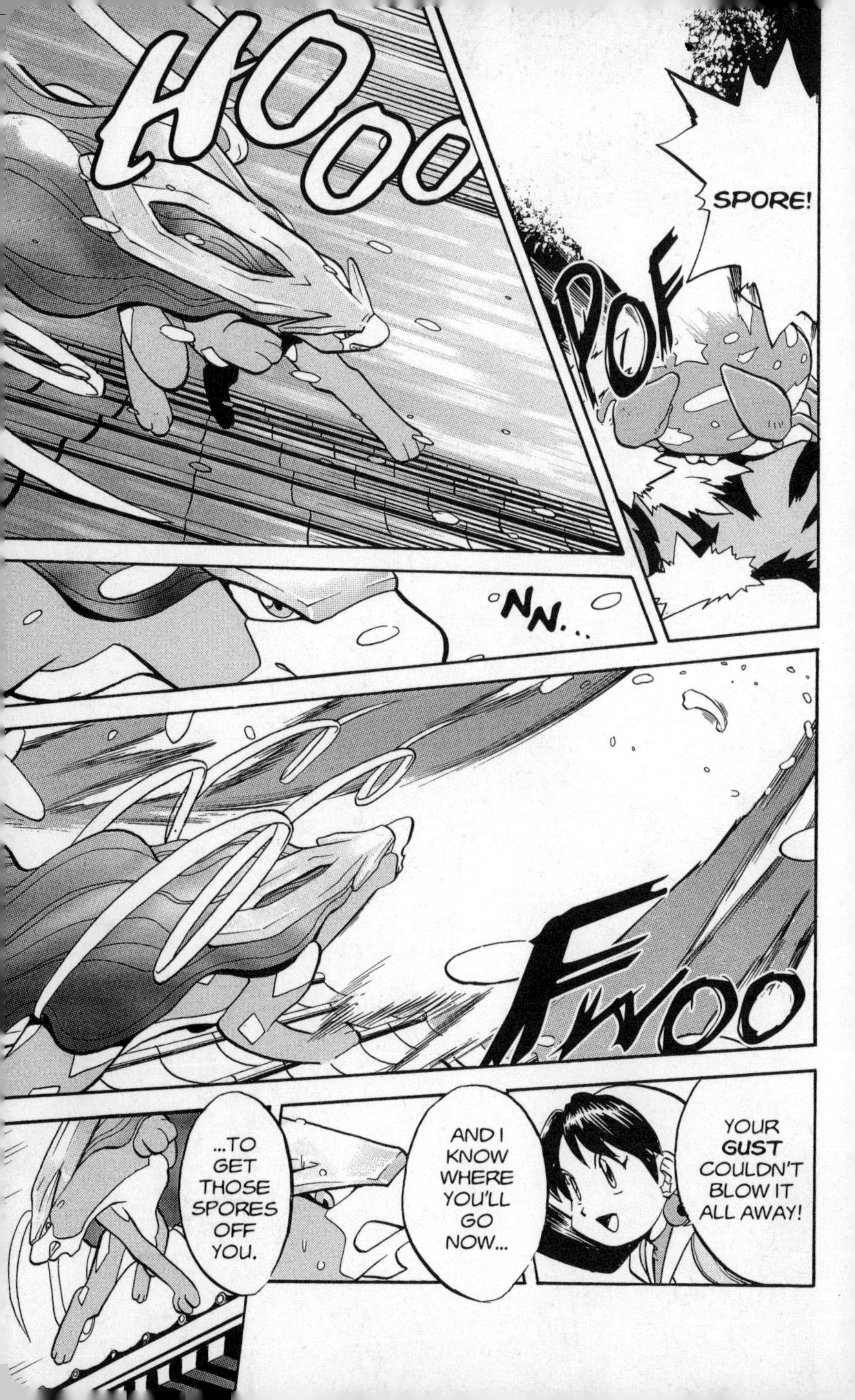
SPORE!
POF
HOOOO
NN...
FWOO
YOUR GUST COULDN'T BLOW IT ALL AWAY!
AND I KNOW WHERE YOU'LL GO NOW...
...TO GET THOSE SPORES OFF YOU.

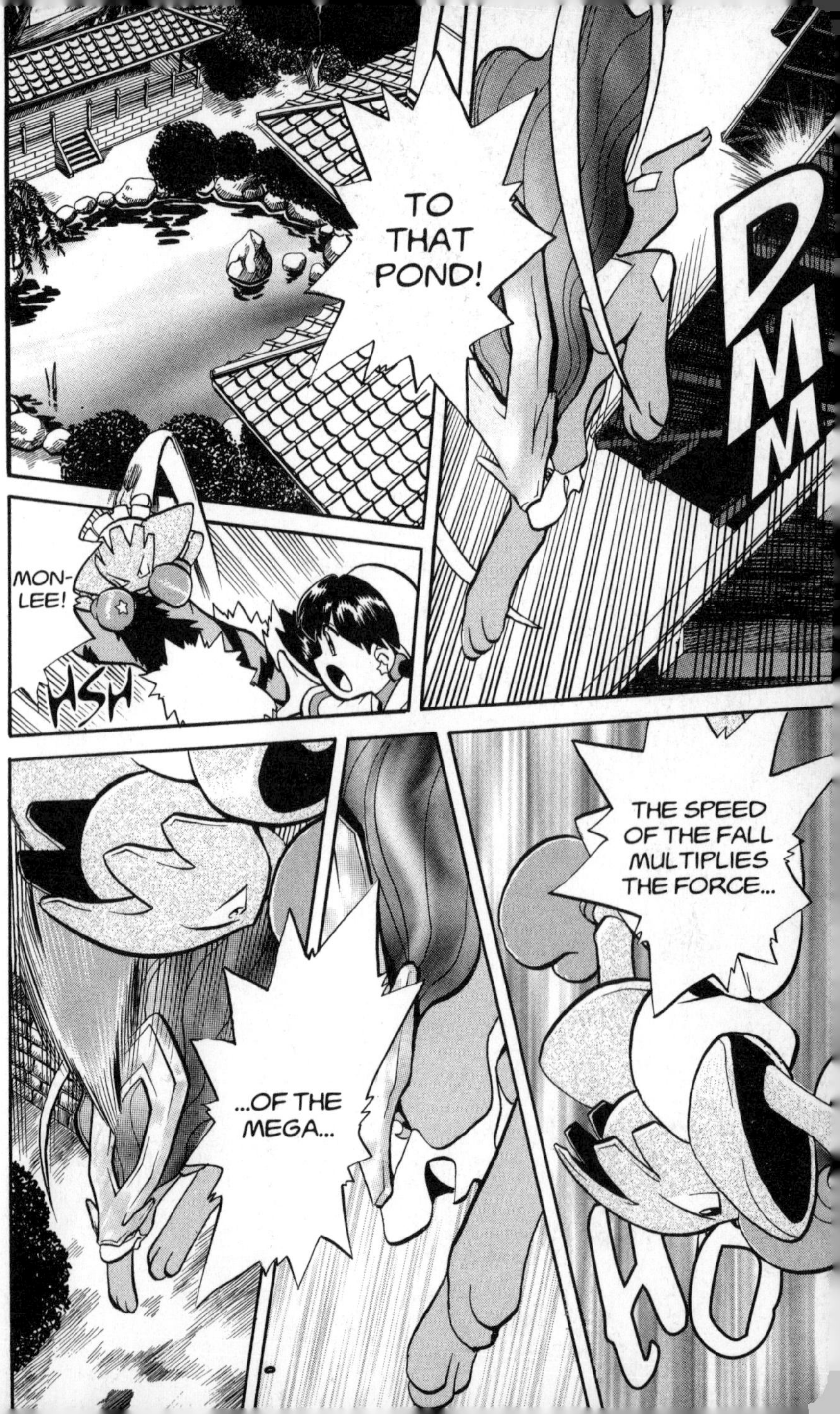
TO THAT POND!
DMMM
MON-LEE!
HSH
THE SPEED OF THE FALL MULTIPLIES THE FORCE...
...OF THE MEGA...

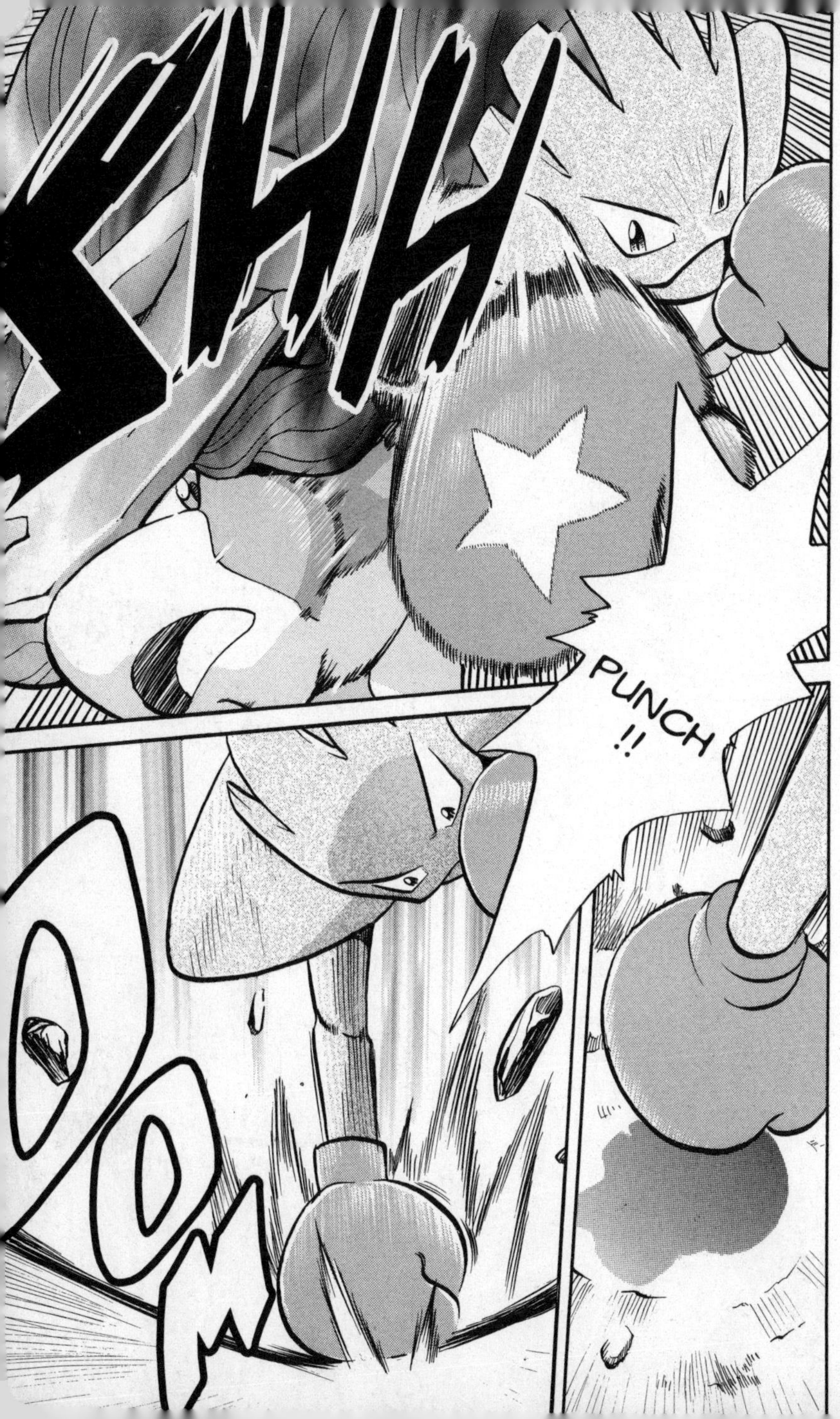
PUNCH !!

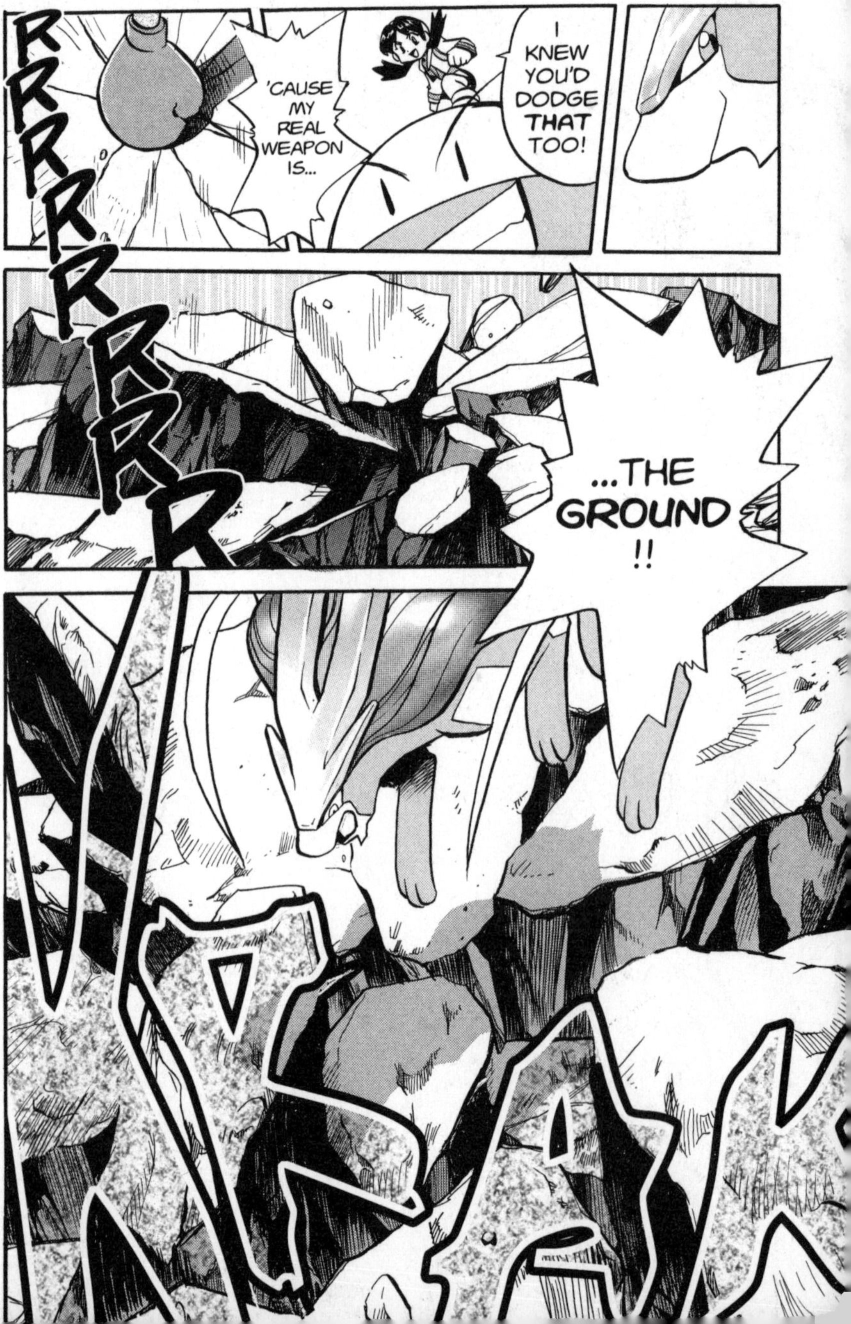
I KNEW YOU'D DODGE THAT TOO!
'CAUSE MY REAL WEAPON IS...
RRRRRRRR
...THE GROUND!!

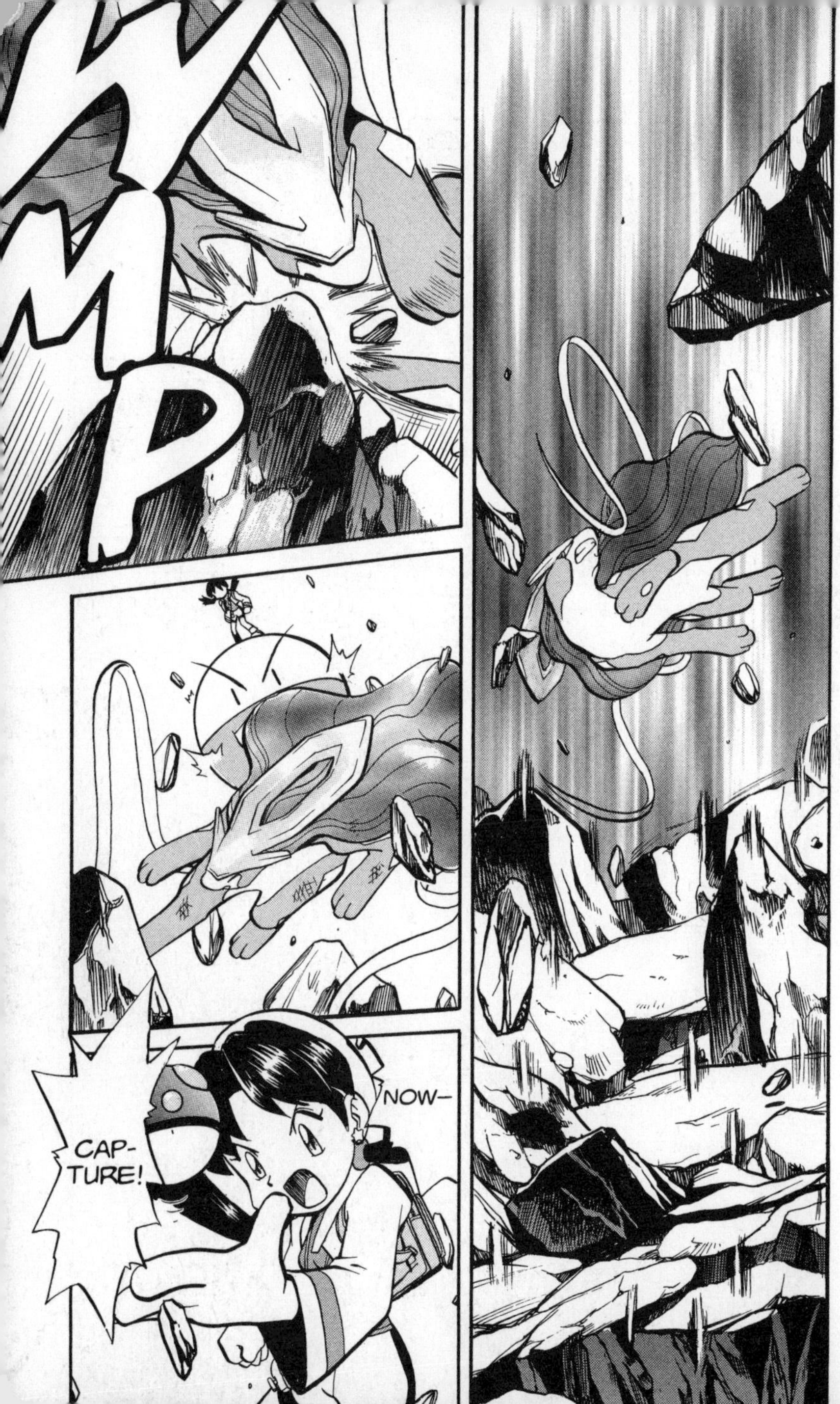
NOW–
CAP-
TURE!

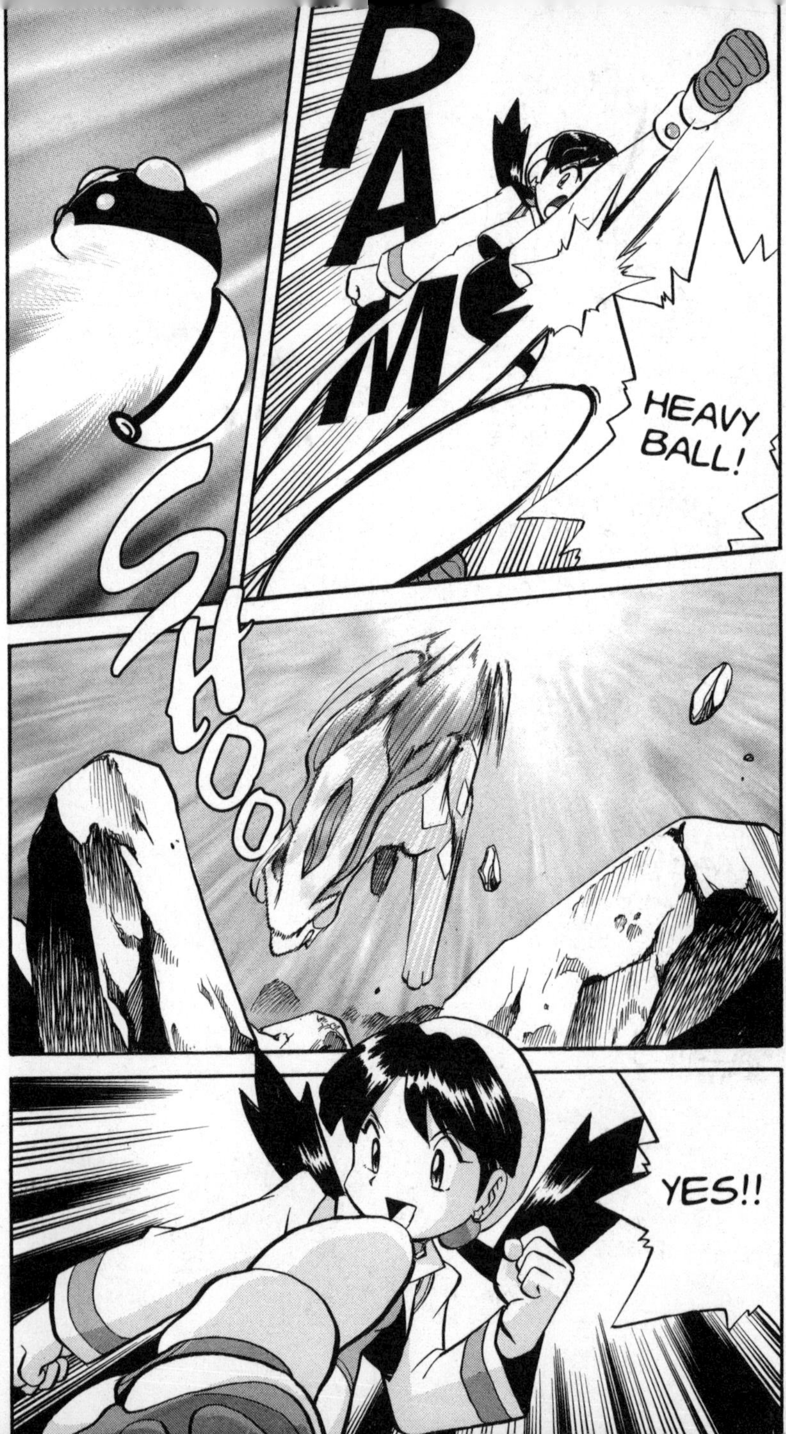
PAM
HEAVY BALL!
SHOOO
YES!!

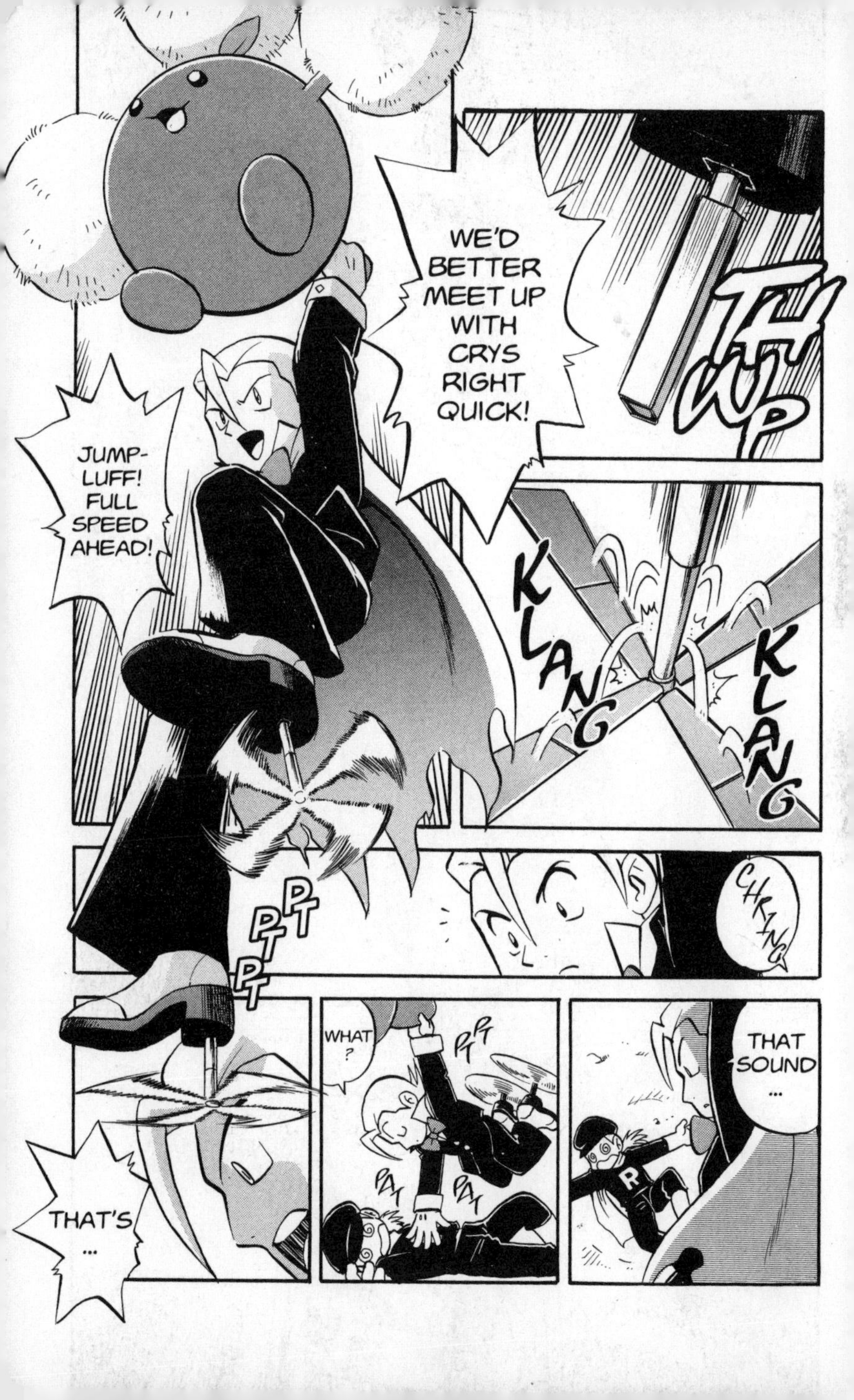
WE'D BETTER MEET UP WITH CRYS RIGHT QUICK!
THWUP
JUMP-LUFF! FULL SPEED AHEAD!
KLANG
KLANG
PT PT PT
CHRING
THAT SOUND...
WHAT?
PT PT
PAT
PAT
THAT'S...

131 Suddenly Suicune (Part 2)

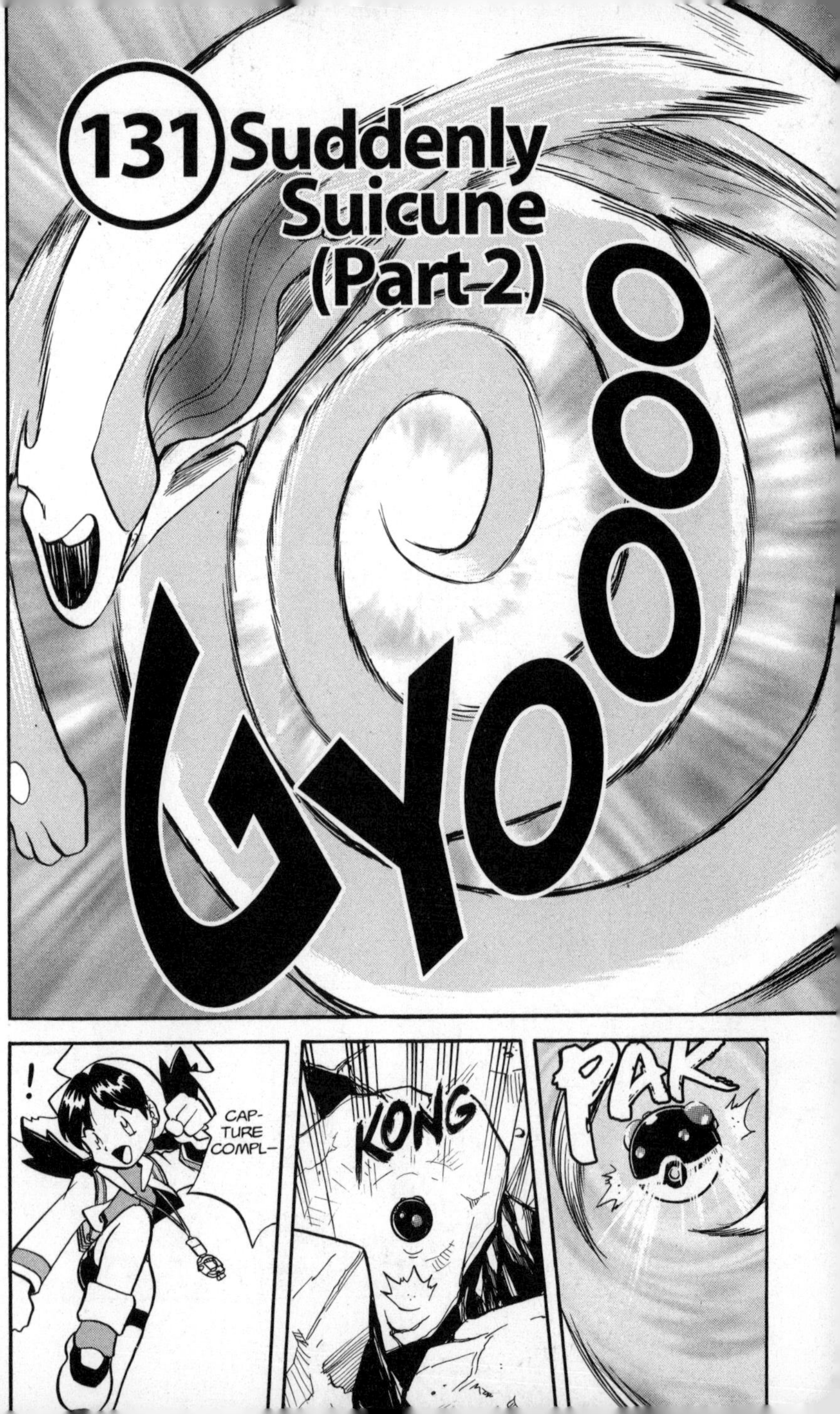
GYOOOOO
PAK
KONG
!
CAP-
TURE
COMPL-

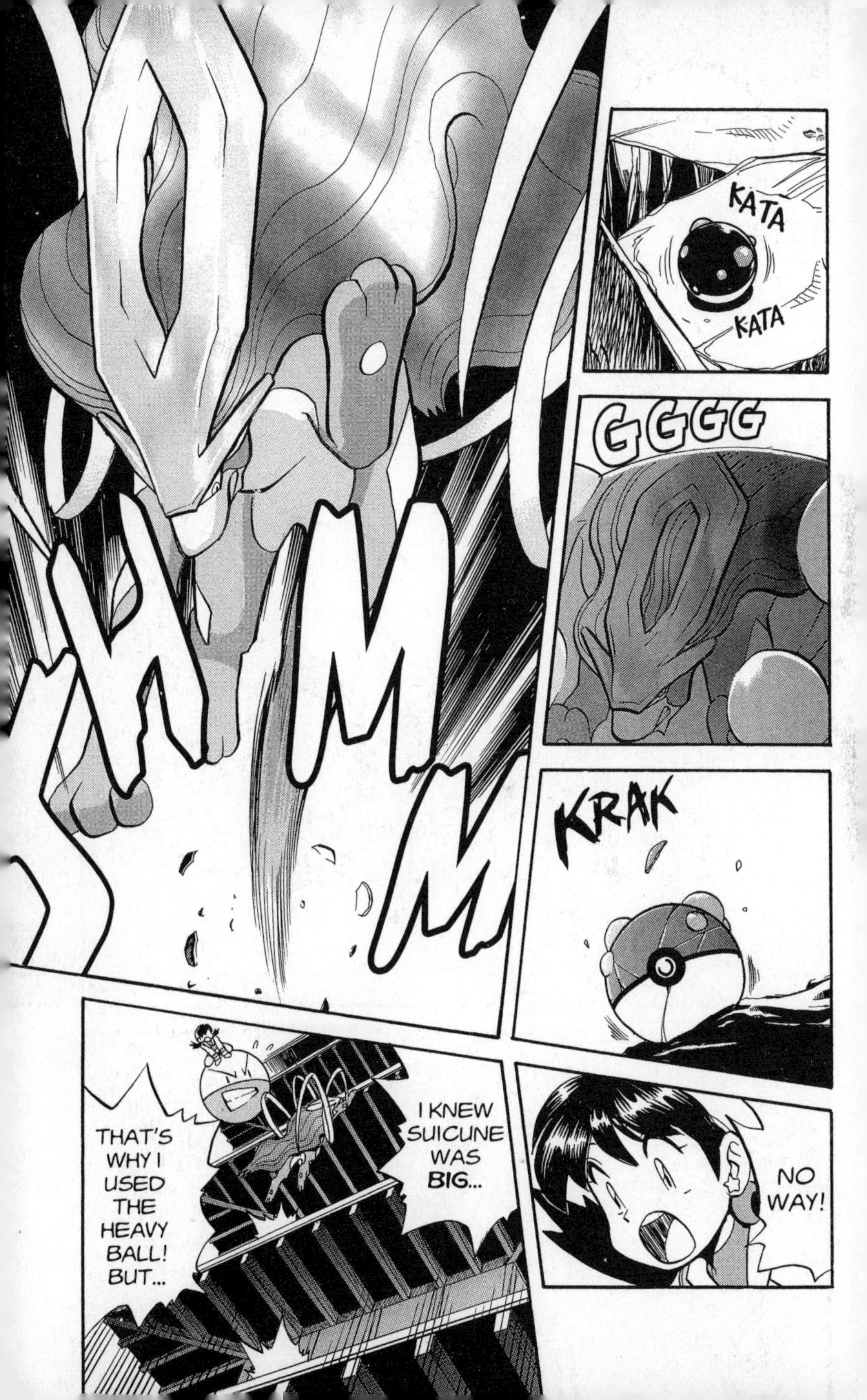
KATA
KATA
GGGG
KRAK
NO WAY!
I KNEW SUICUNE WAS BIG...
THAT'S WHY I USED THE HEAVY BALL! BUT...

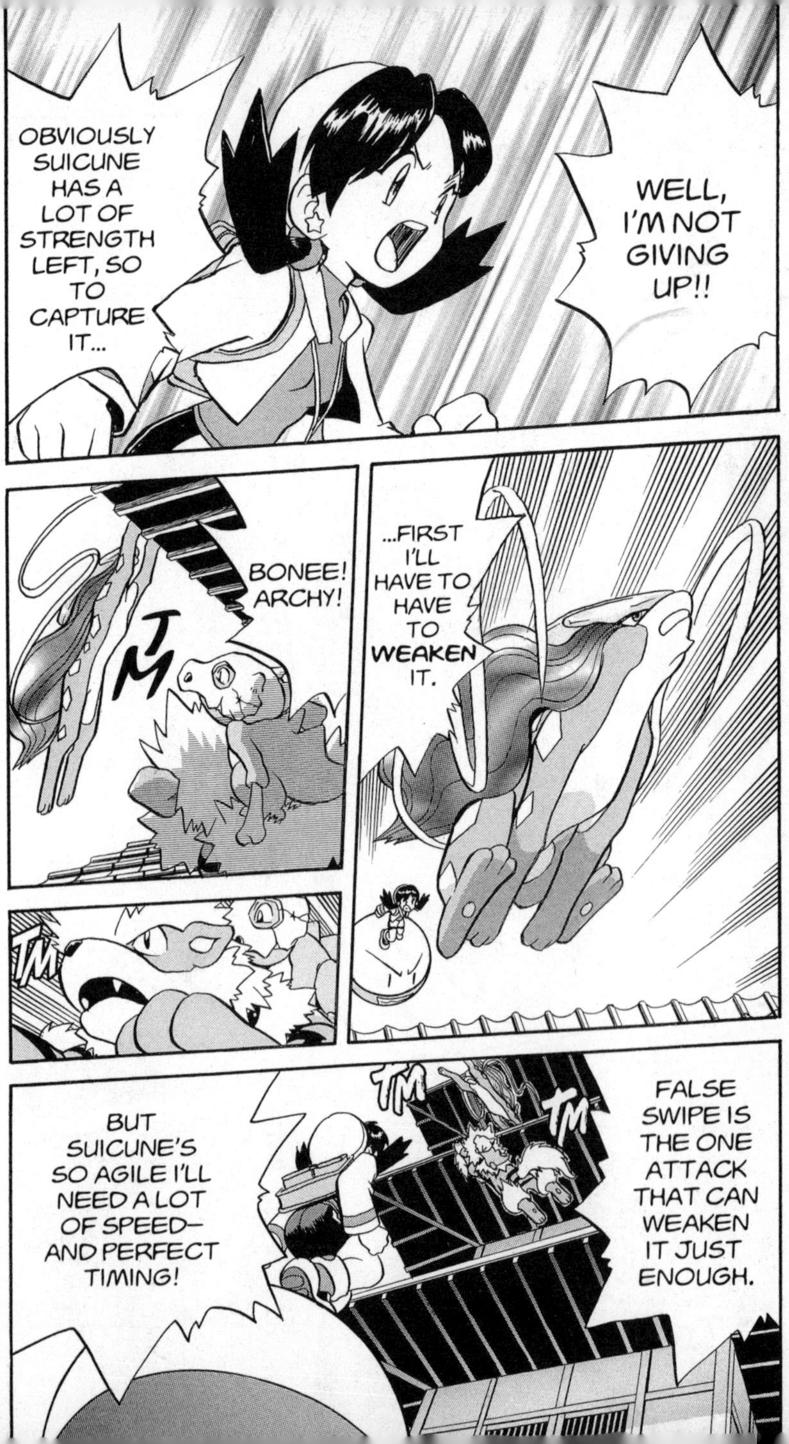
WELL, I'M NOT GIVING UP!!
OBVIOUSLY SUICUNE HAS A LOT OF STRENGTH LEFT, SO TO CAPTURE IT...
...FIRST I'LL HAVE TO HAVE TO WEAKEN IT.
BONEE! ARCHY!
TM
TM
TM
TM
FALSE SWIPE IS THE ONE ATTACK THAT CAN WEAKEN IT JUST ENOUGH.
BUT SUICUNE'S SO AGILE I'LL NEED A LOT OF SPEED— AND PERFECT TIMING!

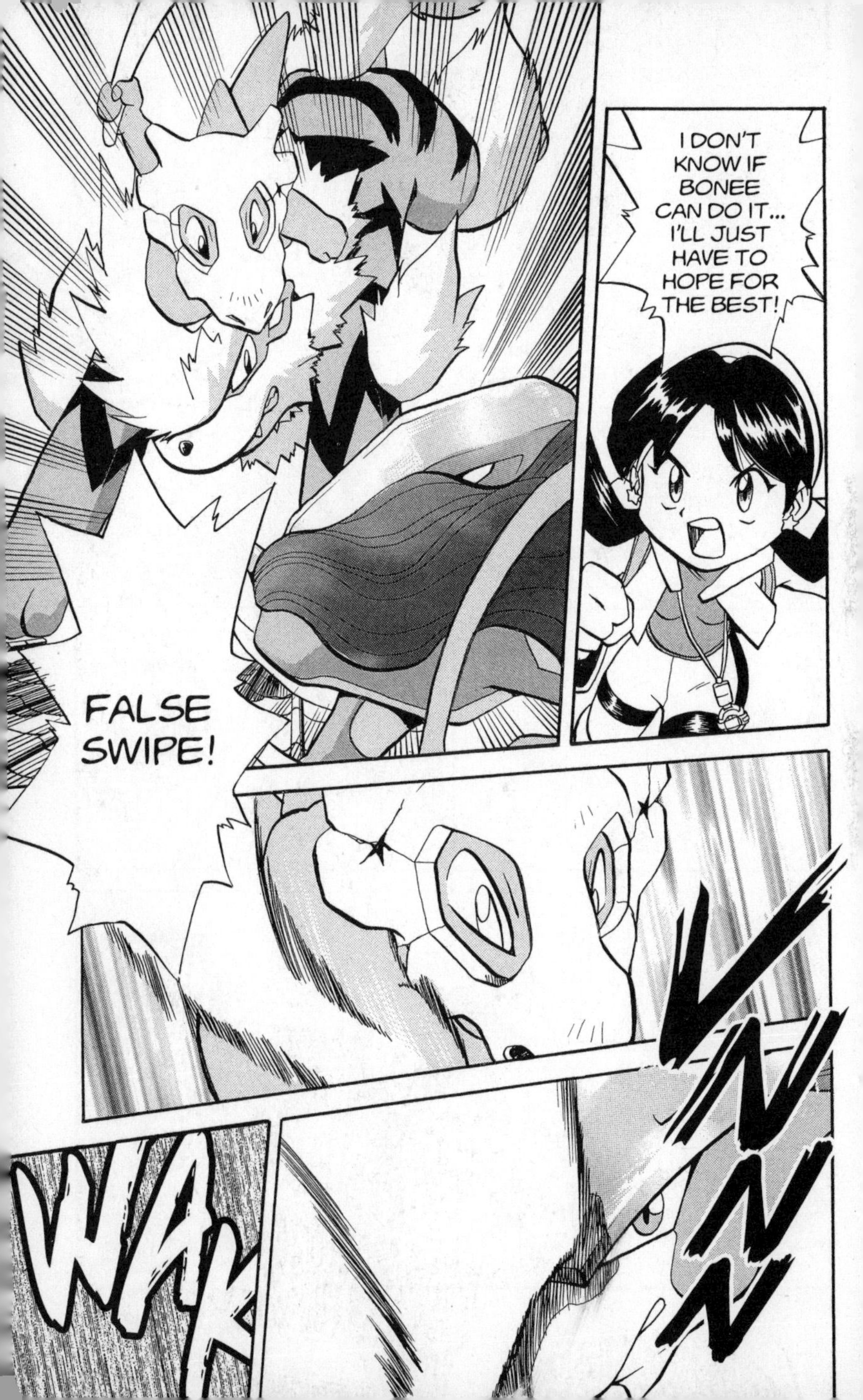
I DON'T KNOW IF BONEE CAN DO IT... I'LL JUST HAVE TO HOPE FOR THE BEST!
FALSE SWIPE!
WHAK
WAK

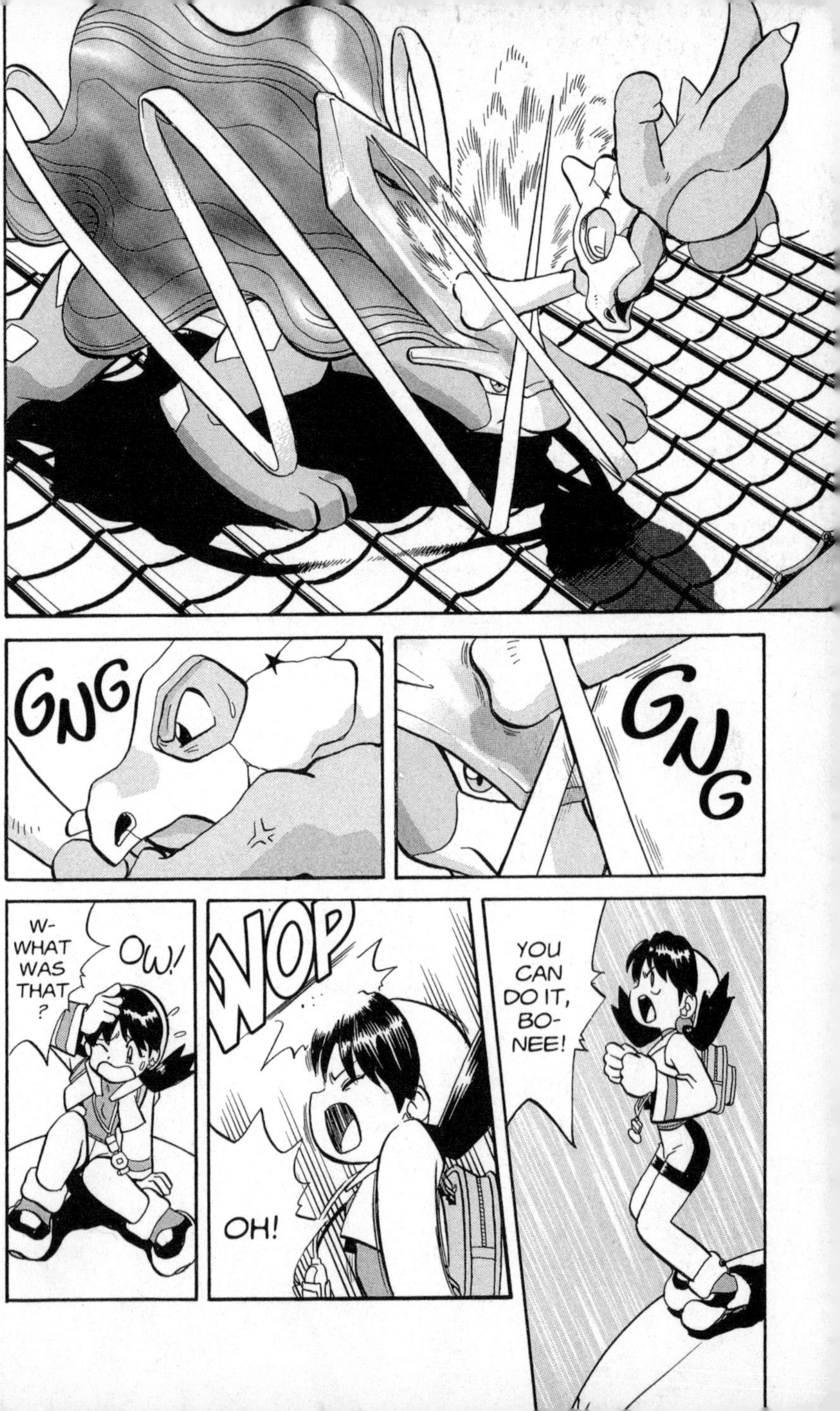
GNG
GNG
YOU CAN DO IT, BO-NEE!
WOP
OH!
OW!
W-WHAT WAS THAT?

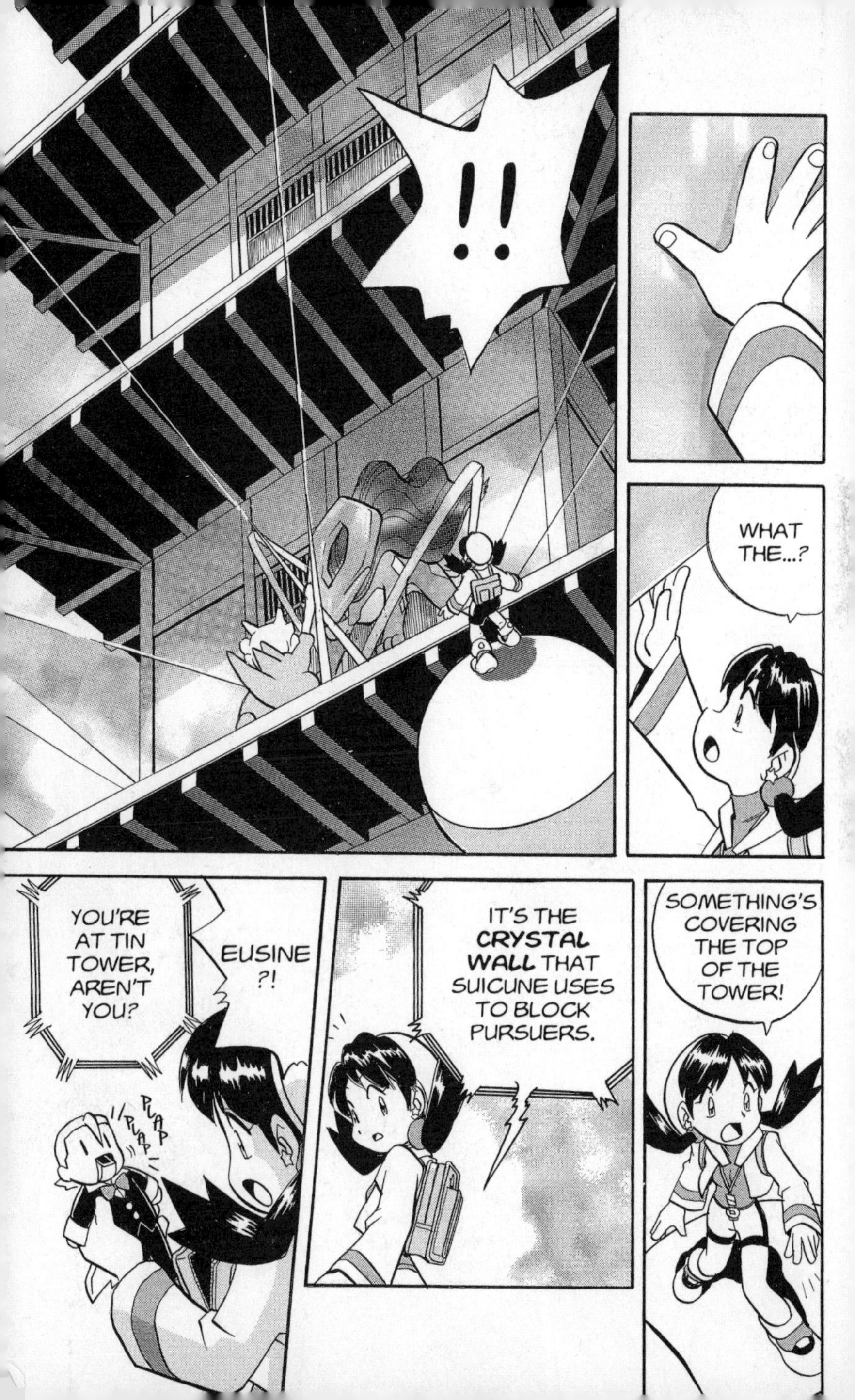
WHAT THE...?
!!
SOMETHING'S COVERING THE TOP OF THE TOWER!
IT'S THE **CRYSTAL WALL** THAT SUICUNE USES TO BLOCK PURSUERS.
EUSINE ?!
YOU'RE AT TIN TOWER, AREN'T YOU?
PLAP PLAP

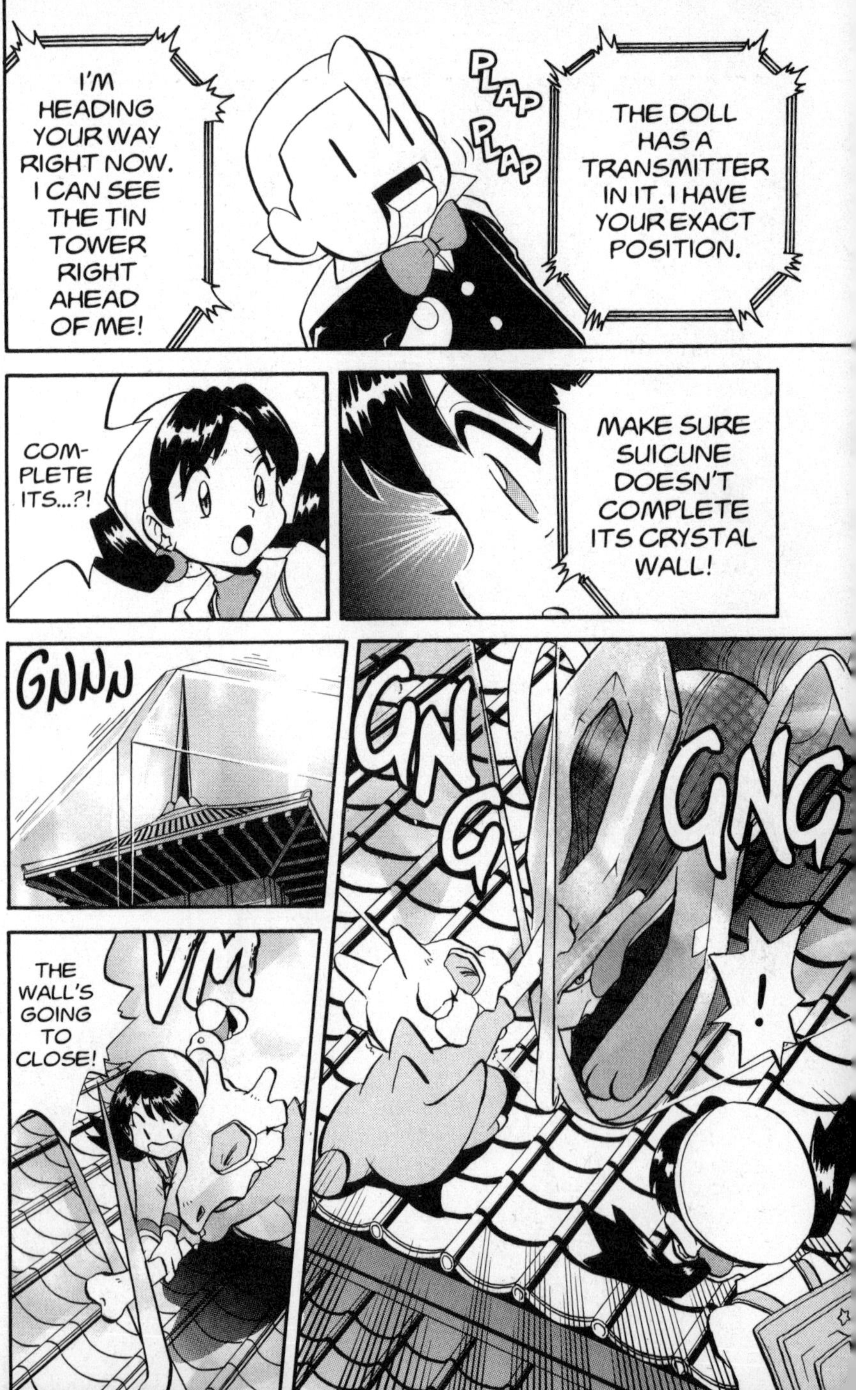
THE DOLL HAS A TRANSMITTER IN IT. I HAVE YOUR EXACT POSITION.
PLAP PLAP
I'M HEADING YOUR WAY RIGHT NOW. I CAN SEE THE TIN TOWER RIGHT AHEAD OF ME!
MAKE SURE SUICUNE DOESN'T COMPLETE ITS CRYSTAL WALL!
COM-PLETE ITS...?!
GNG
GNG
!
GNNN
VM
THE WALL'S GOING TO CLOSE!

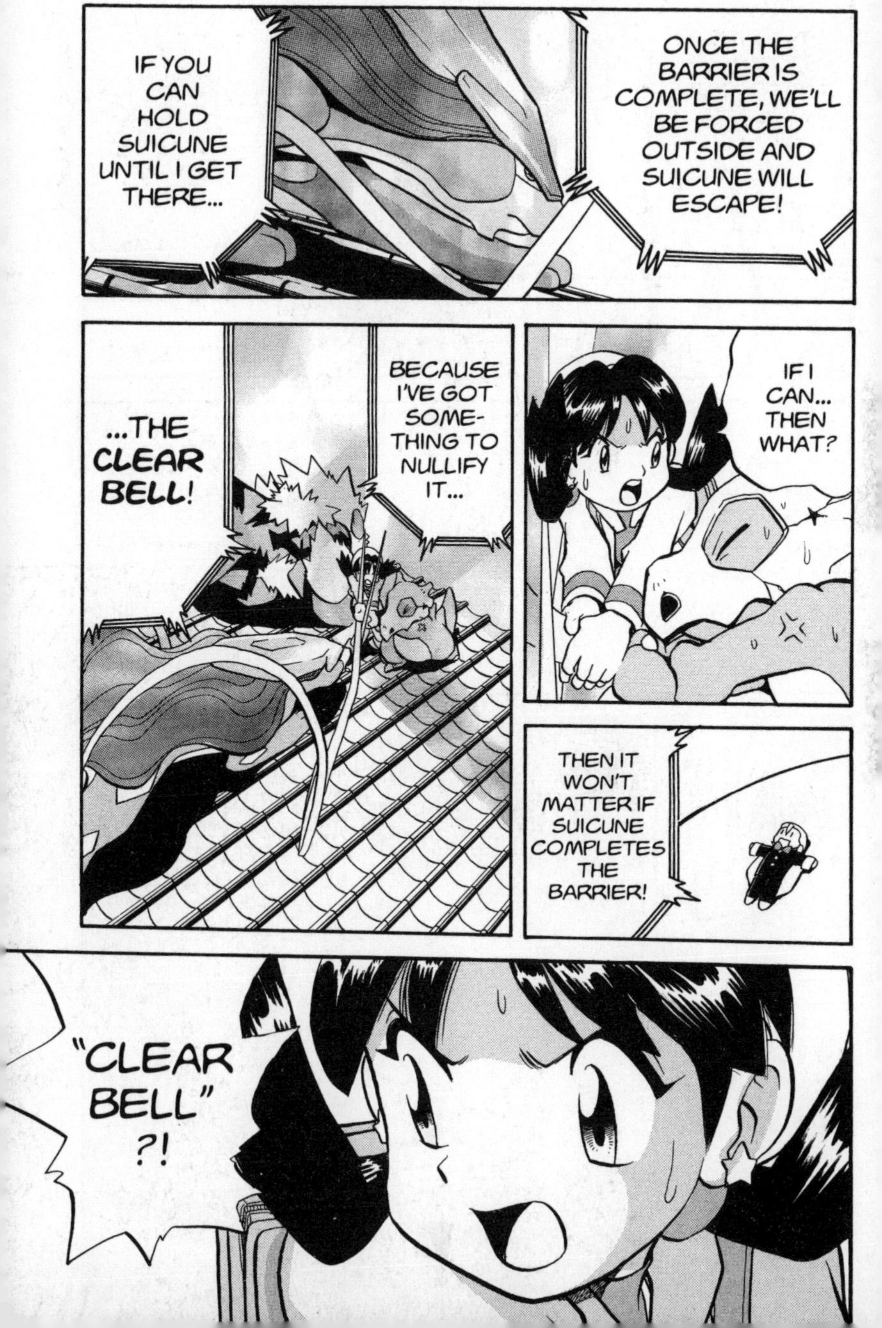
ONCE THE BARRIER IS COMPLETE, WE'LL BE FORCED OUTSIDE AND SUICUNE WILL ESCAPE!
IF YOU CAN HOLD SUICUNE UNTIL I GET THERE...
IF I CAN... THEN WHAT?
THEN IT WON'T MATTER IF SUICUNE COMPLETES THE BARRIER!
BECAUSE I'VE GOT SOME-THING TO NULLIFY IT...
...THE CLEAR BELL!
"CLEAR BELL" ?!

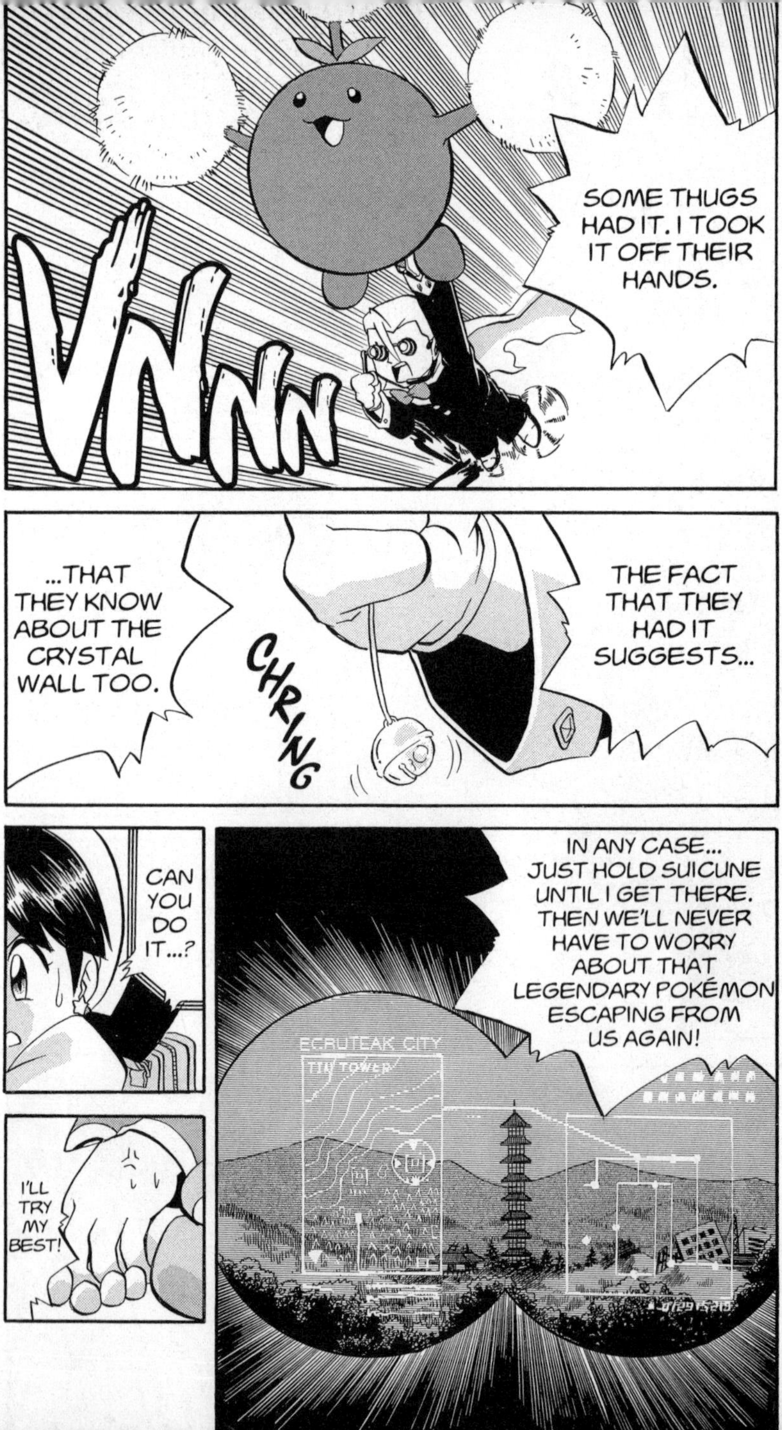
SOME THUGS HAD IT. I TOOK IT OFF THEIR HANDS.
VNNNN
THE FACT THAT THEY HAD IT SUGGESTS...
CHRING
...THAT THEY KNOW ABOUT THE CRYSTAL WALL TOO.
IN ANY CASE... JUST HOLD SUICUNE UNTIL I GET THERE. THEN WE'LL NEVER HAVE TO WORRY ABOUT THAT LEGENDARY POKÉMON ESCAPING FROM US AGAIN!
ECRUTEAK CITY
TIN TOWER
CAN YOU DO IT...?
I'LL TRY MY BEST!

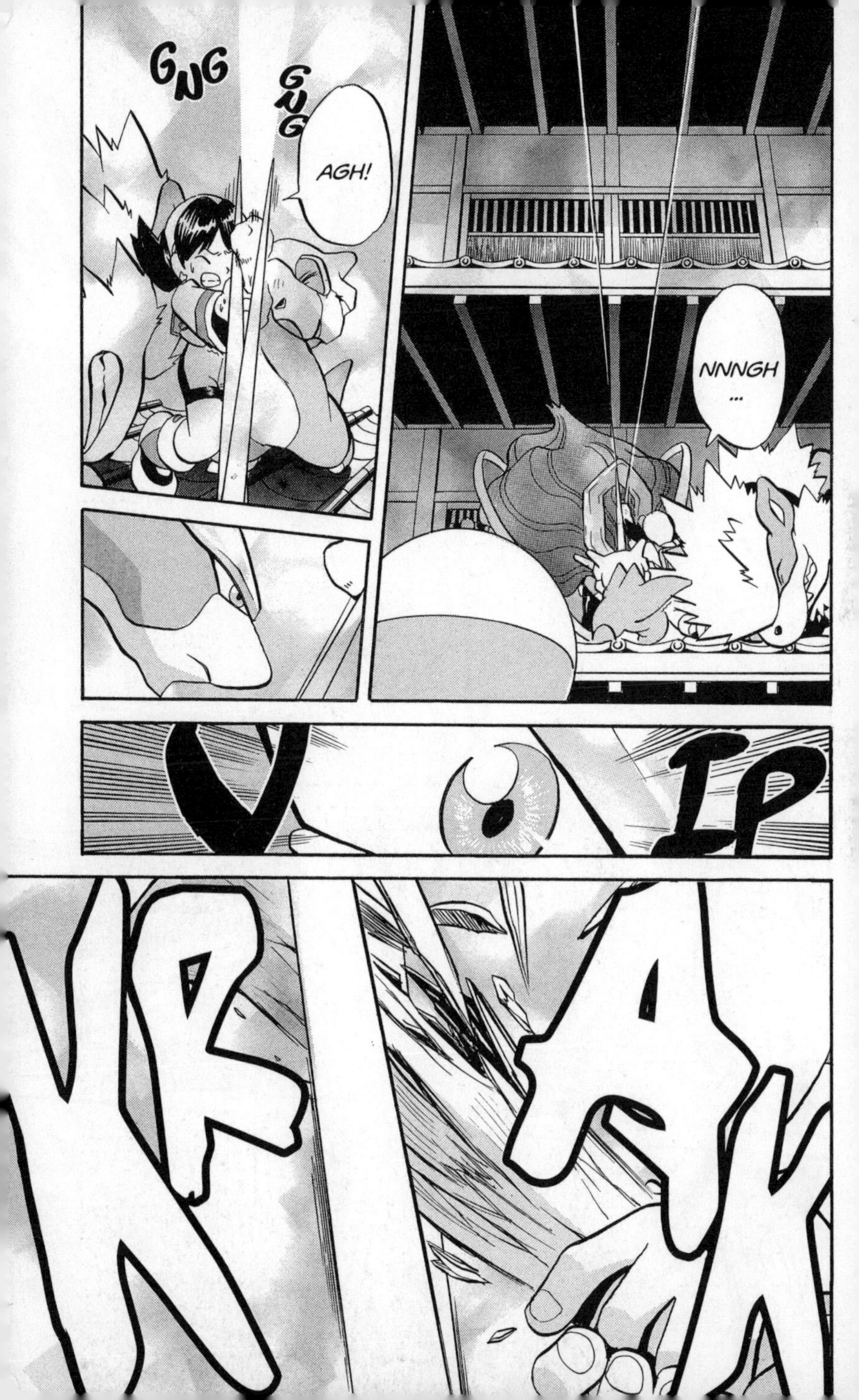
NNNGH...
GNG
GNG
AGH!

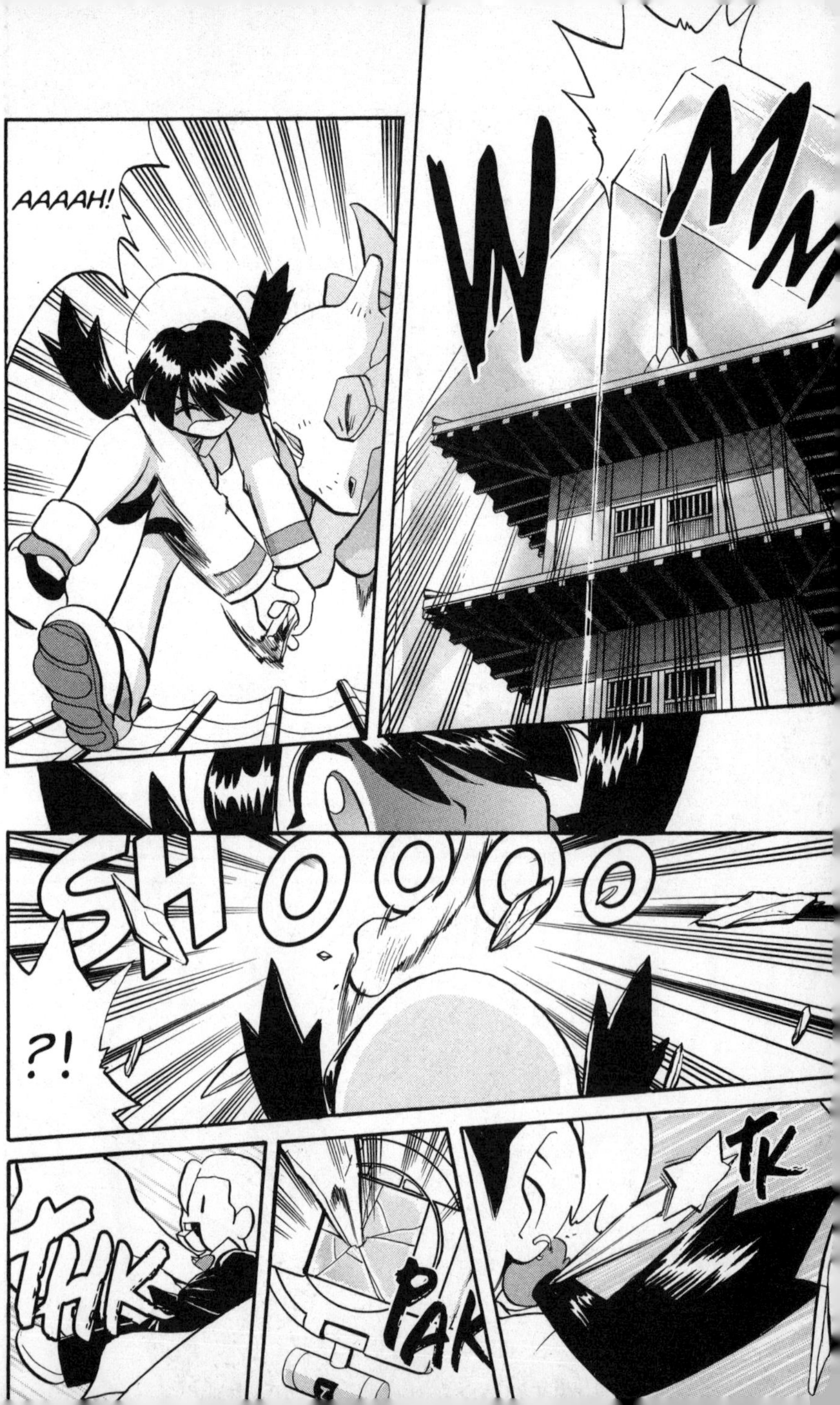
WMMM
AAAAH!
SHOOOO
?!
TK
PAK
THK

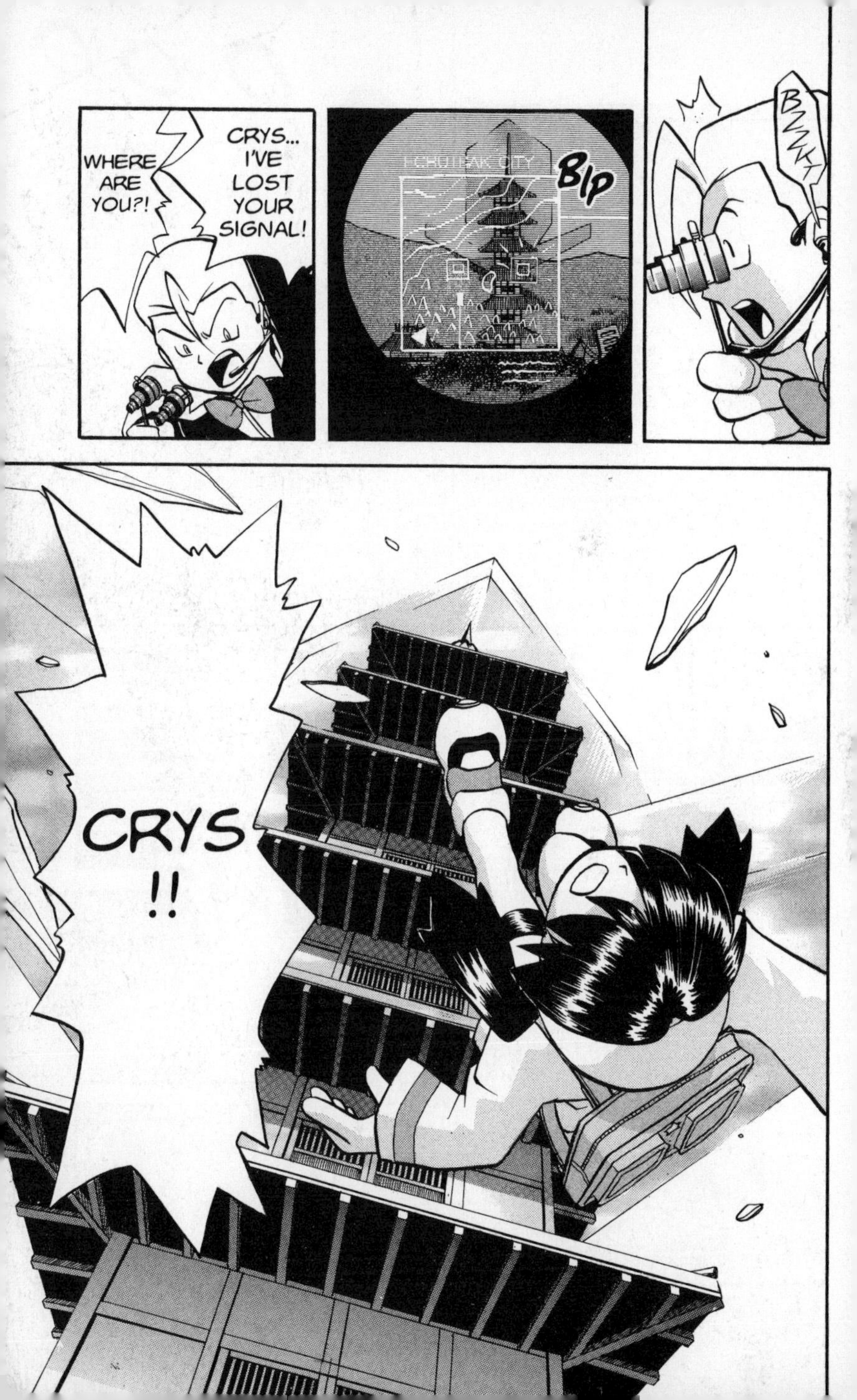
BZZZT
ECRUTEAK CITY
BIP
CRYS... I'VE LOST YOUR SIGNAL!
WHERE ARE YOU?!
CRYS !!

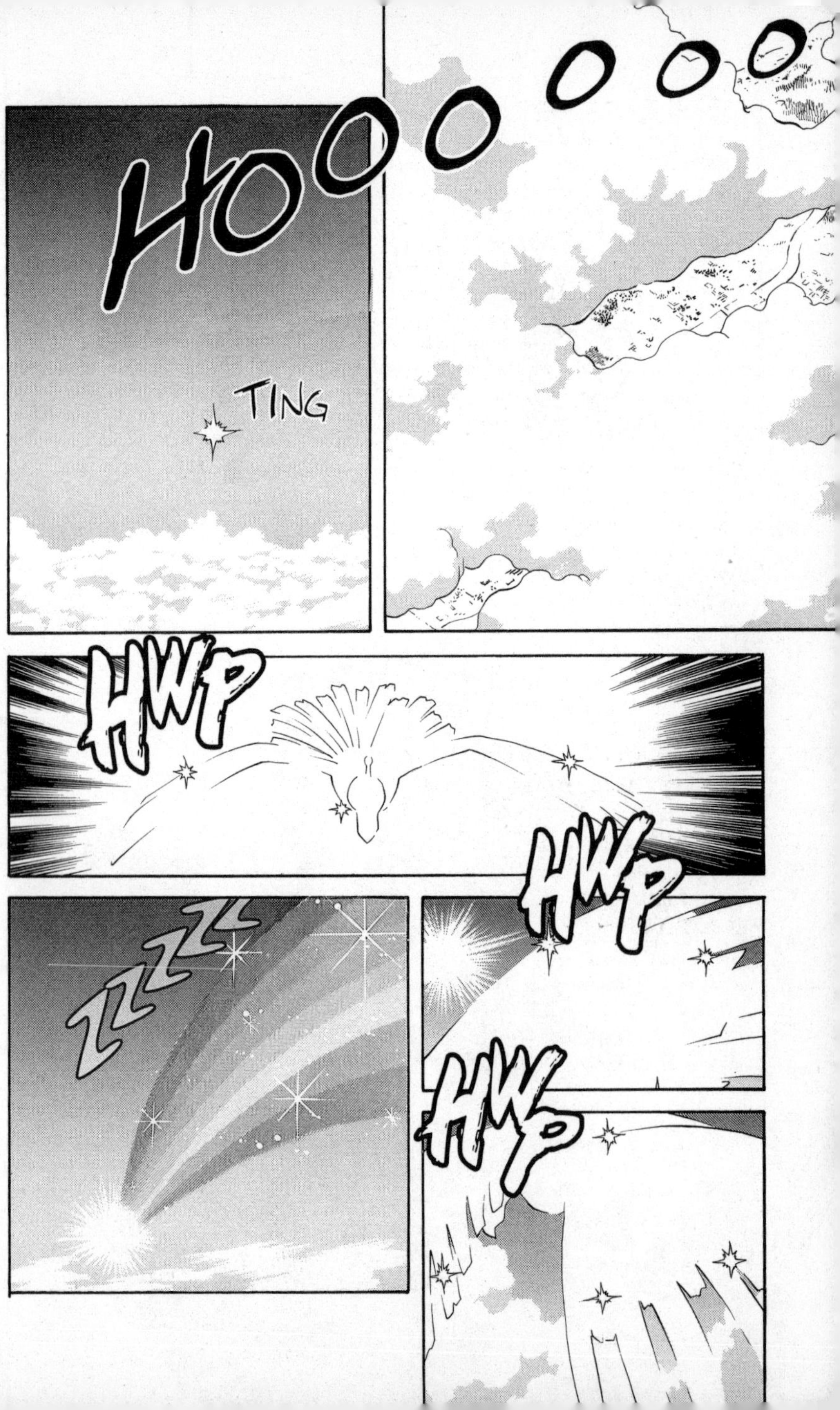
HOOOOOOO
TING
HWP
HWP
HWP
ZZZZZ

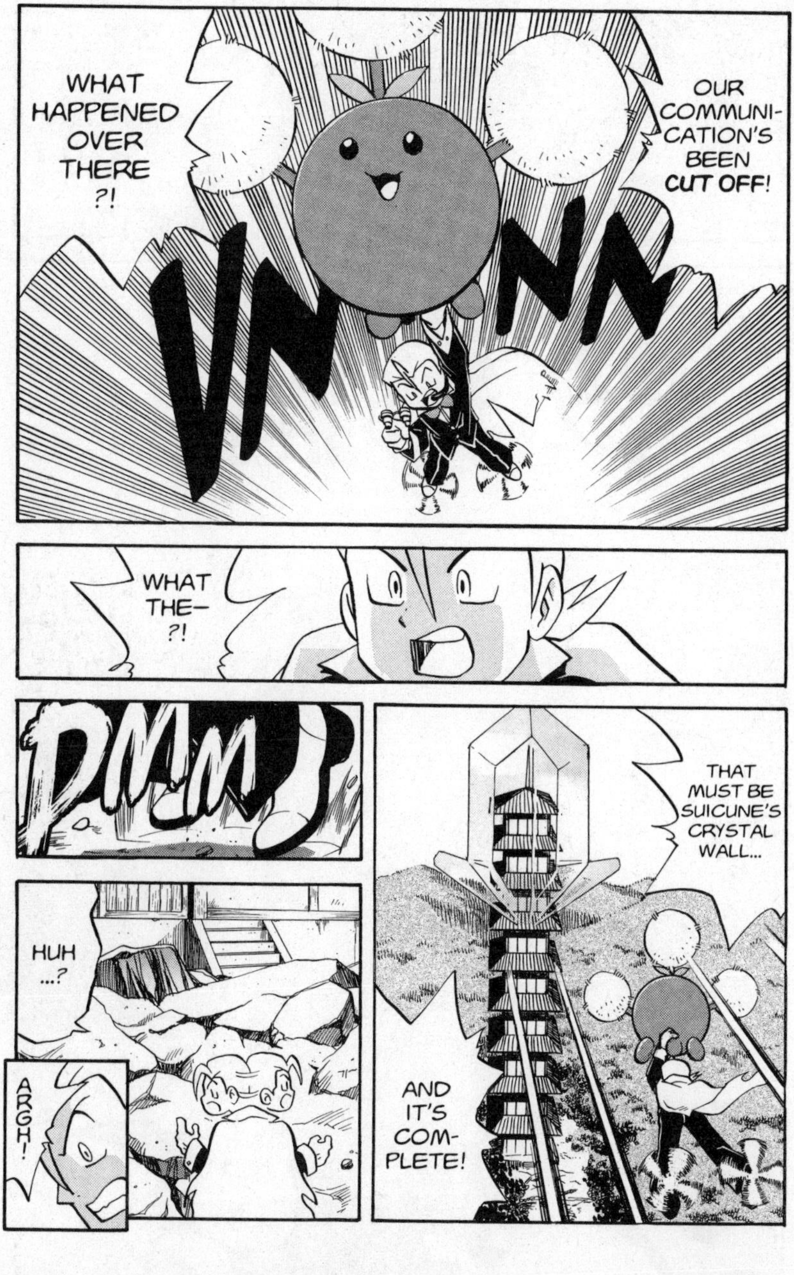
OUR COMMUNICATION'S BEEN CUT OFF!
WHAT HAPPENED OVER THERE ?!
VNNN
WHAT THE— ?!
THAT MUST BE SUICUNE'S CRYSTAL WALL...
AND IT'S COMPLETE!
DMM
HUH ...?
ARGH!

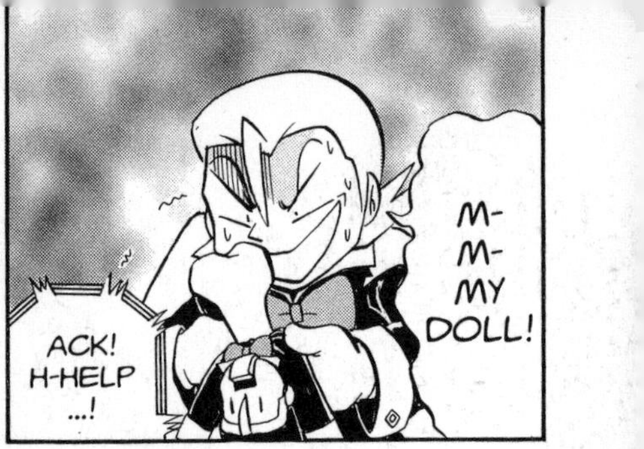
M-
M-
MY
DOLL!
ACK!
H-HELP
...!
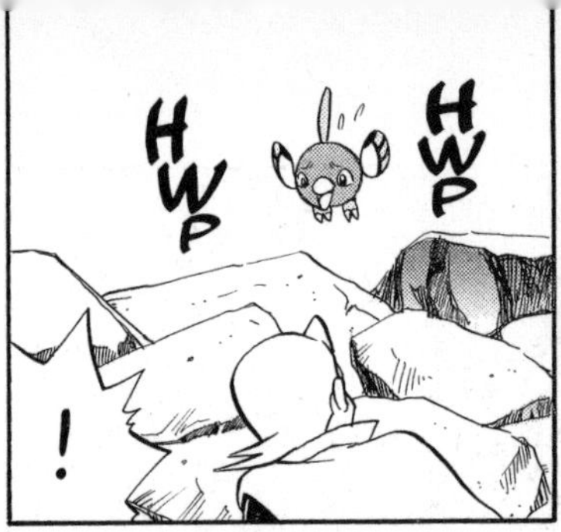
HWP
HWP
!

132 Suddenly Suicune (Part 3)

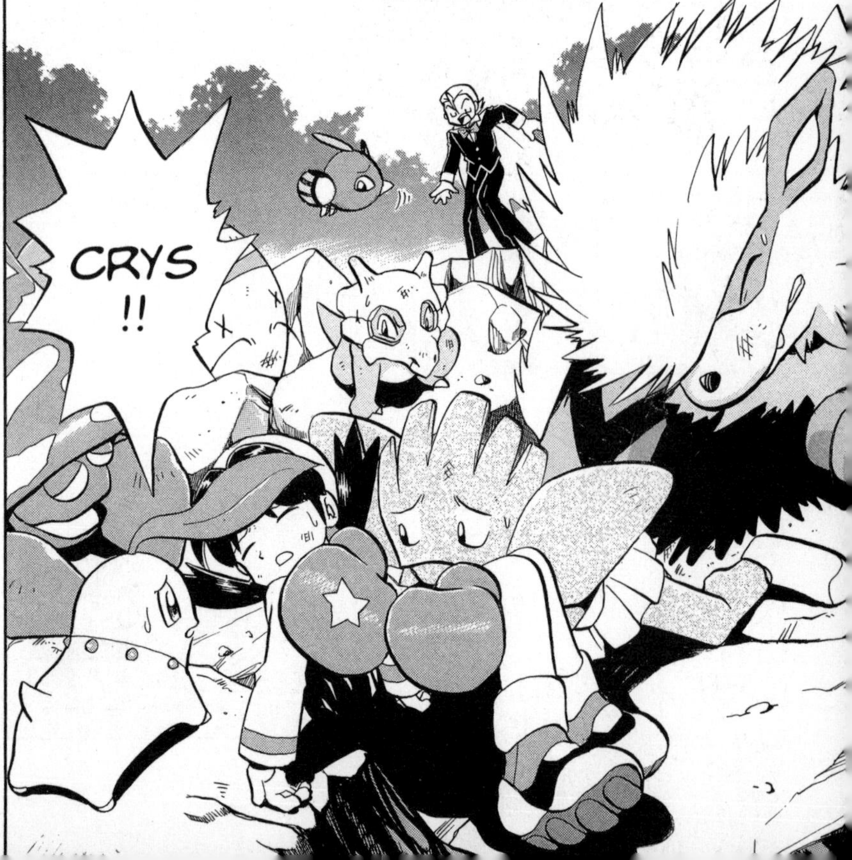
CRYS
!!

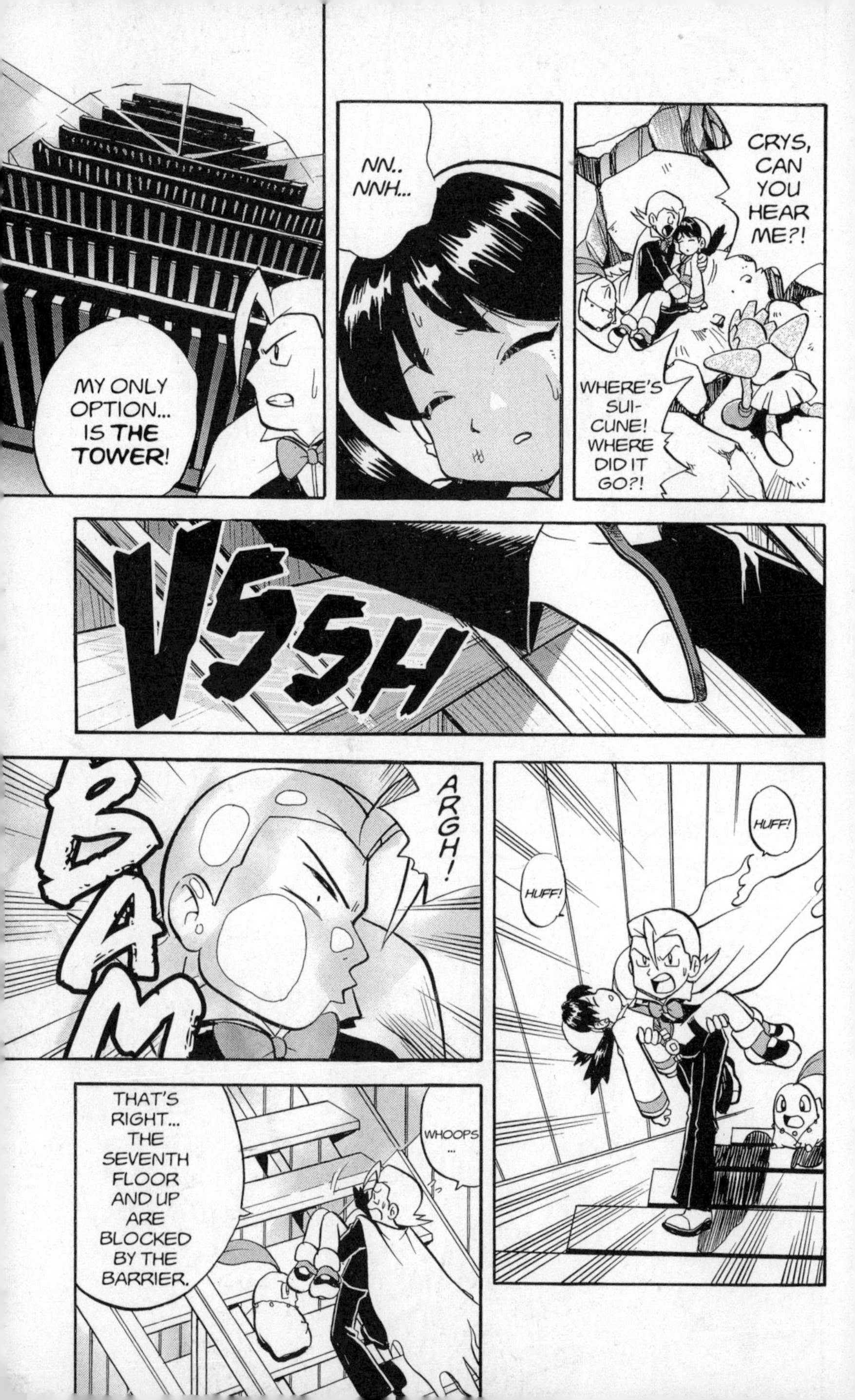
CRYS, CAN YOU HEAR ME?!
WHERE'S SUI-CUNE! WHERE DID IT GO?!
NN.. NNH...
MY ONLY OPTION... IS THE TOWER!
VSSH
HUFF!
HUFF!
ARGH!
BAM
WHOOPS...
THAT'S RIGHT... THE SEVENTH FLOOR AND UP ARE BLOCKED BY THE BARRIER.

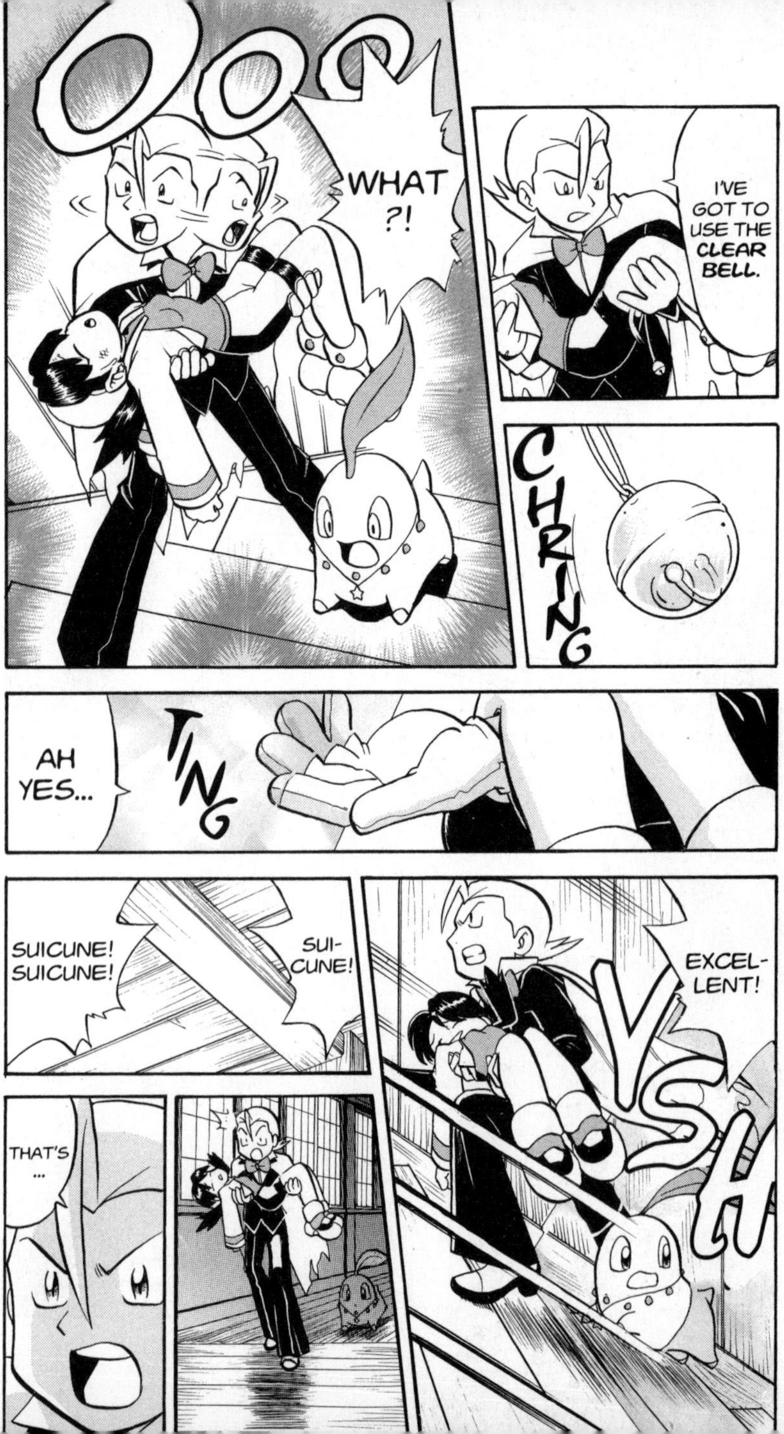
I'VE GOT TO USE THE CLEAR BELL.
CHRING
OOO
WHAT ?!
TING
AH YES...
EXCEL-LENT!
VSSH
SUI-CUNE!
SUICUNE! SUICUNE!
THAT'S ...

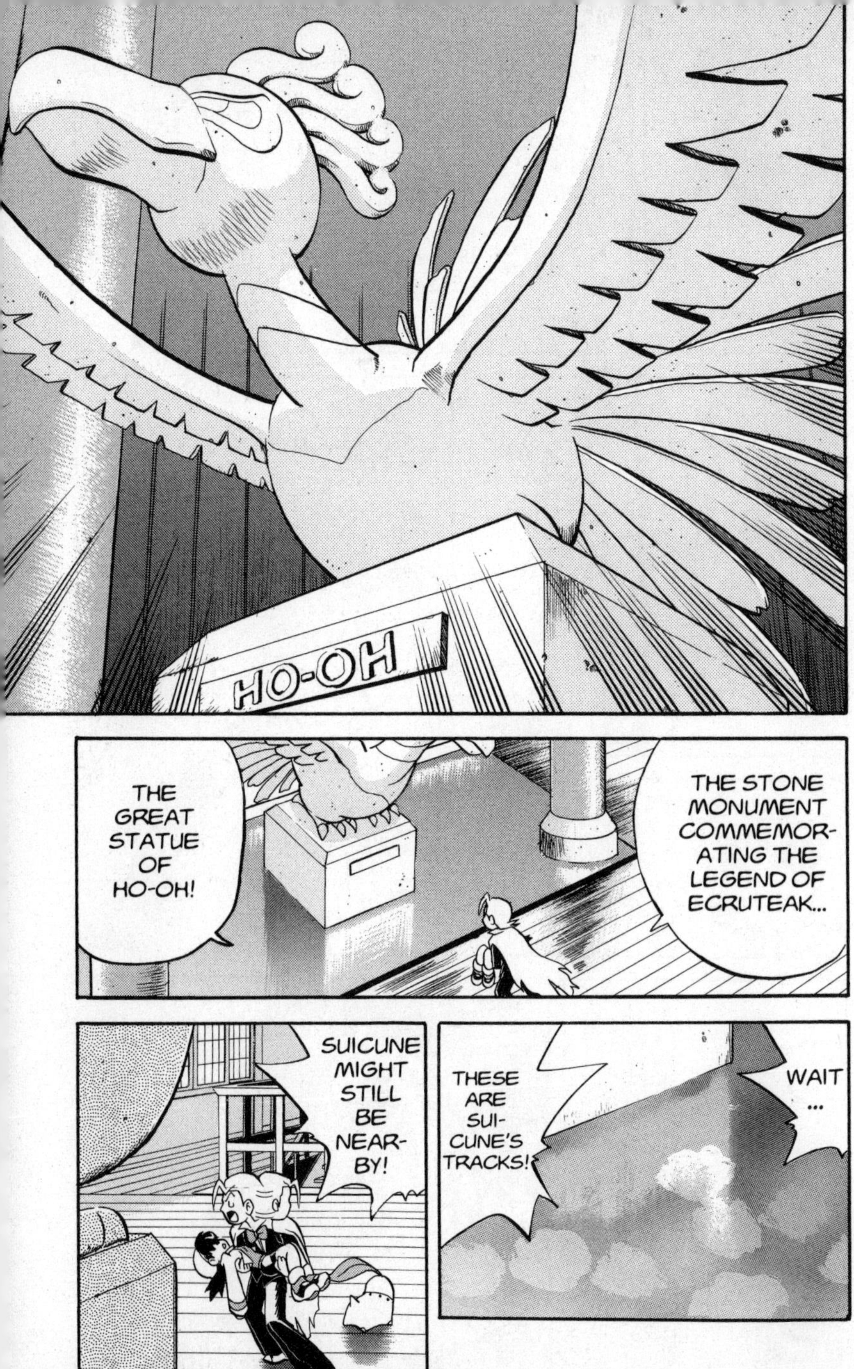
HO-OH
THE STONE MONUMENT COMMEMORATING THE LEGEND OF ECRUTEAK...
THE GREAT STATUE OF HO-OH!
WAIT ...
THESE ARE SUICUNE'S TRACKS!
SUICUNE MIGHT STILL BE NEARBY!

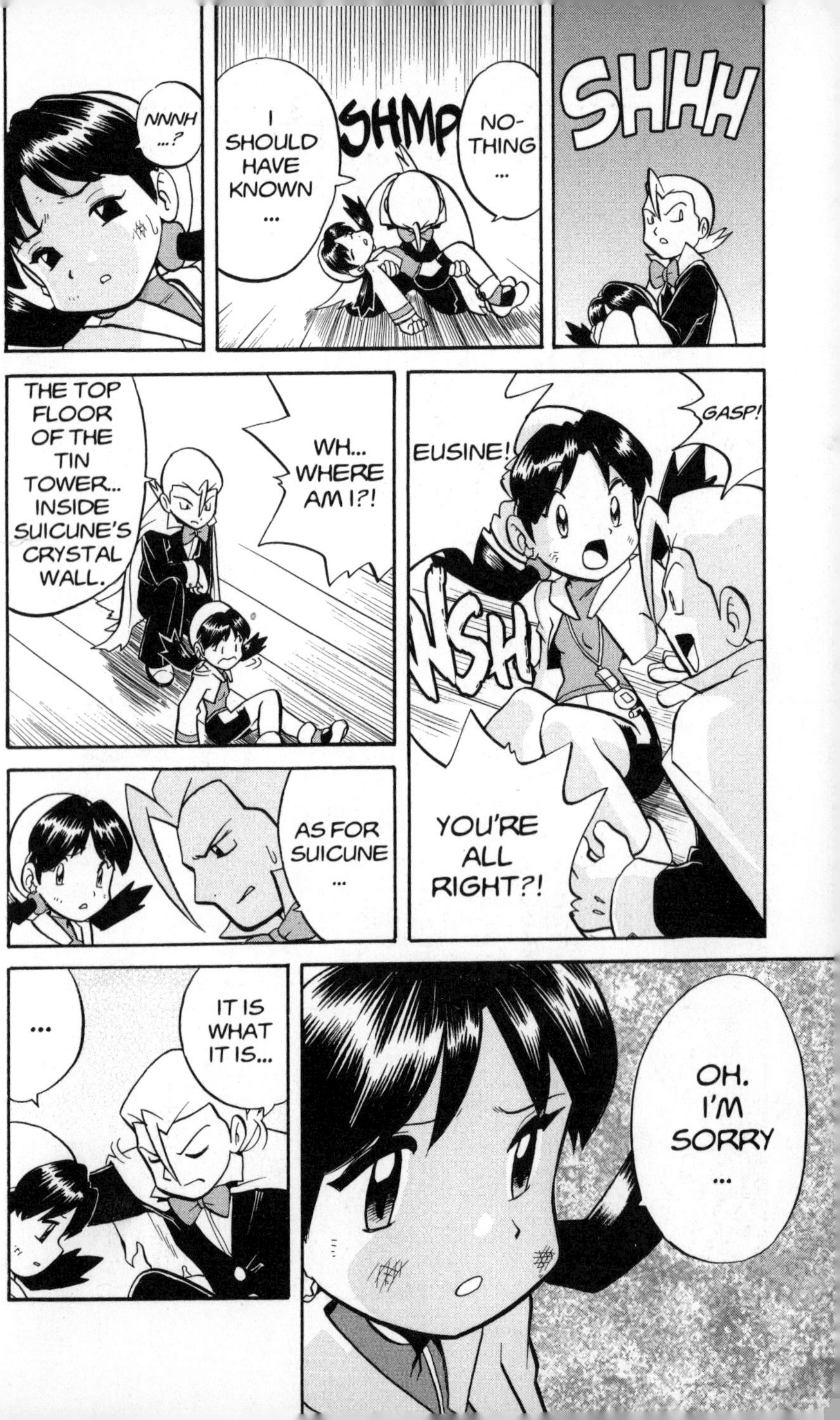
SHHH
NO-THING...
SHMP
I SHOULD HAVE KNOWN...
NNNH...?
GASP!
EUSINE!
WSH
YOU'RE ALL RIGHT?!
WH... WHERE AM I?!
THE TOP FLOOR OF THE TIN TOWER... INSIDE SUICUNE'S CRYSTAL WALL.
AS FOR SUICUNE...
OH. I'M SORRY...
IT IS WHAT IT IS...
...

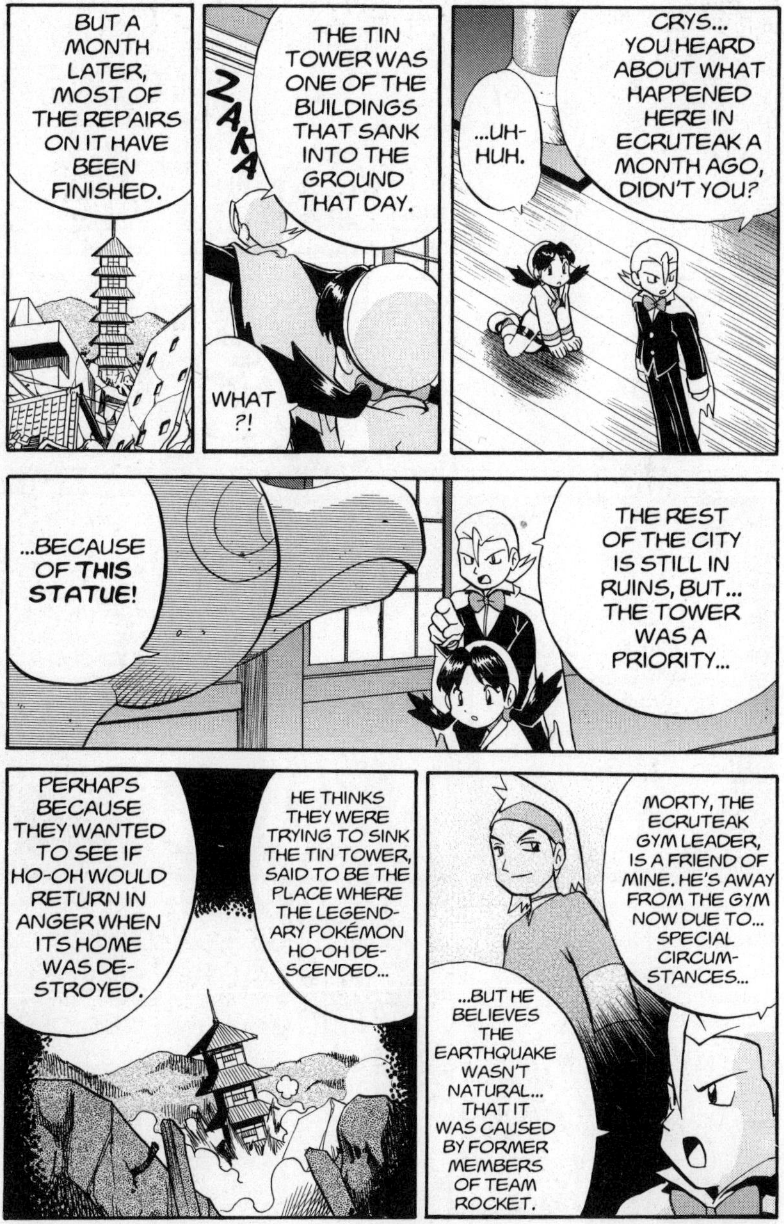
CRYS... YOU HEARD ABOUT WHAT HAPPENED HERE IN ECRUTEAK A MONTH AGO, DIDN'T YOU?
...UH-HUH.
THE TIN TOWER WAS ONE OF THE BUILDINGS THAT SANK INTO THE GROUND THAT DAY.
ZAKA
WHAT ?!
BUT A MONTH LATER, MOST OF THE REPAIRS ON IT HAVE BEEN FINISHED.
THE REST OF THE CITY IS STILL IN RUINS, BUT... THE TOWER WAS A PRIORITY...
...BECAUSE OF **THIS STATUE**!
MORTY, THE ECRUTEAK GYM LEADER, IS A FRIEND OF MINE. HE'S AWAY FROM THE GYM NOW DUE TO... SPECIAL CIRCUMSTANCES...
...BUT HE BELIEVES THE EARTHQUAKE WASN'T NATURAL... THAT IT WAS CAUSED BY FORMER MEMBERS OF TEAM ROCKET.
HE THINKS THEY WERE TRYING TO SINK THE TIN TOWER, SAID TO BE THE PLACE WHERE THE LEGENDARY POKÉMON HO-OH DESCENDED...
PERHAPS BECAUSE THEY WANTED TO SEE IF HO-OH WOULD RETURN IN ANGER WHEN ITS HOME WAS DESTROYED.

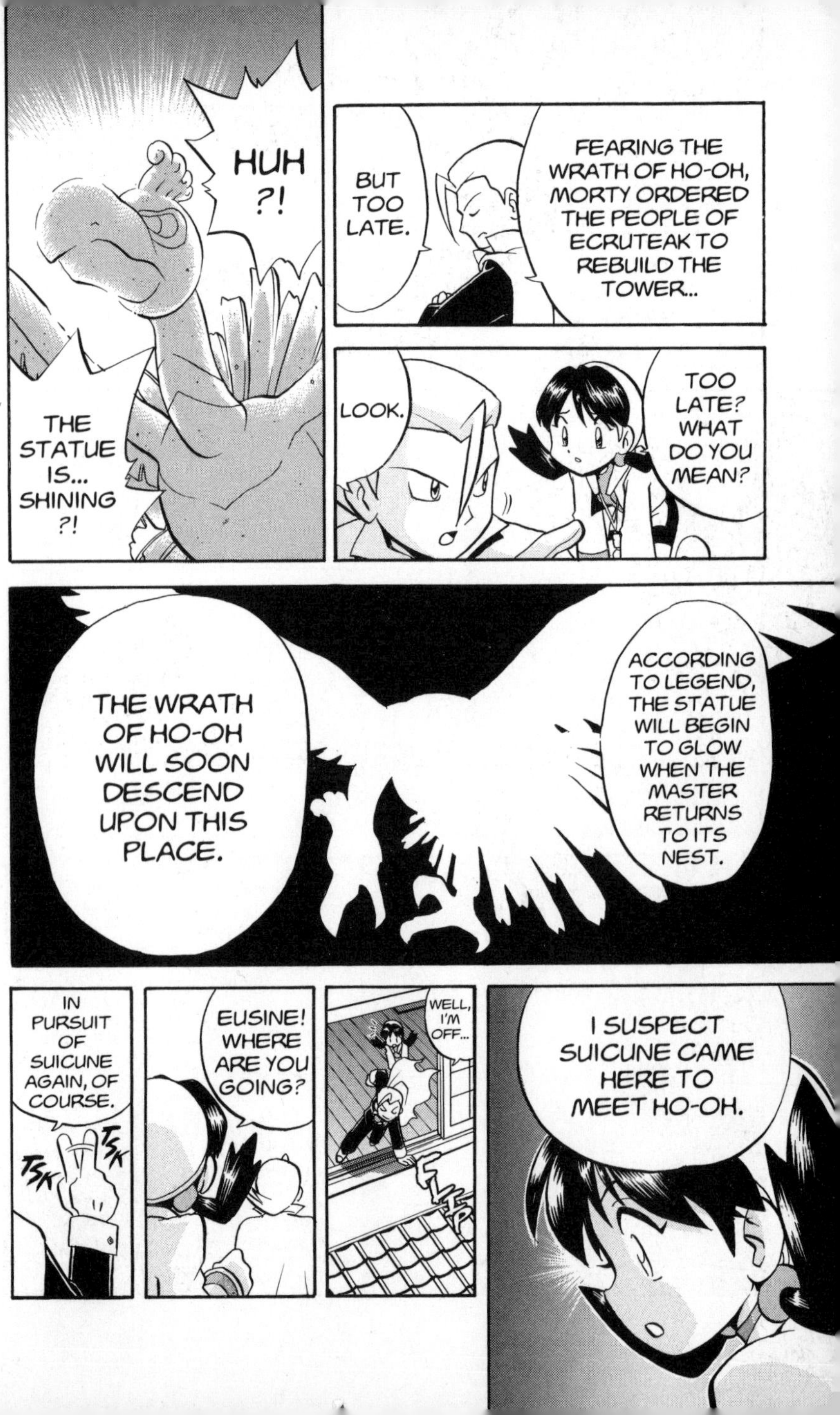
FEARING THE WRATH OF HO-OH, MORTY ORDERED THE PEOPLE OF ECRUTEAK TO REBUILD THE TOWER...
BUT TOO LATE.
TOO LATE? WHAT DO YOU MEAN?
LOOK.
HUH ?!
THE STATUE IS... SHINING ?!
ACCORDING TO LEGEND, THE STATUE WILL BEGIN TO GLOW WHEN THE MASTER RETURNS TO ITS NEST.
THE WRATH OF HO-OH WILL SOON DESCEND UPON THIS PLACE.
I SUSPECT SUICUNE CAME HERE TO MEET HO-OH.
WELL, I'M OFF...
FLIP
EUSINE! WHERE ARE YOU GOING?
IN PURSUIT OF SUICUNE AGAIN, OF COURSE.
TSK
TSK

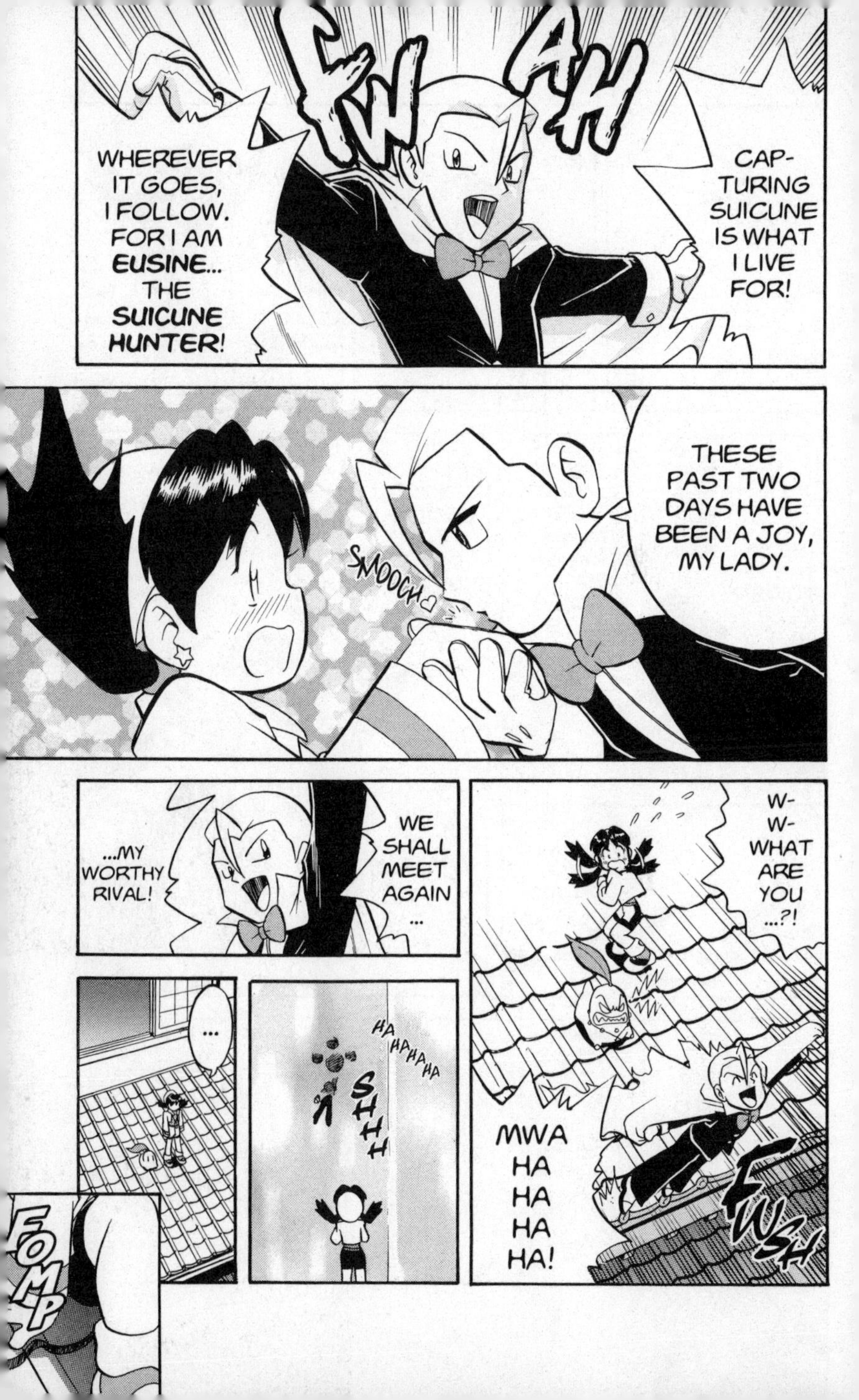
FWAH
CAPTURING SUICUNE IS WHAT I LIVE FOR!
WHEREVER IT GOES, I FOLLOW. FOR I AM EUSINE... THE SUICUNE HUNTER!
THESE PAST TWO DAYS HAVE BEEN A JOY, MY LADY.
SMOOCH♡
W-W-WHAT ARE YOU ...?!
MWA HA HA HA HA!
FWSH
WE SHALL MEET AGAIN ...
...MY WORTHY RIVAL!
HA HA HA HA HA
SHHH
...
FOMP

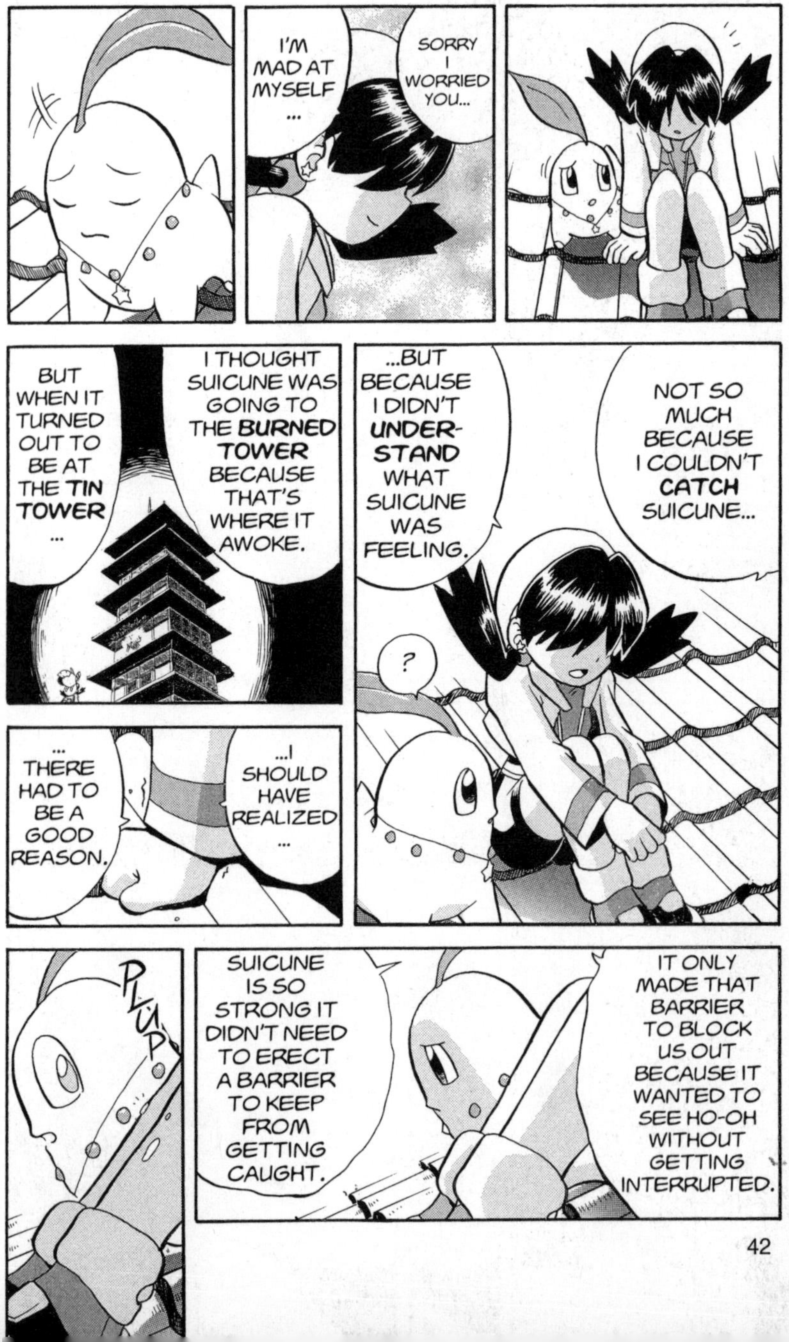
SORRY I WORRIED YOU...
I'M MAD AT MYSELF ...
NOT SO MUCH BECAUSE I COULDN'T CATCH SUICUNE...
...BUT BECAUSE I DIDN'T UNDERSTAND WHAT SUICUNE WAS FEELING.
?
I THOUGHT SUICUNE WAS GOING TO THE BURNED TOWER BECAUSE THAT'S WHERE IT AWOKE.
BUT WHEN IT TURNED OUT TO BE AT THE TIN TOWER ...
...I SHOULD HAVE REALIZED ...
... THERE HAD TO BE A GOOD REASON.
IT ONLY MADE THAT BARRIER TO BLOCK US OUT BECAUSE IT WANTED TO SEE HO-OH WITHOUT GETTING INTERRUPTED.
SUICUNE IS SO STRONG IT DIDN'T NEED TO ERECT A BARRIER TO KEEP FROM GETTING CAUGHT.
PLUP

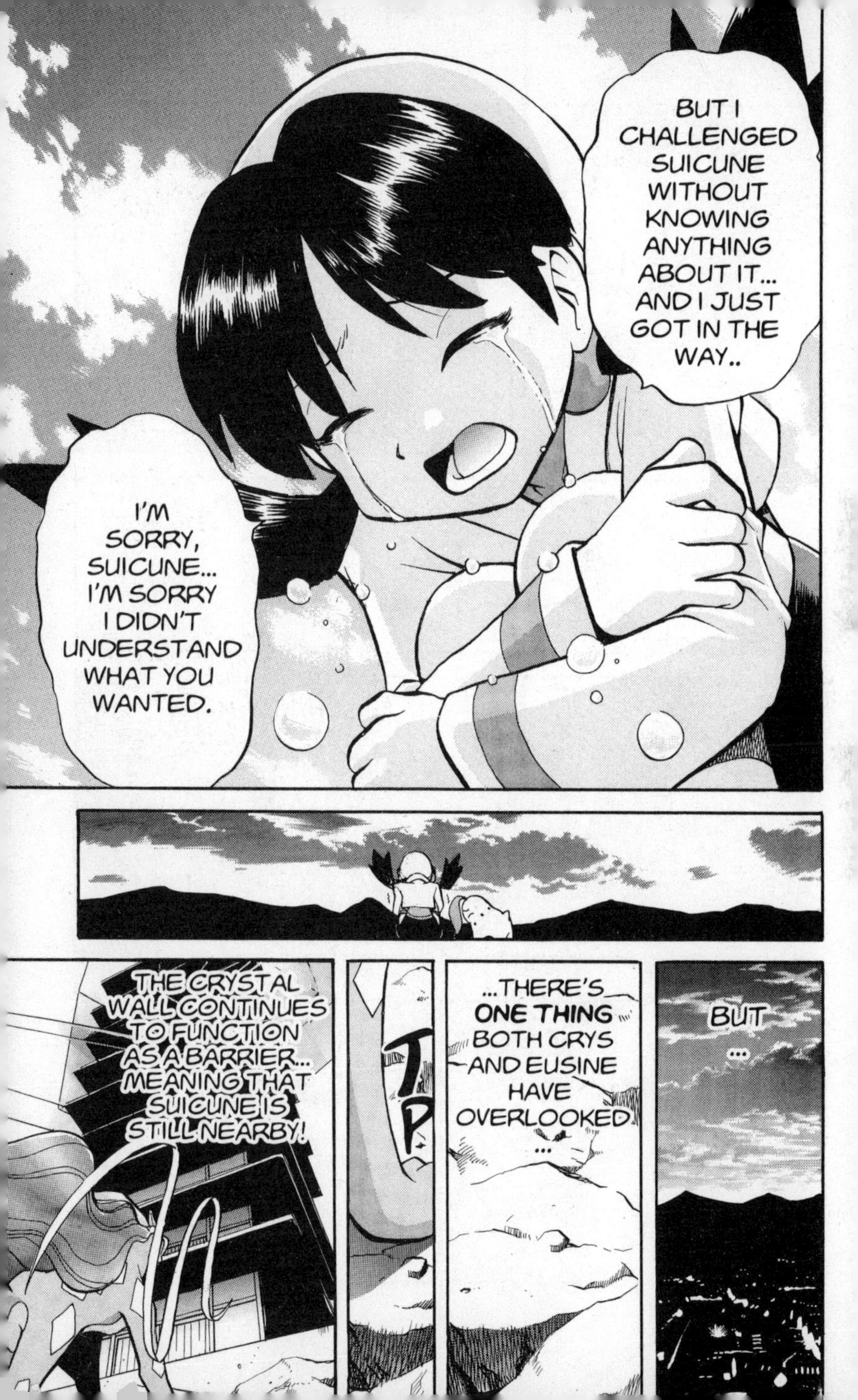
BUT I CHALLENGED SUICUNE WITHOUT KNOWING ANYTHING ABOUT IT... AND I JUST GOT IN THE WAY..
I'M SORRY, SUICUNE... I'M SORRY I DIDN'T UNDERSTAND WHAT YOU WANTED.
BUT ...
...THERE'S ONE THING BOTH CRYS AND EUSINE HAVE OVERLOOKED ...
TP
THE CRYSTAL WALL CONTINUES TO FUNCTION AS A BARRIER... MEANING THAT SUICUNE IS STILL NEARBY!

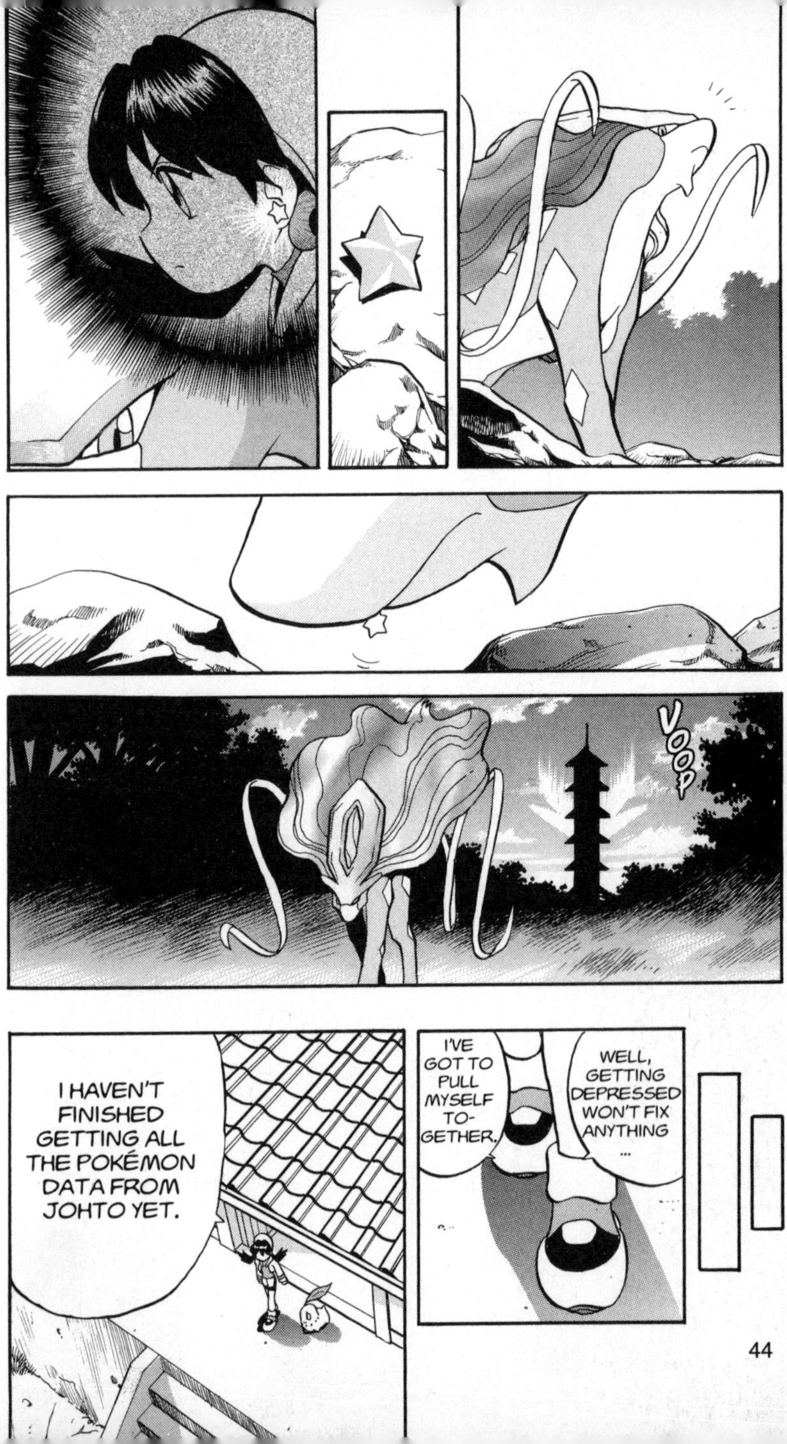
VOOP
WELL, GETTING DEPRESSED WON'T FIX ANYTHING...
I'VE GOT TO PULL MYSELF TO-GETHER.
I HAVEN'T FINISHED GETTING ALL THE POKÉMON DATA FROM JOHTO YET.

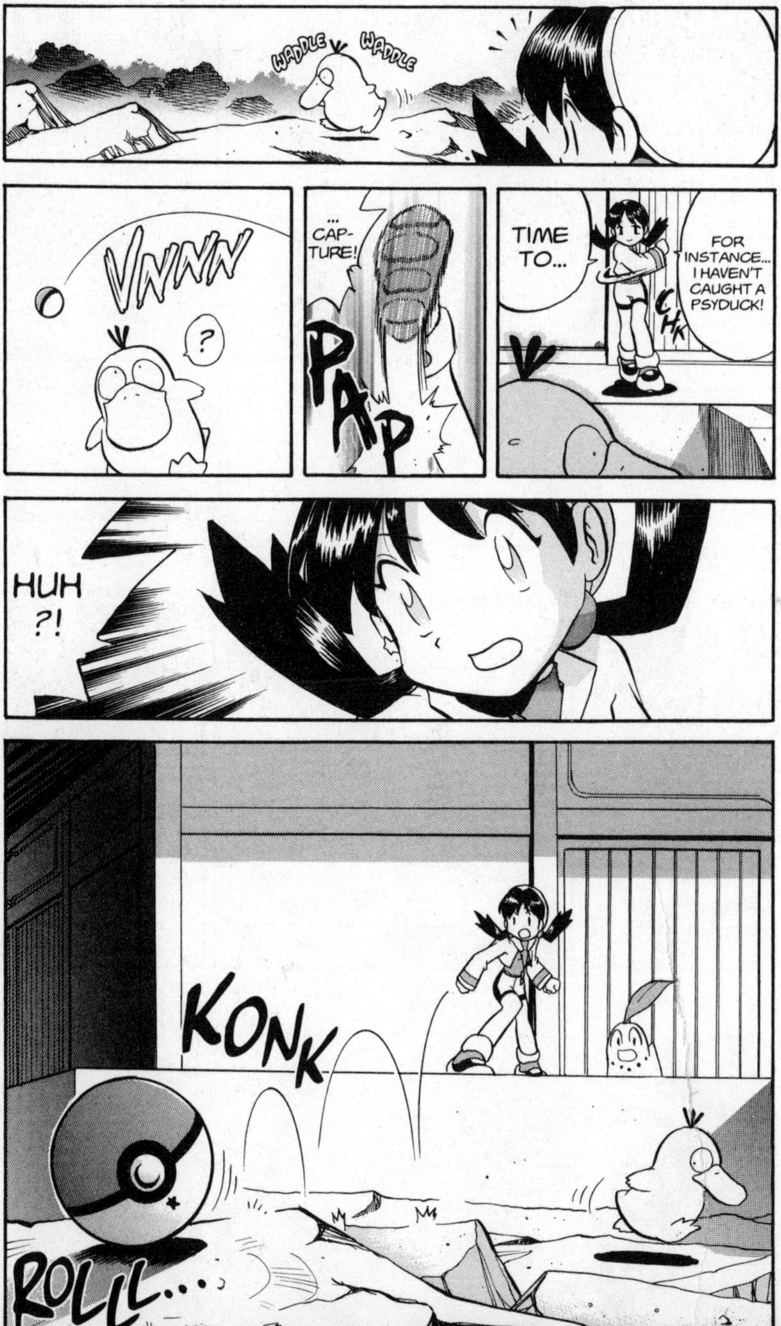
WADDLE WADDLE
FOR INSTANCE... I HAVEN'T CAUGHT A PSYDUCK!
TIME TO...
CHK
... CAPTURE!
PAP
VNNNN
?
HUH ?!
KONK
ROLL...

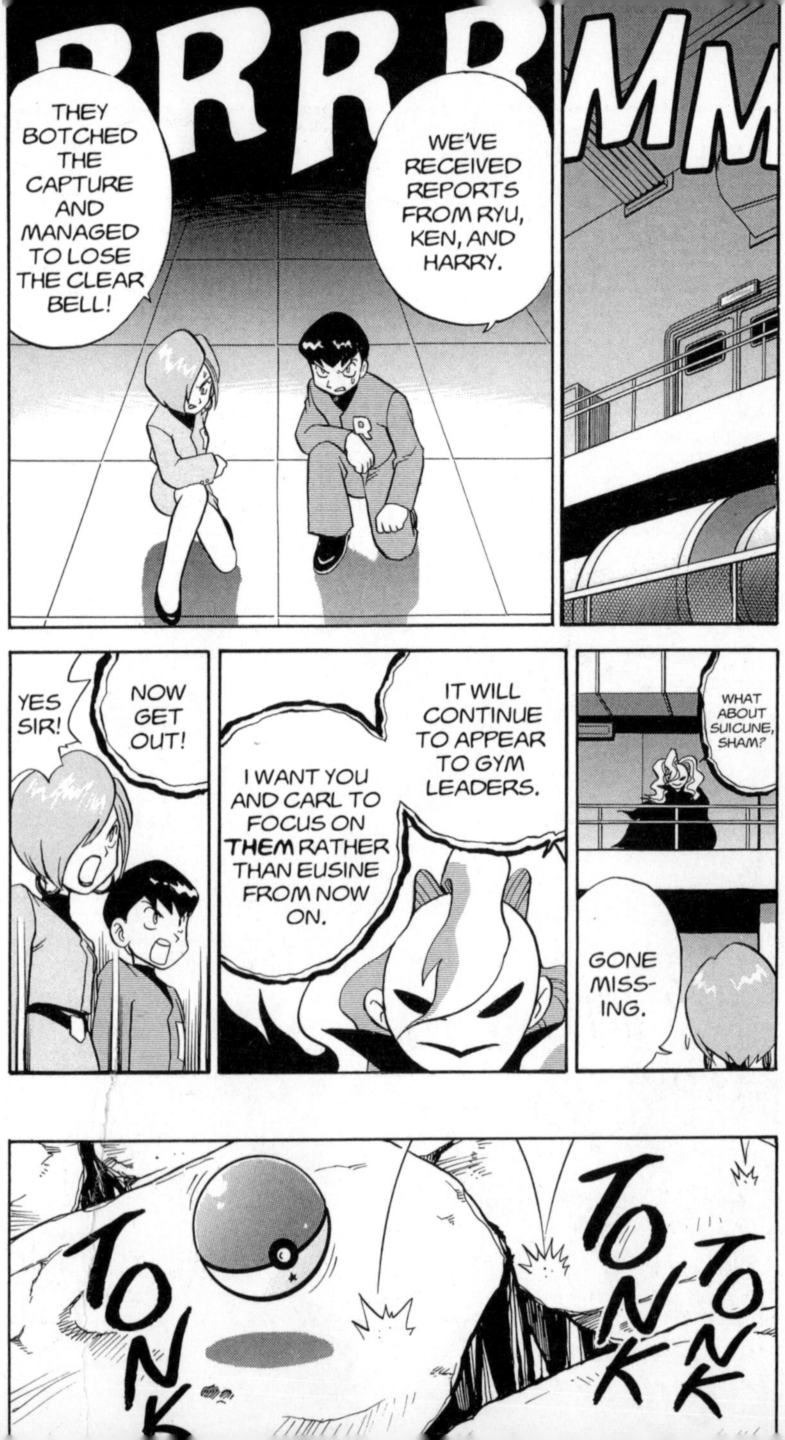
BRRRMM
WE'VE RECEIVED REPORTS FROM RYU, KEN, AND HARRY.
THEY BOTCHED THE CAPTURE AND MANAGED TO LOSE THE CLEAR BELL!
WHAT ABOUT SUICUNE, SHAM?
GONE MISS-ING.
IT WILL CONTINUE TO APPEAR TO GYM LEADERS.
I WANT YOU AND CARL TO FOCUS ON **THEM** RATHER THAN EUSINE FROM NOW ON.
NOW GET OUT!
YES SIR!
TONK
TONK
TONK

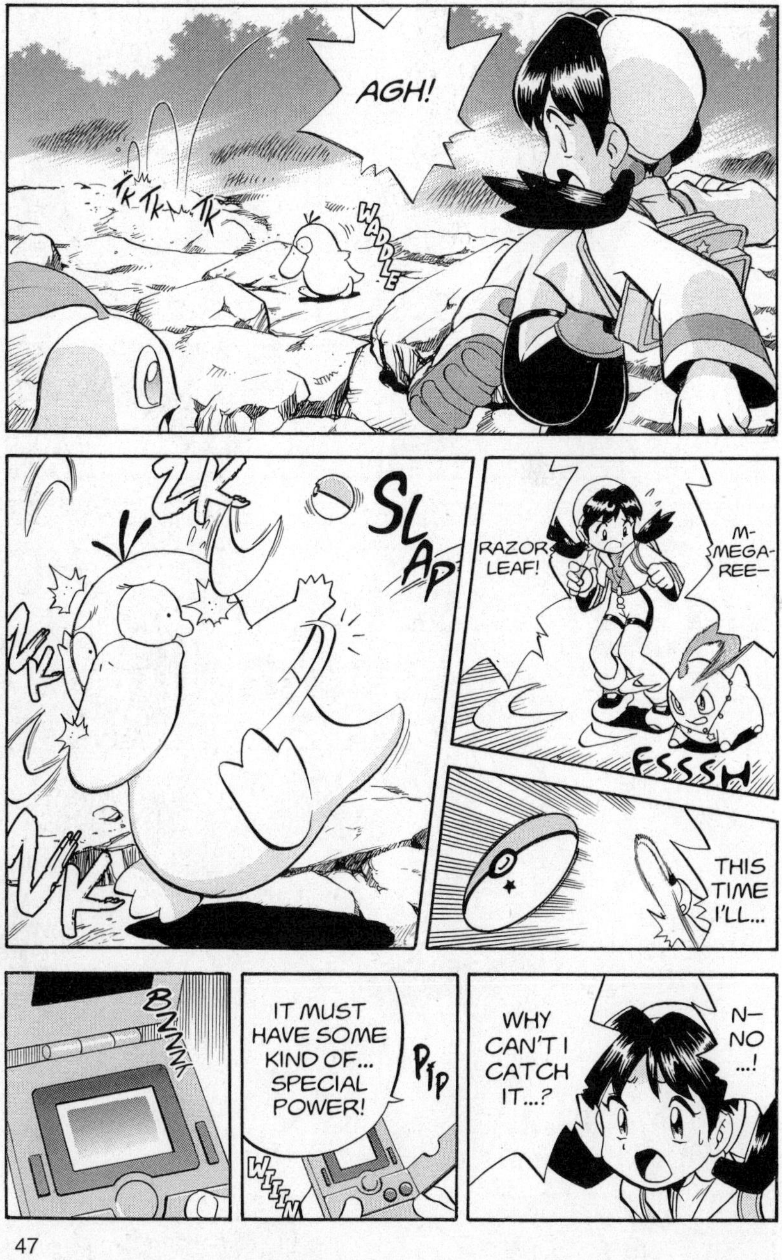
AGH!
TK TK TK
WADDLE
M-MEGA-REE—
RAZOR LEAF!
FSSSH
THIS TIME I'LL...
ZK
SLAP
ZK
ZK
N—NO...!
WHY CAN'T I CATCH IT...?
IT MUST HAVE SOME KIND OF... SPECIAL POWER!
PIP
WIIIN
BZZZZ

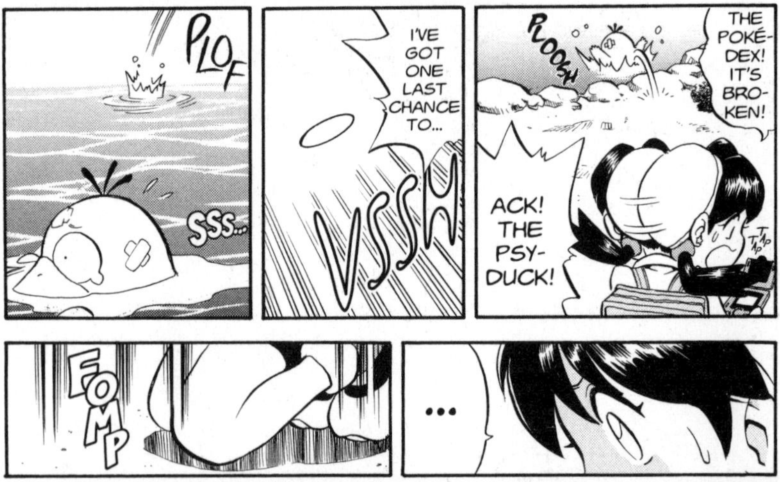
THE POKÉ-DEX! IT'S BRO-KEN!
PLOOSH
ACK! THE PSY-DUCK!
TAP TAP
I'VE GOT ONE LAST CHANCE TO...
VSSH
PLOF
SSS...
...
FOMP

133 Absolutely Azumarill

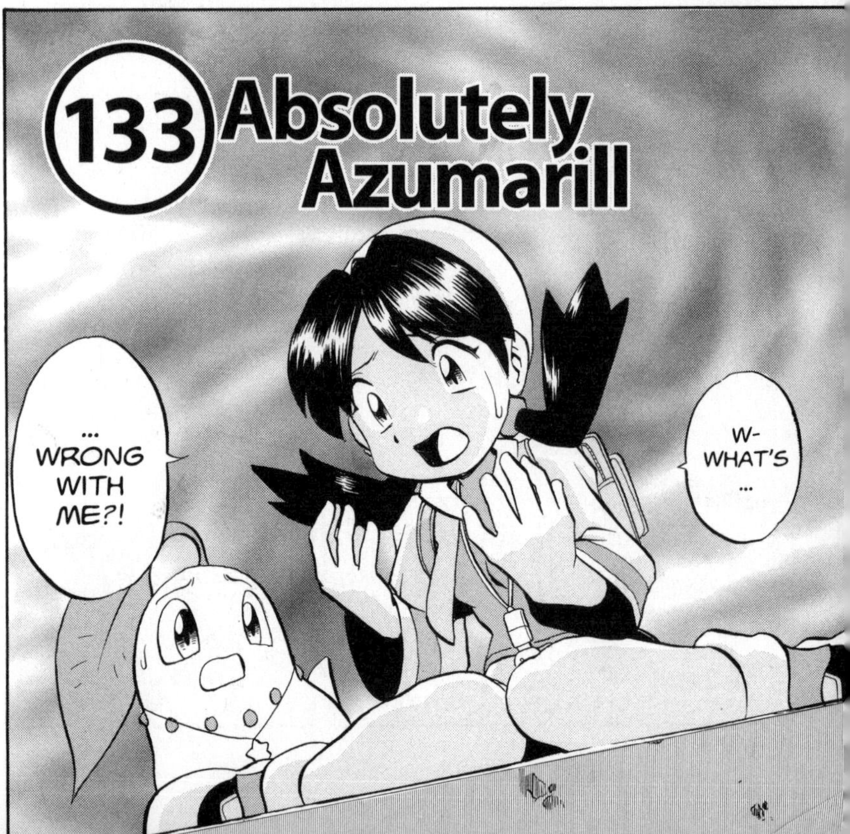
W-WHAT'S ...
... WRONG WITH ME?!

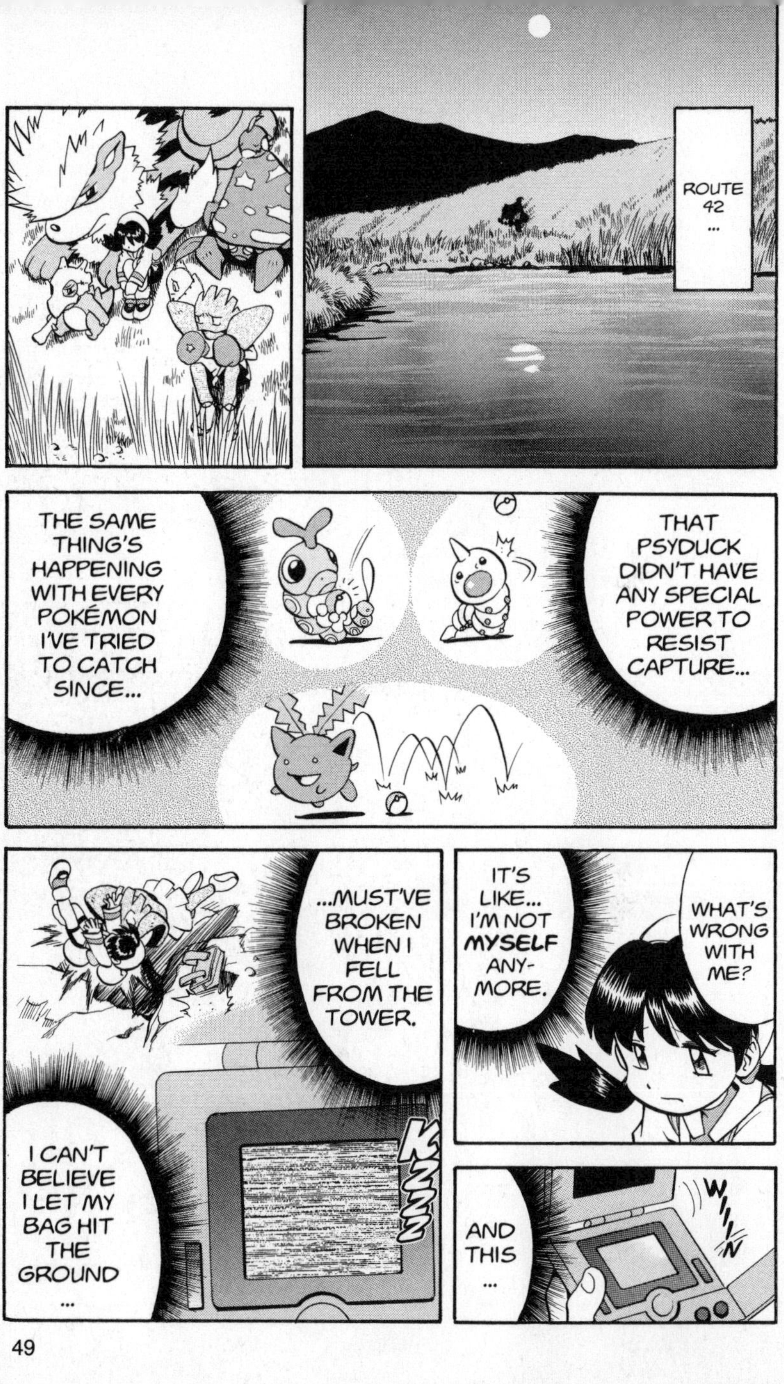
ROUTE 42 ...
THAT PSYDUCK DIDN'T HAVE ANY SPECIAL POWER TO RESIST CAPTURE...
THE SAME THING'S HAPPENING WITH EVERY POKÉMON I'VE TRIED TO CATCH SINCE...
WHAT'S WRONG WITH ME?
IT'S LIKE... I'M NOT **MYSELF** ANY-MORE.
AND THIS ...
WIIIN
...MUST'VE BROKEN WHEN I FELL FROM THE TOWER.
KZZZ
I CAN'T BELIEVE I LET MY BAG HIT THE GROUND ...

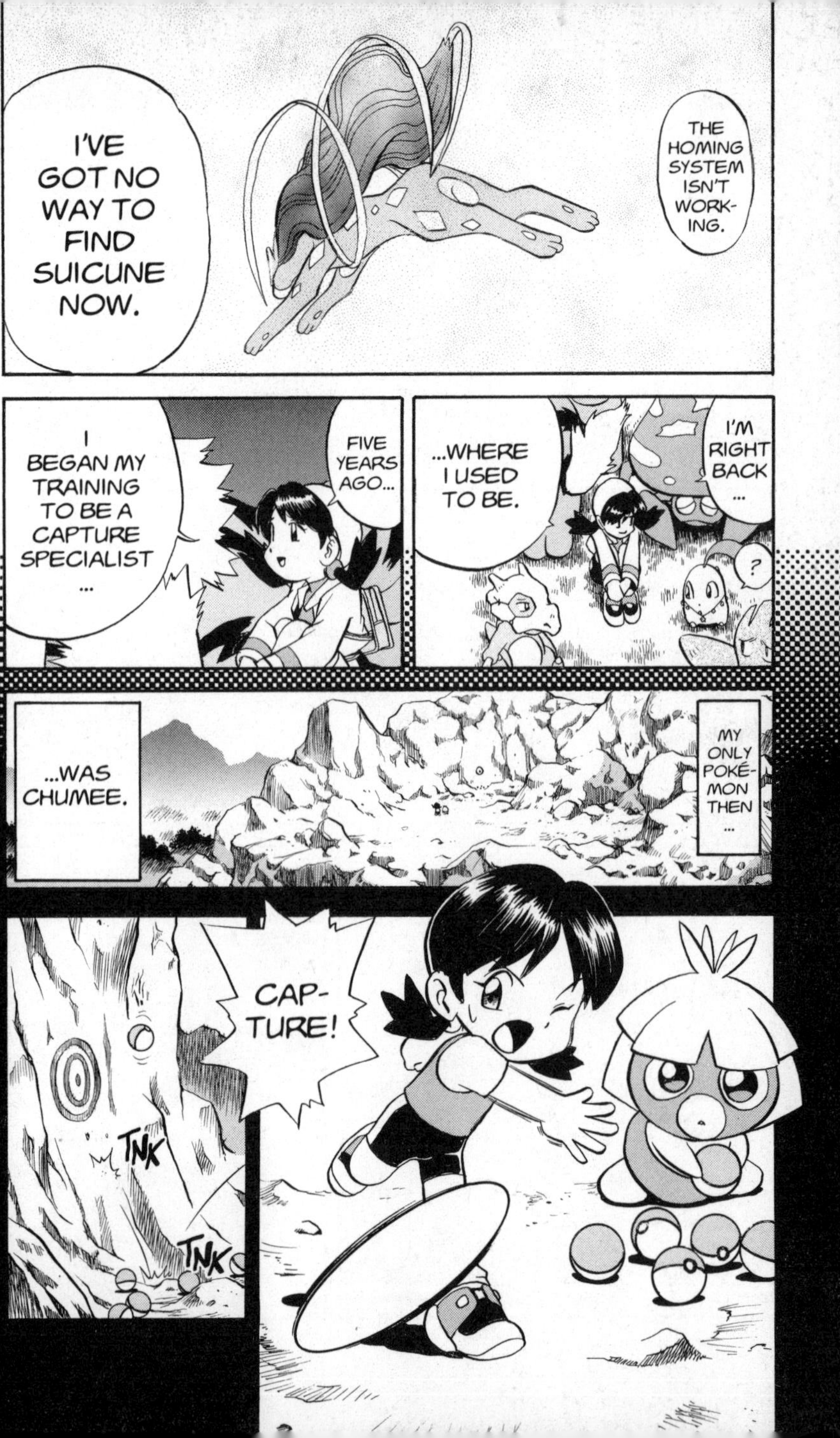
THE HOMING SYSTEM ISN'T WORK-ING.
I'VE GOT NO WAY TO FIND SUICUNE NOW.
I'M RIGHT BACK ...
...WHERE I USED TO BE.
?
FIVE YEARS AGO...
I BEGAN MY TRAINING TO BE A CAPTURE SPECIALIST ...
MY ONLY POKÉ-MON THEN ...
...WAS CHUMEE.
CAP-TURE!
TNK
TNK

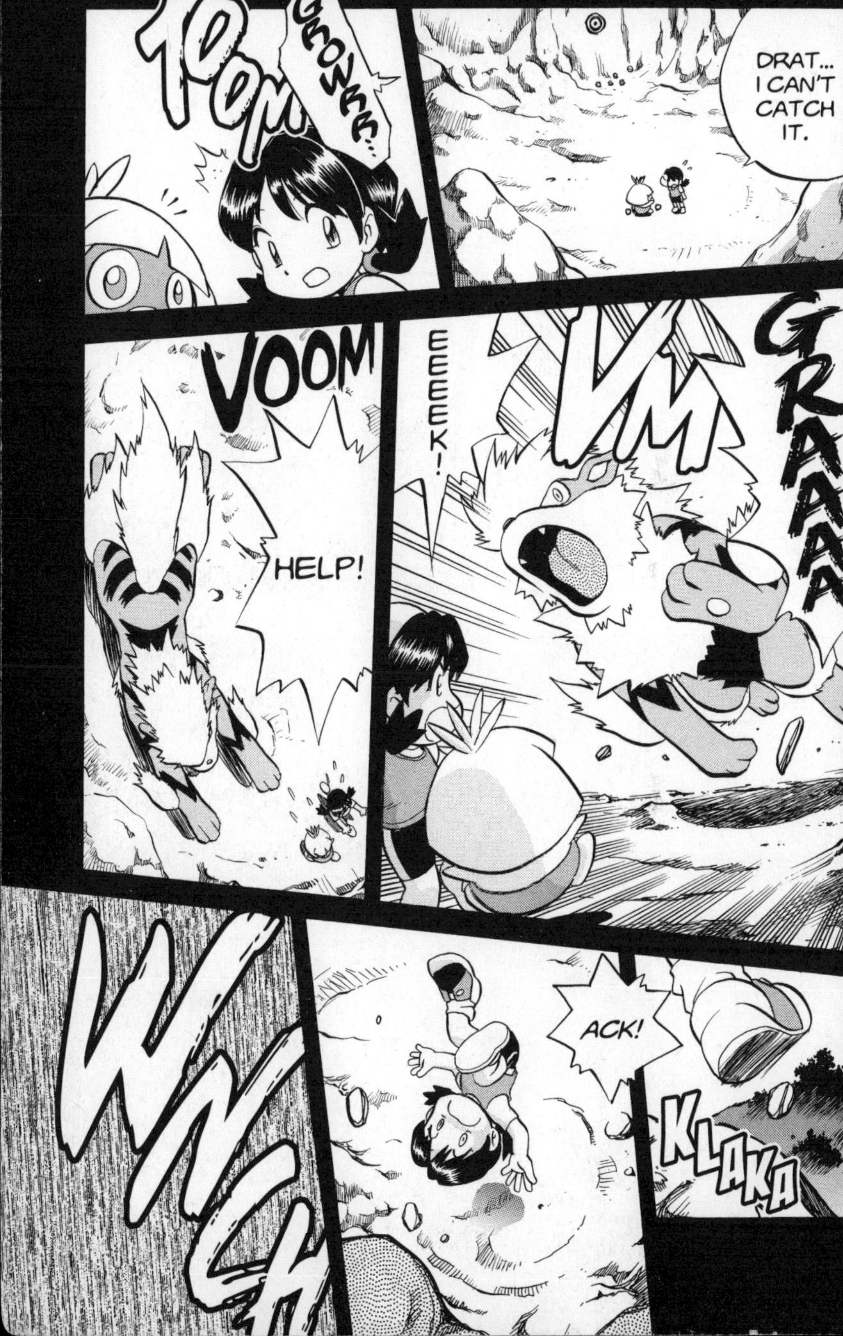
DRAT... I CAN'T CATCH IT.
GROWRR...
TOOM
GRAAAA
VM
EEEEEK!
VOOM
HELP!
ACK!
KLAKA

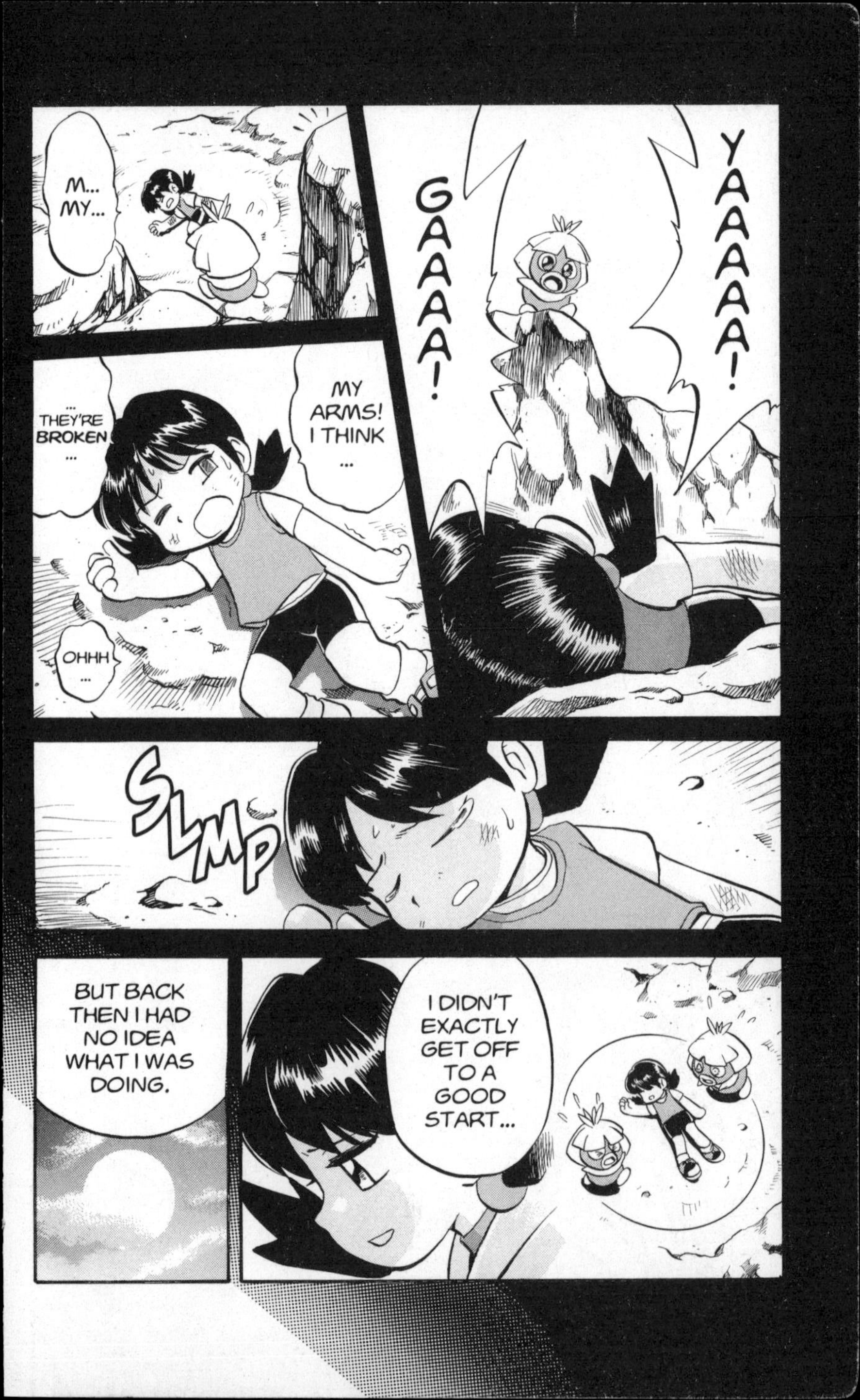
YAAAAAA!
GAAAA!
M... MY...
MY ARMS! I THINK ...
... THEY'RE BROKEN ...
OHHH ...
SLMP
I DIDN'T EXACTLY GET OFF TO A GOOD START...
BUT BACK THEN I HAD NO IDEA WHAT I WAS DOING.

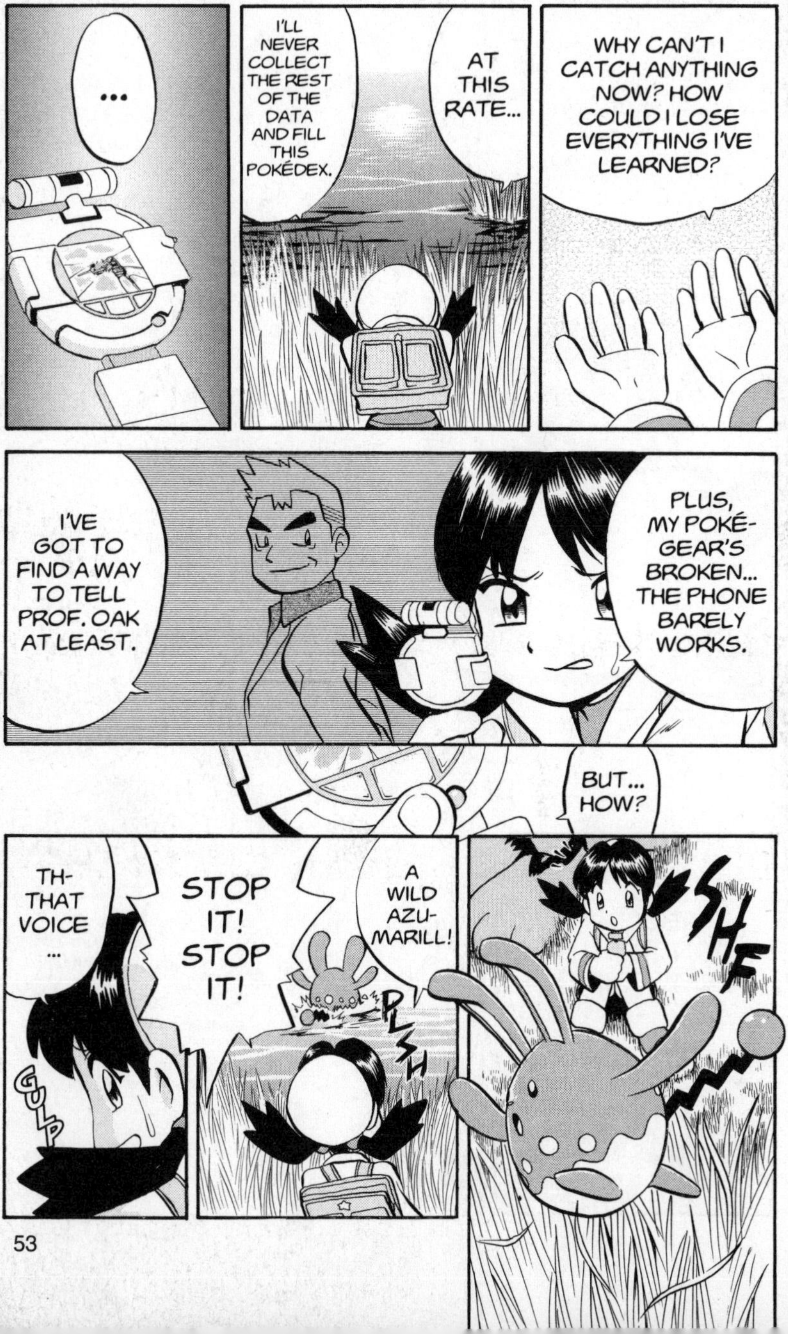
WHY CAN'T I CATCH ANYTHING NOW? HOW COULD I LOSE EVERYTHING I'VE LEARNED?
AT THIS RATE...
I'LL NEVER COLLECT THE REST OF THE DATA AND FILL THIS POKÉDEX.
...
PLUS, MY POKÉ-GEAR'S BROKEN... THE PHONE BARELY WORKS.
I'VE GOT TO FIND A WAY TO TELL PROF. OAK AT LEAST.
BUT... HOW?
SHE
A WILD AZU-MARILL!
STOP IT! STOP IT!
PLSH
TH-THAT VOICE ...
GULP

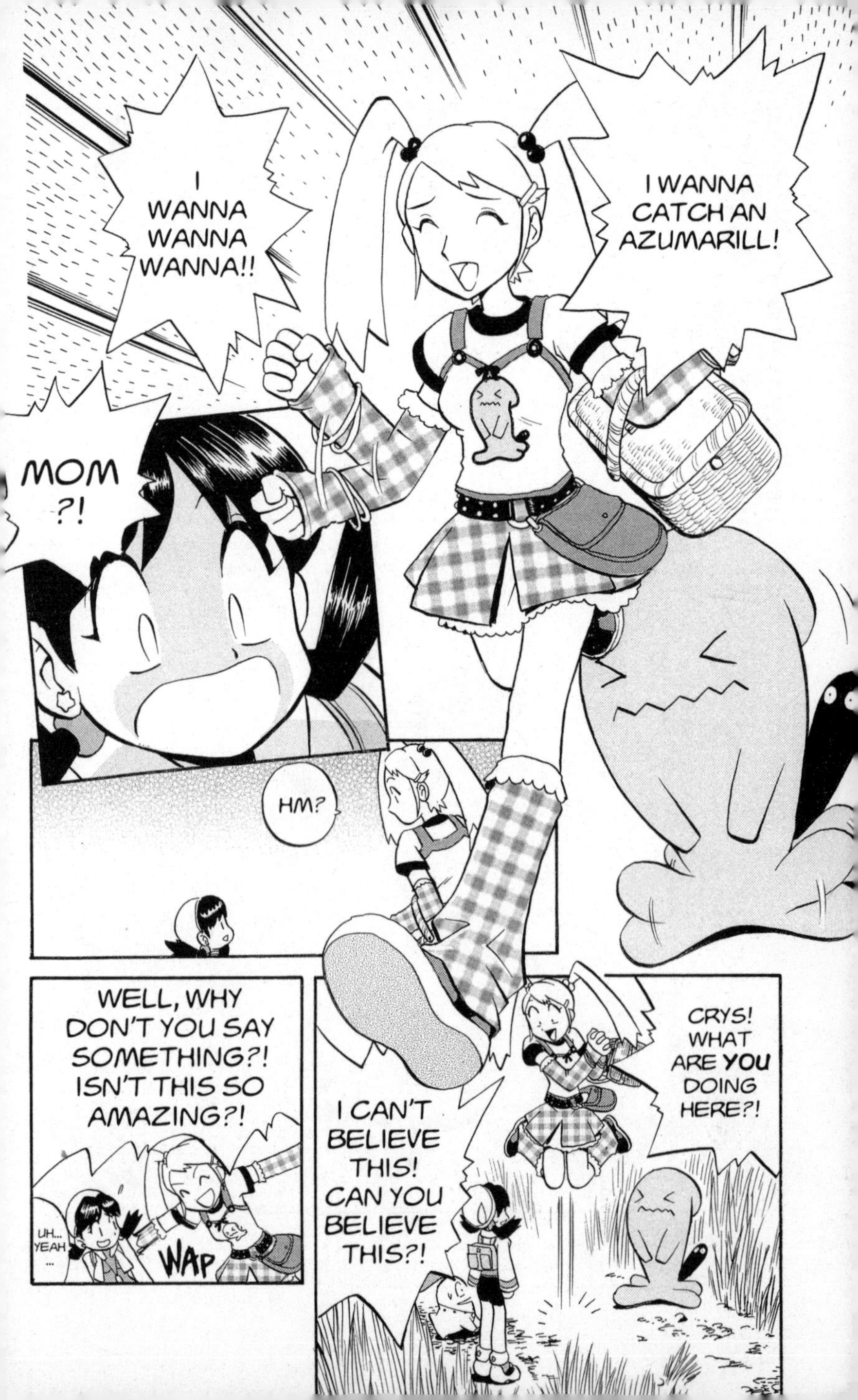
I WANNA CATCH AN AZUMARILL!
I WANNA WANNA WANNA!!
MOM ?!
HM?
CRYS! WHAT ARE **YOU** DOING HERE?!
I CAN'T BELIEVE THIS! CAN YOU BELIEVE THIS?!
WELL, WHY DON'T YOU SAY SOMETHING?! ISN'T THIS SO AMAZING?!
UH... YEAH ...
WAP

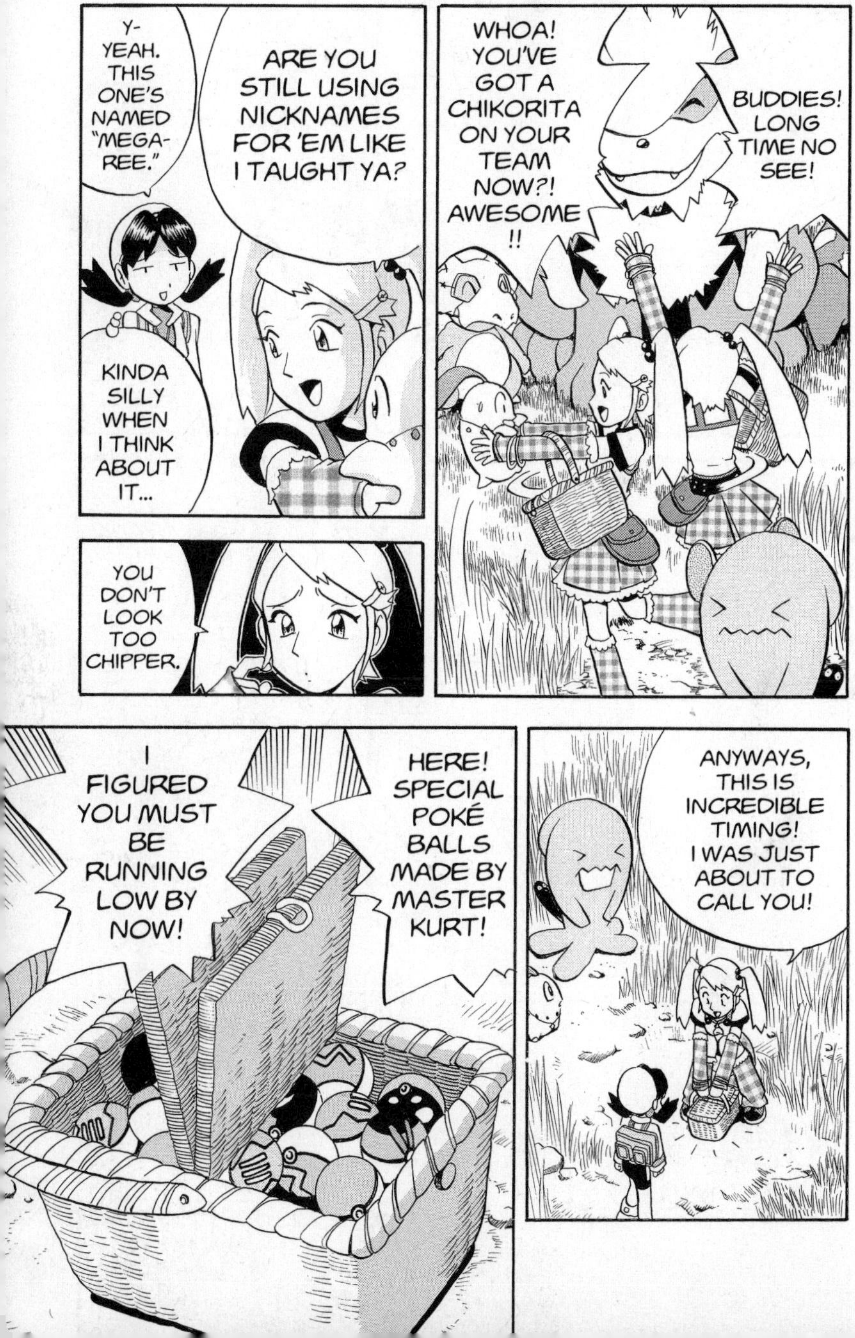
BUDDIES! LONG TIME NO SEE!
WHOA! YOU'VE GOT A CHIKORITA ON YOUR TEAM NOW?! AWESOME!!
ARE YOU STILL USING NICKNAMES FOR 'EM LIKE I TAUGHT YA?
Y-YEAH. THIS ONE'S NAMED "MEGA-REE."
KINDA SILLY WHEN I THINK ABOUT IT...
YOU DON'T LOOK TOO CHIPPER.
ANYWAYS, THIS IS INCREDIBLE TIMING! I WAS JUST ABOUT TO CALL YOU!
HERE! SPECIAL POKÉ BALLS MADE BY MASTER KURT!
I FIGURED YOU MUST BE RUNNING LOW BY NOW!

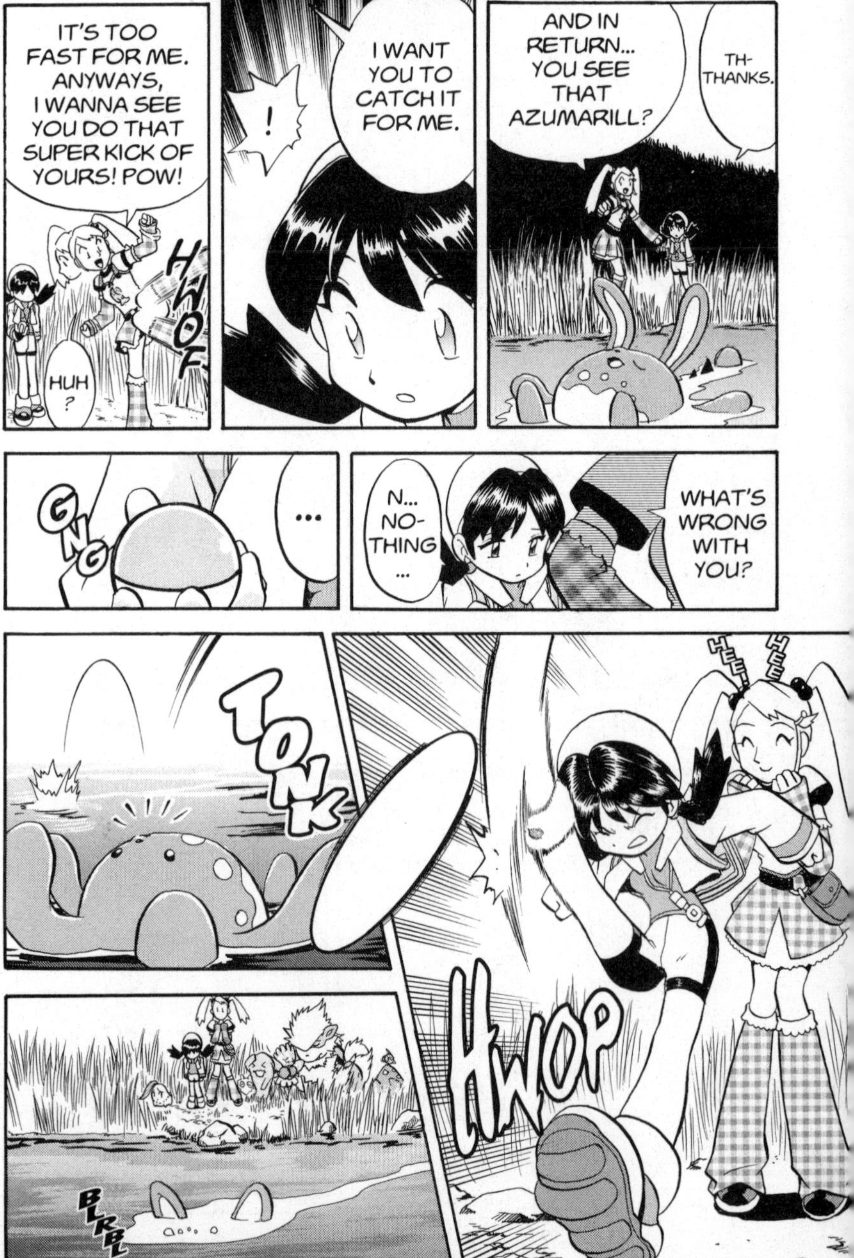
TH-THANKS.
AND IN RETURN... YOU SEE THAT AZUMARILL?
I WANT YOU TO CATCH IT FOR ME.
!
IT'S TOO FAST FOR ME. ANYWAYS, I WANNA SEE YOU DO THAT SUPER KICK OF YOURS! POW!
HWOF
HUH?
WHAT'S WRONG WITH YOU?
N... NO-THING...
...
GNG
HEE HEE
HWOP
TONK
BLRBL

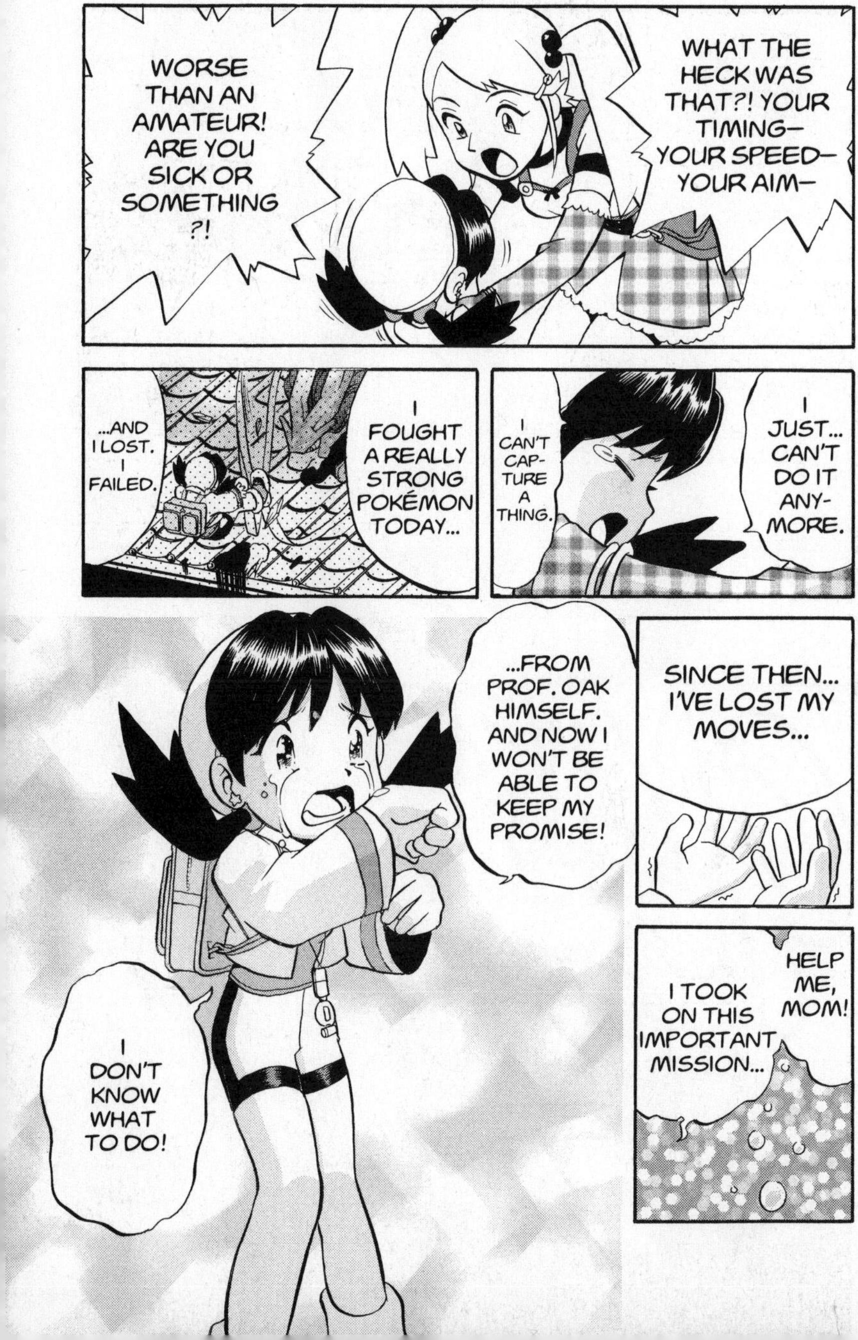
WHAT THE HECK WAS THAT?! YOUR TIMING— YOUR SPEED— YOUR AIM—
WORSE THAN AN AMATEUR! ARE YOU SICK OR SOMETHING ?!
I JUST... CAN'T DO IT ANY-MORE.
I CAN'T CAP-TURE A THING.
I FOUGHT A REALLY STRONG POKÉMON TODAY...
...AND I LOST. I FAILED.
SINCE THEN... I'VE LOST MY MOVES...
HELP ME, MOM!
I TOOK ON THIS IMPORTANT MISSION...
...FROM PROF. OAK HIMSELF. AND NOW I WON'T BE ABLE TO KEEP MY PROMISE!
I DON'T KNOW WHAT TO DO!

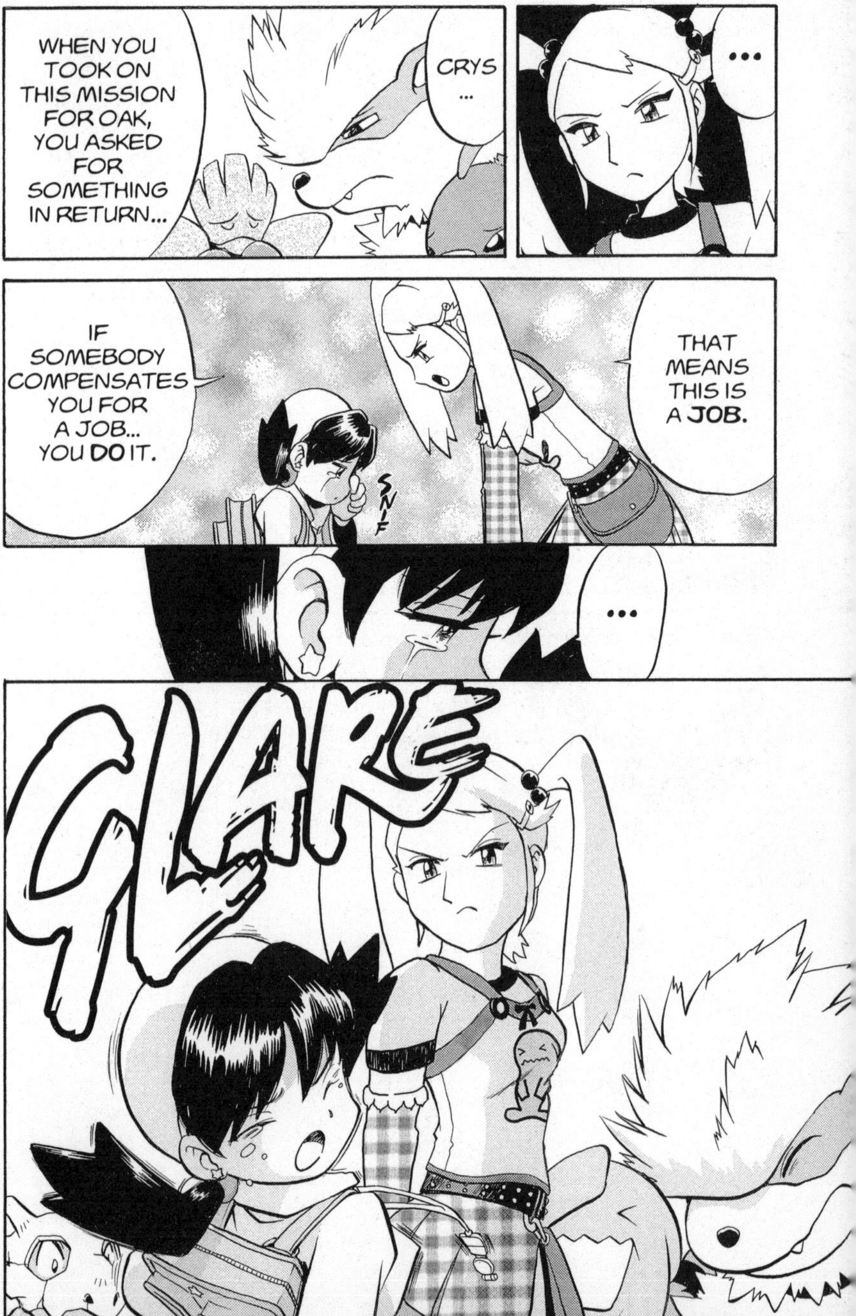
...
CRYS ...
WHEN YOU TOOK ON THIS MISSION FOR OAK, YOU ASKED FOR SOMETHING IN RETURN...
THAT MEANS THIS IS A JOB.
IF SOMEBODY COMPENSATES YOU FOR A JOB... YOU DO IT.
SNIF
...
GLARE

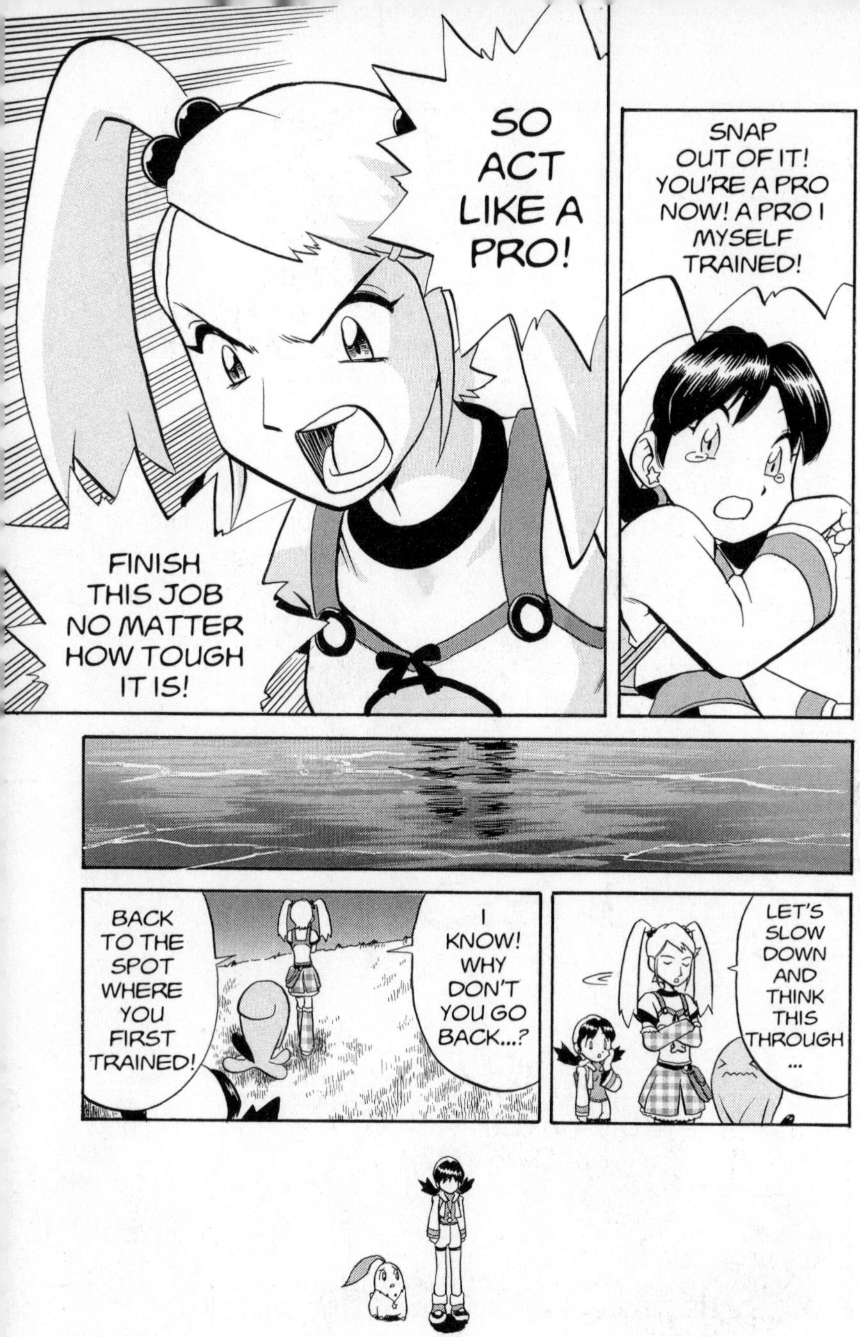
SNAP OUT OF IT! YOU'RE A PRO NOW! A PRO I MYSELF TRAINED!
SO ACT LIKE A PRO!
FINISH THIS JOB NO MATTER HOW TOUGH IT IS!
LET'S SLOW DOWN AND THINK THIS THROUGH...
I KNOW! WHY DON'T YOU GO BACK...?
BACK TO THE SPOT WHERE YOU FIRST TRAINED!

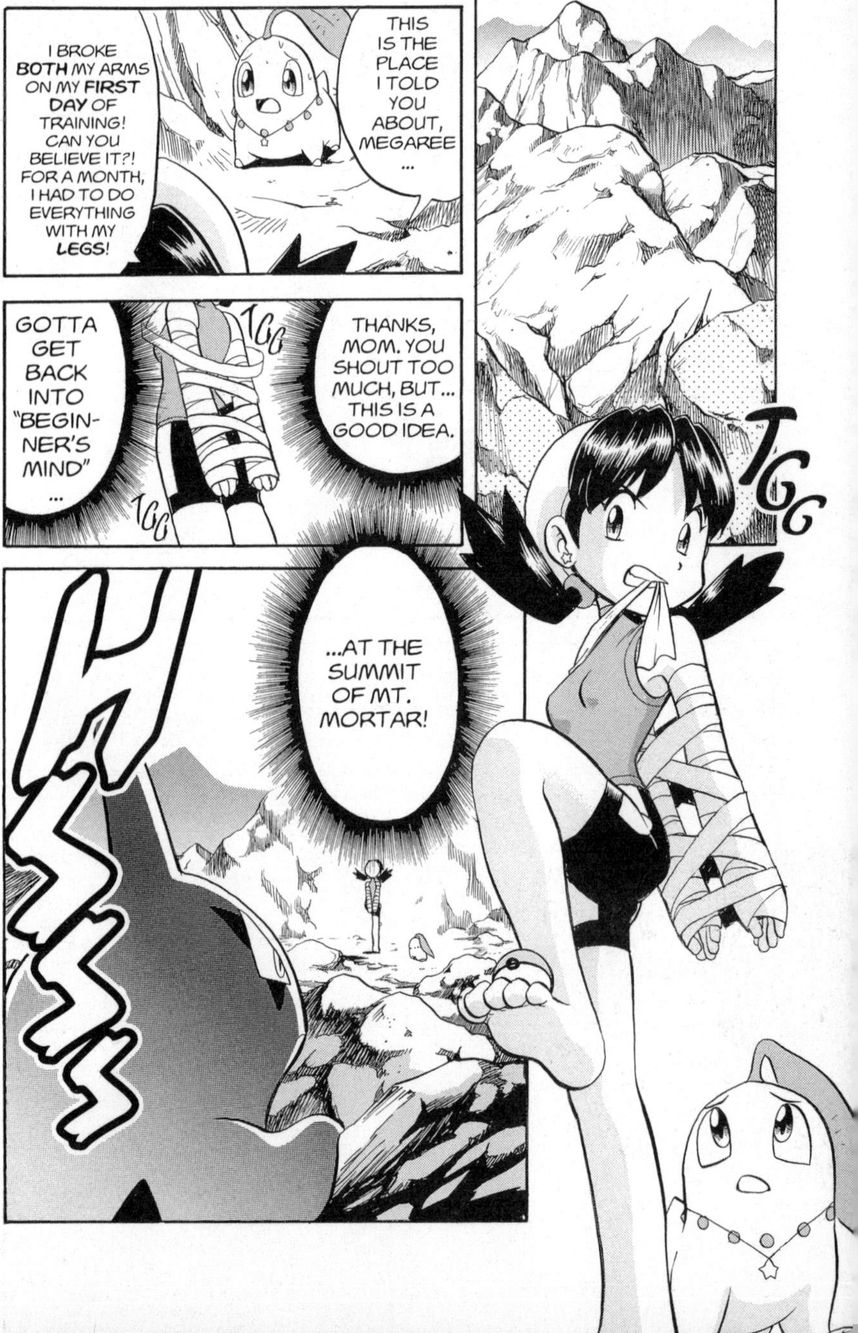
TGG
THIS IS THE PLACE I TOLD YOU ABOUT, MEGAREE...
I BROKE **BOTH** MY ARMS ON MY **FIRST DAY** OF TRAINING! CAN YOU BELIEVE IT?! FOR A MONTH, I HAD TO DO EVERYTHING WITH MY **LEGS**!
TGG
THANKS, MOM. YOU SHOUT TOO MUCH, BUT... THIS IS A GOOD IDEA.
GOTTA GET BACK INTO "BEGINNER'S MIND"...
TGG
...AT THE SUMMIT OF MT. MORTAR!

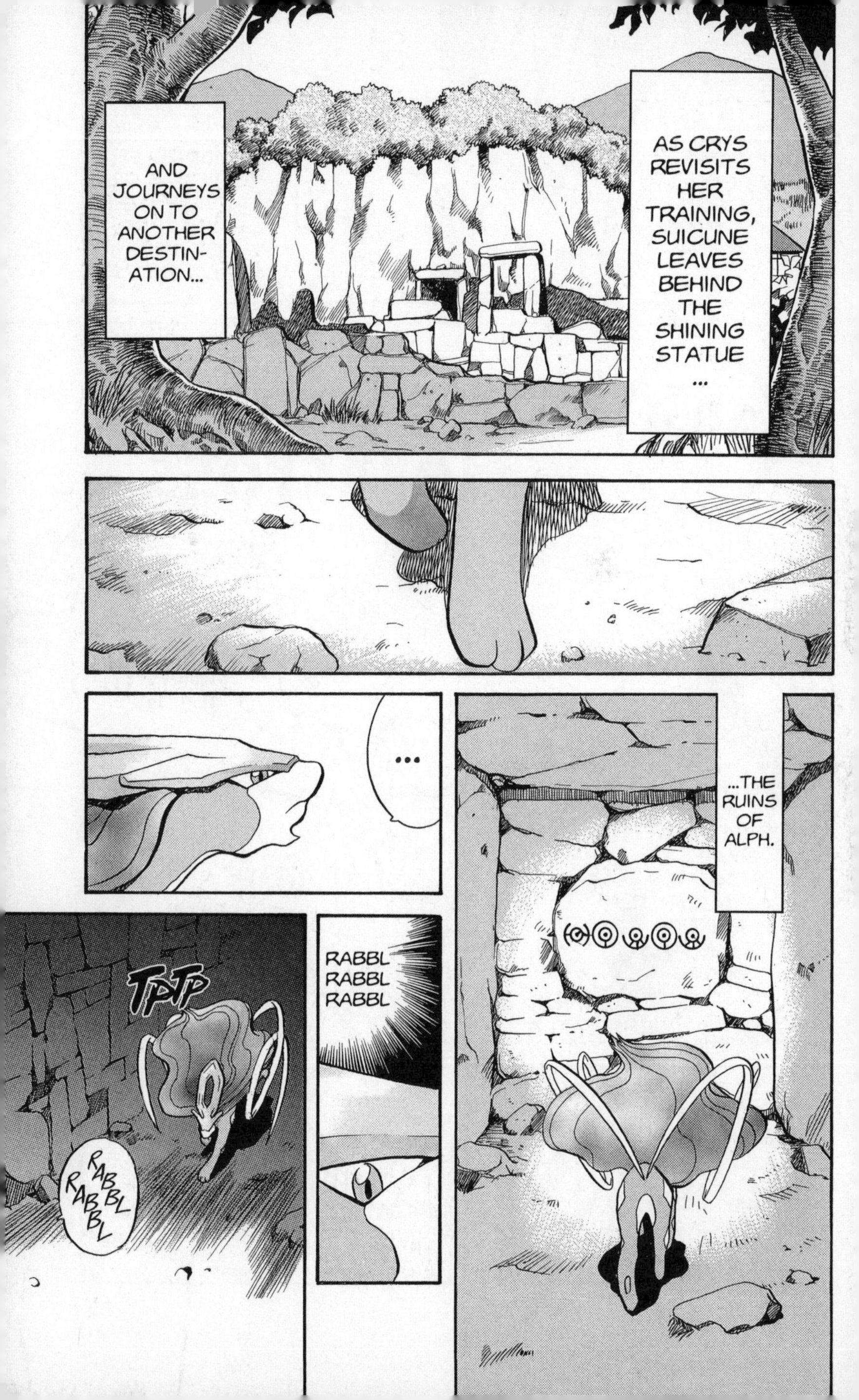
AS CRYS REVISITS HER TRAINING, SUICUNE LEAVES BEHIND THE SHINING STATUE ...
AND JOURNEYS ON TO ANOTHER DESTIN-ATION...
...THE RUINS OF ALPH.
...
RABBL RABBL RABBL
TPTP
RABBL RABBL

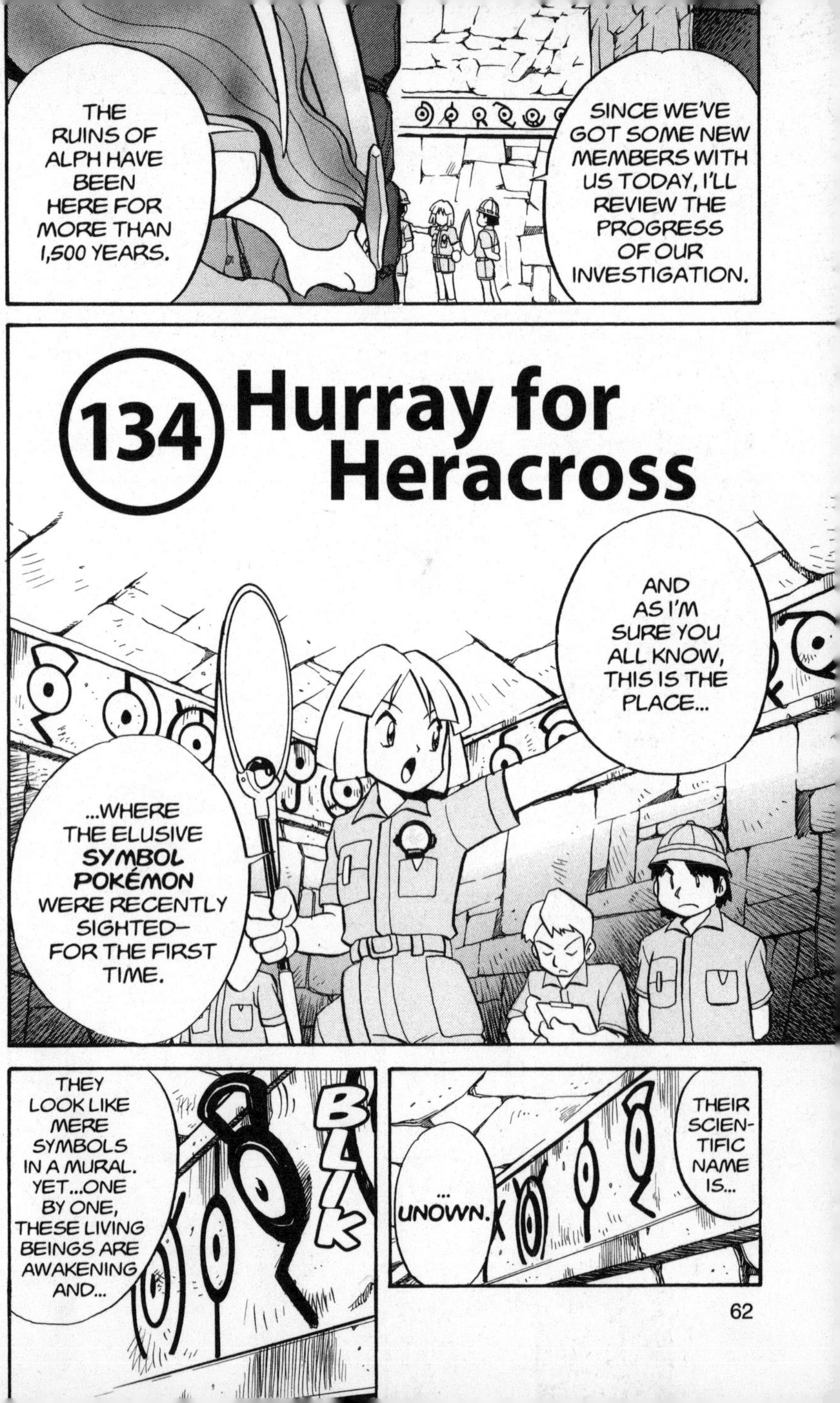
SINCE WE'VE GOT SOME NEW MEMBERS WITH US TODAY, I'LL REVIEW THE PROGRESS OF OUR INVESTIGATION.
THE RUINS OF ALPH HAVE BEEN HERE FOR MORE THAN 1,500 YEARS.
134 Hurray for Heracross
AND AS I'M SURE YOU ALL KNOW, THIS IS THE PLACE...
...WHERE THE ELUSIVE **SYMBOL POKÉMON** WERE RECENTLY SIGHTED—FOR THE FIRST TIME.
THEIR SCIEN-TIFIC NAME IS...
...UNOWN.
THEY LOOK LIKE MERE SYMBOLS IN A MURAL. YET...ONE BY ONE, THESE LIVING BEINGS ARE AWAKENING AND...
BLIK

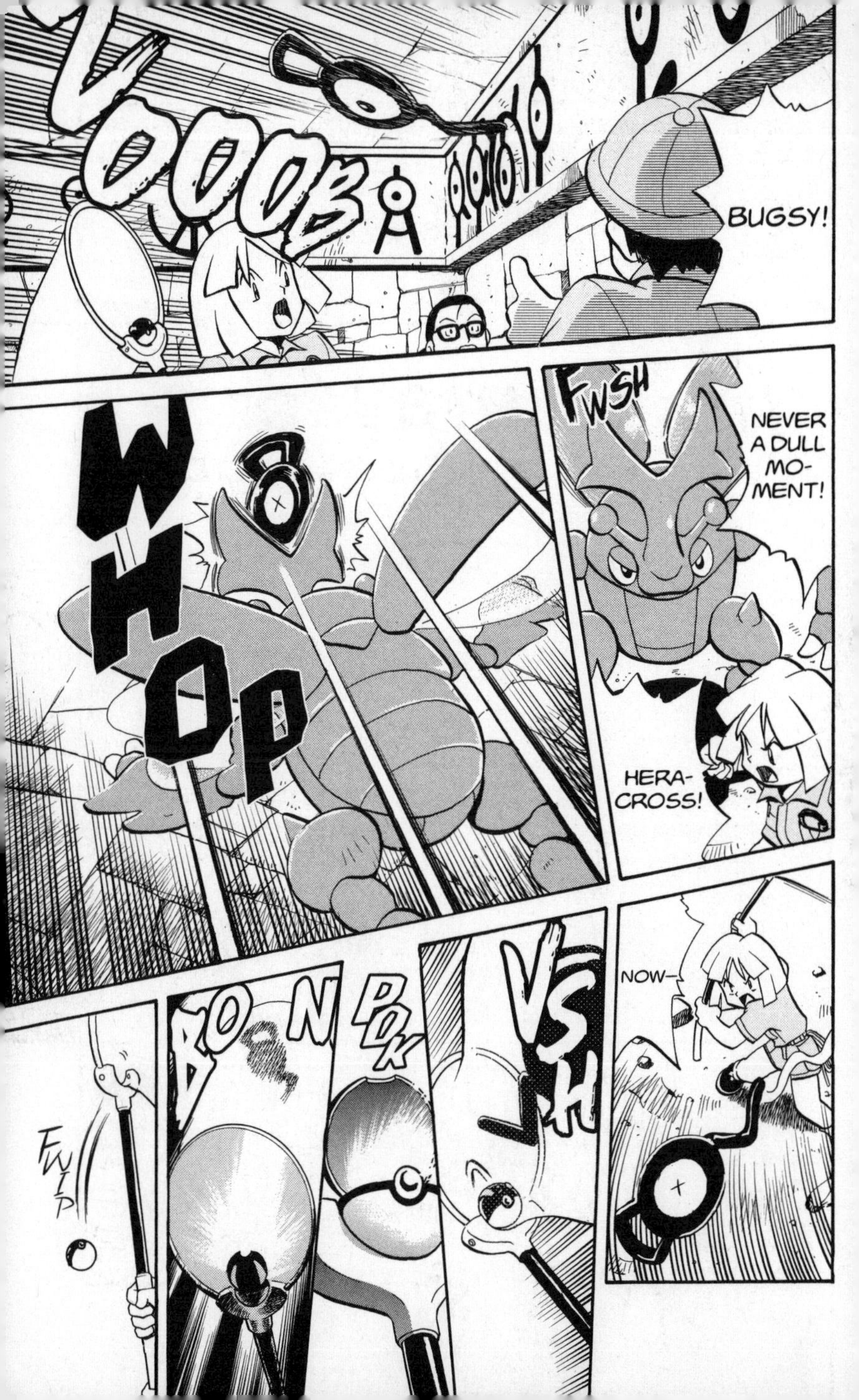
BUGSY!
VOOOOB
NEVER A DULL MO-MENT!
FWSH
HERA-CROSS!
WHOP
NOW—
VSH
POK
BON
FWIP

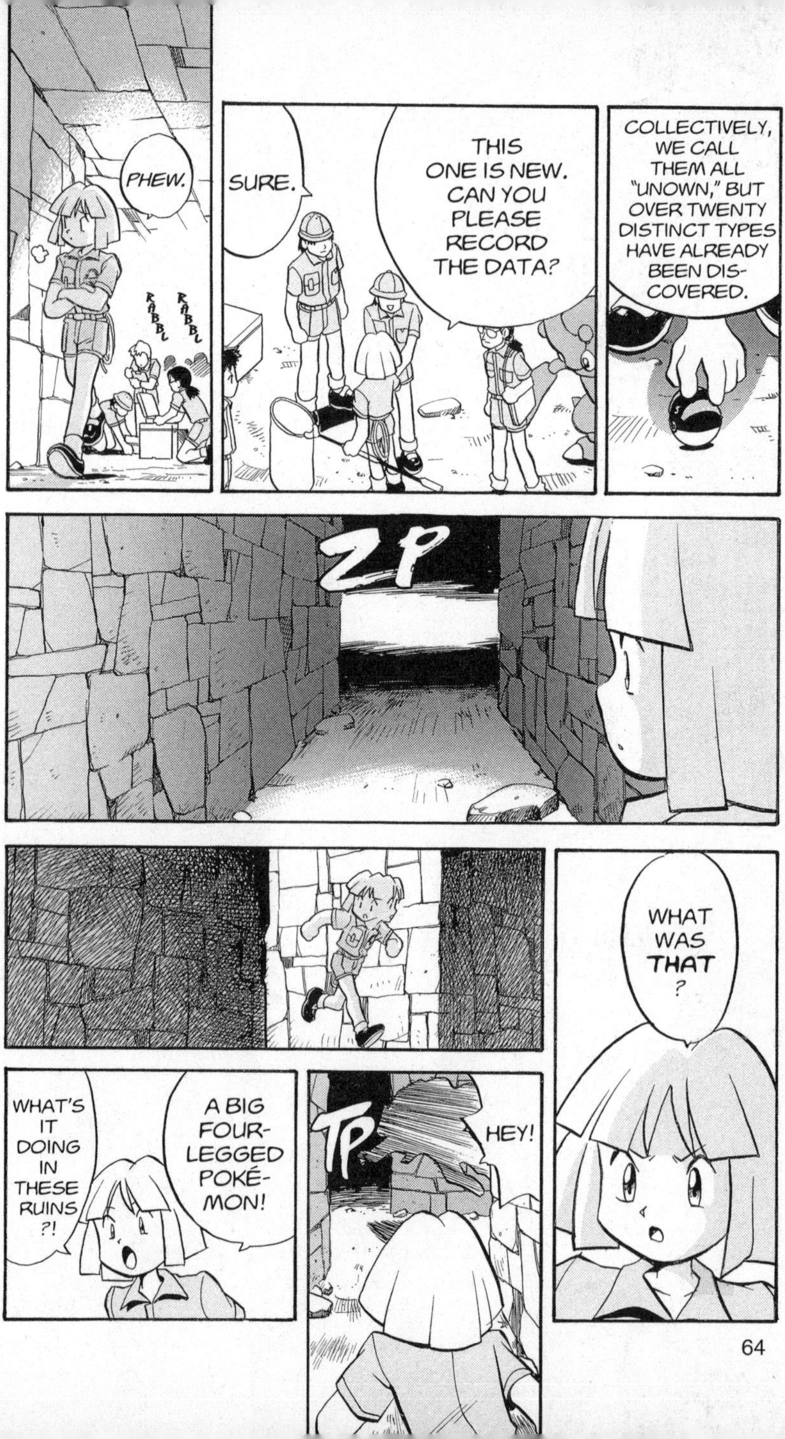
COLLECTIVELY, WE CALL THEM ALL "UNOWN," BUT OVER TWENTY DISTINCT TYPES HAVE ALREADY BEEN DIS-COVERED.
THIS ONE IS NEW. CAN YOU PLEASE RECORD THE DATA?
SURE.
PHEW.
RABBL
RABBL
ZP
WHAT WAS THAT?
HEY!
TP
A BIG FOUR-LEGGED POKÉ-MON!
WHAT'S IT DOING IN THESE RUINS?!

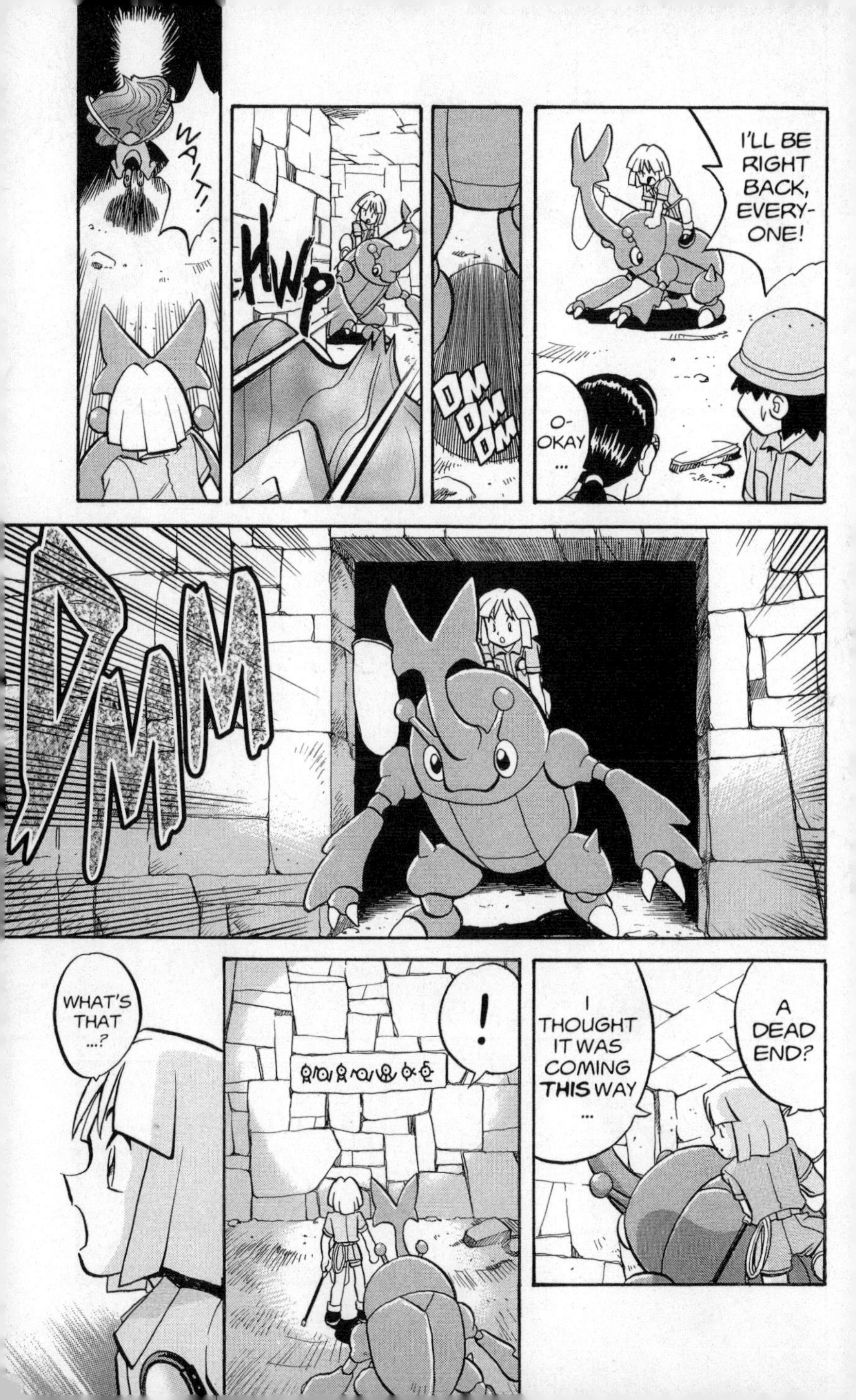
I'LL BE RIGHT BACK, EVERYONE!
O-OKAY ...
DM DM DM
HWP
WAIT!
DMM
A DEAD END?
I THOUGHT IT WAS COMING **THIS** WAY ...
!
WHAT'S THAT ...?

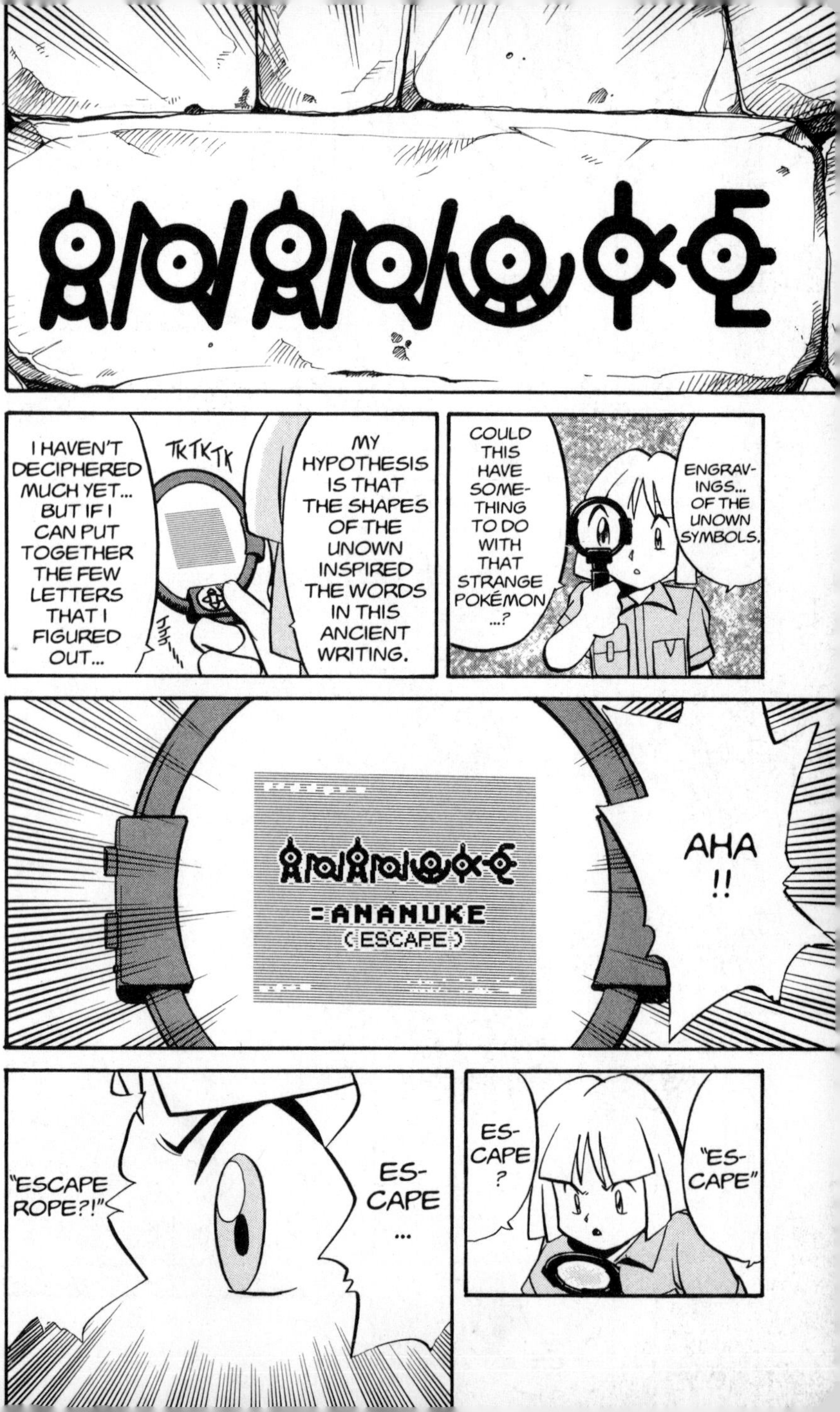
ENGRAVINGS... OF THE UNOWN SYMBOLS.
COULD THIS HAVE SOMETHING TO DO WITH THAT STRANGE POKÉMON...?
MY HYPOTHESIS IS THAT THE SHAPES OF THE UNOWN INSPIRED THE WORDS IN THIS ANCIENT WRITING.
TKTKTK
I HAVEN'T DECIPHERED MUCH YET... BUT IF I CAN PUT TOGETHER THE FEW LETTERS THAT I FIGURED OUT...
AHA!!
=ANANUKE
(ESCAPE)
"ESCAPE"
ESCAPE?
ESCAPE...
"ESCAPE ROPE?!"

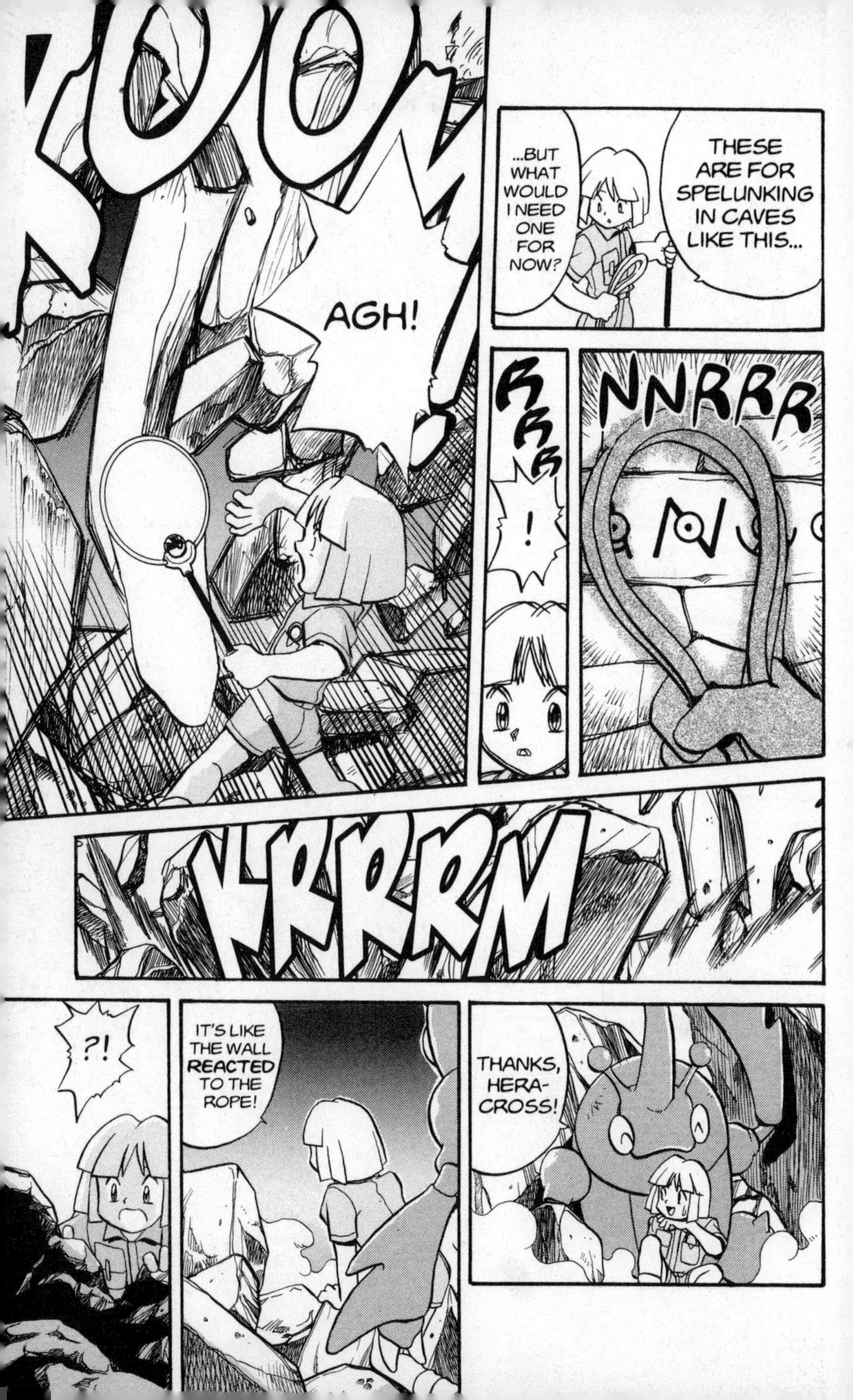

THESE ARE FOR SPELUNKING IN CAVES LIKE THIS...
...BUT WHAT WOULD I NEED ONE FOR NOW?
NNRRR
RRRR
!
AGH!
KRRRM
THANKS, HERA-CROSS!
IT'S LIKE THE WALL **REACTED** TO THE ROPE!
?!

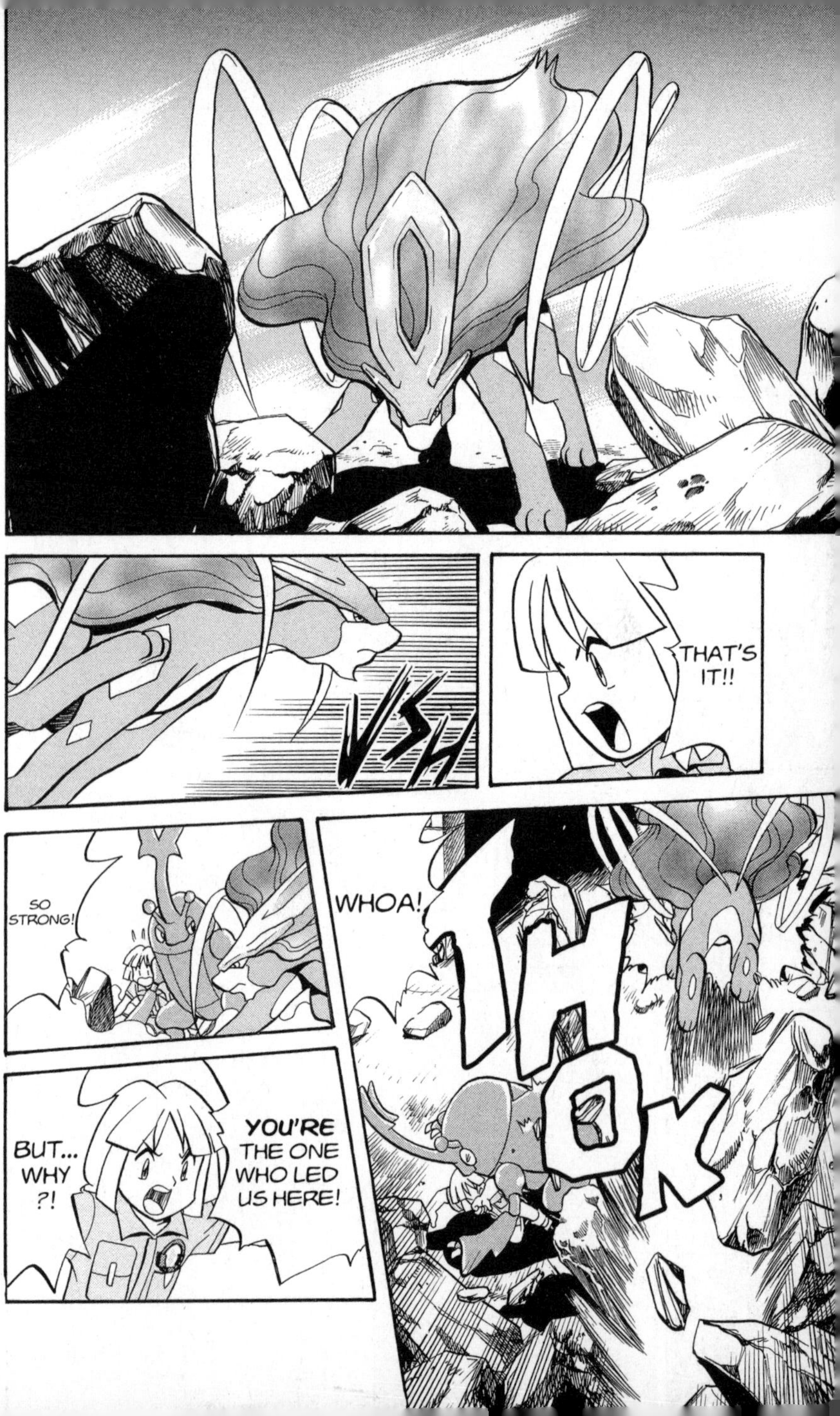
THAT'S IT!!
VSSH
WHOA!
THOK
SO STRONG!
YOU'RE THE ONE WHO LED US HERE!
BUT... WHY?!

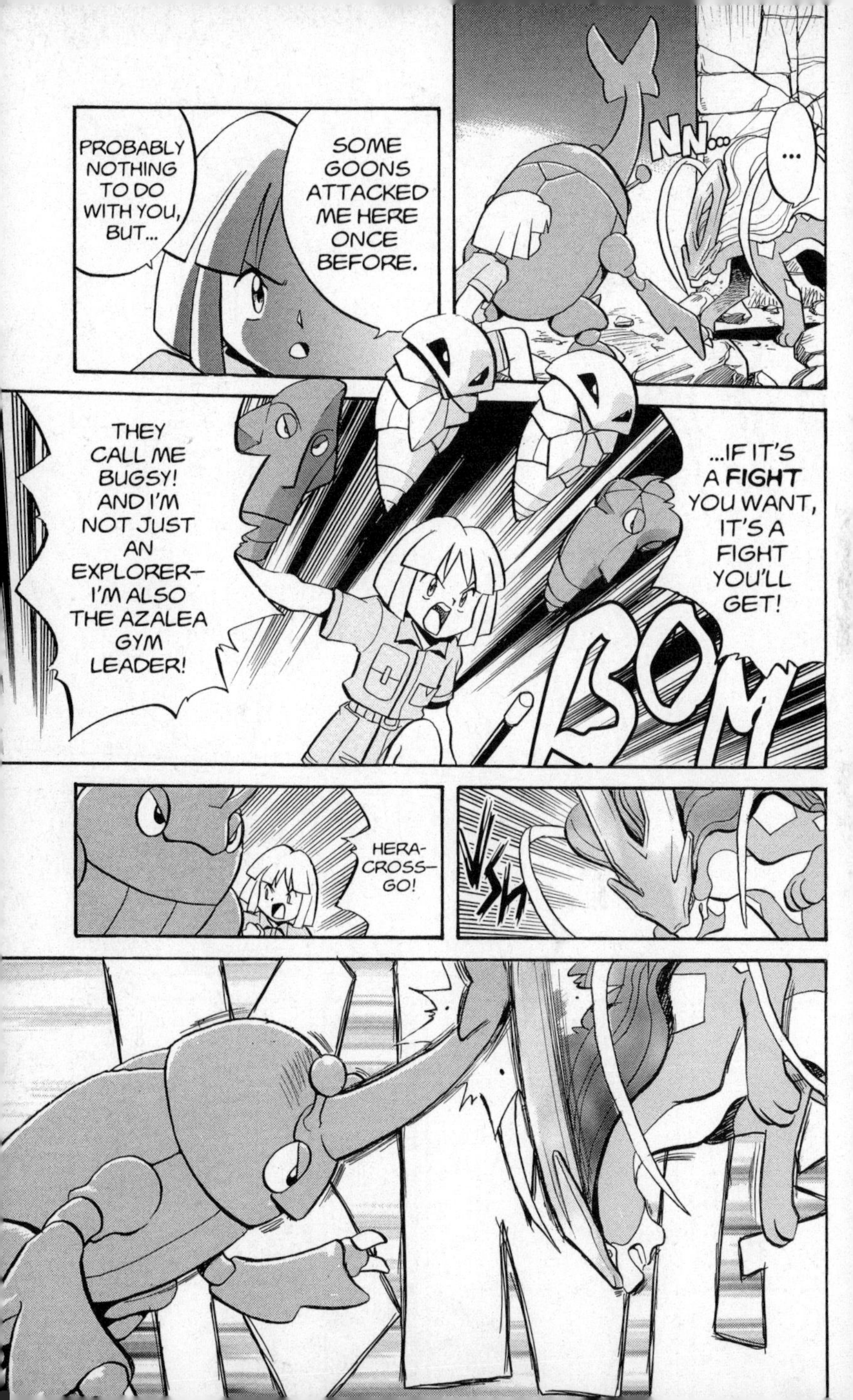
...
NN...
SOME GOONS ATTACKED ME HERE ONCE BEFORE.
PROBABLY NOTHING TO DO WITH YOU, BUT...
...IF IT'S A **FIGHT** YOU WANT, IT'S A FIGHT YOU'LL GET!
BOM
THEY CALL ME BUGSY! AND I'M NOT JUST AN EXPLORER— I'M ALSO THE AZALEA GYM LEADER!
VSH
HERA-CROSS-GO!

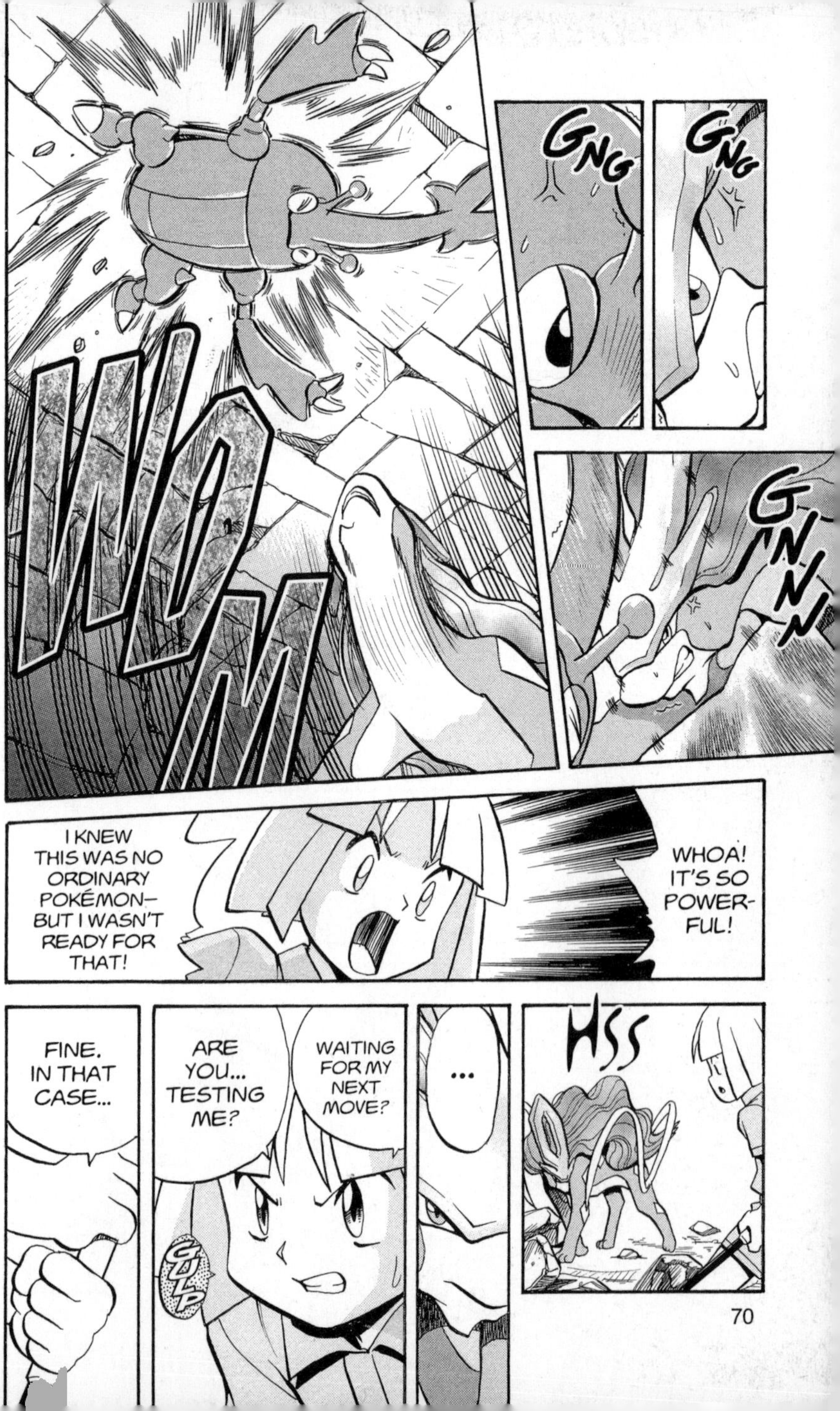

GNG
GNG
GNNNN
WOM
WHOA! IT'S SO POWERFUL!
I KNEW THIS WAS NO ORDINARY POKÉMON—BUT I WASN'T READY FOR THAT!
HSS
...
WAITING FOR MY NEXT MOVE?
ARE YOU... TESTING ME?
GULP
FINE. IN THAT CASE...

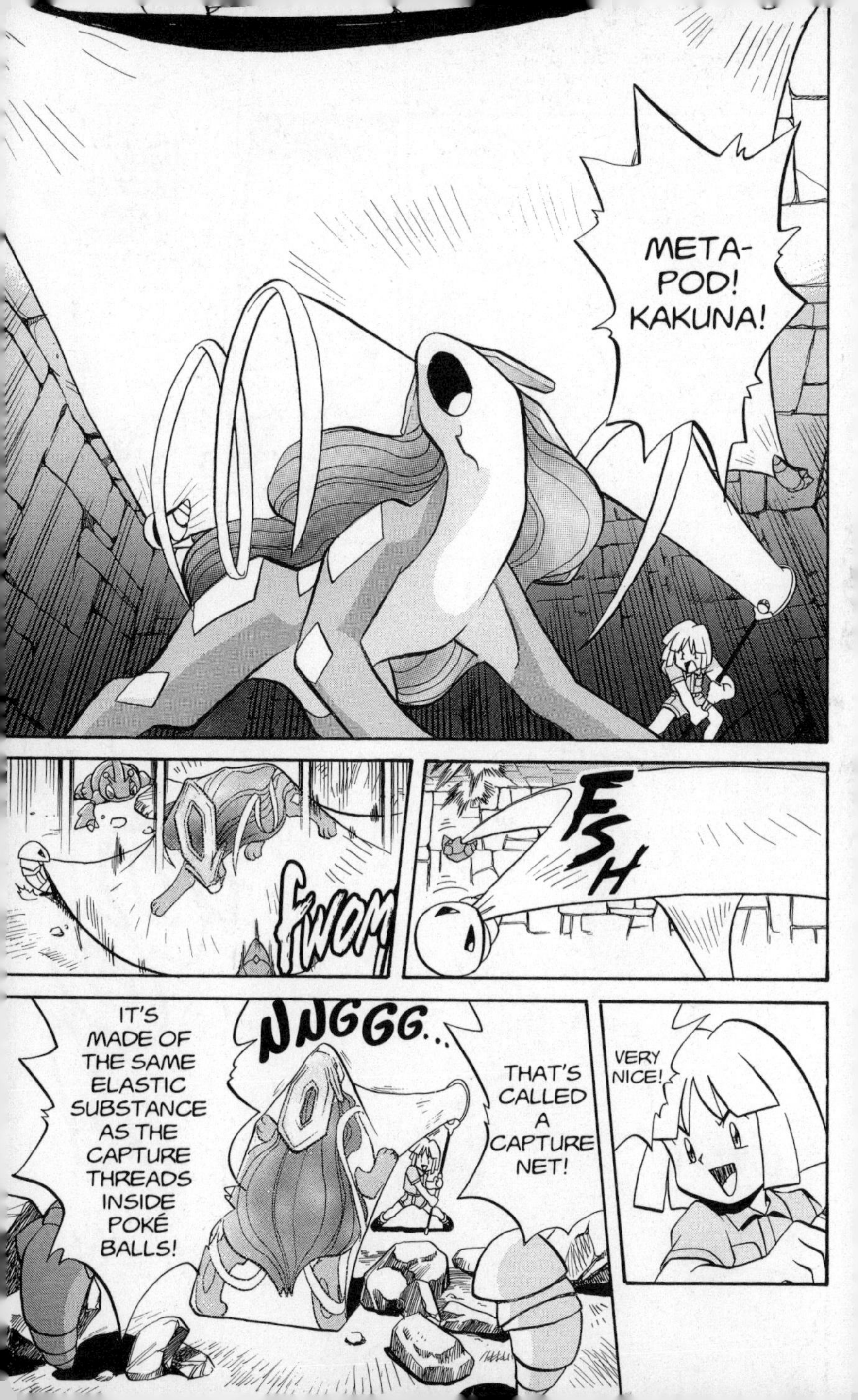
META-
POD!
KAKUNA!
FSH
fwom
VERY
NICE!
NNGGG...
THAT'S
CALLED
A
CAPTURE
NET!
IT'S
MADE OF
THE SAME
ELASTIC
SUBSTANCE
AS THE
CAPTURE
THREADS
INSIDE
POKÉ
BALLS!

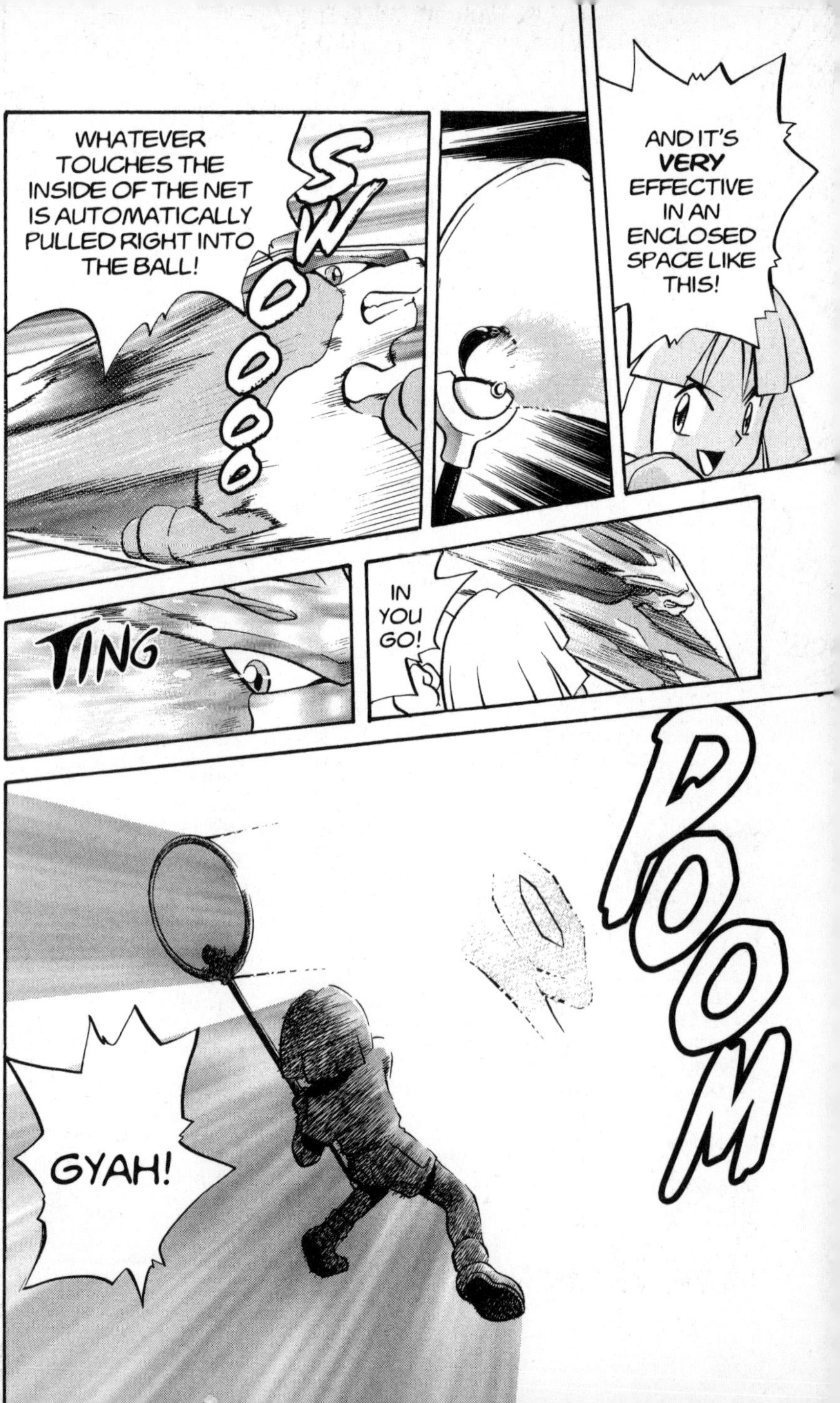
AND IT'S **VERY** EFFECTIVE IN AN ENCLOSED SPACE LIKE THIS!
WHATEVER TOUCHES THE INSIDE OF THE NET IS AUTOMATICALLY PULLED RIGHT INTO THE BALL!
SWOOOOO
IN YOU GO!
TING
DOOM
GYAH!

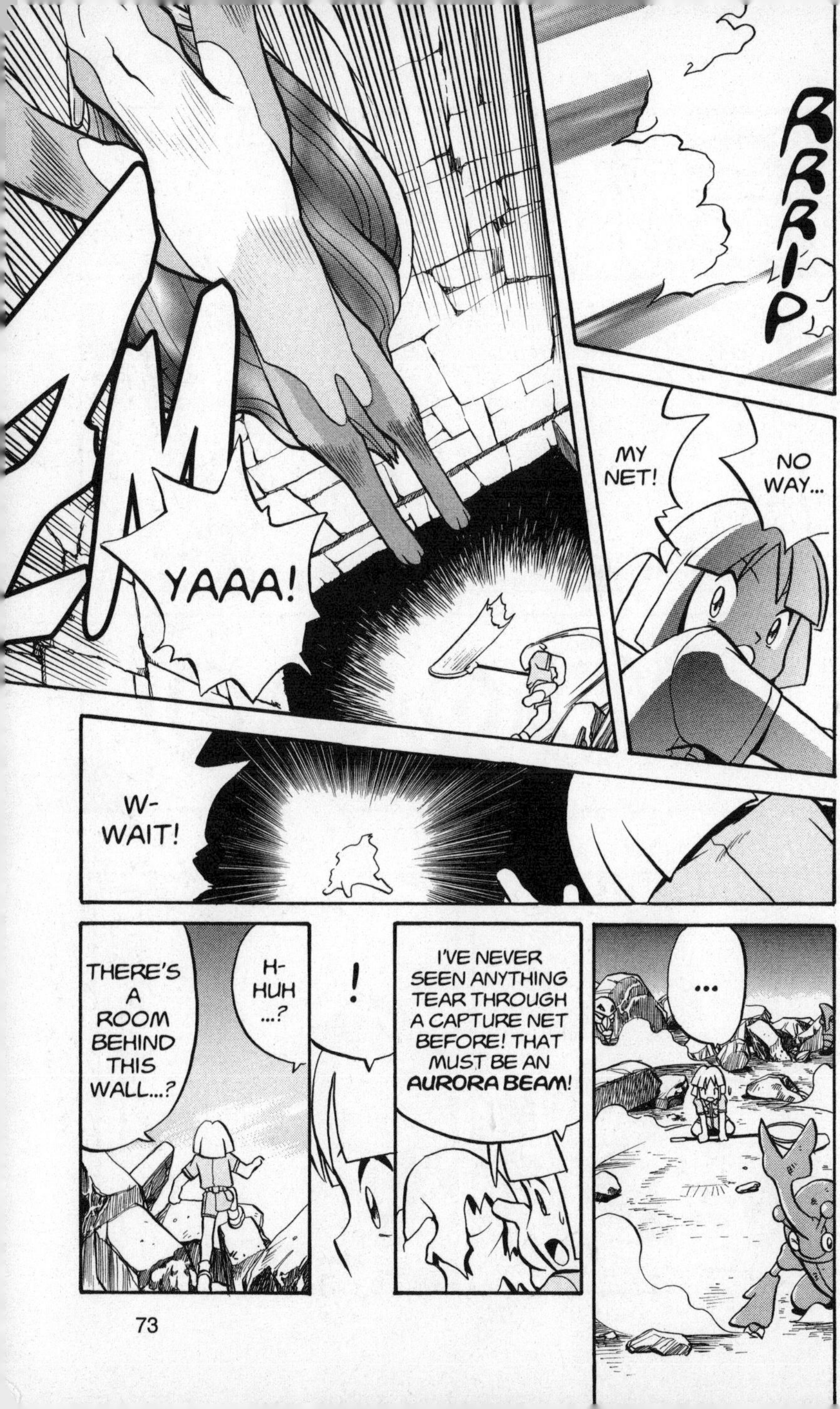
RRRIP
NO WAY...
MY NET!
YAAA!
W-WAIT!
...
I'VE NEVER SEEN ANYTHING TEAR THROUGH A CAPTURE NET BEFORE! THAT MUST BE AN AURORA BEAM!
!
H-HUH ...?
THERE'S A ROOM BEHIND THIS WALL...?

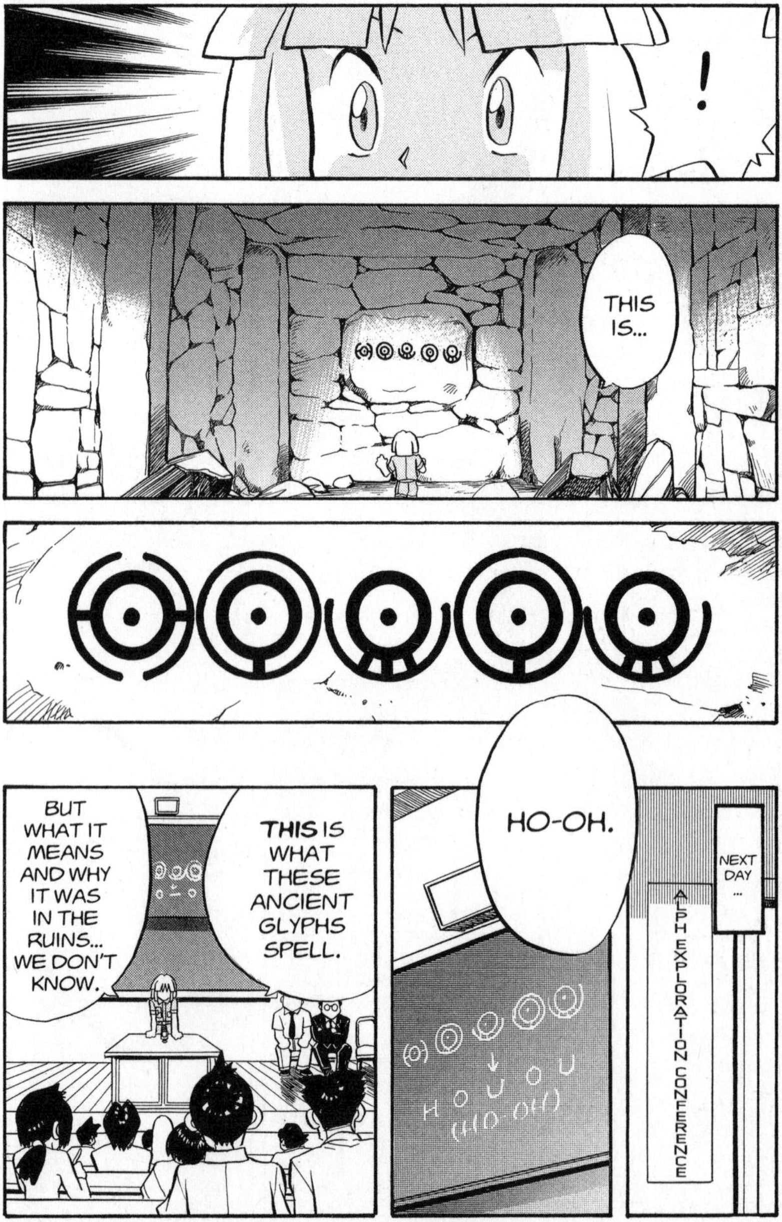
!
THIS IS...
NEXT DAY ...
ALPH EXPLORATION CONFERENCE
HO-OH.
H O U O U
(HO-OH)
THIS IS WHAT THESE ANCIENT GLYPHS SPELL.
BUT WHAT IT MEANS AND WHY IT WAS IN THE RUINS... WE DON'T KNOW.

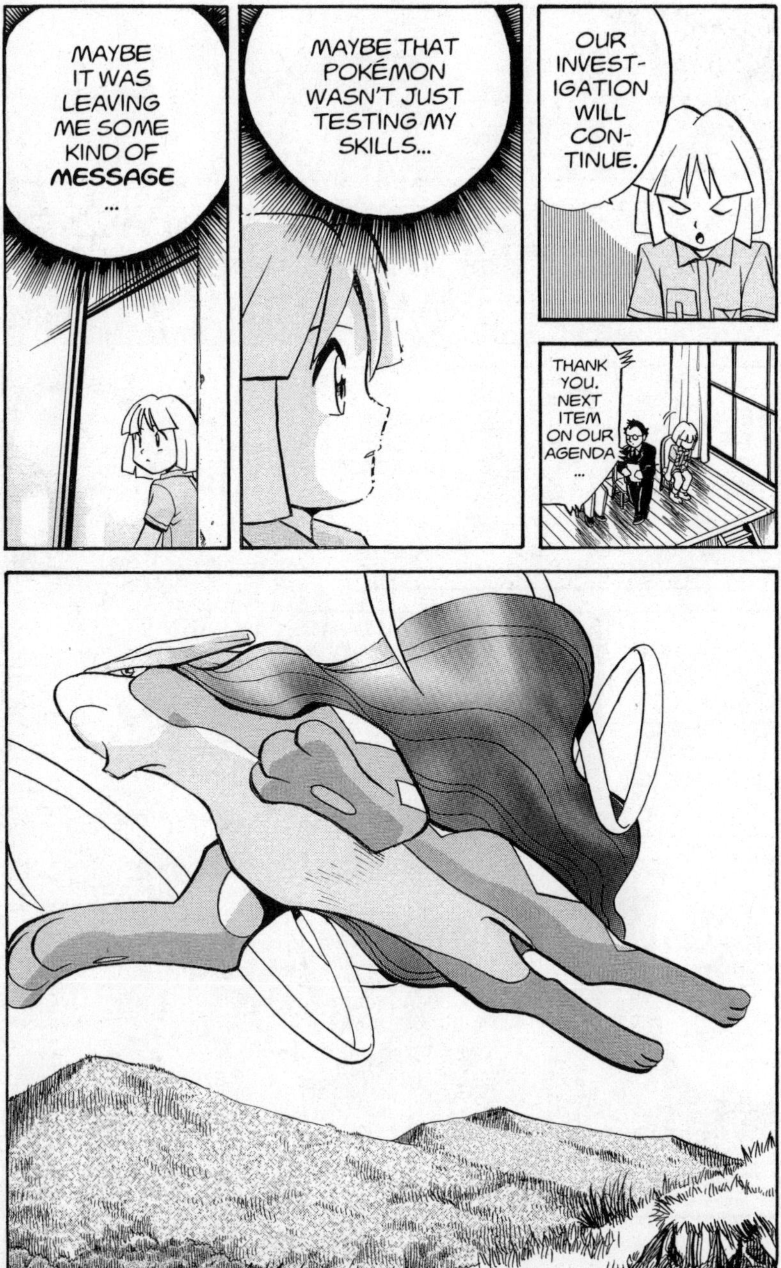
OUR INVEST-IGATION WILL CON-TINUE.
THANK YOU. NEXT ITEM ON OUR AGENDA...
MAYBE THAT POKÉMON WASN'T JUST TESTING MY SKILLS...
MAYBE IT WAS LEAVING ME SOME KIND OF MESSAGE...

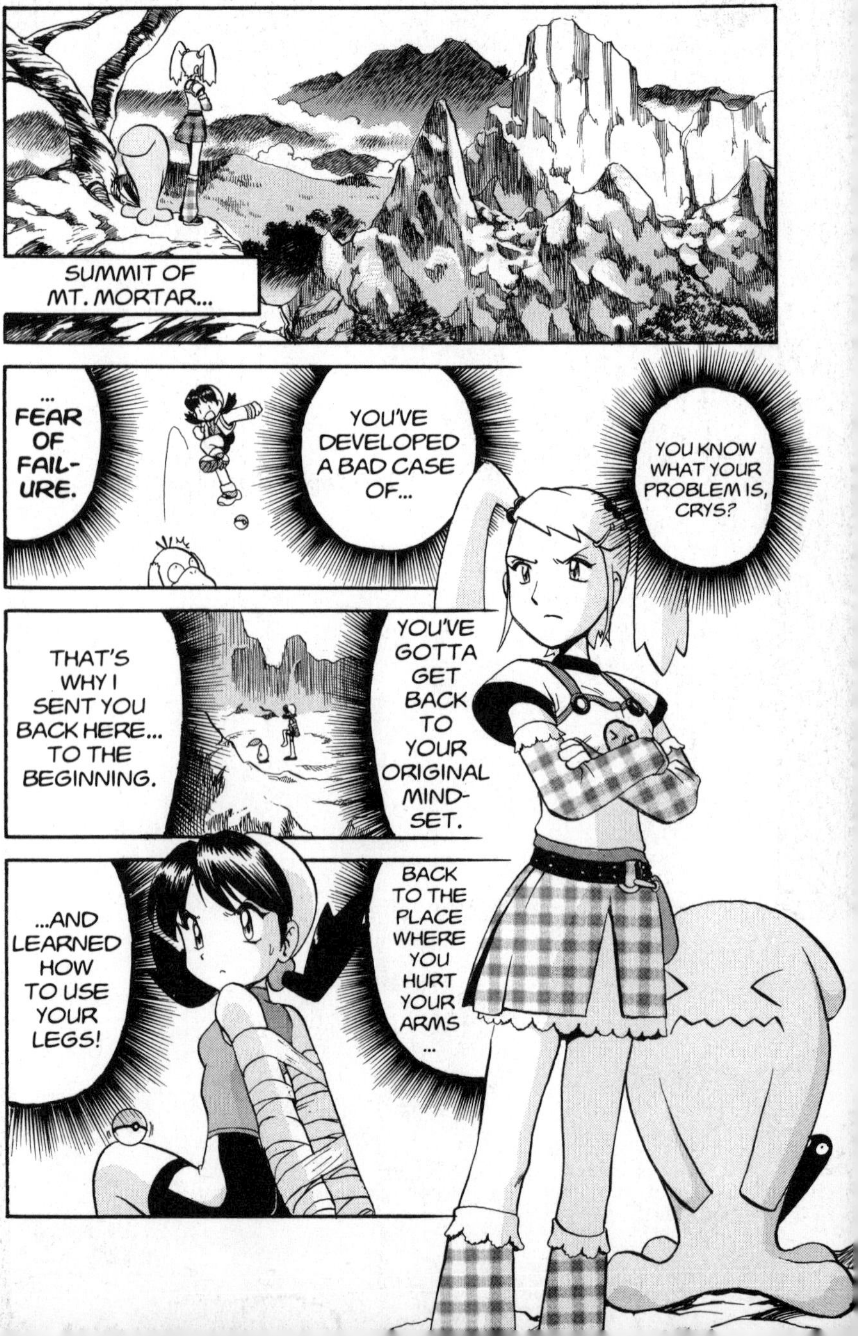
SUMMIT OF MT. MORTAR...
YOU KNOW WHAT YOUR PROBLEM IS, CRYS?
YOU'VE DEVELOPED A BAD CASE OF...
... FEAR OF FAILURE.
YOU'VE GOTTA GET BACK TO YOUR ORIGINAL MINDSET.
THAT'S WHY I SENT YOU BACK HERE... TO THE BEGINNING.
BACK TO THE PLACE WHERE YOU HURT YOUR ARMS ...
...AND LEARNED HOW TO USE YOUR LEGS!

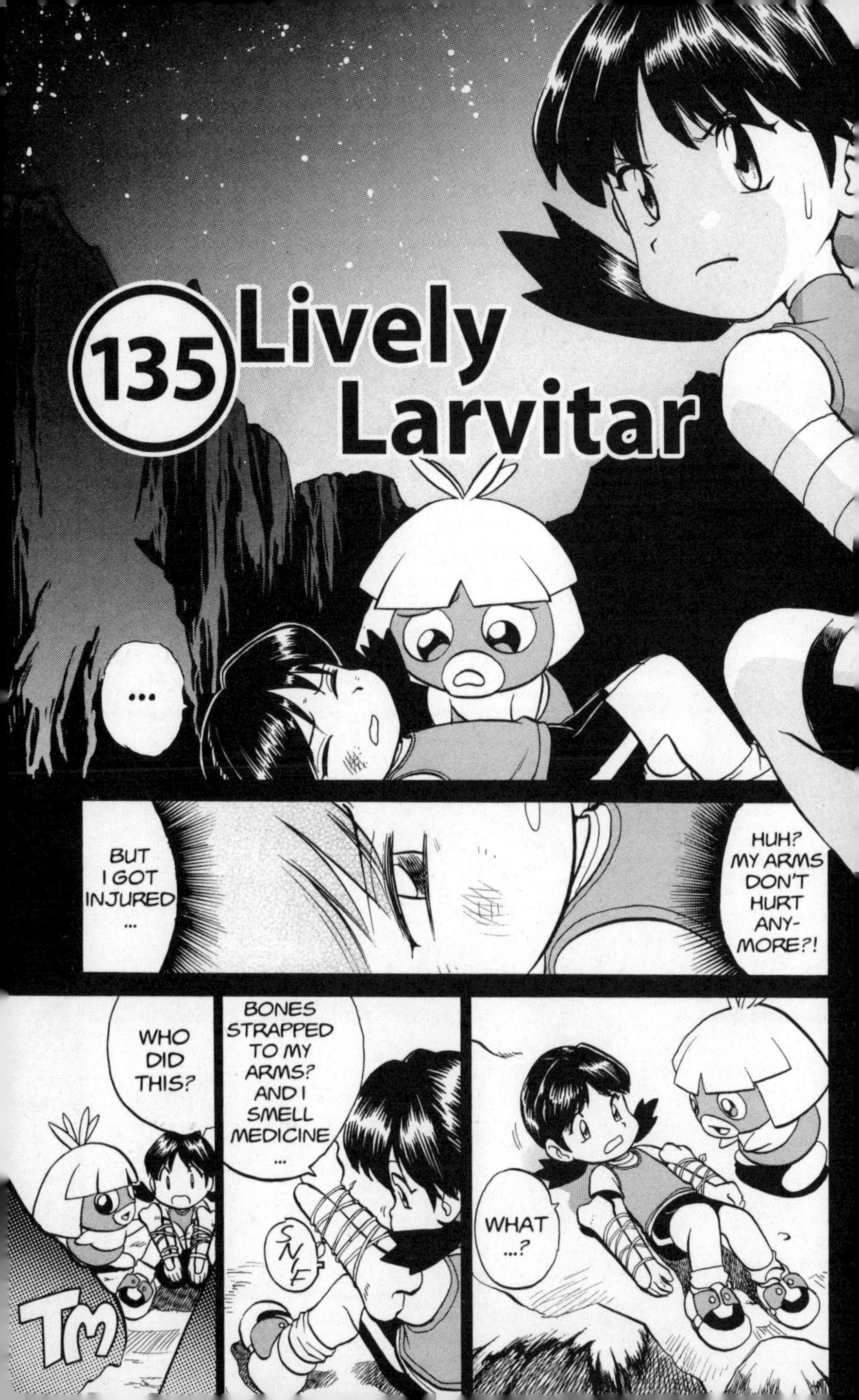
135 Lively Larvitar
...
HUH? MY ARMS DON'T HURT ANYMORE?!
BUT I GOT INJURED ...
WHAT ...?
BONES STRAPPED TO MY ARMS? AND I SMELL MEDICINE ...
SNIF
WHO DID THIS?
TM

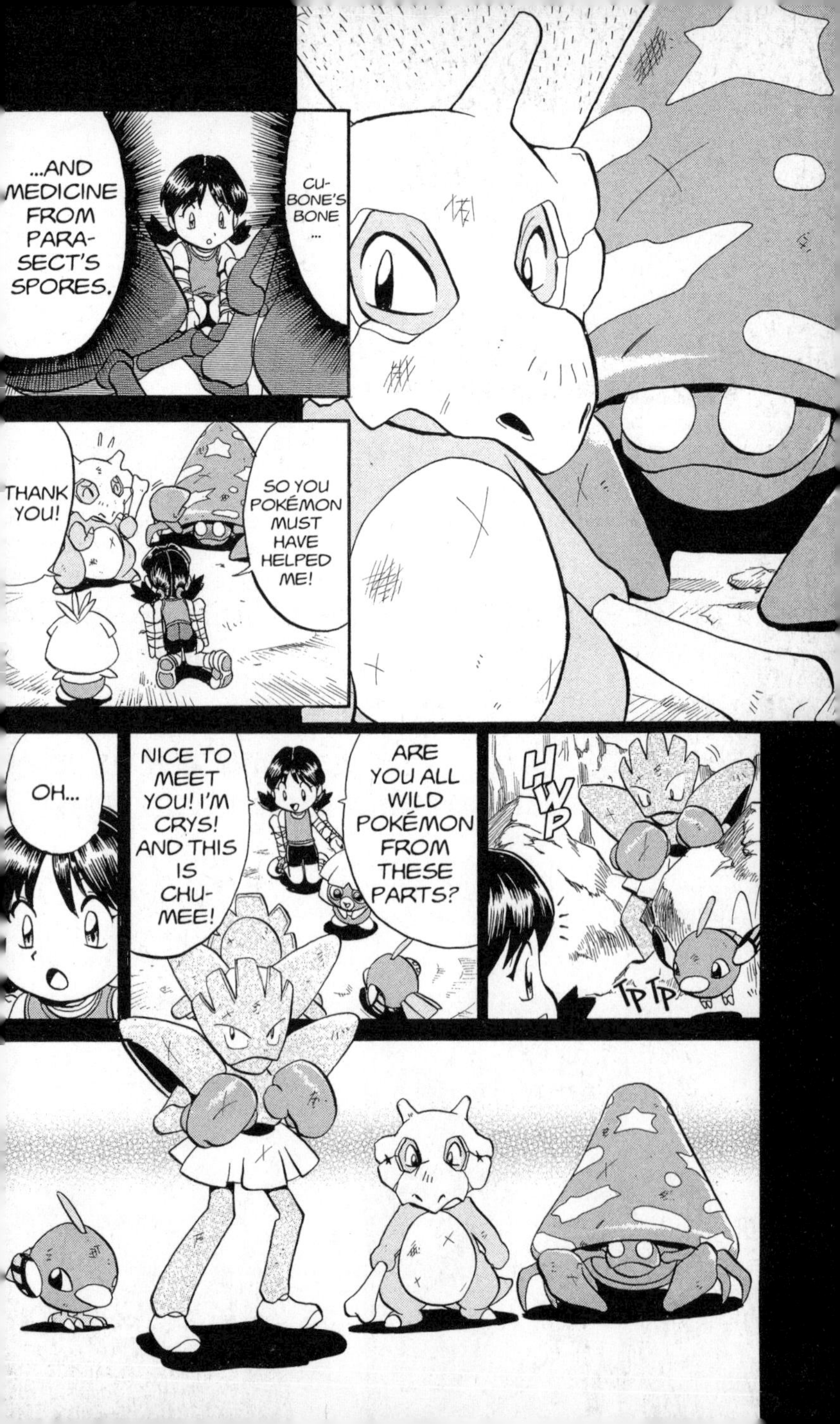
CU-BONE'S BONE ...
...AND MEDICINE FROM PARA-SECT'S SPORES.
SO YOU POKÉMON MUST HAVE HELPED ME!
THANK YOU!
HWP
TP TP
ARE YOU ALL WILD POKÉMON FROM THESE PARTS?
NICE TO MEET YOU! I'M CRYS! AND THIS IS CHU-MEE!
OH...

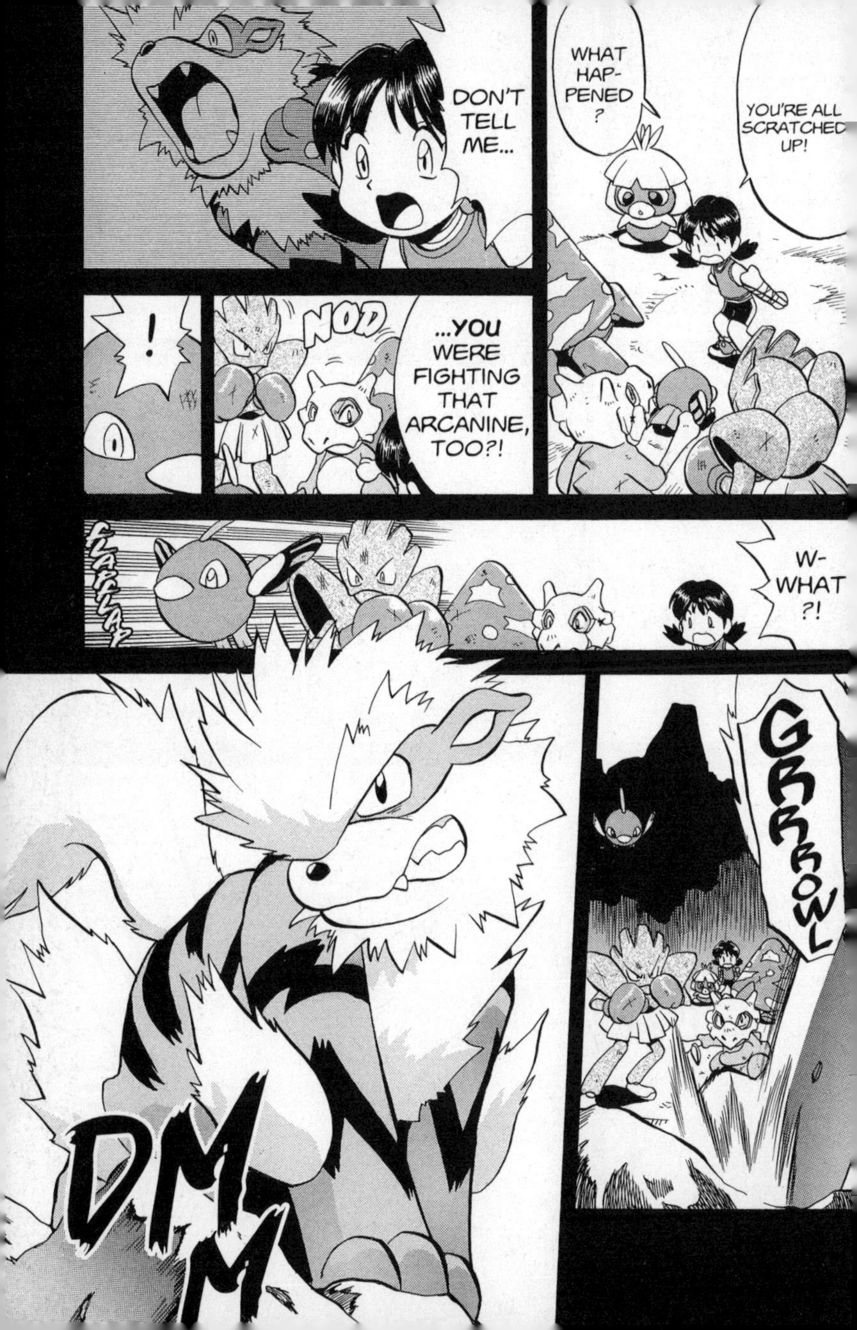
WHAT HAP-PENED ?
YOU'RE ALL SCRATCHED UP!
DON'T TELL ME...
NOD
...YOU WERE FIGHTING THAT ARCANINE, TOO?!
!
W- WHAT ?!
FLAPFLAP
GRRROWL
DMM

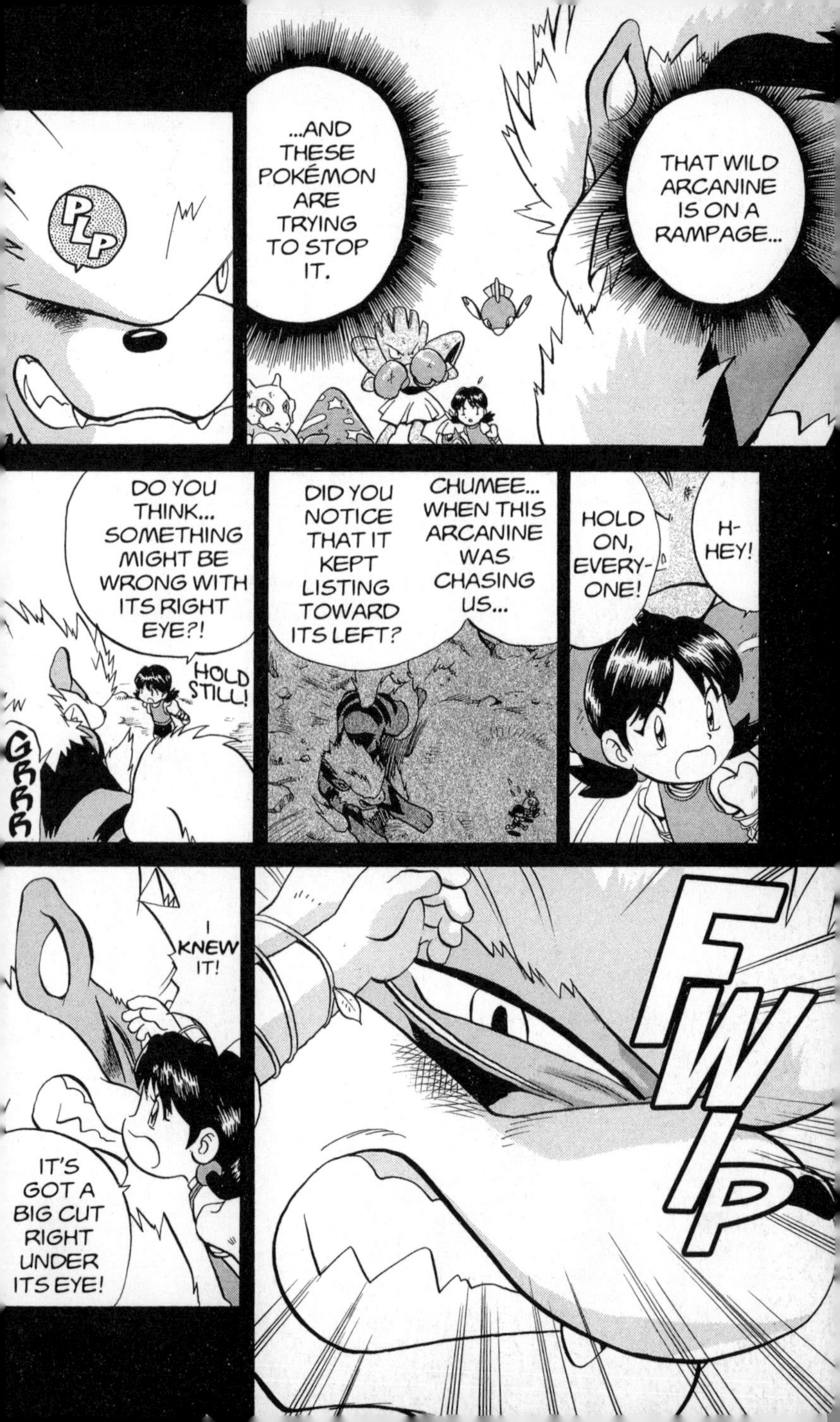
THAT WILD ARCANINE IS ON A RAMPAGE...
...AND THESE POKÉMON ARE TRYING TO STOP IT.
PLP
H-HEY!
HOLD ON, EVERY-ONE!
CHUMEE... WHEN THIS ARCANINE WAS CHASING US...
DID YOU NOTICE THAT IT KEPT LISTING TOWARD ITS LEFT?
DO YOU THINK... SOMETHING MIGHT BE WRONG WITH ITS RIGHT EYE?!
HOLD STILL!
GRRRR
FWIP
I KNEW IT!
IT'S GOT A BIG CUT RIGHT UNDER ITS EYE!

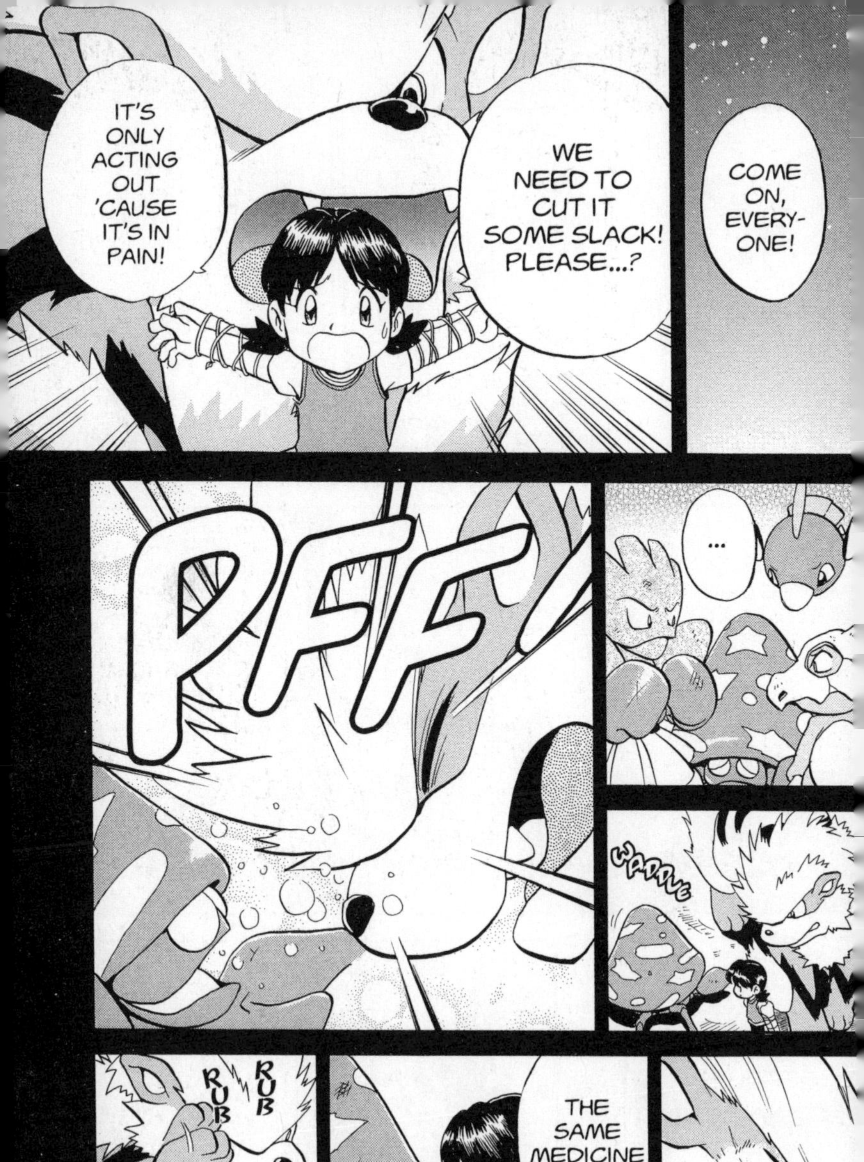
COME ON, EVERYONE!
WE NEED TO CUT IT SOME SLACK! PLEASE...?
IT'S ONLY ACTING OUT 'CAUSE IT'S IN PAIN!
...
WADDLE
PFF
THE SAME MEDICINE YOU PUT ON ME...?
RUB RUB

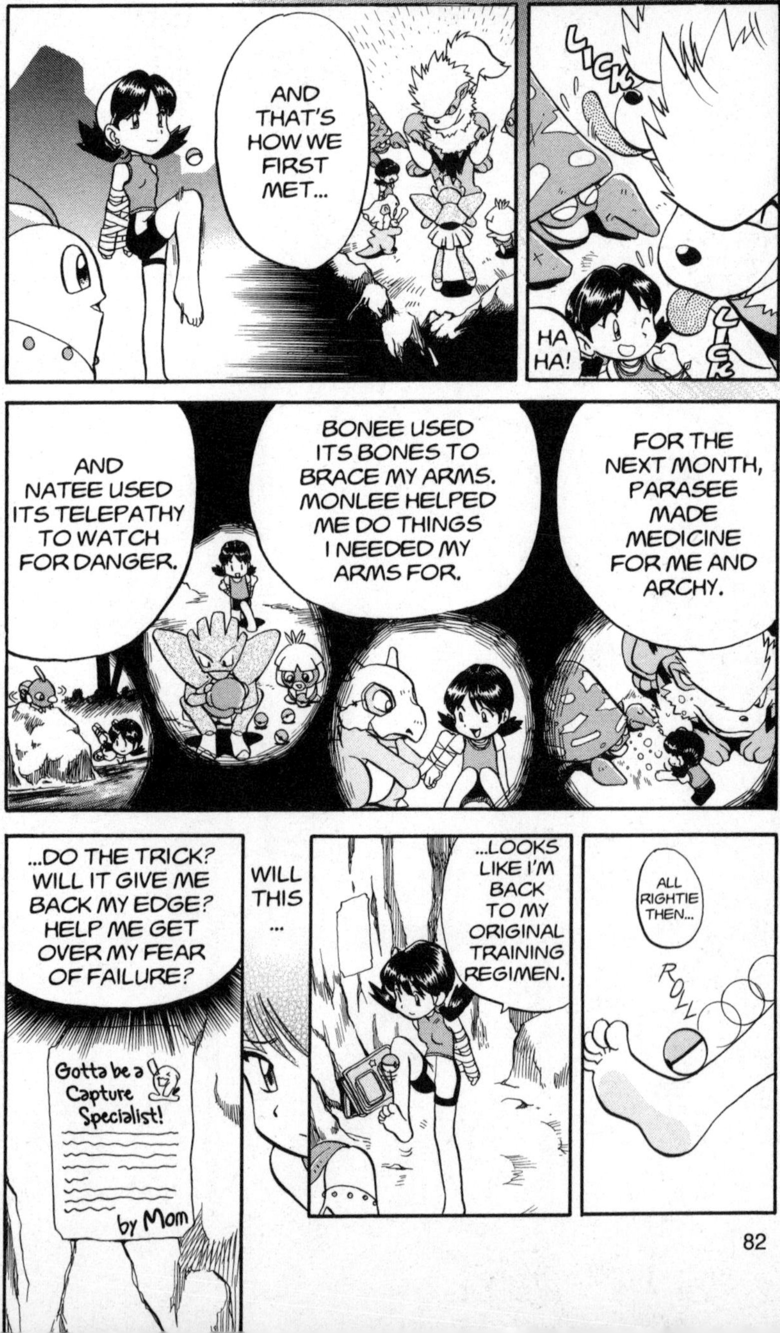

LICK
HA HA!
LICK
AND THAT'S HOW WE FIRST MET...
FOR THE NEXT MONTH, PARASEE MADE MEDICINE FOR ME AND ARCHY.
BONEE USED ITS BONES TO BRACE MY ARMS. MONLEE HELPED ME DO THINGS I NEEDED MY ARMS FOR.
AND NATEE USED ITS TELEPATHY TO WATCH FOR DANGER.
ALL RIGHTIE THEN...
ROLL
...LOOKS LIKE I'M BACK TO MY ORIGINAL TRAINING REGIMEN.
WILL THIS...
...DO THE TRICK? WILL IT GIVE ME BACK MY EDGE? HELP ME GET OVER MY FEAR OF FAILURE?
Gotta be a Capture Specialist!
by Mom

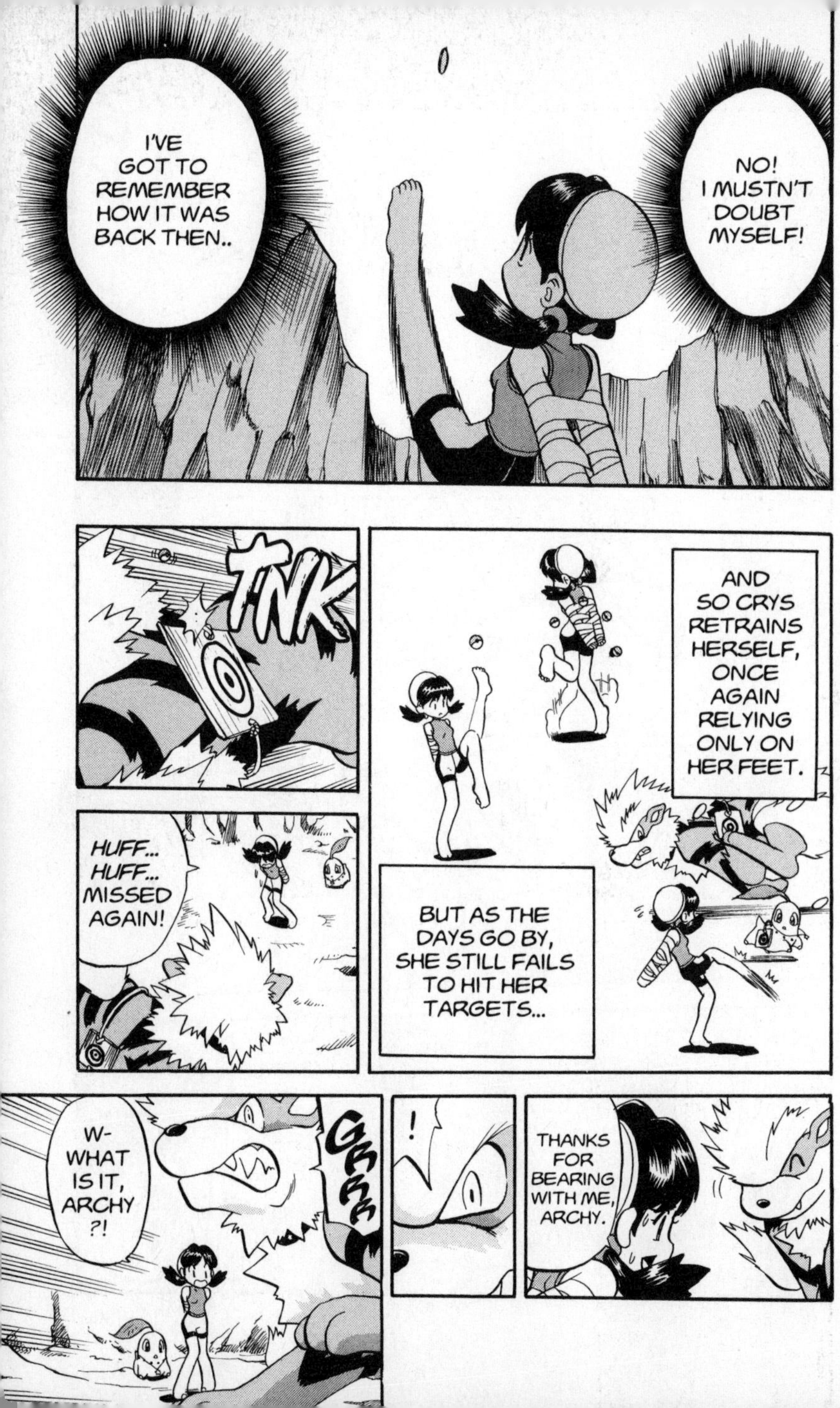
NO! I MUSTN'T DOUBT MYSELF!
I'VE GOT TO REMEMBER HOW IT WAS BACK THEN..
AND SO CRYS RETRAINS HERSELF, ONCE AGAIN RELYING ONLY ON HER FEET.
BUT AS THE DAYS GO BY, SHE STILL FAILS TO HIT HER TARGETS...
TNK
HUFF... HUFF... MISSED AGAIN!
THANKS FOR BEARING WITH ME, ARCHY.
!
GRRR
W-WHAT IS IT, ARCHY?!

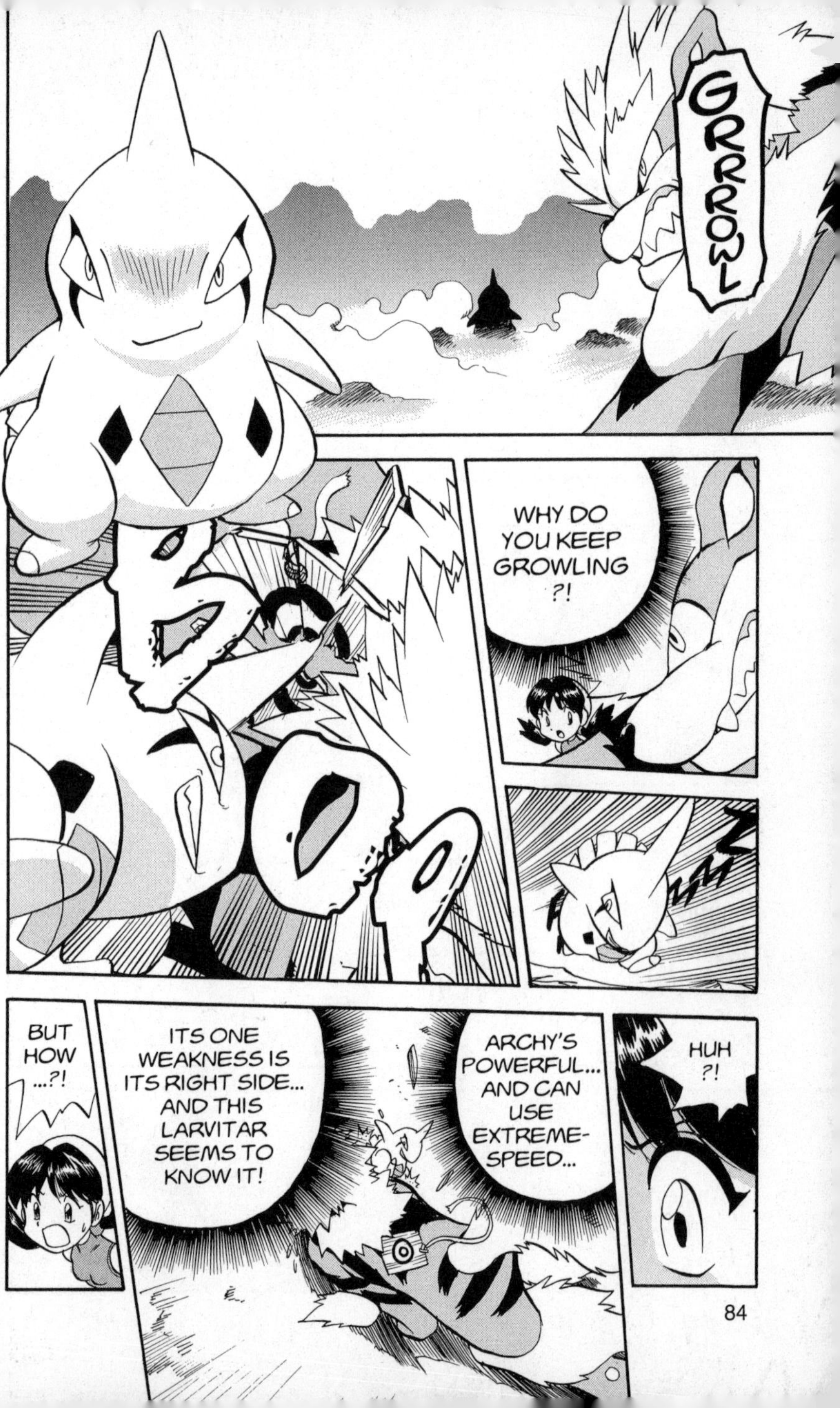
GRRROWL
WHY DO YOU KEEP GROWLING ?!
HUH ?!
ARCHY'S POWERFUL... AND CAN USE EXTREME-SPEED...
ITS ONE WEAKNESS IS ITS RIGHT SIDE... AND THIS LARVITAR SEEMS TO KNOW IT!
BUT HOW ...?!

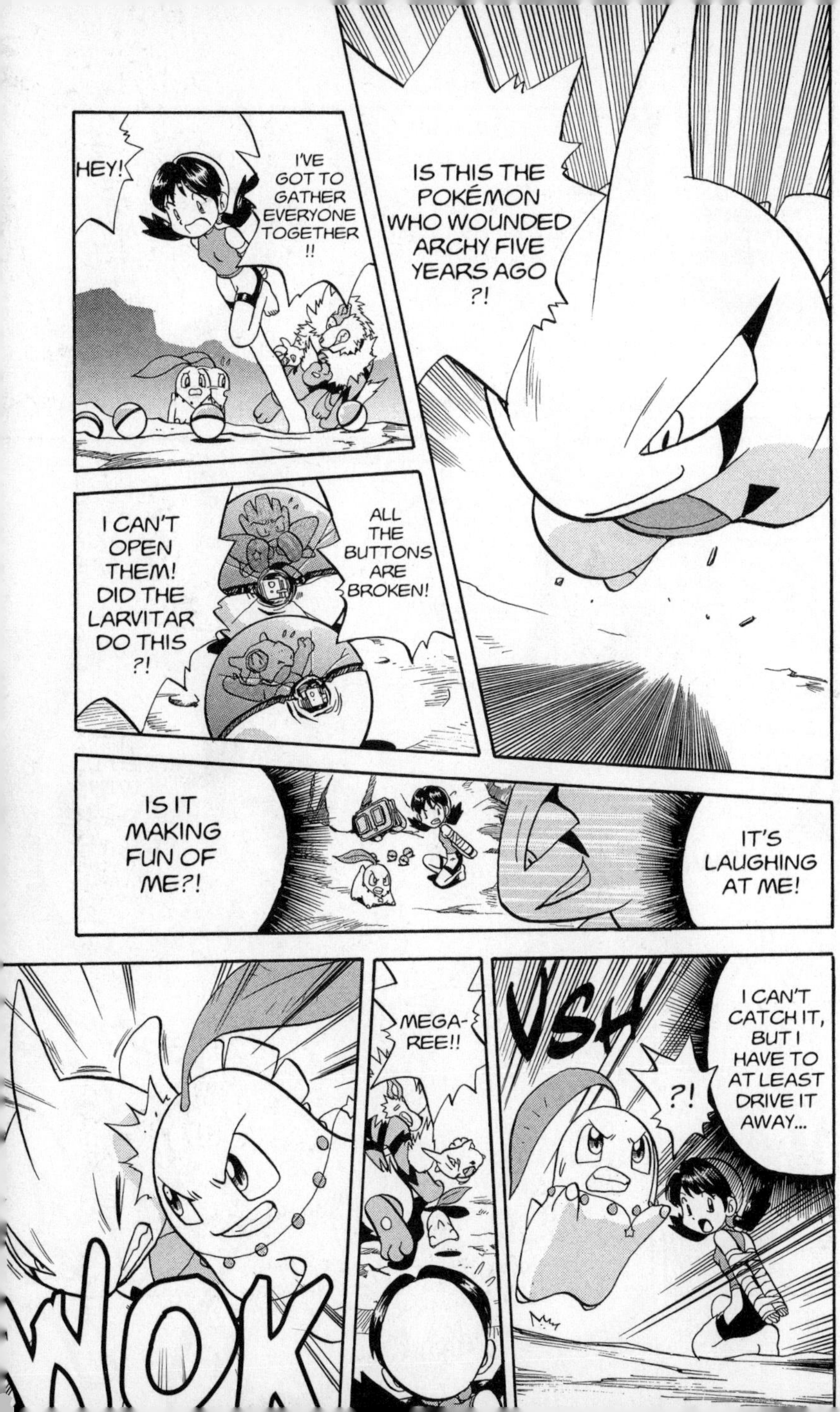
IS THIS THE POKÉMON WHO WOUNDED ARCHY FIVE YEARS AGO ?!
I'VE GOT TO GATHER EVERYONE TOGETHER !!
HEY!
ALL THE BUTTONS ARE BROKEN!
I CAN'T OPEN THEM! DID THE LARVITAR DO THIS ?!
IT'S LAUGHING AT ME!
IS IT MAKING FUN OF ME?!
I CAN'T CATCH IT, BUT I HAVE TO AT LEAST DRIVE IT AWAY...
VSH
?!
MEGA-REE!!
WOK

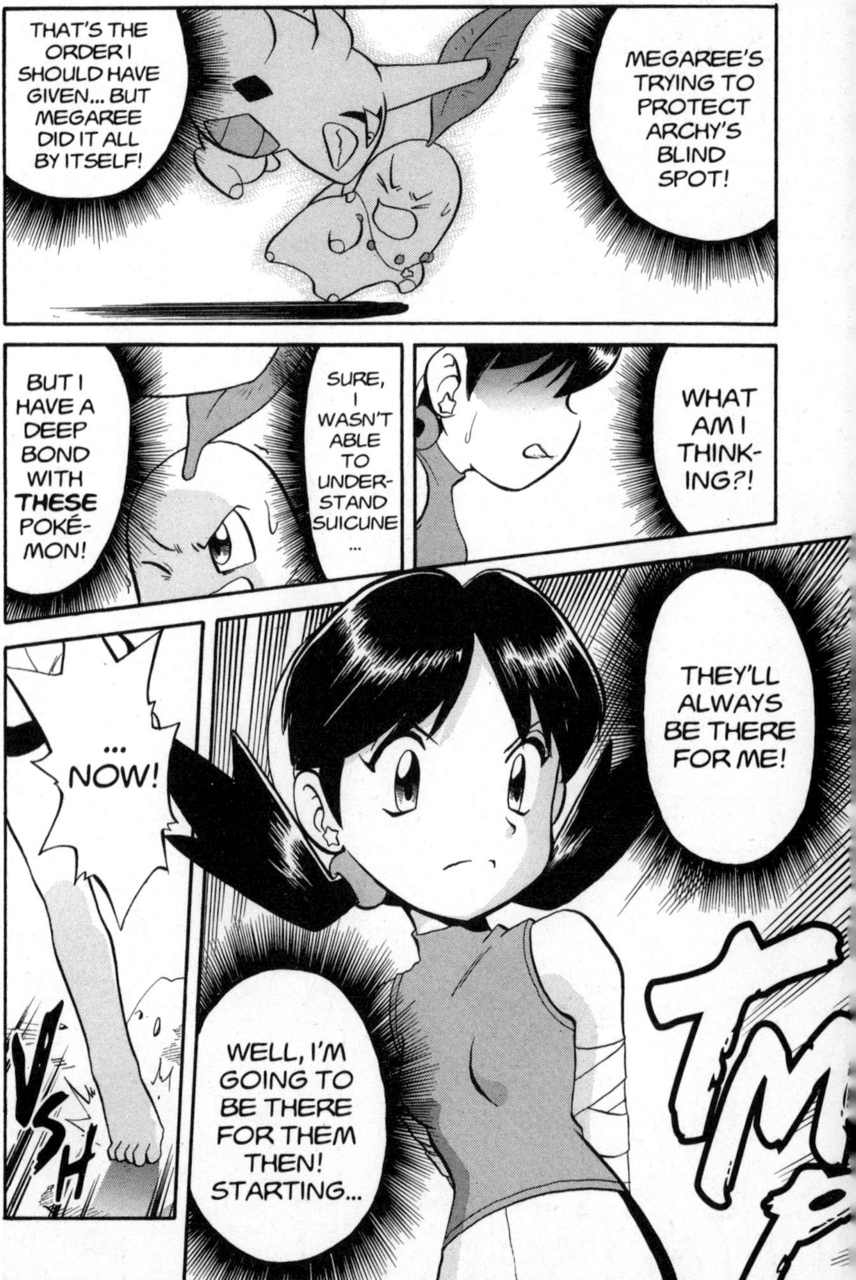
MEGAREE'S TRYING TO PROTECT ARCHY'S BLIND SPOT!
THAT'S THE ORDER I SHOULD HAVE GIVEN... BUT MEGAREE DID IT ALL BY ITSELF!
WHAT AM I THINKING?!
SURE, I WASN'T ABLE TO UNDERSTAND SUICUNE ...
BUT I HAVE A DEEP BOND WITH **THESE** POKÉMON!
THEY'LL ALWAYS BE THERE FOR ME!
WELL, I'M GOING TO BE THERE FOR THEM THEN! STARTING...
TMP
... NOW!
VSH!

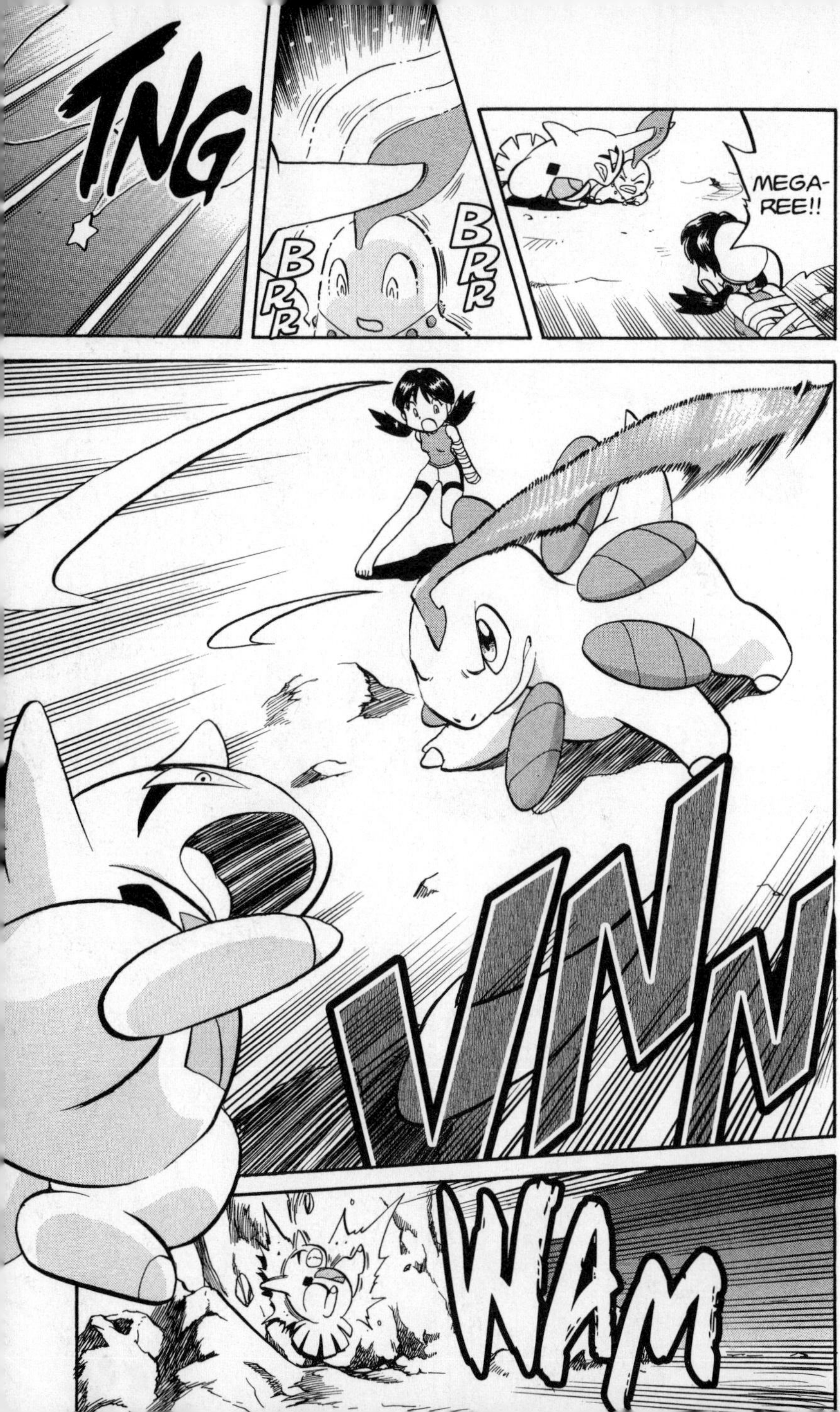
MEGA-REE!!
BRR
BRR
TNG
WINN
WAM

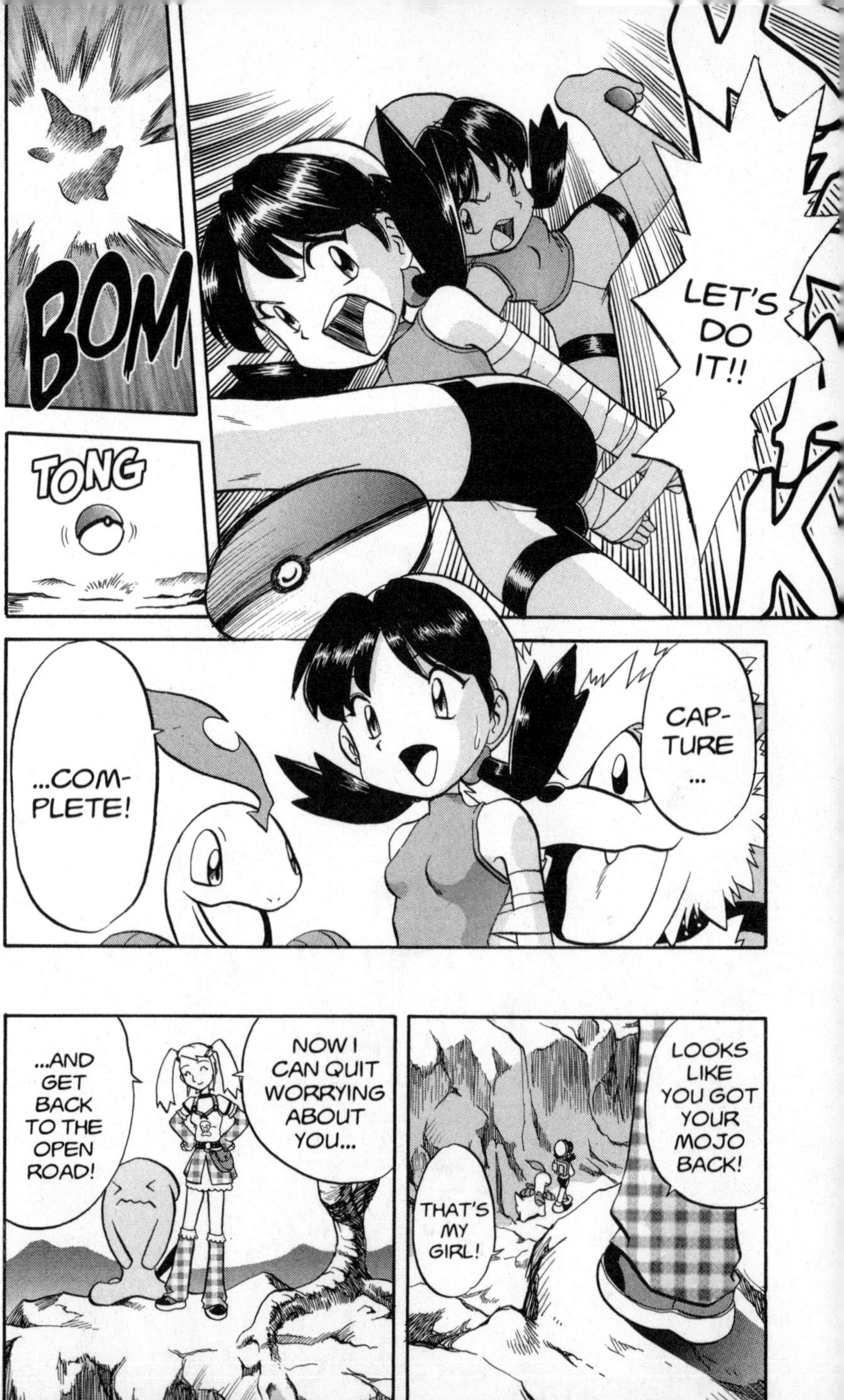
LET'S DO IT!!
BOM
TONG
CAP-TURE ...
...COM-PLETE!
LOOKS LIKE YOU GOT YOUR MOJO BACK!
THAT'S MY GIRL!
NOW I CAN QUIT WORRYING ABOUT YOU...
...AND GET BACK TO THE OPEN ROAD!

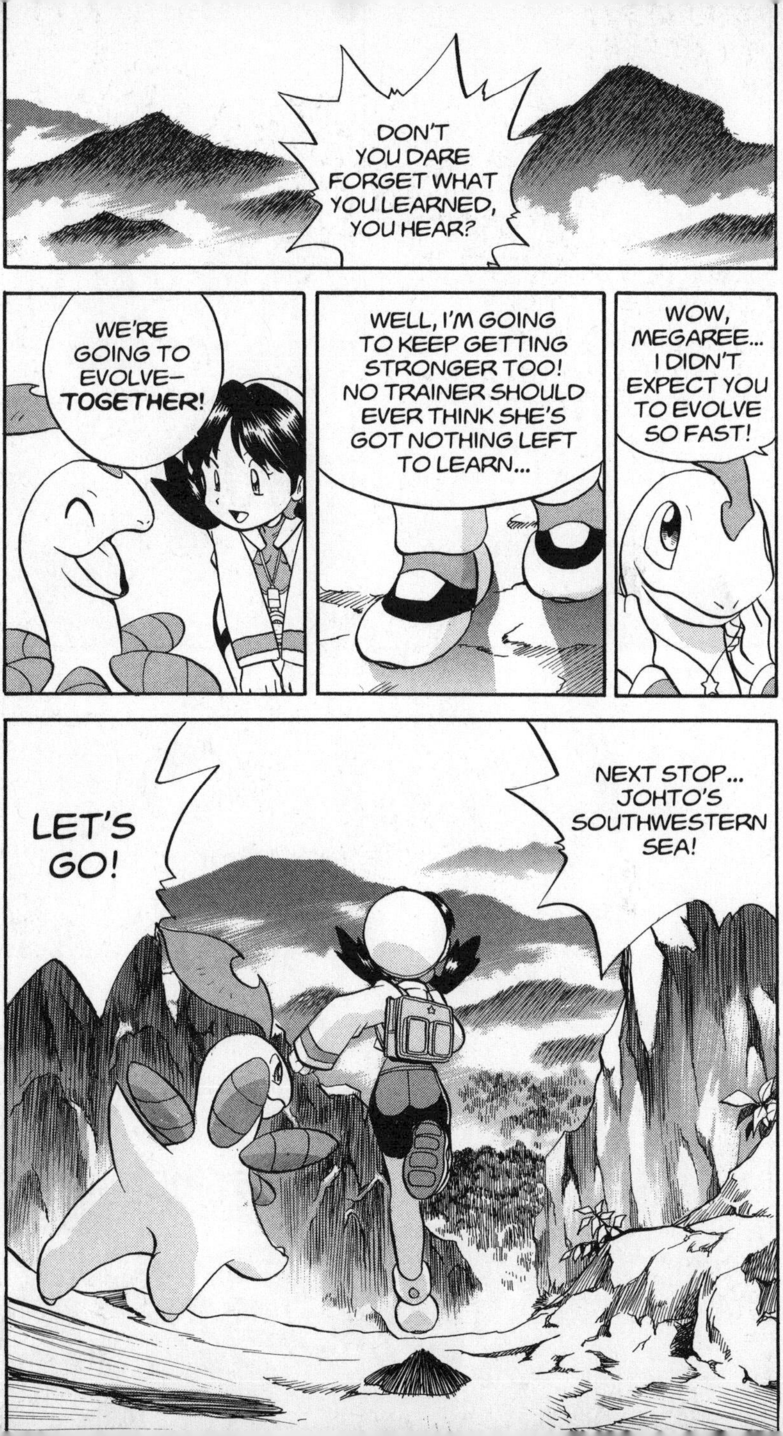
DON'T YOU DARE FORGET WHAT YOU LEARNED, YOU HEAR?
WOW, MEGAREE... I DIDN'T EXPECT YOU TO EVOLVE SO FAST!
WELL, I'M GOING TO KEEP GETTING STRONGER TOO! NO TRAINER SHOULD EVER THINK SHE'S GOT NOTHING LEFT TO LEARN...
WE'RE GOING TO EVOLVE—TOGETHER!
NEXT STOP... JOHTO'S SOUTHWESTERN SEA!
LET'S GO!

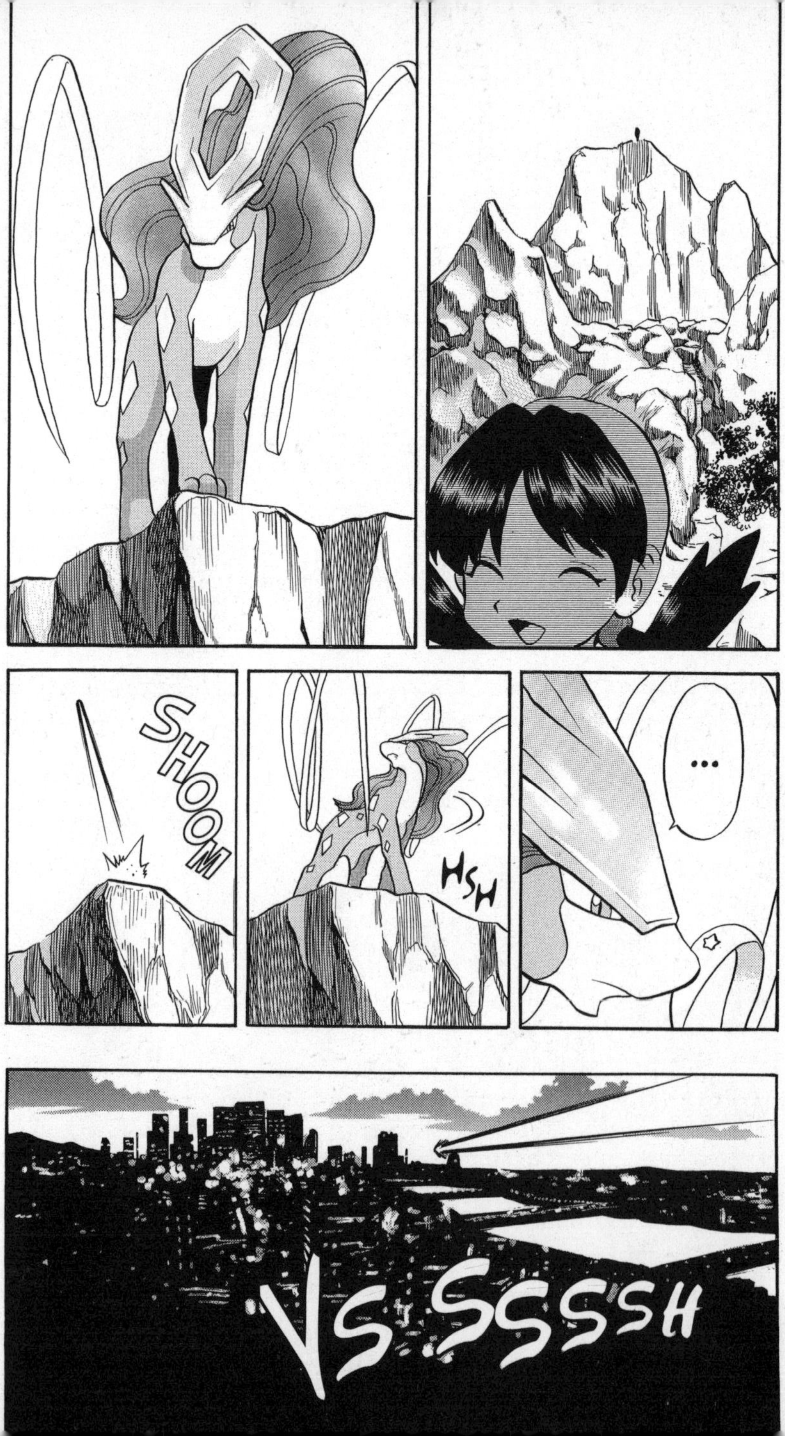
...
HSH
SHOOM
VSSSSSH

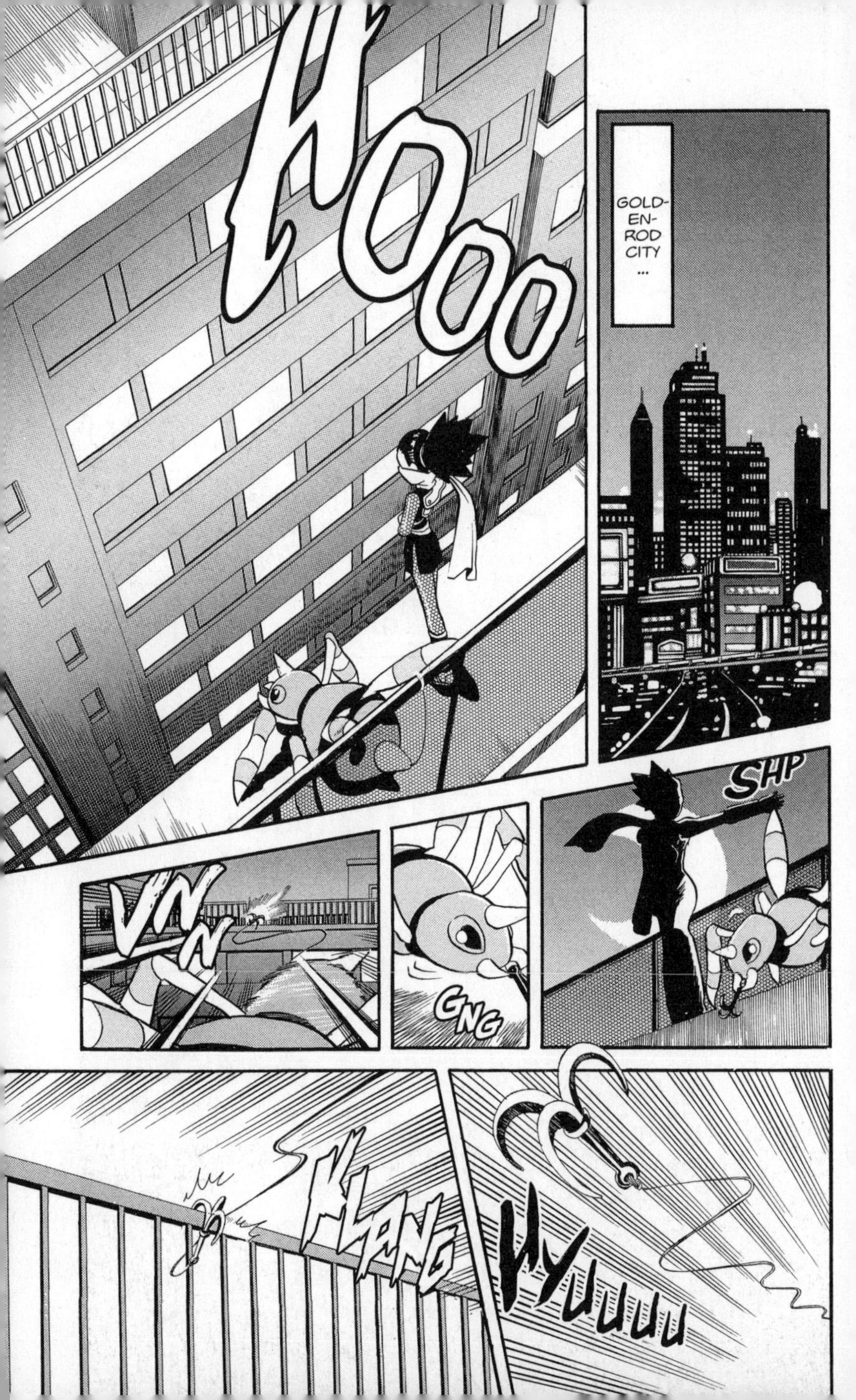
GOLD-
EN-
ROD
CITY
...
HOOOO
SHP
GNG
VNN
WYUUUUU
KLANG

136 Crossing Crobat

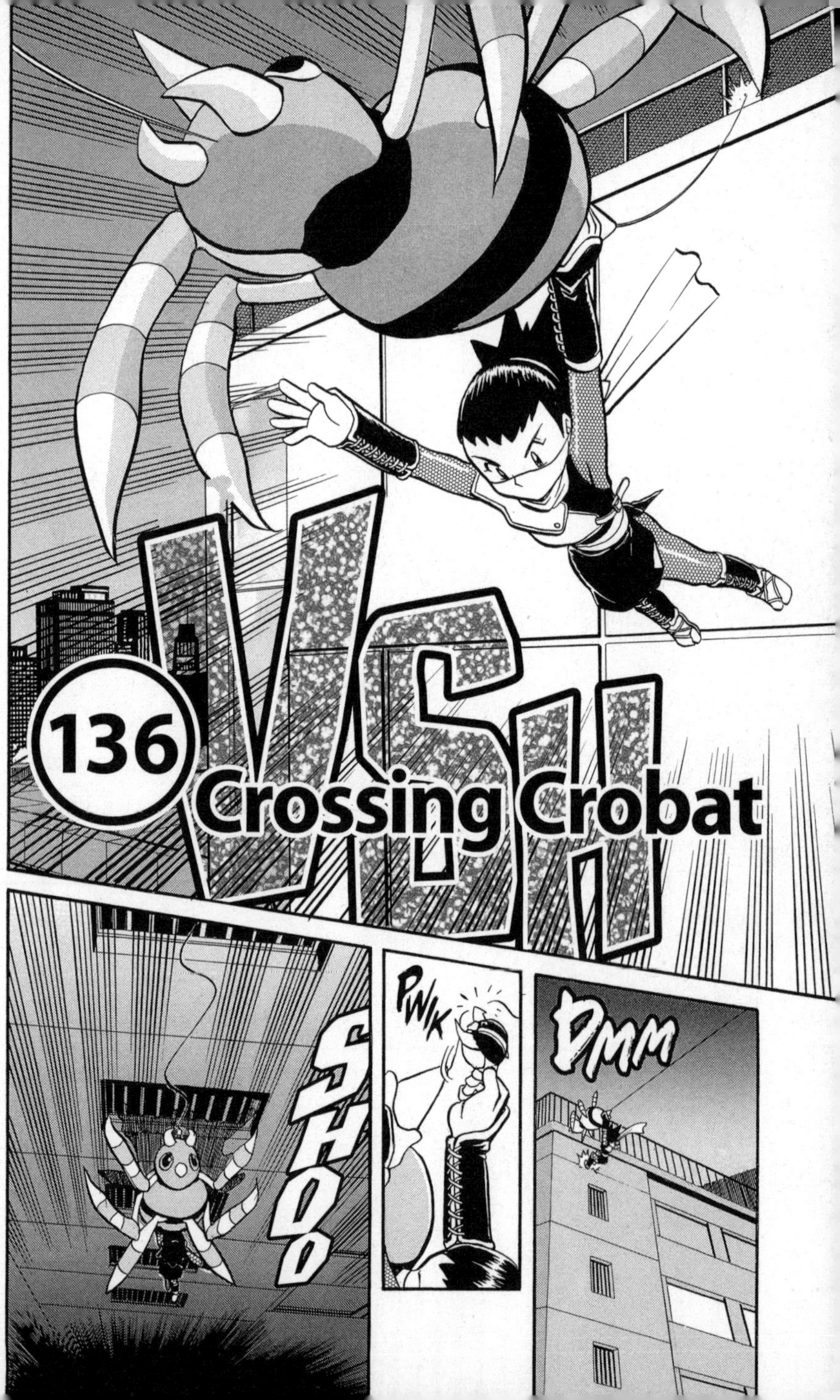
VS!!
DMM
PWIK
SHOO

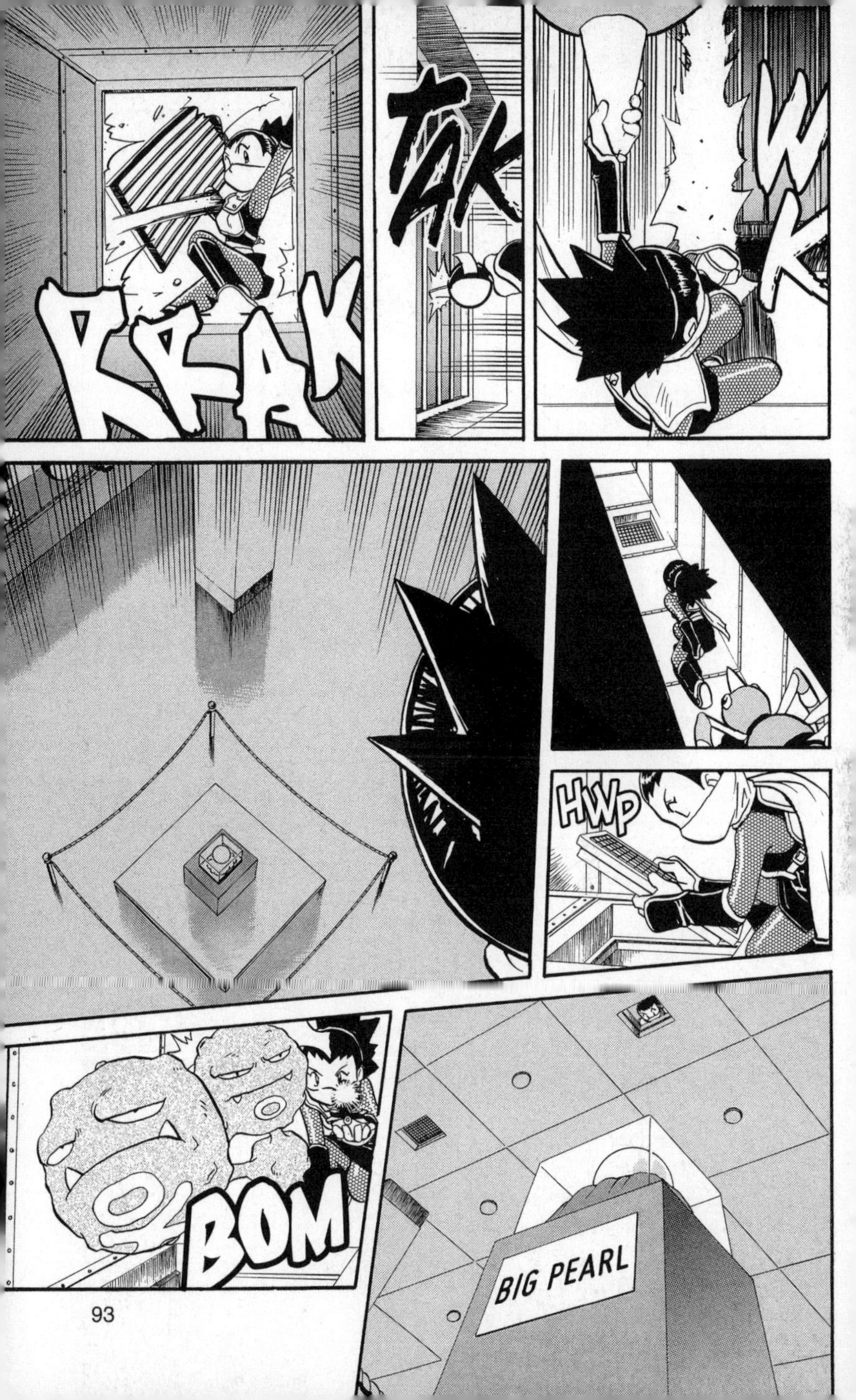
RRAK
HWP
BIG PEARL
BOM

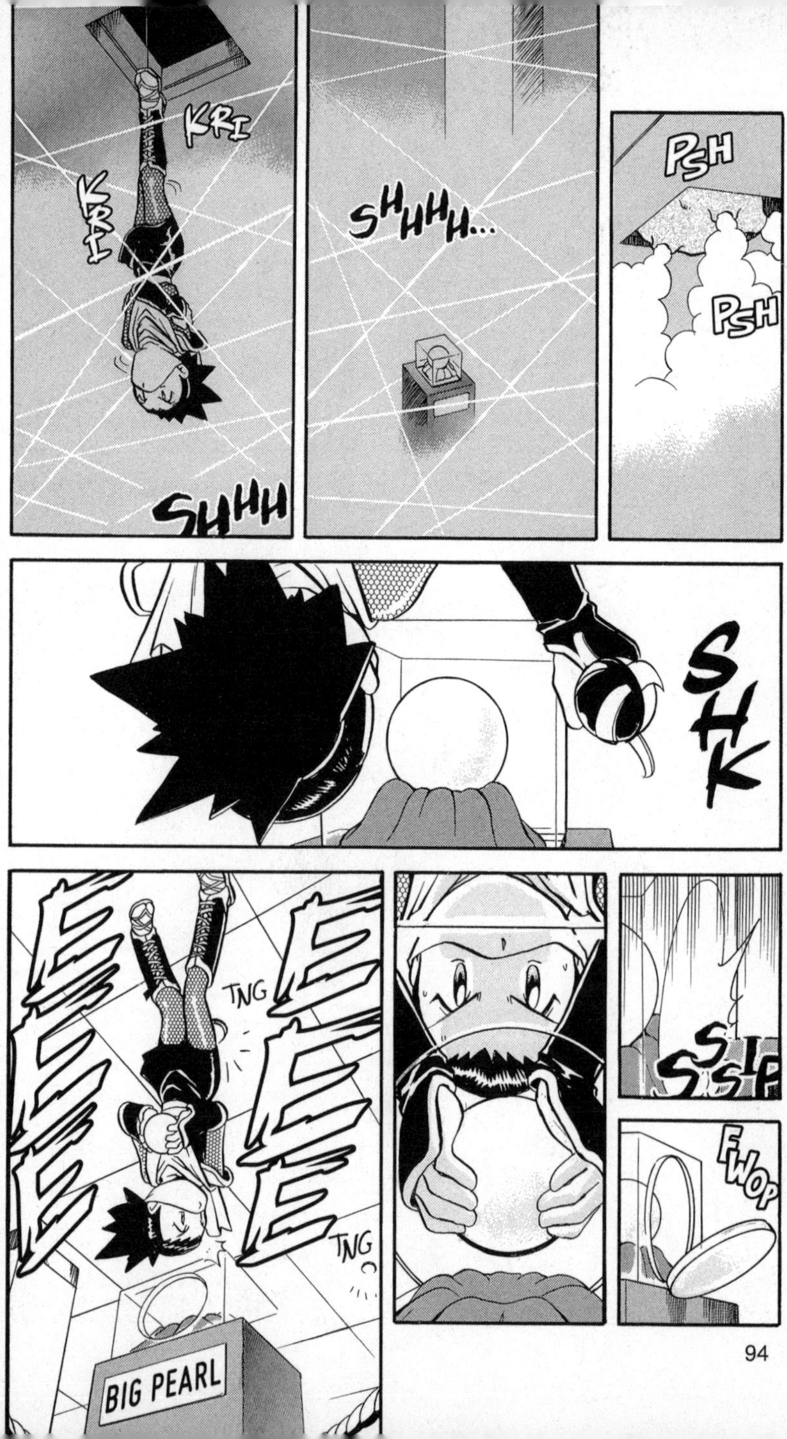
PSH
PSH
SHHHH...
KRI
KRI
SHHH
SHK
SSIP
FWOP
EEEEEEE
TNG
TNG
BIG PEARL

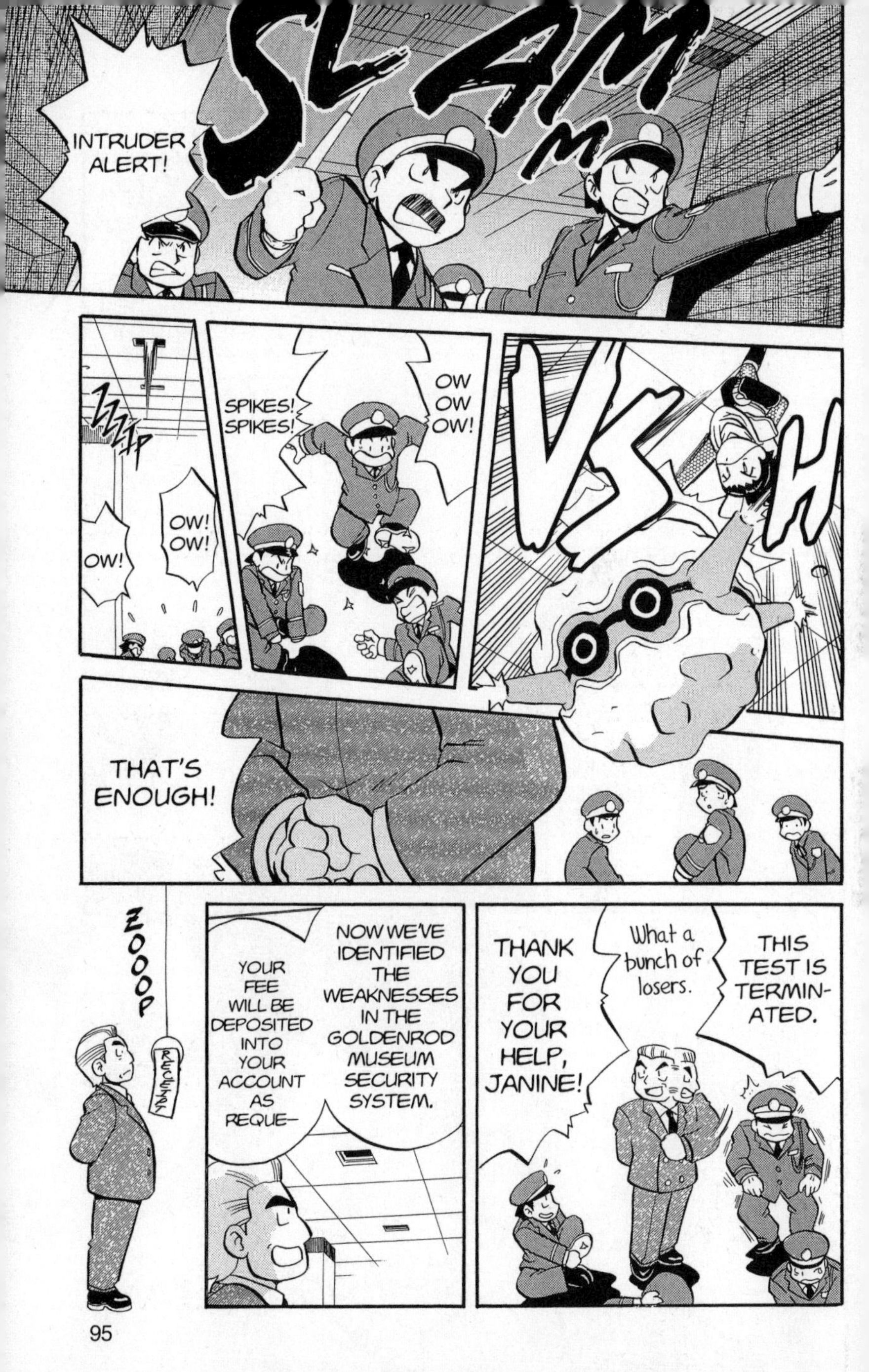
SLAM
INTRUDER ALERT!
VSSH
OW OW OW!
SPIKES! SPIKES!
OW! OW!
OW!
THAT'S ENOUGH!
THIS TEST IS TERMINATED.
What a bunch of losers.
THANK YOU FOR YOUR HELP, JANINE!
NOW WE'VE IDENTIFIED THE WEAKNESSES IN THE GOLDENROD MUSEUM SECURITY SYSTEM.
YOUR FEE WILL BE DEPOSITED INTO YOUR ACCOUNT AS REQUE–
ZOOOP

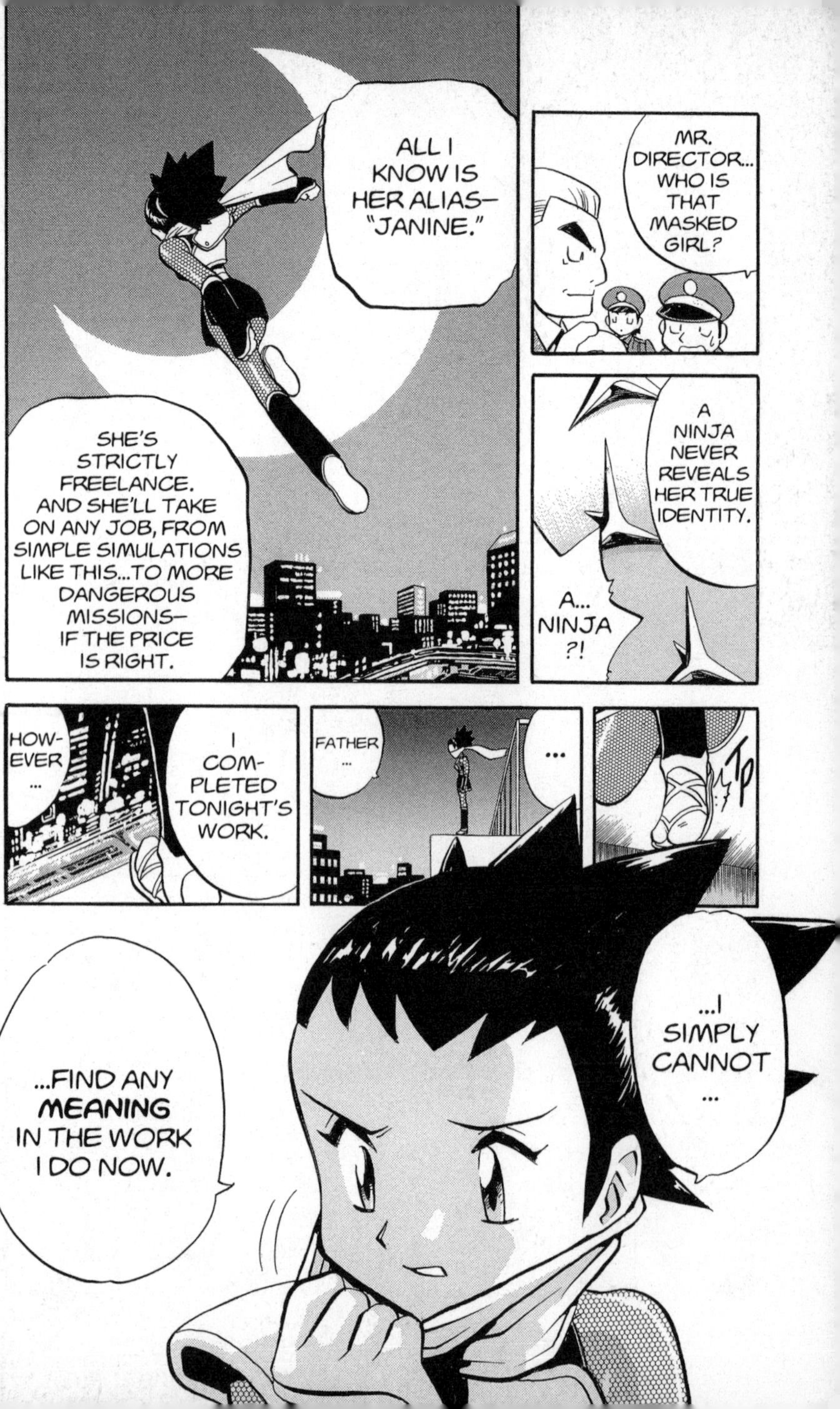
MR. DIRECTOR... WHO IS THAT MASKED GIRL?
A NINJA NEVER REVEALS HER TRUE IDENTITY.
A... NINJA?!
ALL I KNOW IS HER ALIAS— "JANINE."
SHE'S STRICTLY FREELANCE. AND SHE'LL TAKE ON ANY JOB, FROM SIMPLE SIMULATIONS LIKE THIS...TO MORE DANGEROUS MISSIONS— IF THE PRICE IS RIGHT.
TP
...
FATHER...
I COMPLETED TONIGHT'S WORK.
HOWEVER...
...I SIMPLY CANNOT...
...FIND ANY MEANING IN THE WORK I DO NOW.

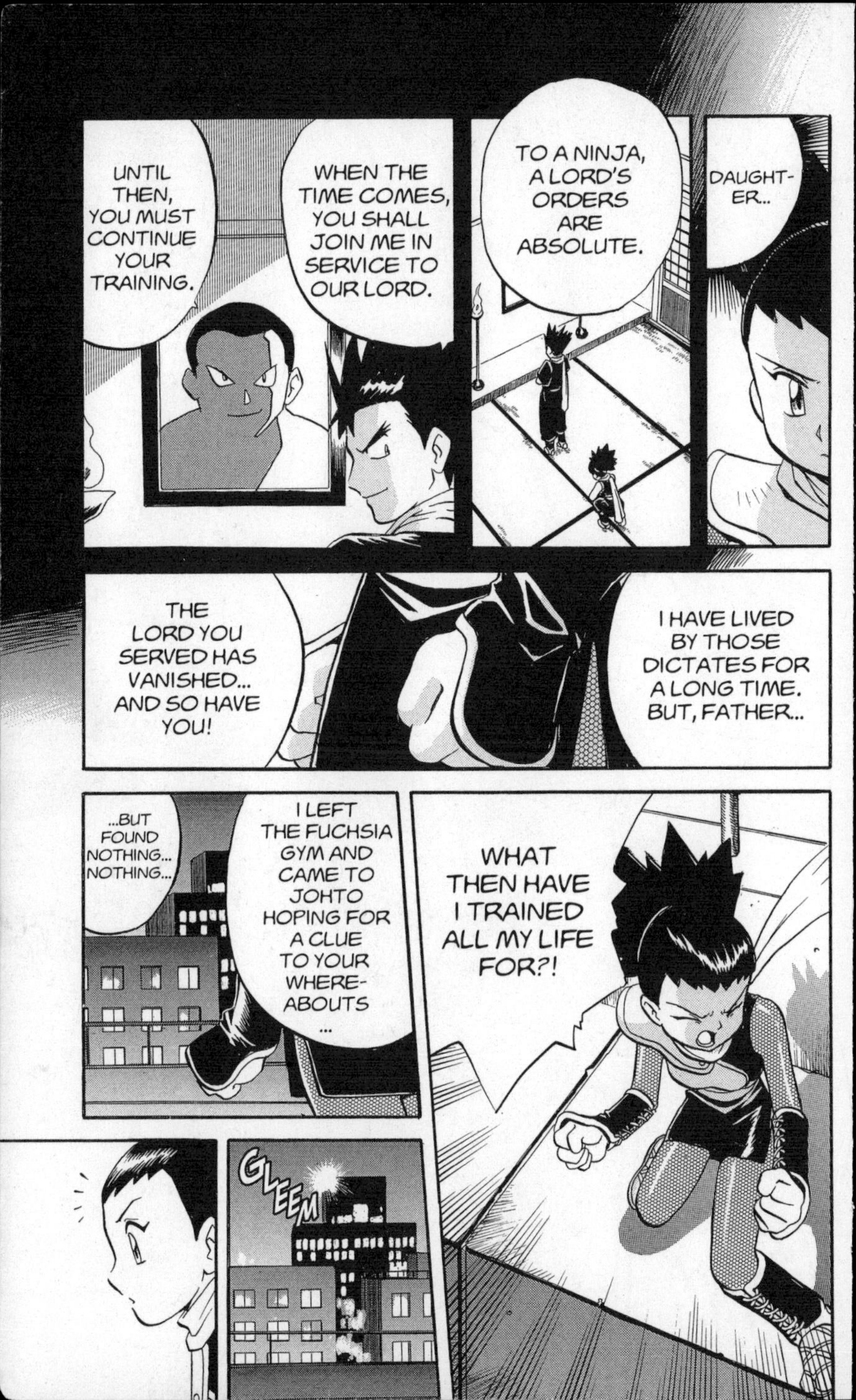
DAUGHTER-ER...
TO A NINJA, A LORD'S ORDERS ARE ABSOLUTE.
WHEN THE TIME COMES, YOU SHALL JOIN ME IN SERVICE TO OUR LORD.
UNTIL THEN, YOU MUST CONTINUE YOUR TRAINING.
I HAVE LIVED BY THOSE DICTATES FOR A LONG TIME. BUT, FATHER...
THE LORD YOU SERVED HAS VANISHED... AND SO HAVE YOU!
WHAT THEN HAVE I TRAINED ALL MY LIFE FOR?!
I LEFT THE FUCHSIA GYM AND CAME TO JOHTO HOPING FOR A CLUE TO YOUR WHEREABOUTS...
...BUT FOUND NOTHING... NOTHING...
GLEEM

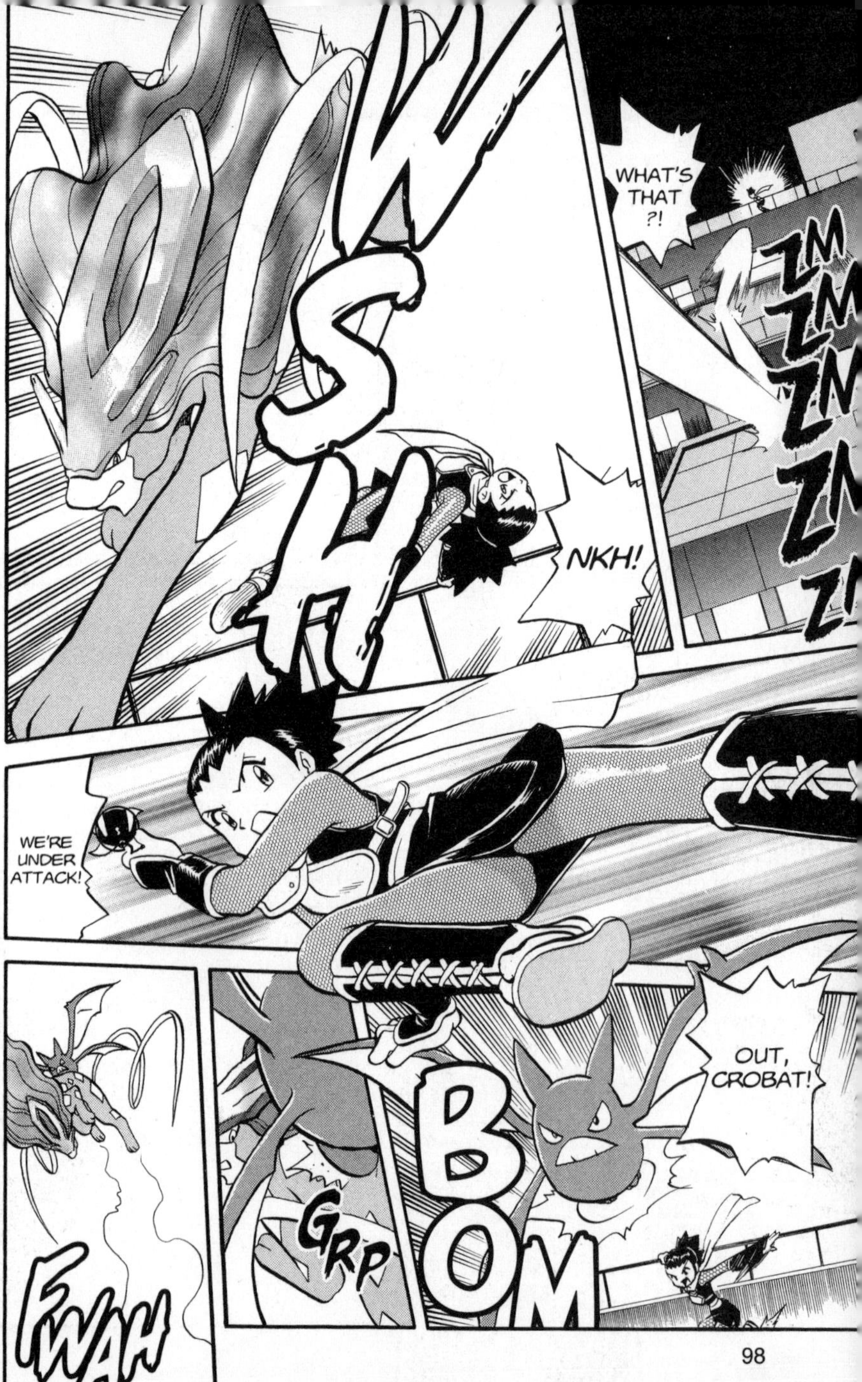
WHAT'S THAT ?!
ZM ZM ZM ZM ZM ZM
WHSH
NKH!
WE'RE UNDER ATTACK!
OUT, CROBAT!
BOOM
GRP
FWAH

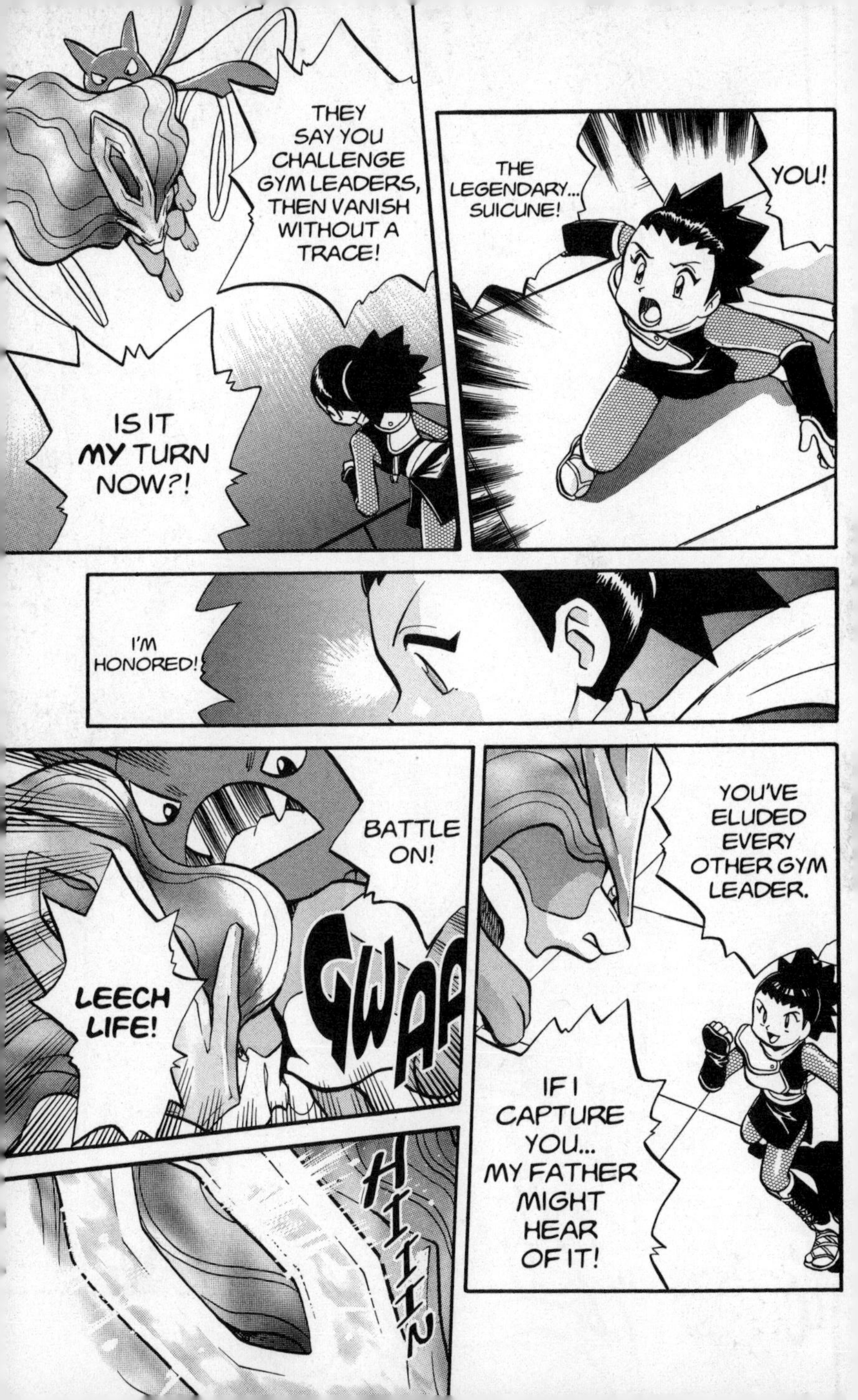
YOU!
THE LEGENDARY... SUICUNE!
THEY SAY YOU CHALLENGE GYM LEADERS, THEN VANISH WITHOUT A TRACE!
IS IT **MY** TURN NOW?!
I'M HONORED!
YOU'VE ELUDED EVERY OTHER GYM LEADER.
IF I CAPTURE YOU... MY FATHER MIGHT HEAR OF IT!
BATTLE ON!
LEECH LIFE!
GWAA
HIIIN

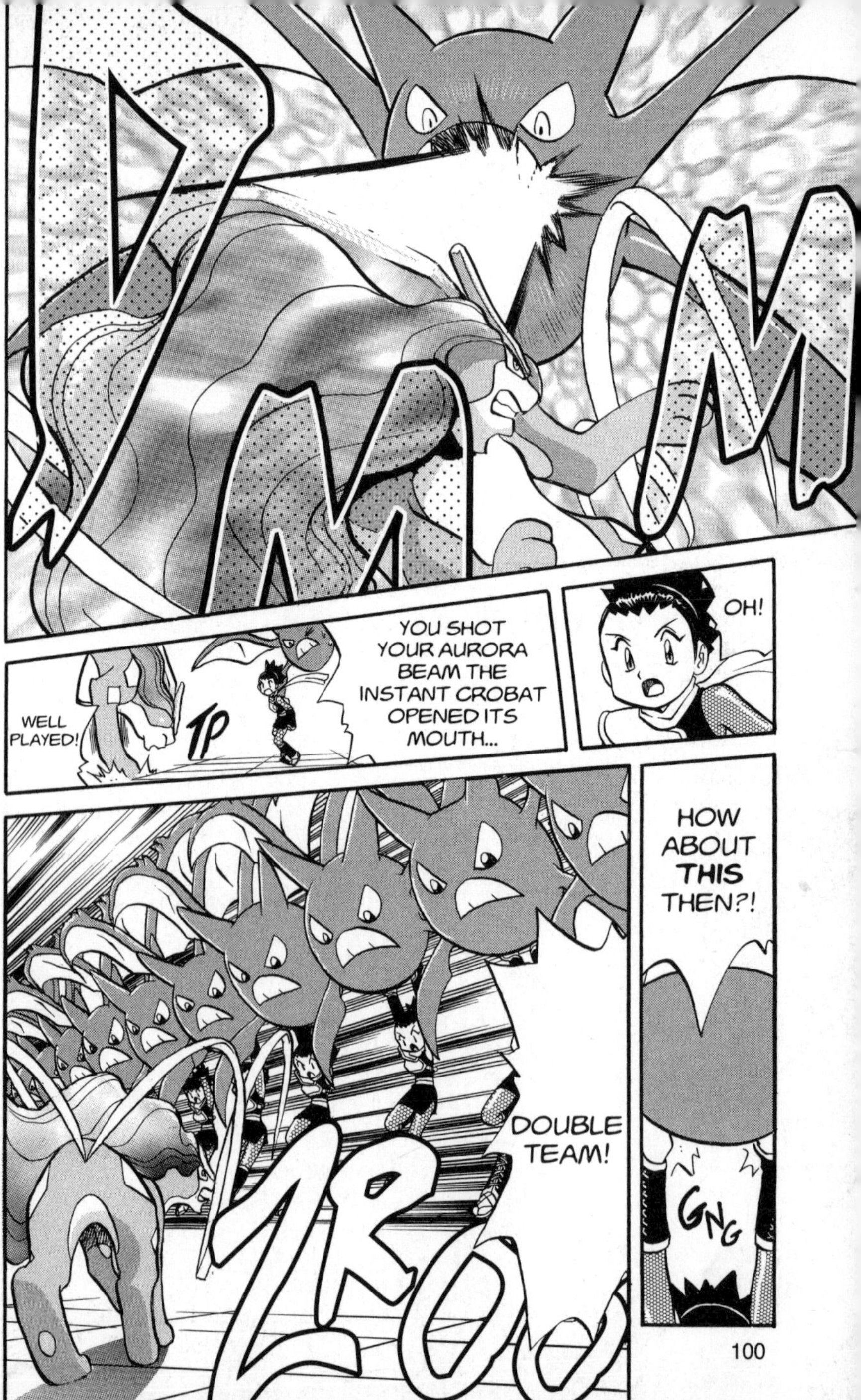
OH!
YOU SHOT YOUR AURORA BEAM THE INSTANT CROBAT OPENED ITS MOUTH...
WELL PLAYED!
TP
HOW ABOUT **THIS** THEN?!
GNG
DOUBLE TEAM!

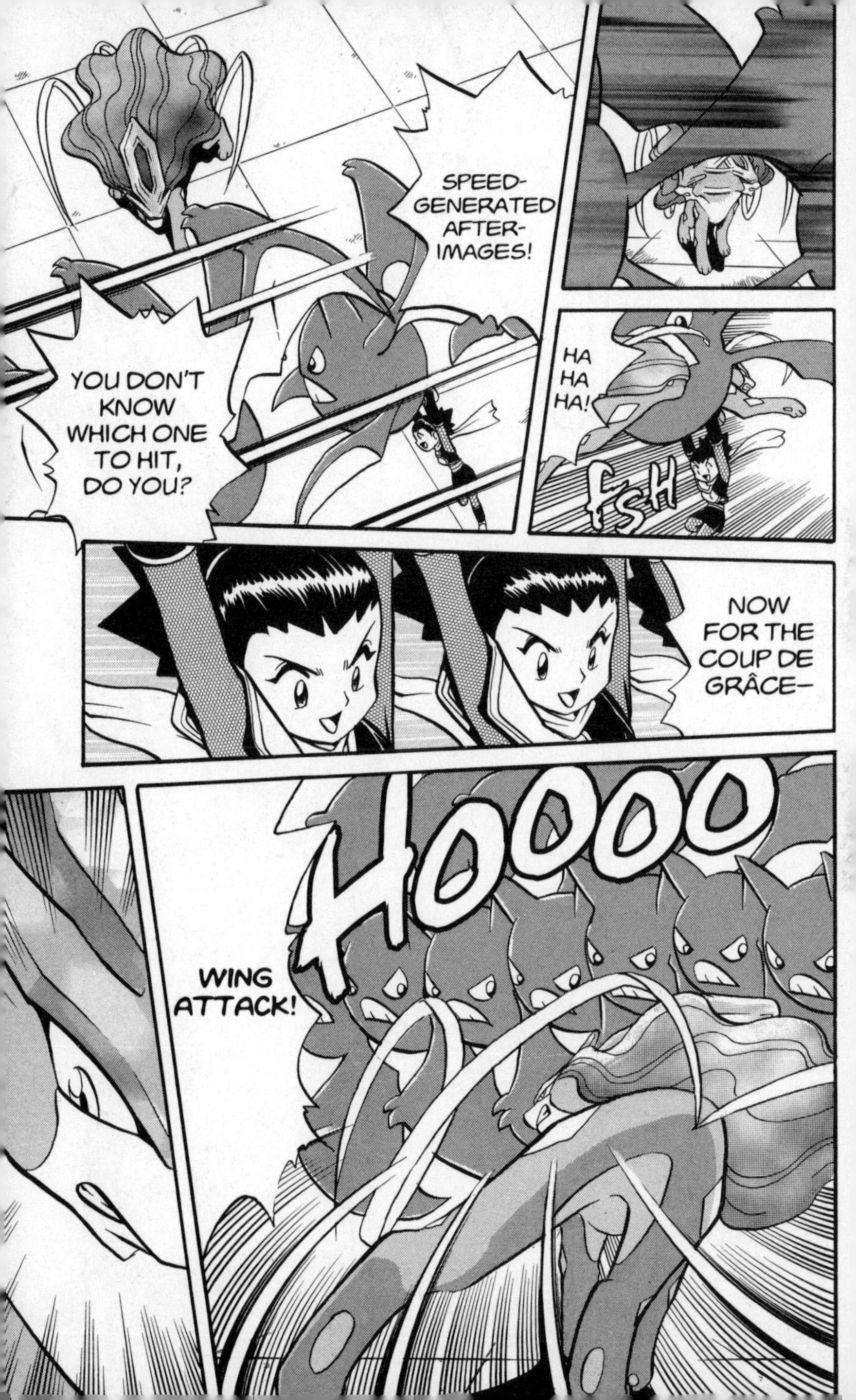
HA HA HA!
FSH
SPEED-GENERATED AFTER-IMAGES!
YOU DON'T KNOW WHICH ONE TO HIT, DO YOU?
NOW FOR THE COUP DE GRÂCE—
HOOOO
WING ATTACK!

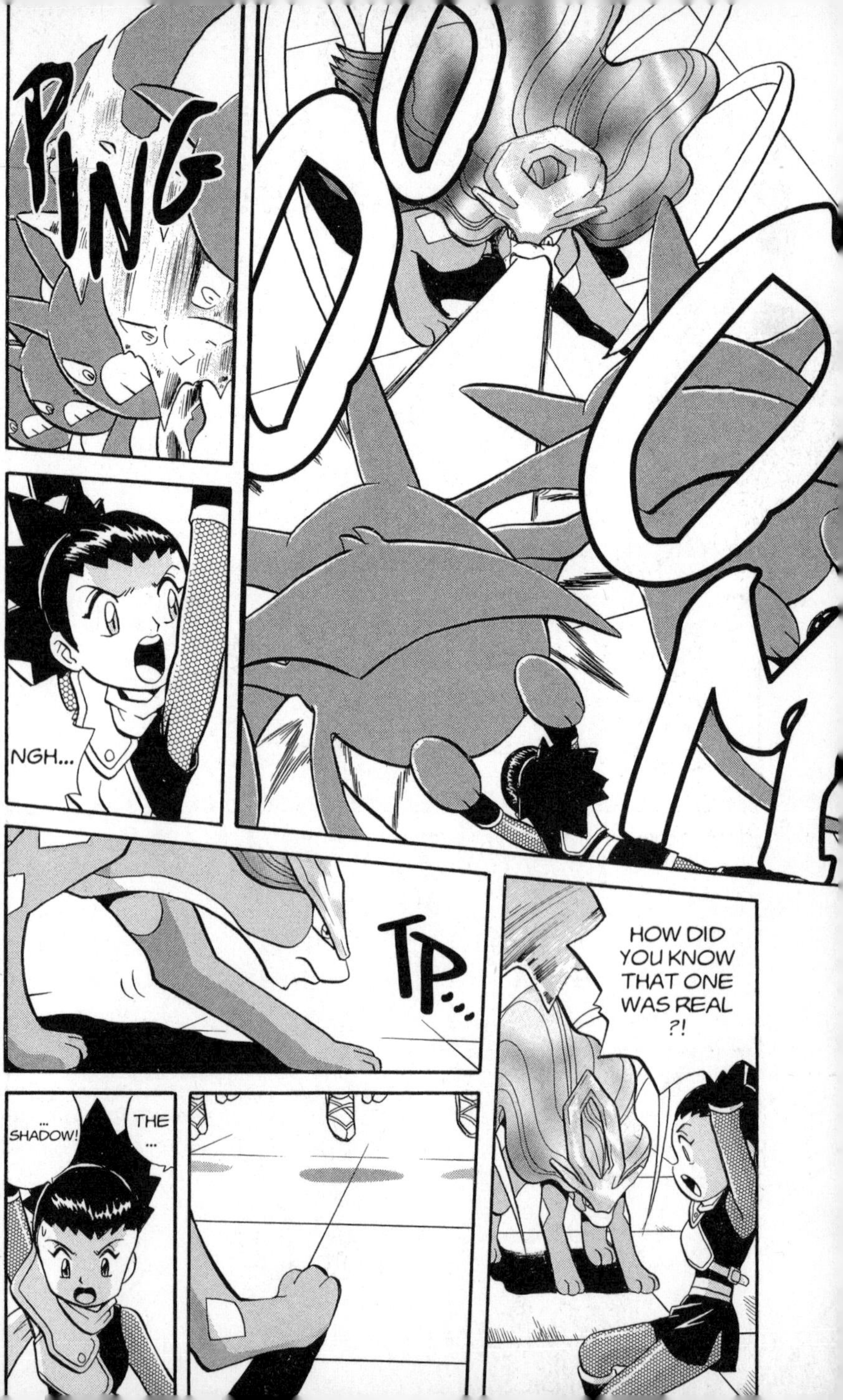
DOOM
PING
NGH...
HOW DID YOU KNOW THAT ONE WAS REAL ?!
TP...
THE ...
... SHADOW!

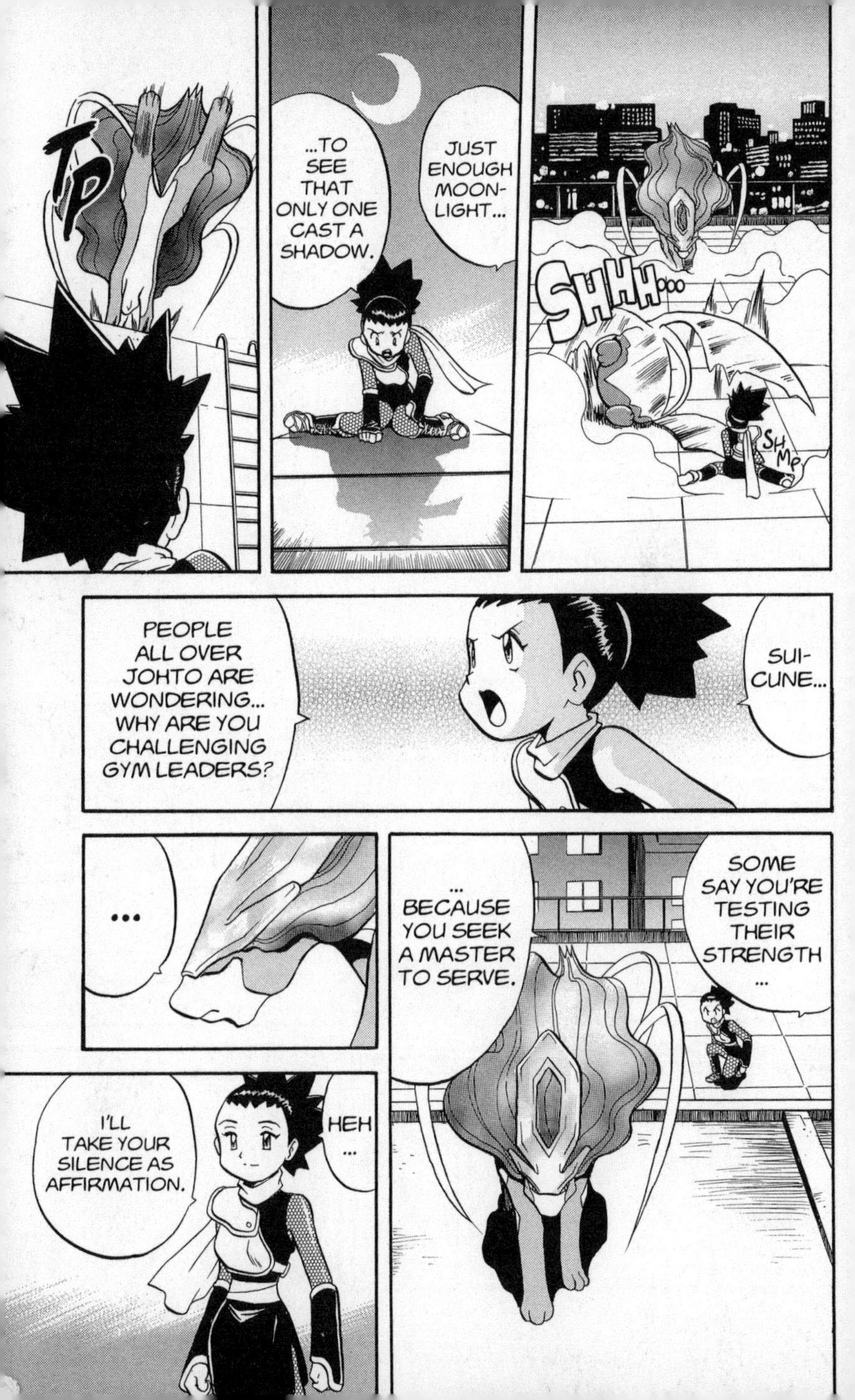
SHHH...
SHMP
JUST ENOUGH MOONLIGHT...
...TO SEE THAT ONLY ONE CAST A SHADOW.
TP
SUICUNE...
PEOPLE ALL OVER JOHTO ARE WONDERING... WHY ARE YOU CHALLENGING GYM LEADERS?
SOME SAY YOU'RE TESTING THEIR STRENGTH...
...BECAUSE YOU SEEK A MASTER TO SERVE.
...
HEH...
I'LL TAKE YOUR SILENCE AS AFFIRMATION.

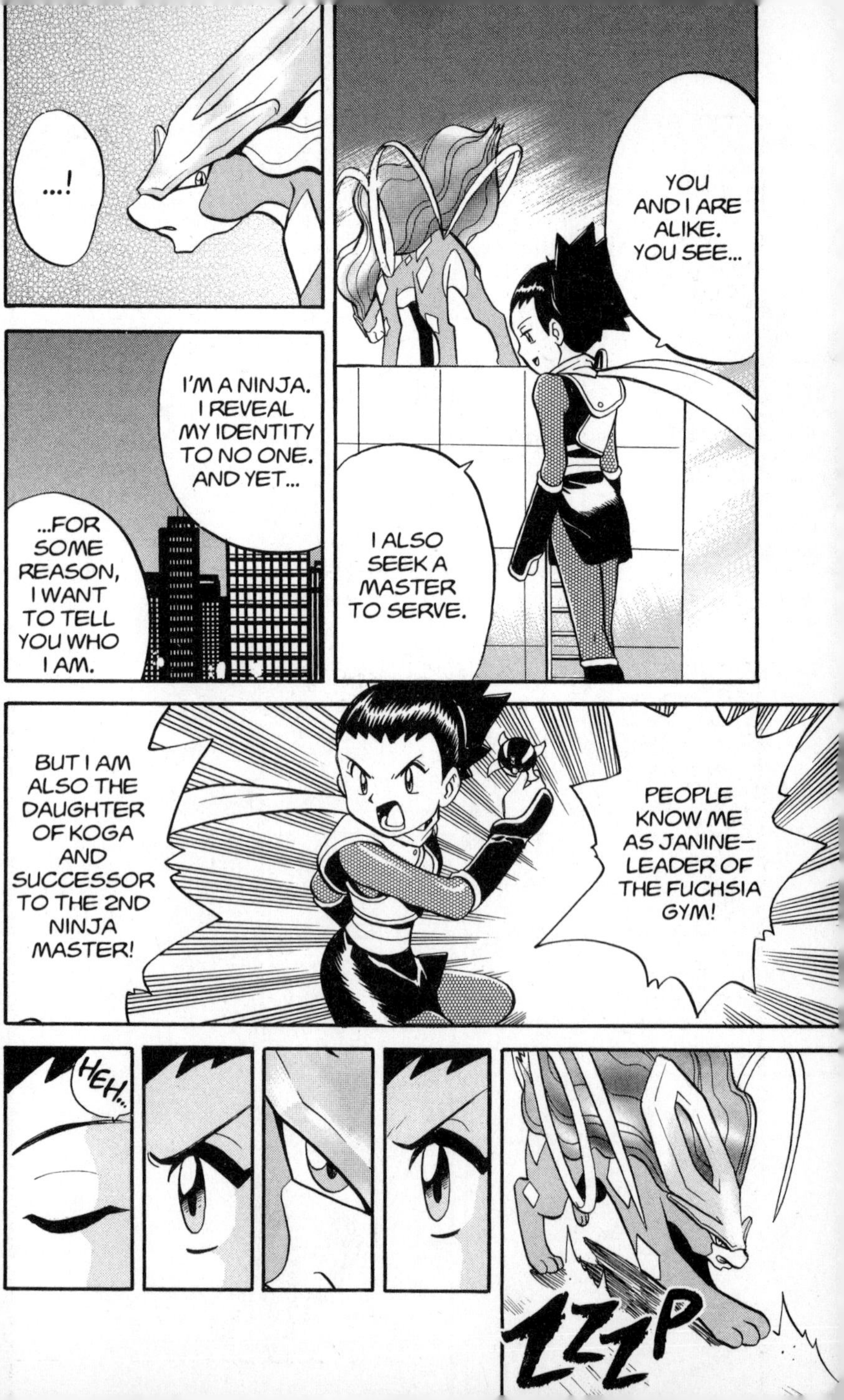
YOU AND I ARE ALIKE. YOU SEE...
I ALSO SEEK A MASTER TO SERVE.
...!
I'M A NINJA. I REVEAL MY IDENTITY TO NO ONE. AND YET...
...FOR SOME REASON, I WANT TO TELL YOU WHO I AM.
PEOPLE KNOW ME AS JANINE—LEADER OF THE FUCHSIA GYM!
BUT I AM ALSO THE DAUGHTER OF KOGA AND SUCCESSOR TO THE 2ND NINJA MASTER!
ZZZP
HEH...

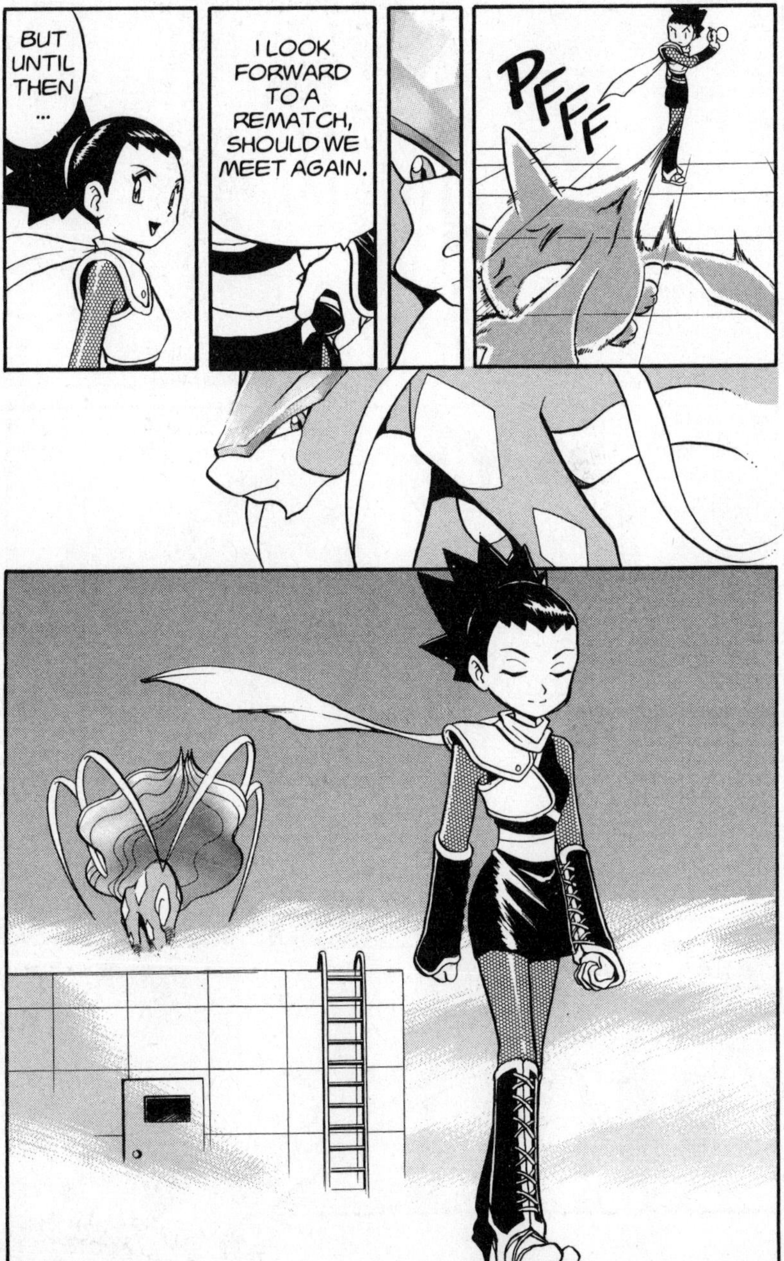
PFFFF
I LOOK FORWARD TO A REMATCH, SHOULD WE MEET AGAIN.
BUT UNTIL THEN ...

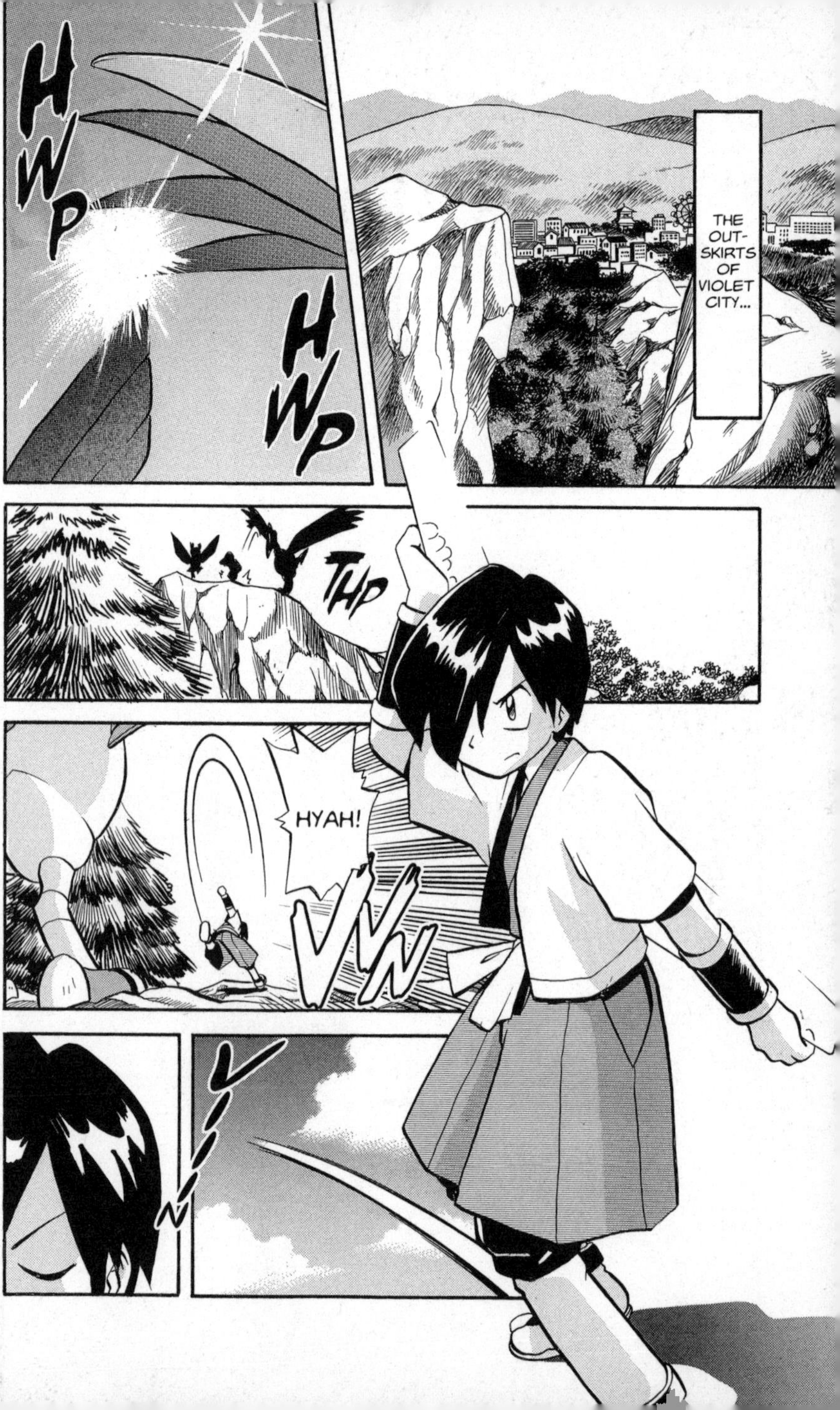
THE OUT-SKIRTS OF VIOLET CITY...
HWP
HWP
THP
HYAH!
VNN
V---N

137 Really Raikou & Entirely Entei (Part 1)

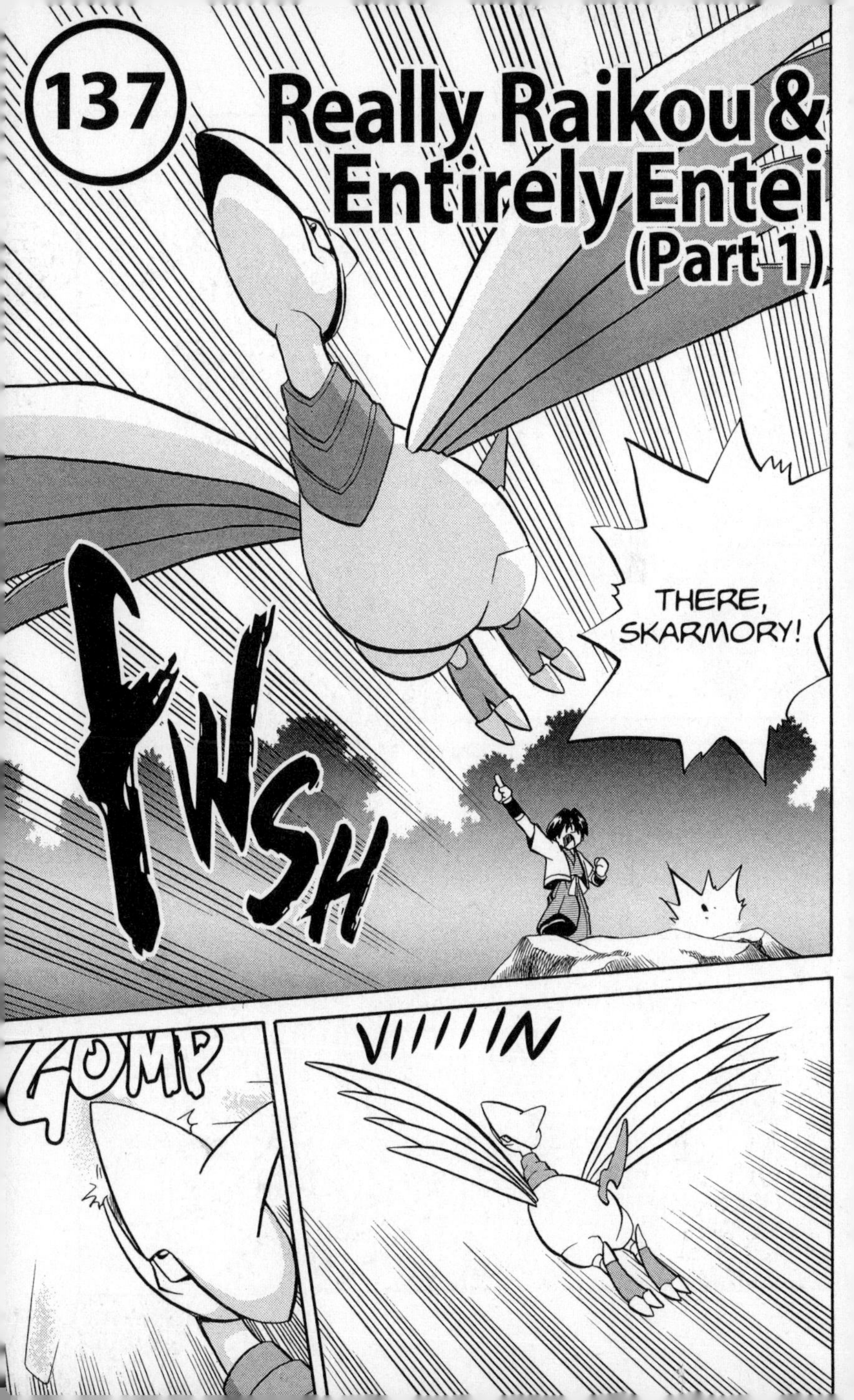
THERE, SKARMORY!
FWSH
VIIIIIN
GOMP

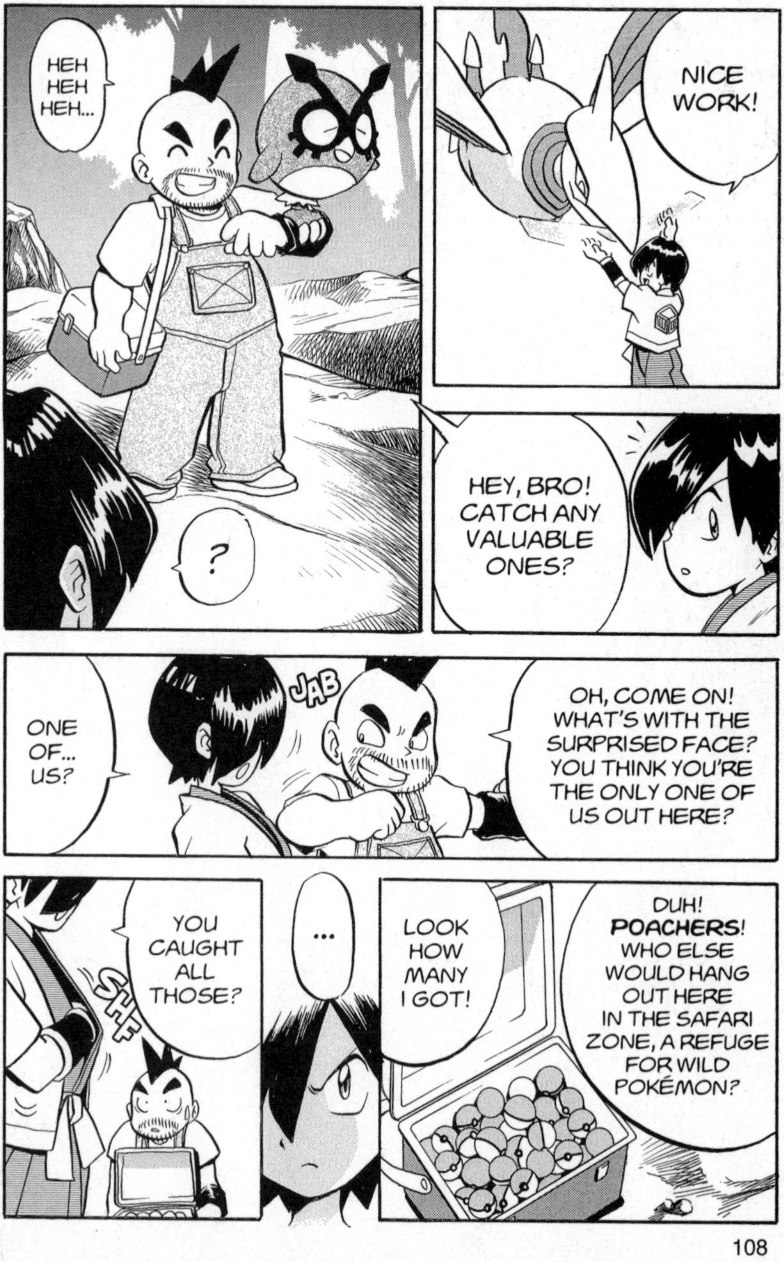
NICE WORK!
HEY, BRO! CATCH ANY VALUABLE ONES?
HEH HEH HEH...
?
OH, COME ON! WHAT'S WITH THE SURPRISED FACE? YOU THINK YOU'RE THE ONLY ONE OF US OUT HERE?
JAB
ONE OF... US?
DUH! **POACHERS**! WHO ELSE WOULD HANG OUT HERE IN THE SAFARI ZONE, A REFUGE FOR WILD POKÉMON?
LOOK HOW MANY I GOT!
...
YOU CAUGHT ALL THOSE?
SHF

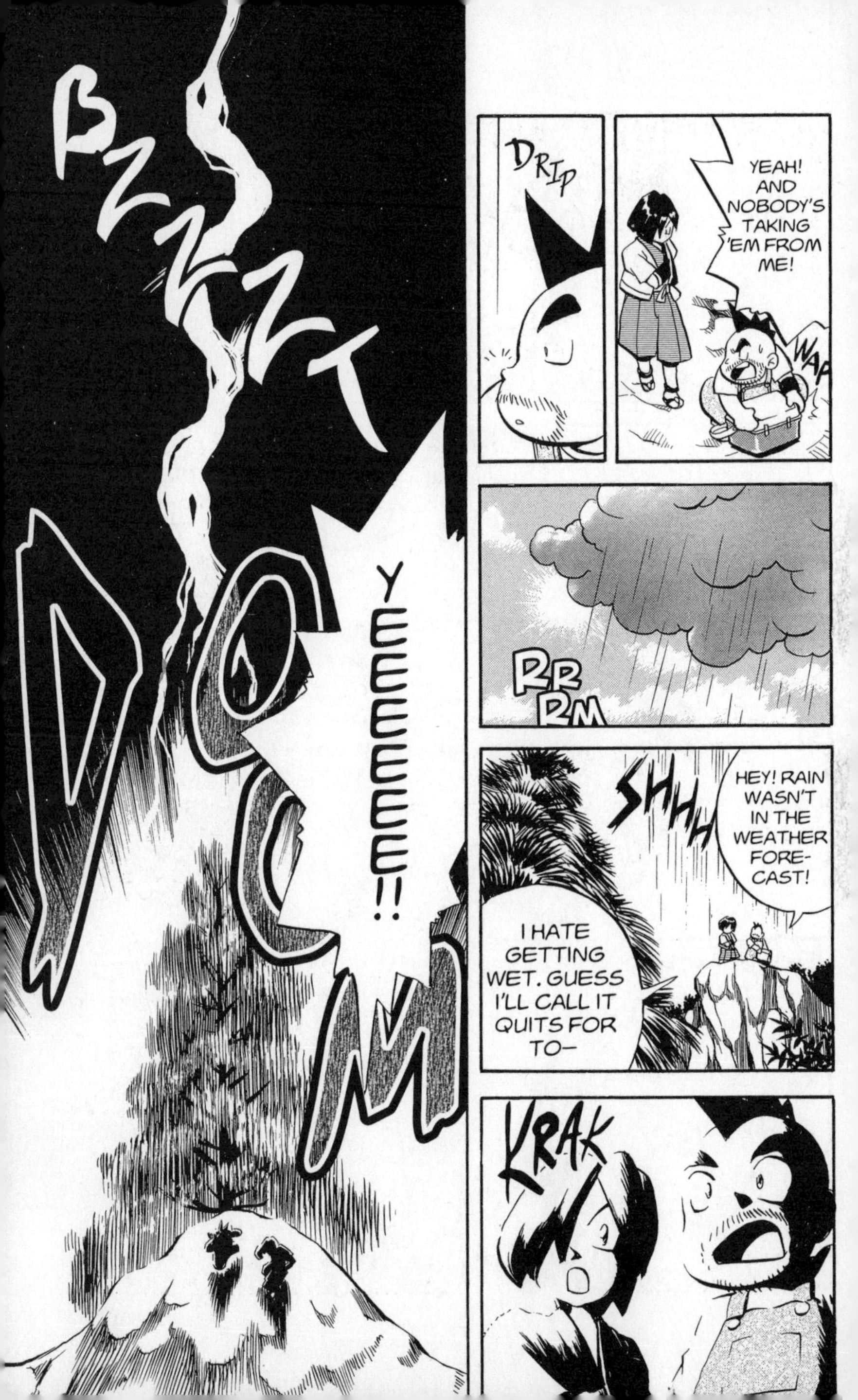
YEAH! AND NOBODY'S TAKING 'EM FROM ME!
WAP
DRIP
RRRM
SHHH
HEY! RAIN WASN'T IN THE WEATHER FORE-CAST!
I HATE GETTING WET. GUESS I'LL CALL IT QUITS FOR TO—
KRAK
BZZZZT
DOOM
YEEEEEEE!!

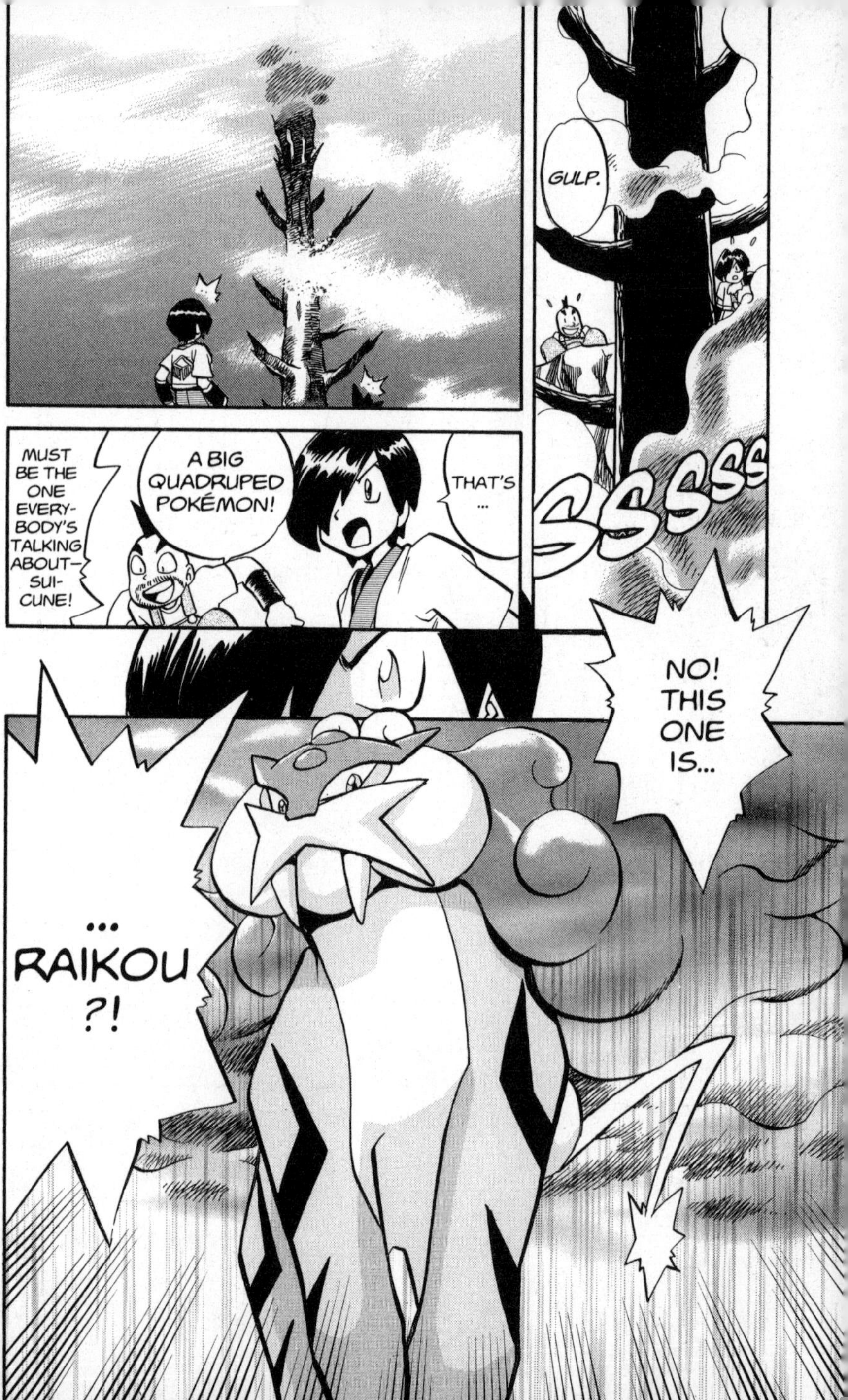
GULP.
SSSSS
THAT'S ...
A BIG QUADRUPED POKÉMON!
MUST BE THE ONE EVERY-BODY'S TALKING ABOUT—SUI-CUNE!
NO! THIS ONE IS...
... RAIKOU ?!

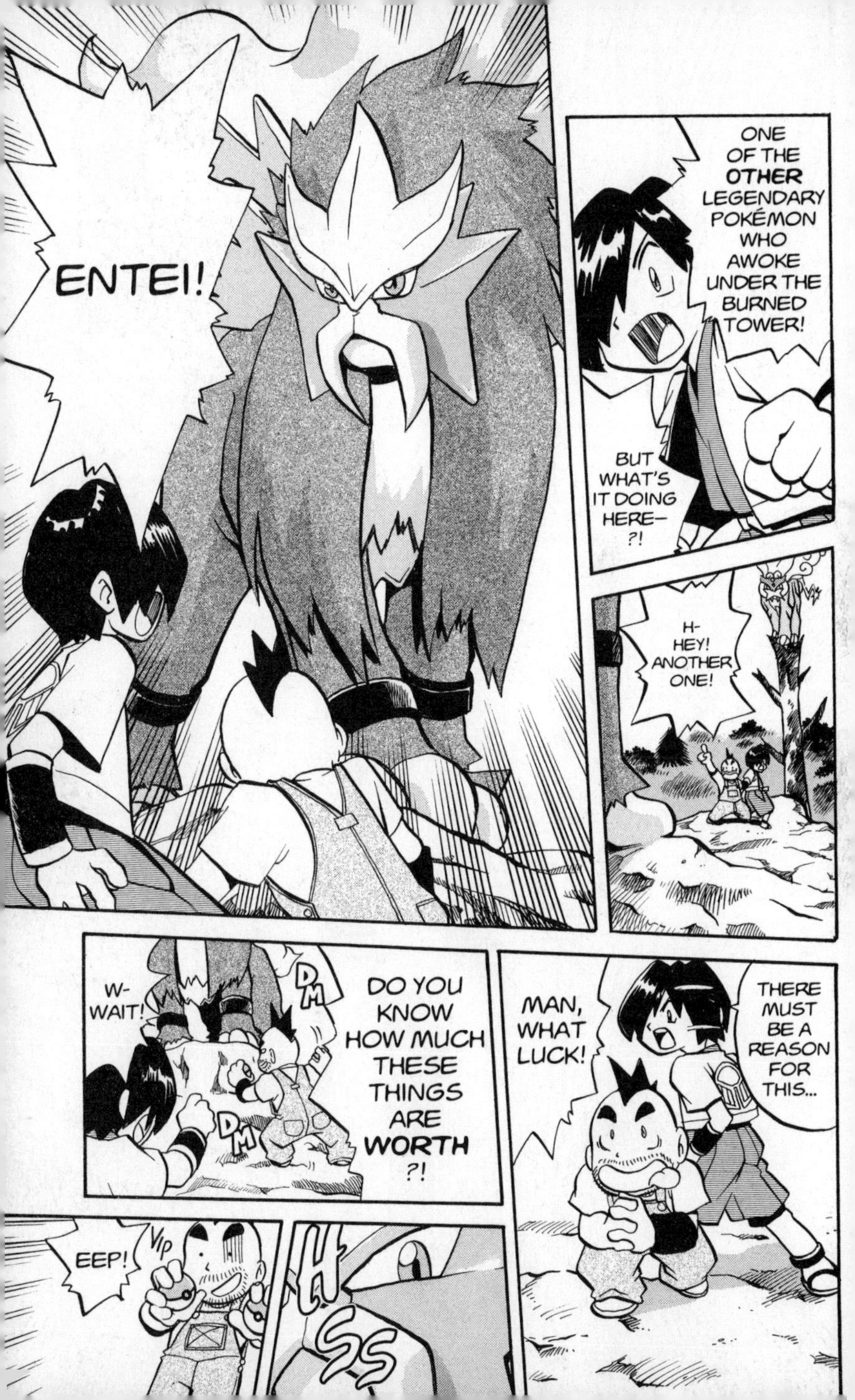
ONE OF THE OTHER LEGENDARY POKÉMON WHO AWOKE UNDER THE BURNED TOWER!
BUT WHAT'S IT DOING HERE–?!
H-HEY! ANOTHER ONE!
ENTEI!
THERE MUST BE A REASON FOR THIS...
MAN, WHAT LUCK!
DM
DO YOU KNOW HOW MUCH THESE THINGS ARE WORTH?!
W-WAIT!
DM
HSSS
VIP
EEP!

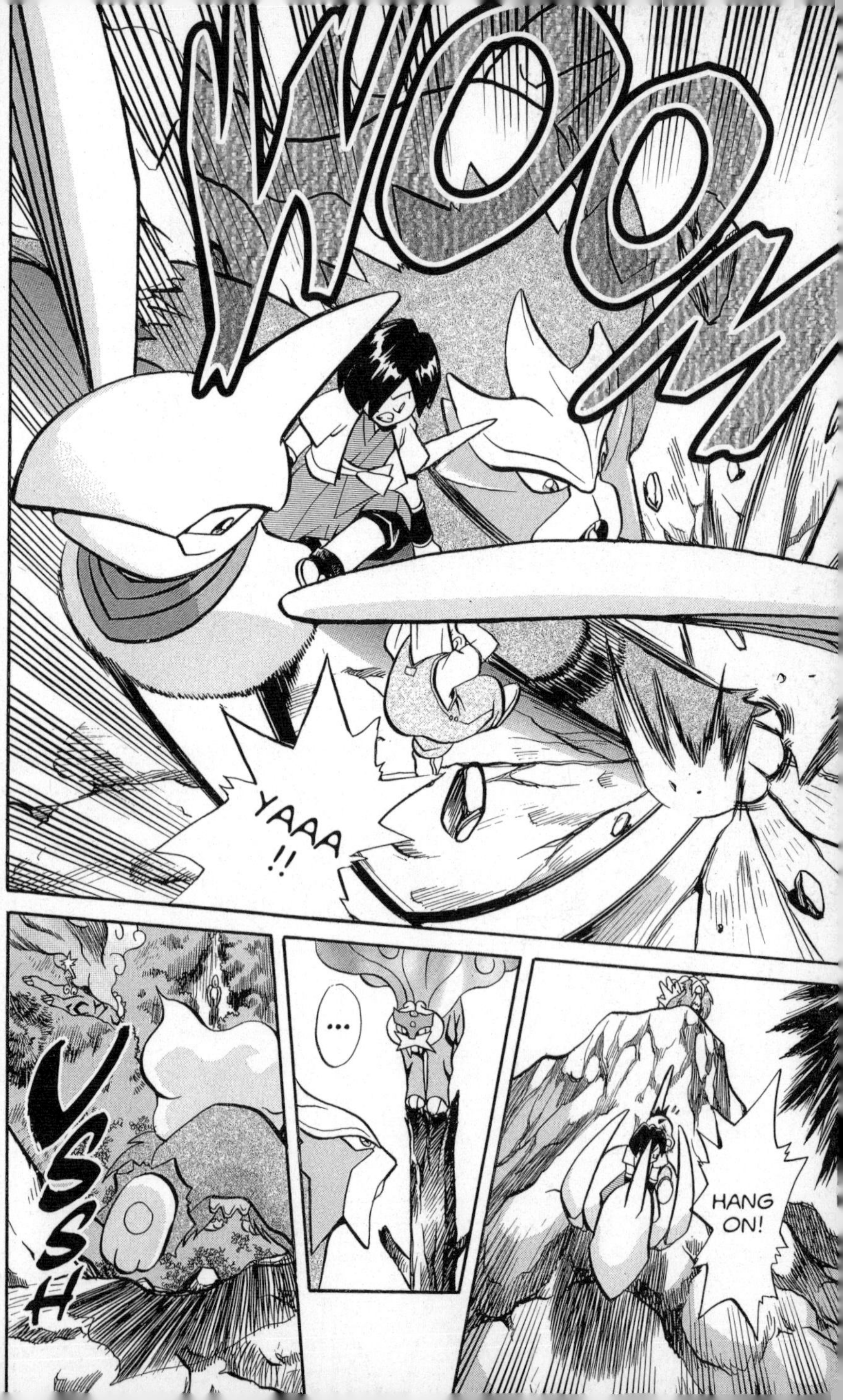
WHOOM
YAAA!!
HANG ON!
...
VSSH

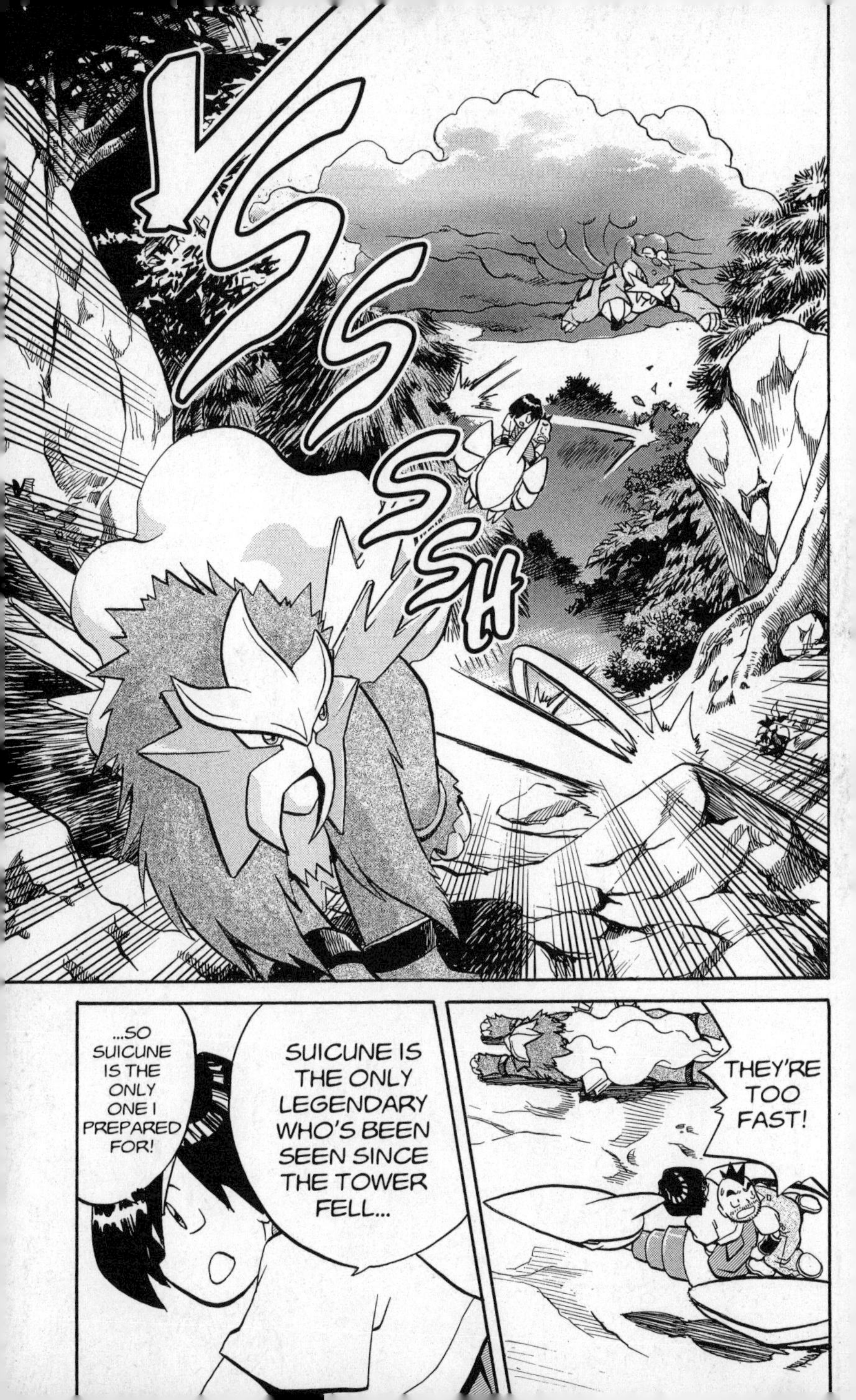
VSSSSH
THEY'RE TOO FAST!
SUICUNE IS THE ONLY LEGENDARY WHO'S BEEN SEEN SINCE THE TOWER FELL...
...SO SUICUNE IS THE ONLY ONE I PREPARED FOR!

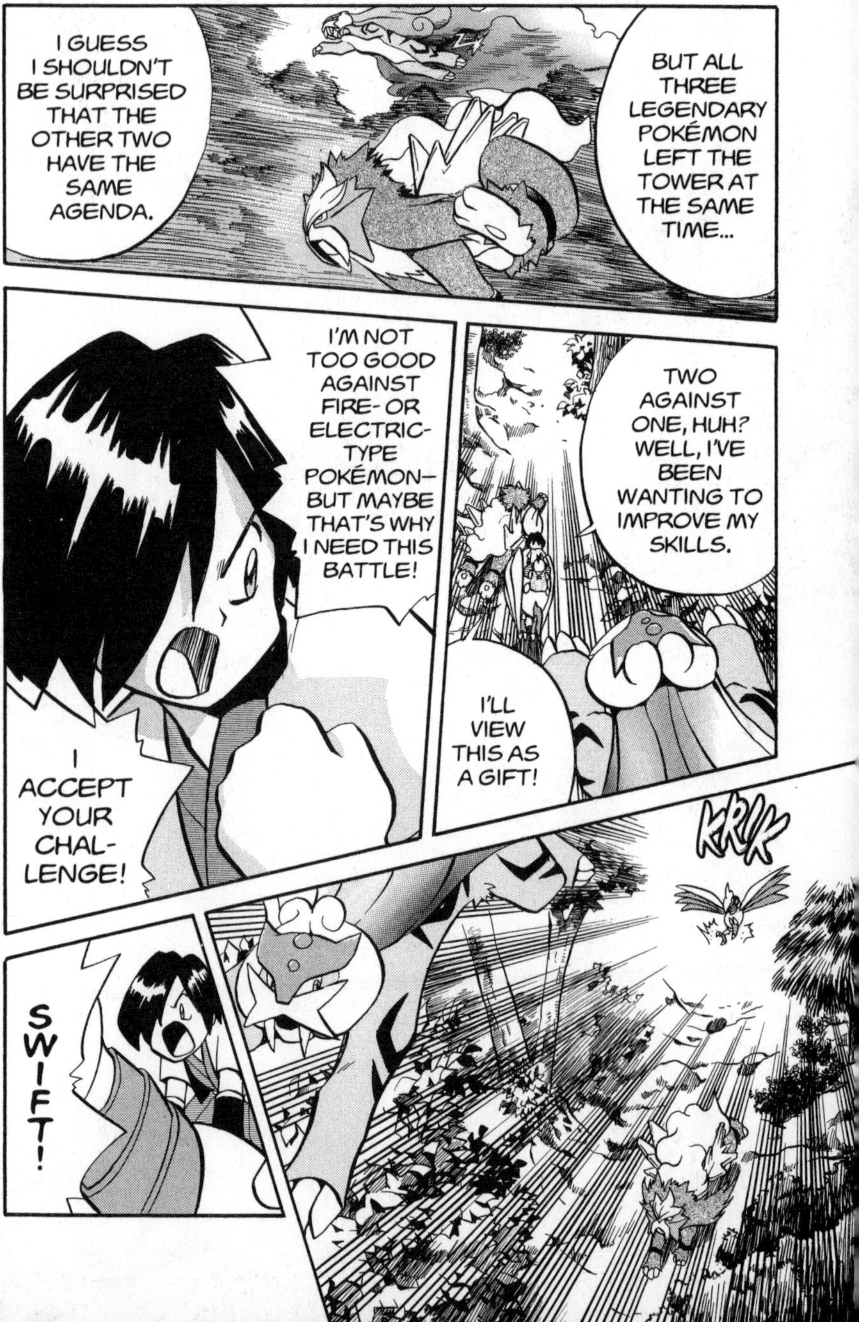
BUT ALL THREE LEGENDARY POKÉMON LEFT THE TOWER AT THE SAME TIME...
I GUESS I SHOULDN'T BE SURPRISED THAT THE OTHER TWO HAVE THE SAME AGENDA.
TWO AGAINST ONE, HUH? WELL, I'VE BEEN WANTING TO IMPROVE MY SKILLS.
I'LL VIEW THIS AS A GIFT!
I'M NOT TOO GOOD AGAINST FIRE- OR ELECTRIC-TYPE POKÉMON— BUT MAYBE THAT'S WHY I NEED THIS BATTLE!
I ACCEPT YOUR CHAL-LENGE!
KRUK
SWIFT!

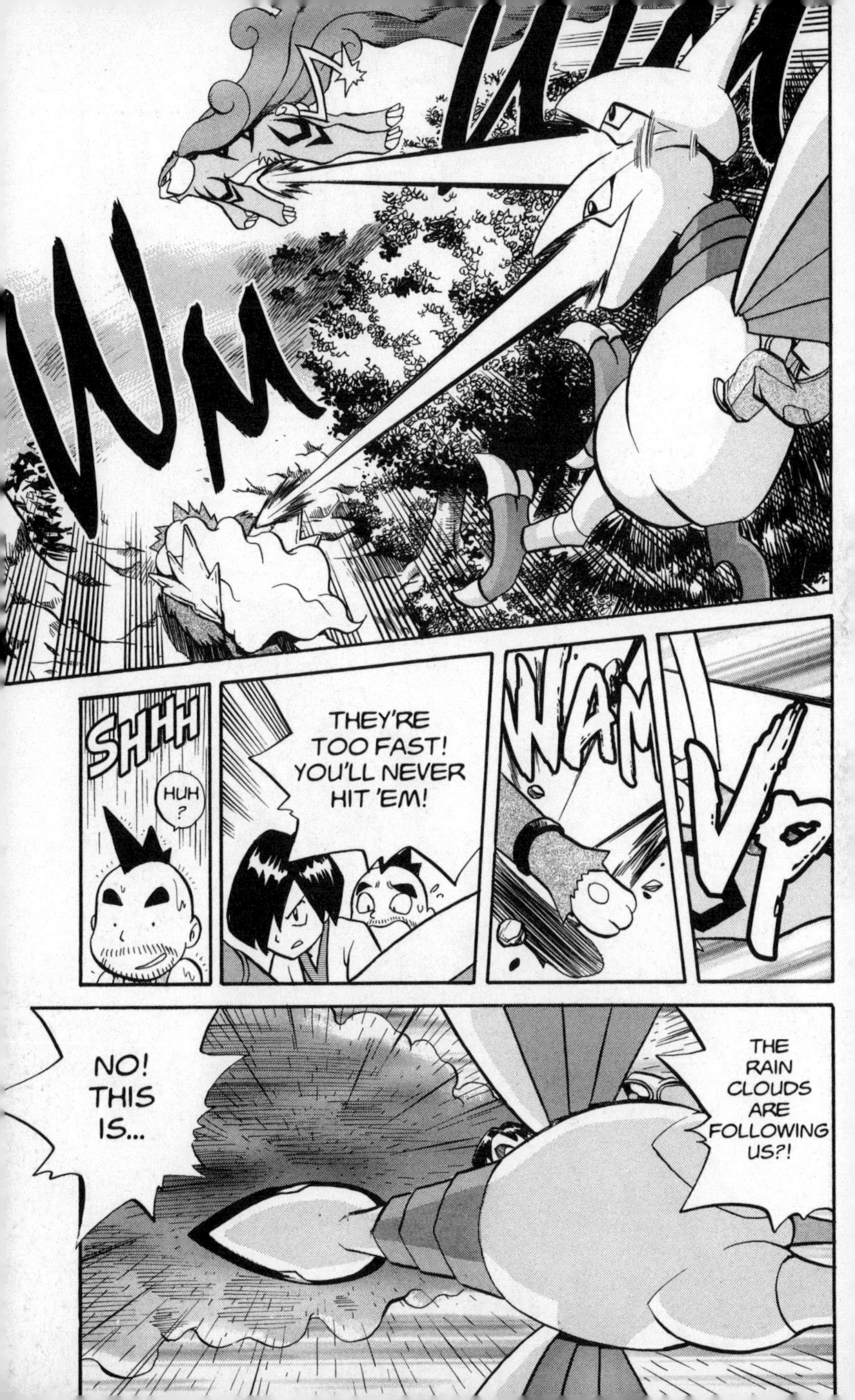
WAM
THEY'RE TOO FAST! YOU'LL NEVER HIT 'EM!
SHHH
HUH?
THE RAIN CLOUDS ARE FOLLOWING US?!
NO! THIS IS...

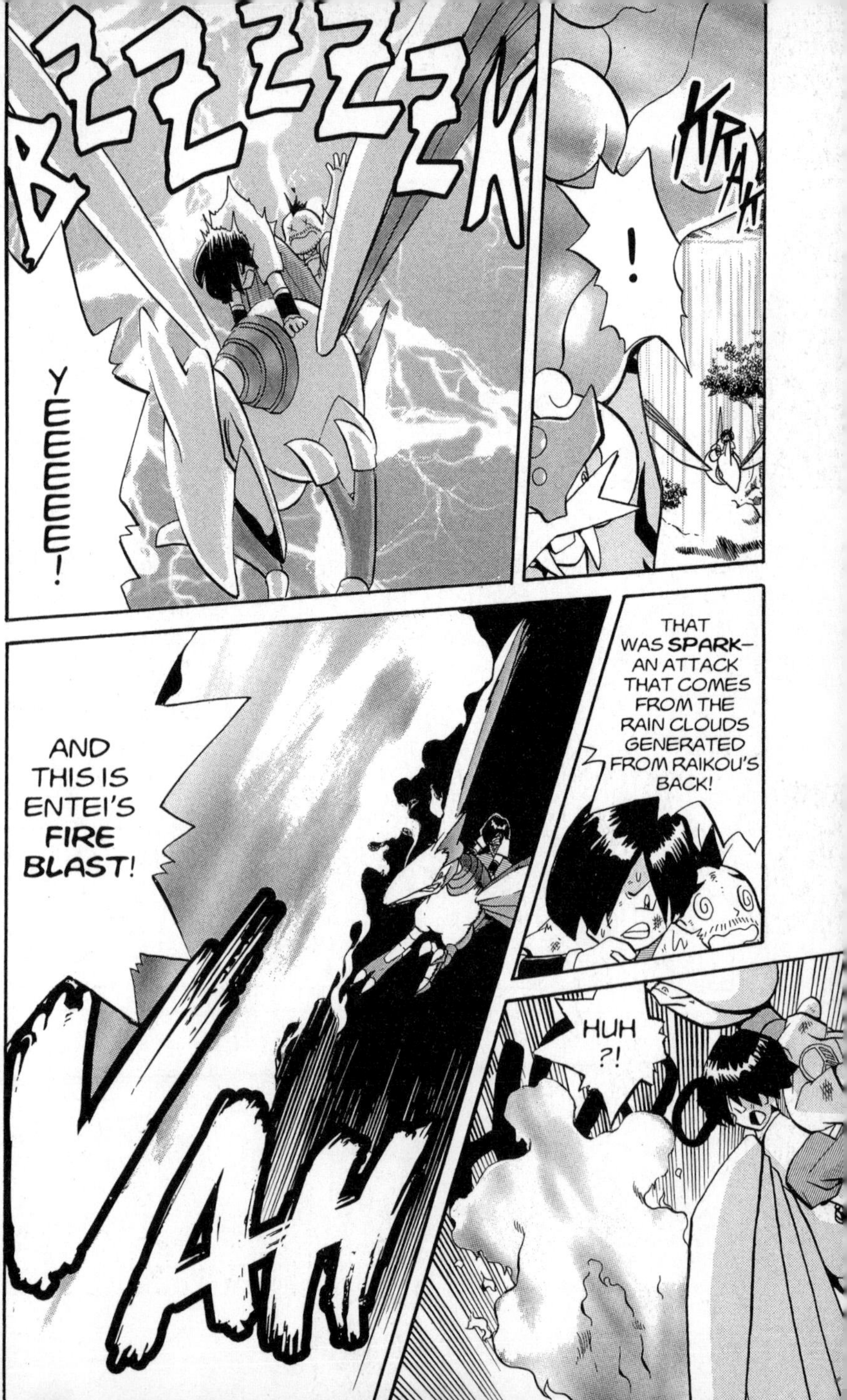
KRAK
!
BZZZZZZK
YEEEEEE!
THAT WAS SPARK—AN ATTACK THAT COMES FROM THE RAIN CLOUDS GENERATED FROM RAIKOU'S BACK!
HUH ?!
AND THIS IS ENTEI'S FIRE BLAST!

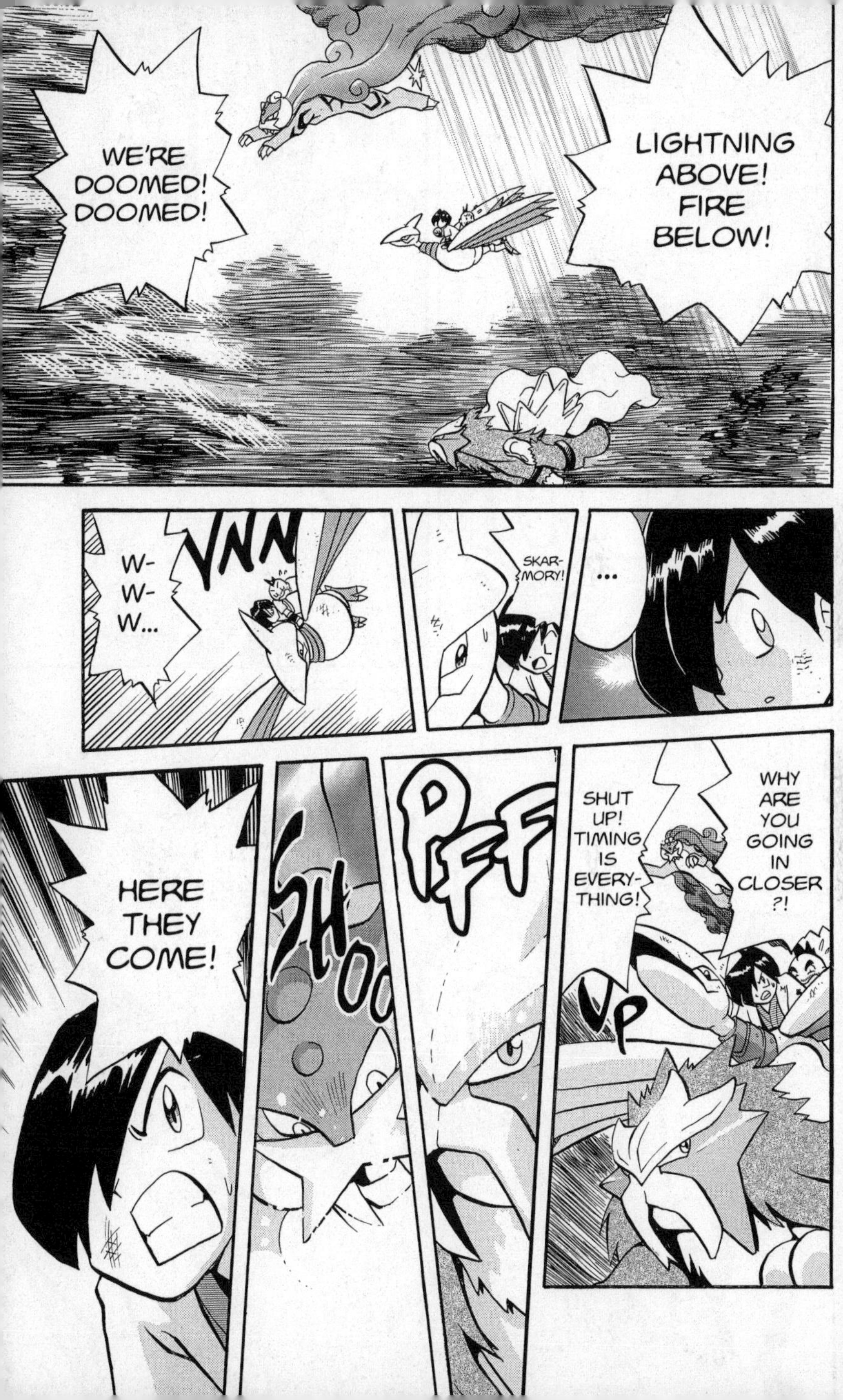
LIGHTNING ABOVE! FIRE BELOW!
WE'RE DOOMED! DOOMED!
...
SKARMORY!
VNN
W- W- W...
WHY ARE YOU GOING IN CLOSER?!
SHUT UP! TIMING IS EVERYTHING!
UP
PFF
SHOO
HERE THEY COME!

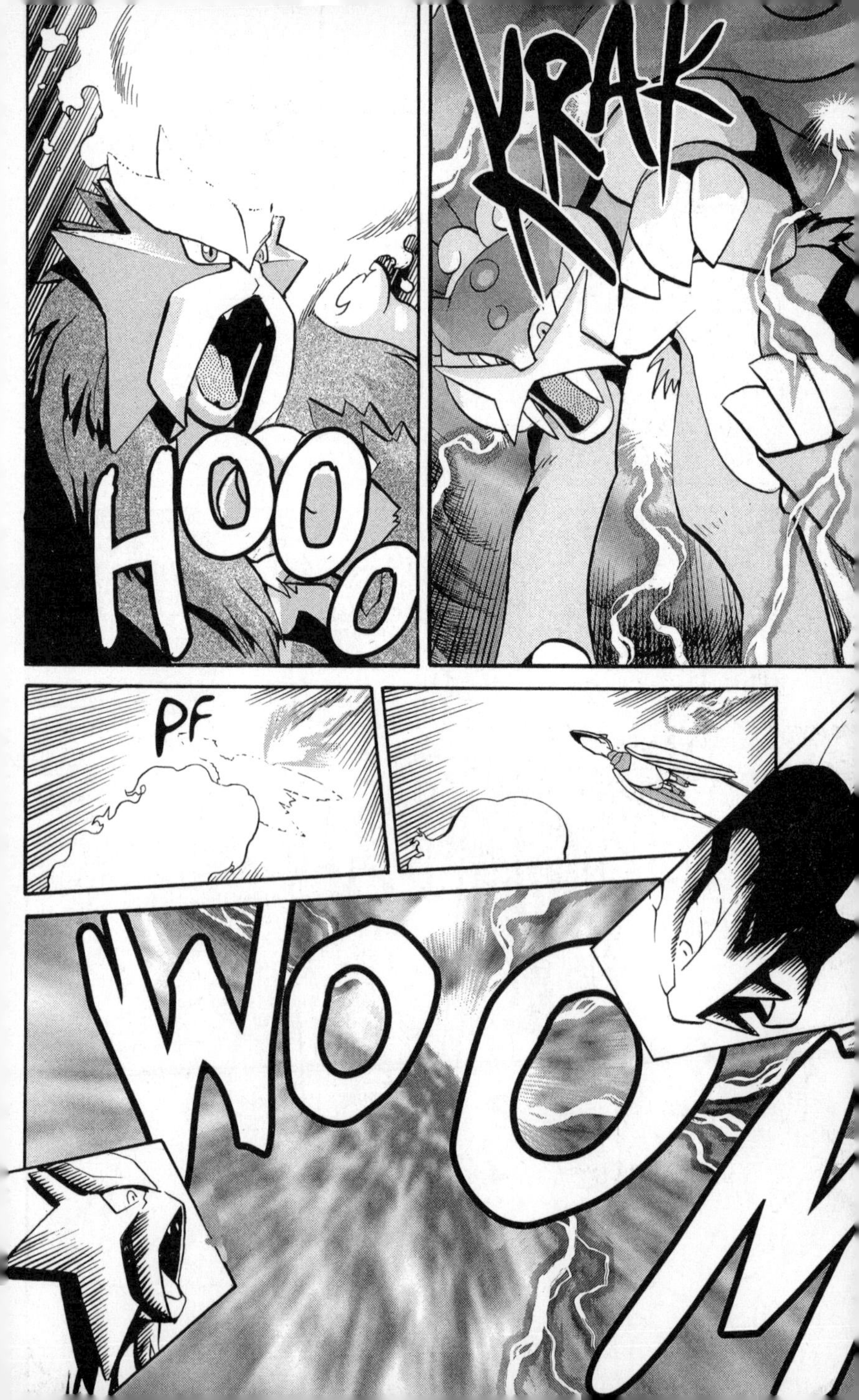
VRAK
HOOOO
PF
WOOM

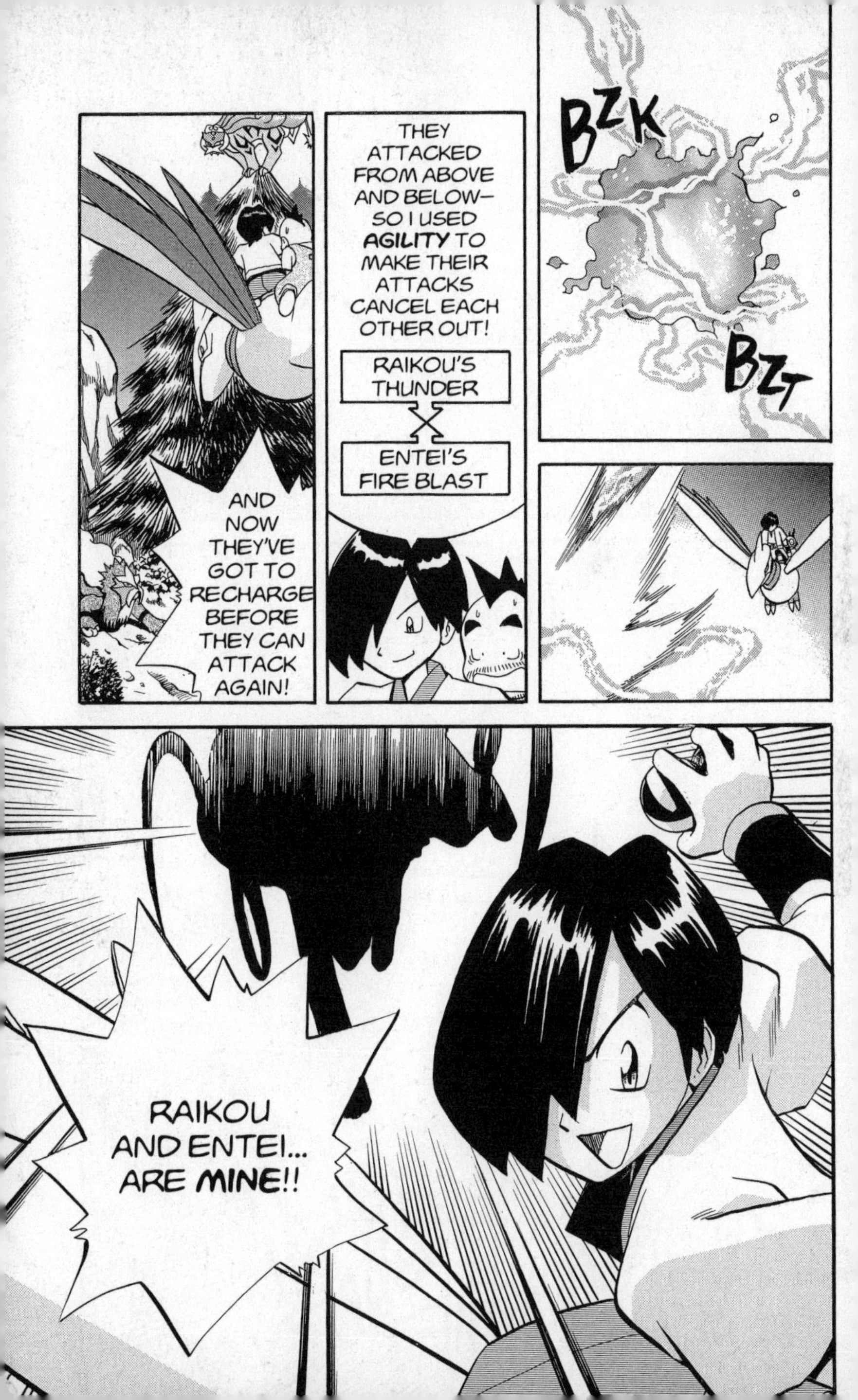
BZK
BZT
THEY ATTACKED FROM ABOVE AND BELOW— SO I USED **AGILITY** TO MAKE THEIR ATTACKS CANCEL EACH OTHER OUT!
RAIKOU'S THUNDER
ENTEI'S FIRE BLAST
AND NOW THEY'VE GOT TO RECHARGE BEFORE THEY CAN ATTACK AGAIN!
RAIKOU AND ENTEI... ARE **MINE**!!

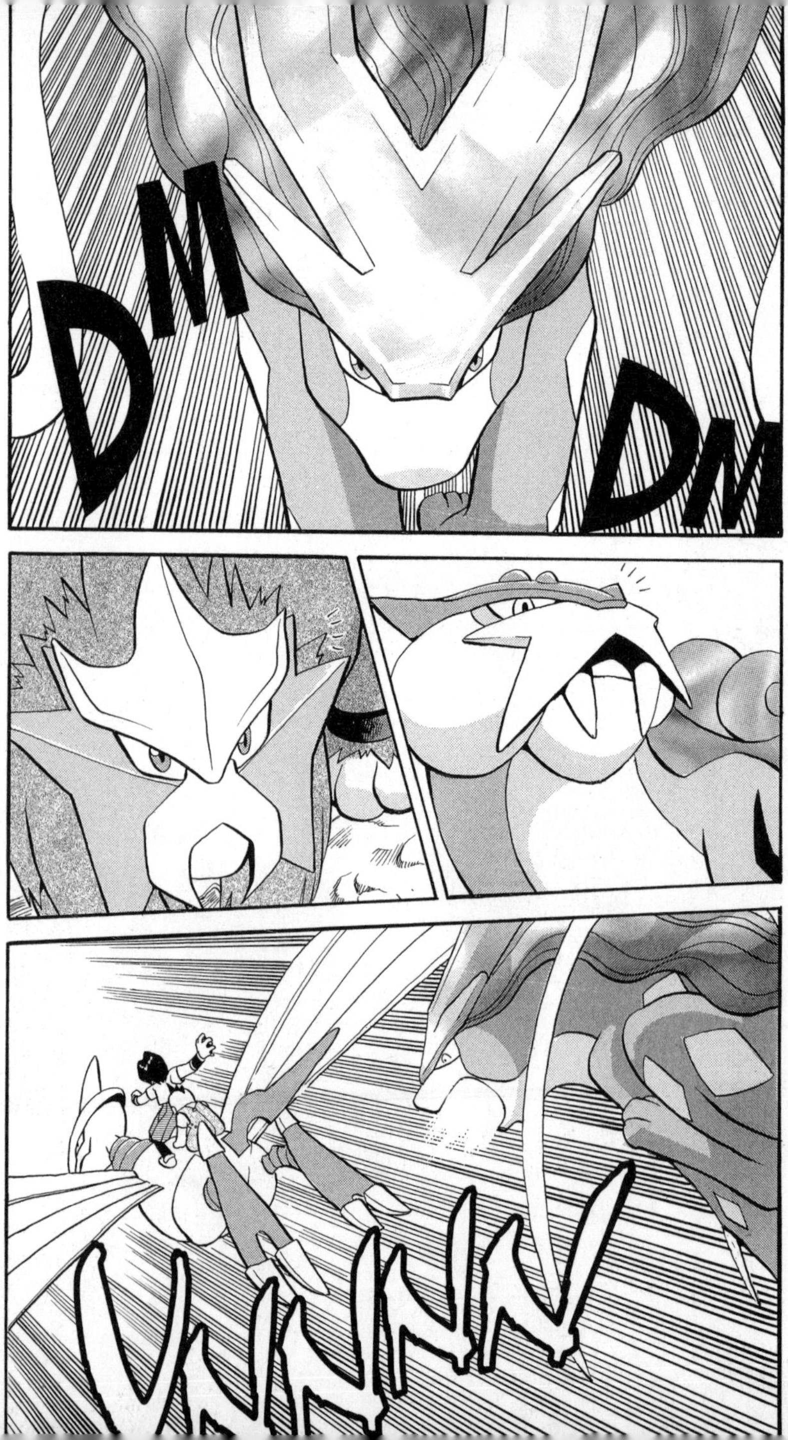
DM
DM

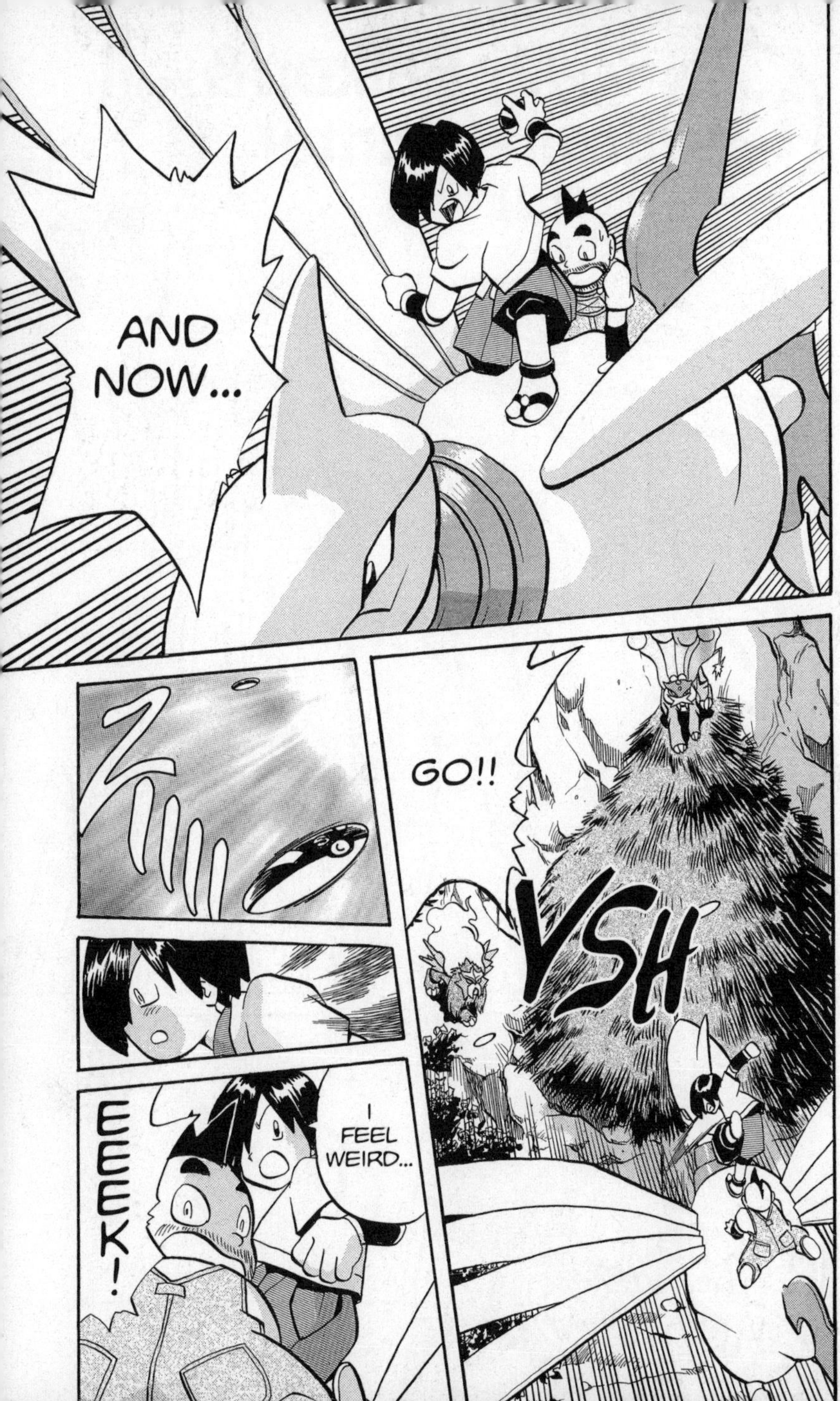
AND NOW...
GO!!
YSH
I FEEL WEIRD...
EEEEK!

138 Really Raikou & Entirely Entei (Part 2)

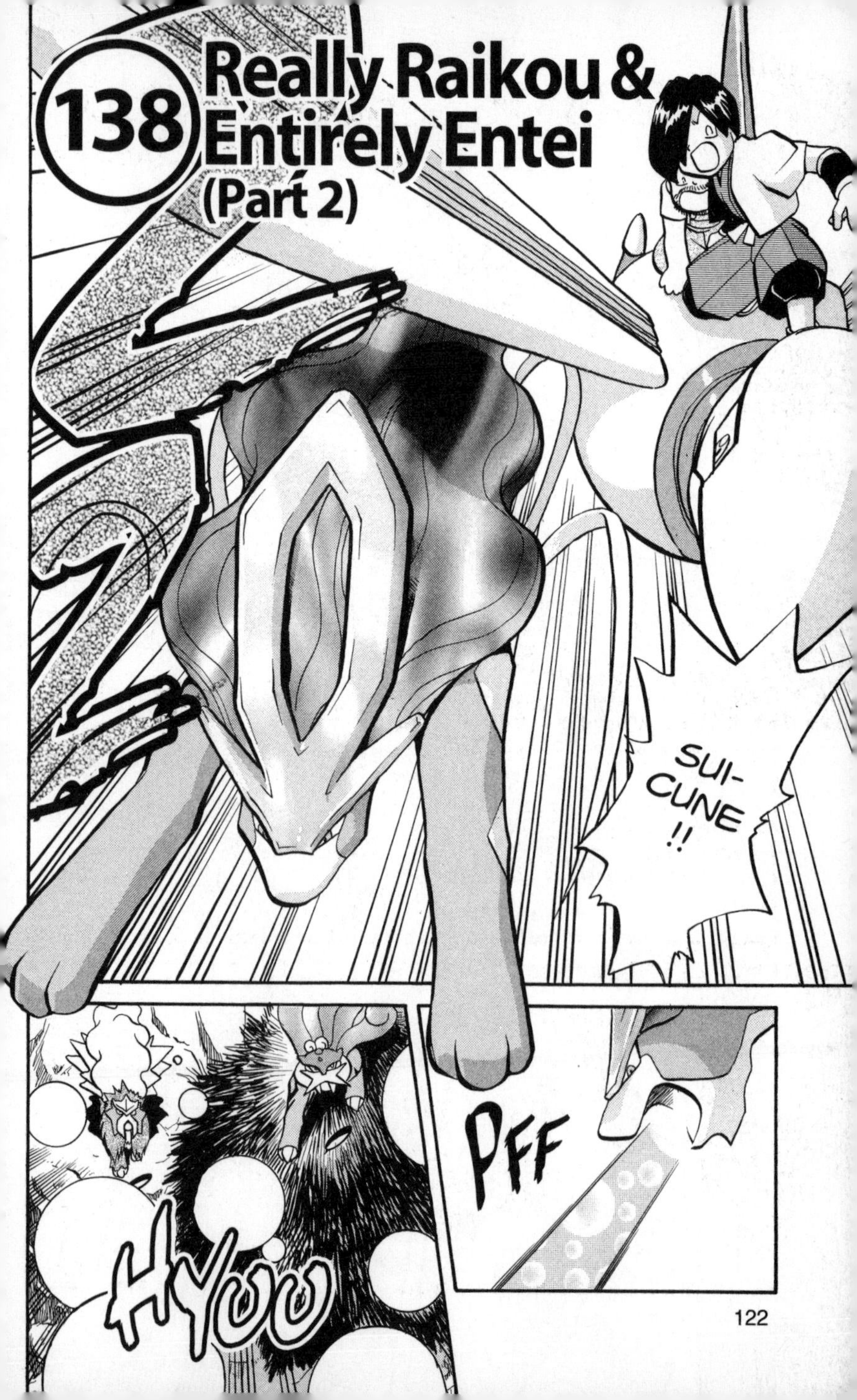
SUI-CUNE!!
PFF
HYUU

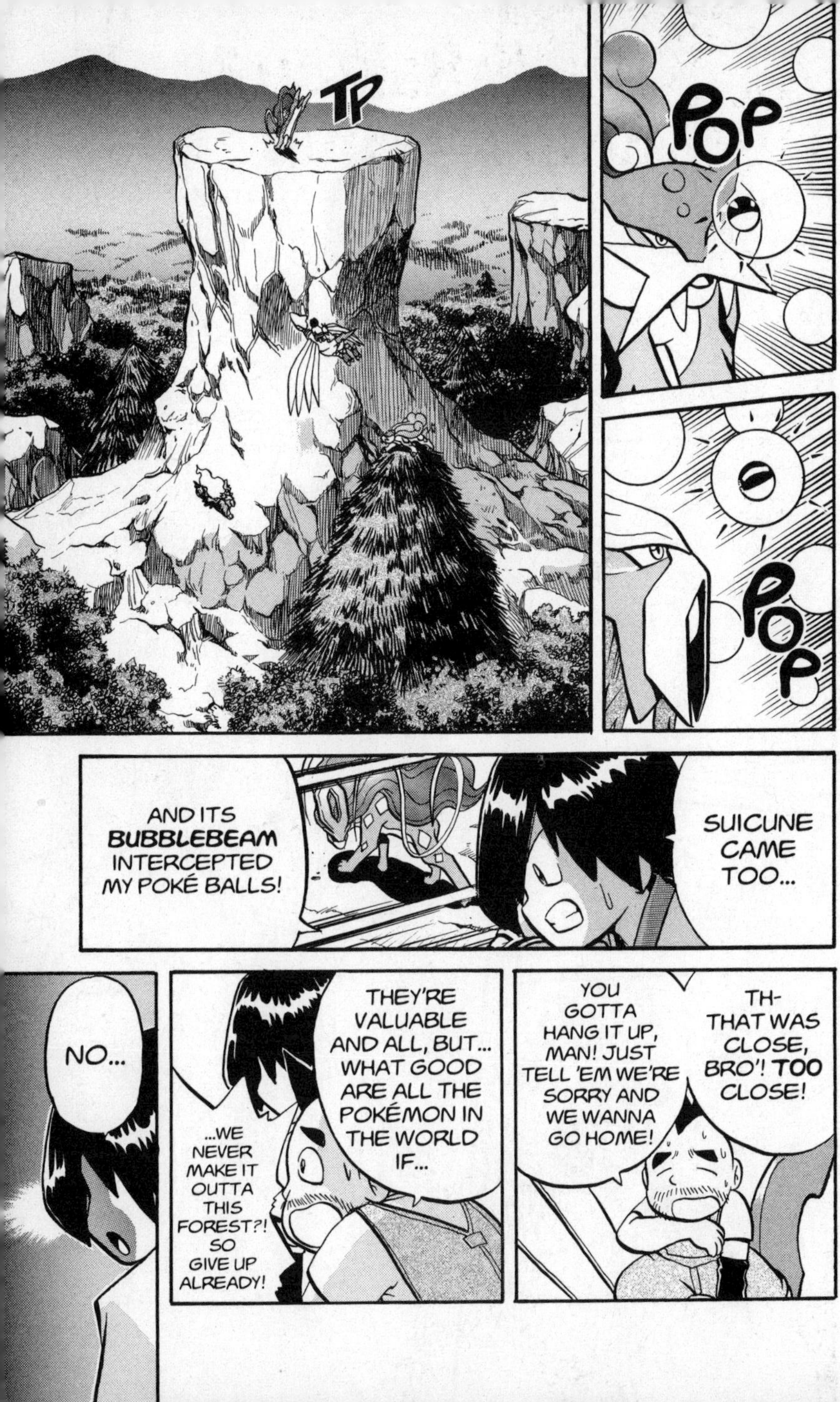
POP
POP POP
TP
SUICUNE CAME TOO...
AND ITS BUBBLEBEAM INTERCEPTED MY POKÉ BALLS!
TH-THAT WAS CLOSE, BRO'! TOO CLOSE!
YOU GOTTA HANG IT UP, MAN! JUST TELL 'EM WE'RE SORRY AND WE WANNA GO HOME!
THEY'RE VALUABLE AND ALL, BUT... WHAT GOOD ARE ALL THE POKÉMON IN THE WORLD IF...
...WE NEVER MAKE IT OUTTA THIS FOREST?! SO GIVE UP ALREADY!
NO...

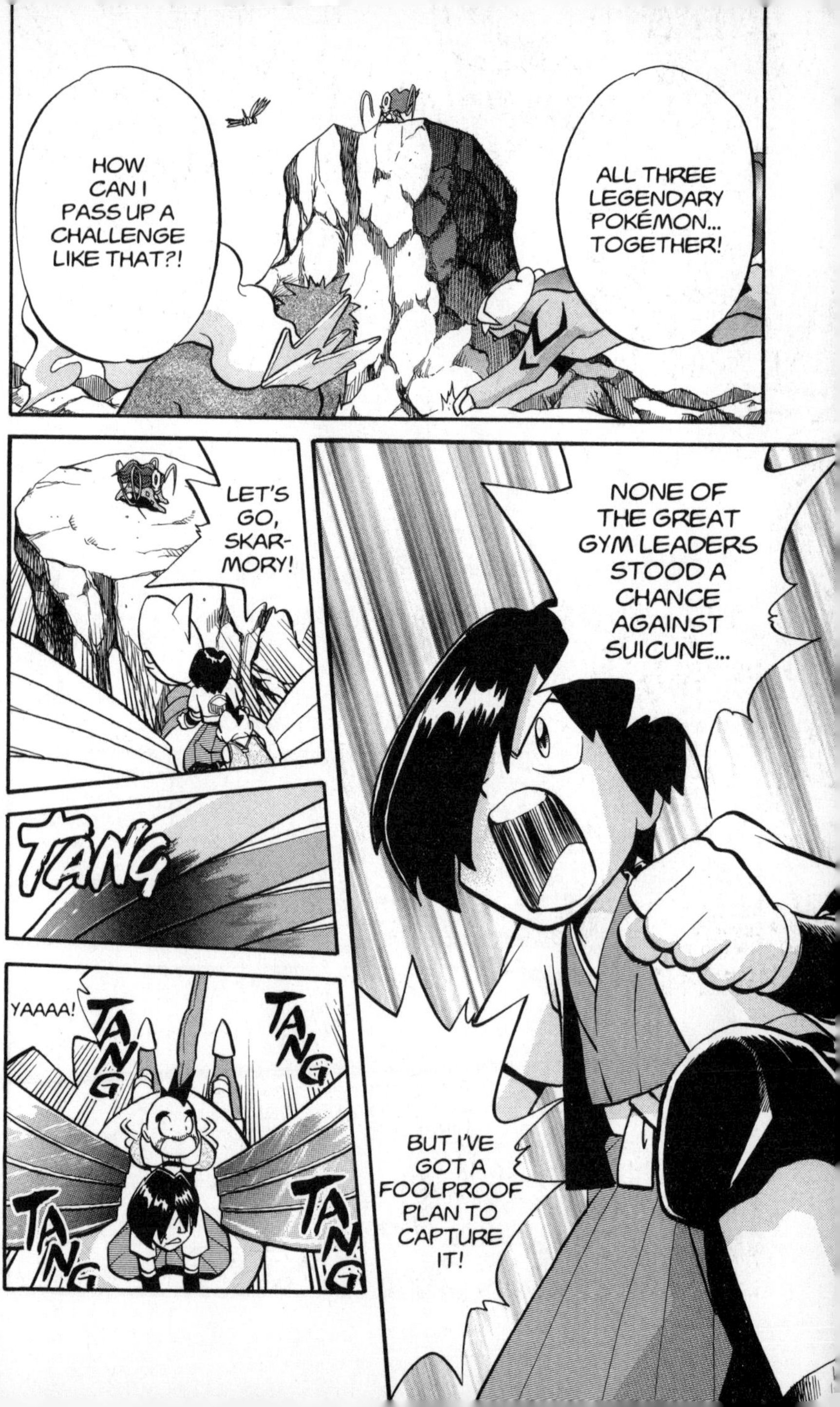
ALL THREE LEGENDARY POKÉMON... TOGETHER!
HOW CAN I PASS UP A CHALLENGE LIKE THAT?!
NONE OF THE GREAT GYM LEADERS STOOD A CHANCE AGAINST SUICUNE...
BUT I'VE GOT A FOOLPROOF PLAN TO CAPTURE IT!
LET'S GO, SKAR-MORY!
TANG
TANG TANG
YAAAA!
TANG TANG
TANG TANG
TANG TANG

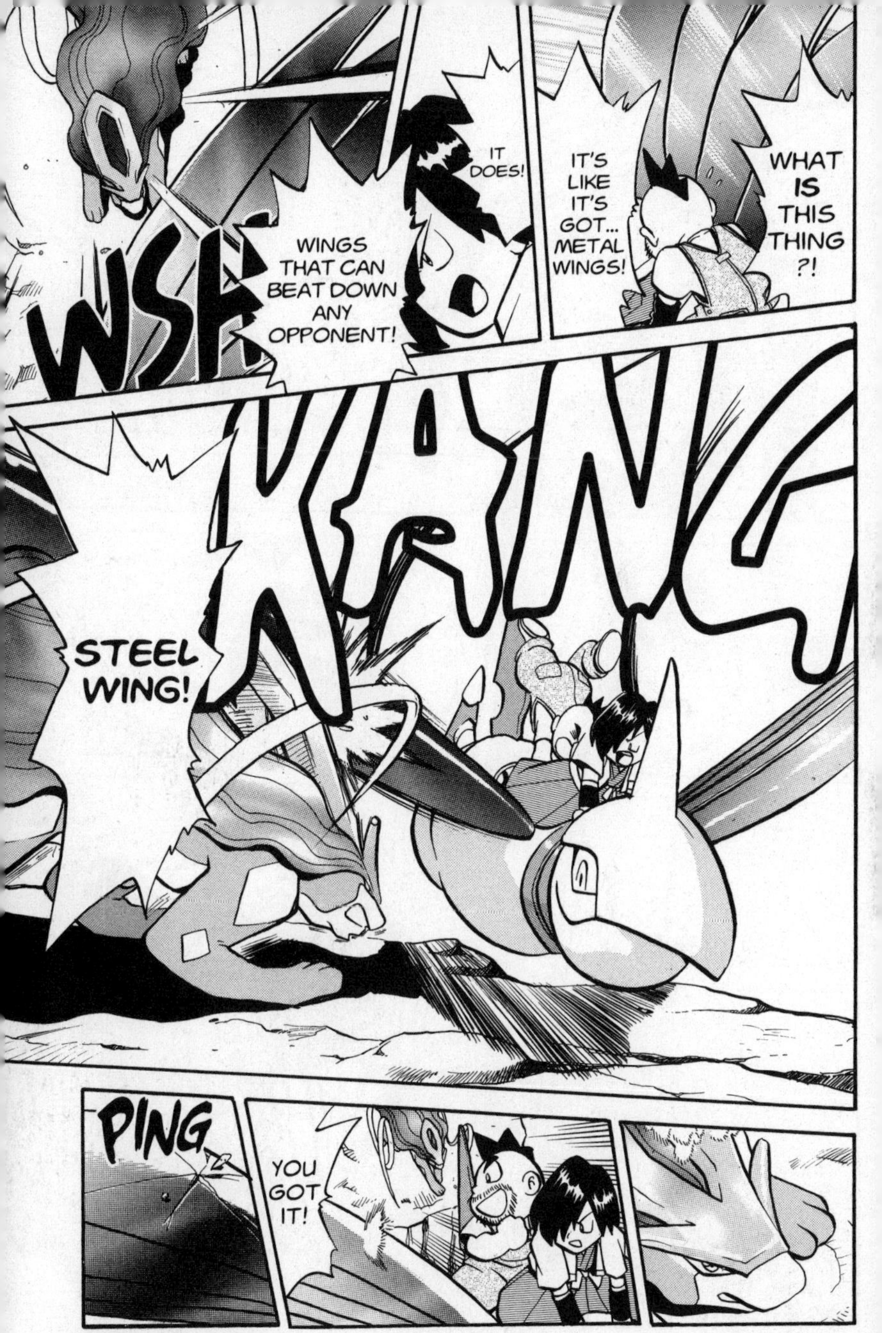
WHAT IS THIS THING?!
IT'S LIKE IT'S GOT... METAL WINGS!
IT DOES!
WINGS THAT CAN BEAT DOWN ANY OPPONENT!
WSH
KANG
STEEL WING!
YOU GOT IT!
PING

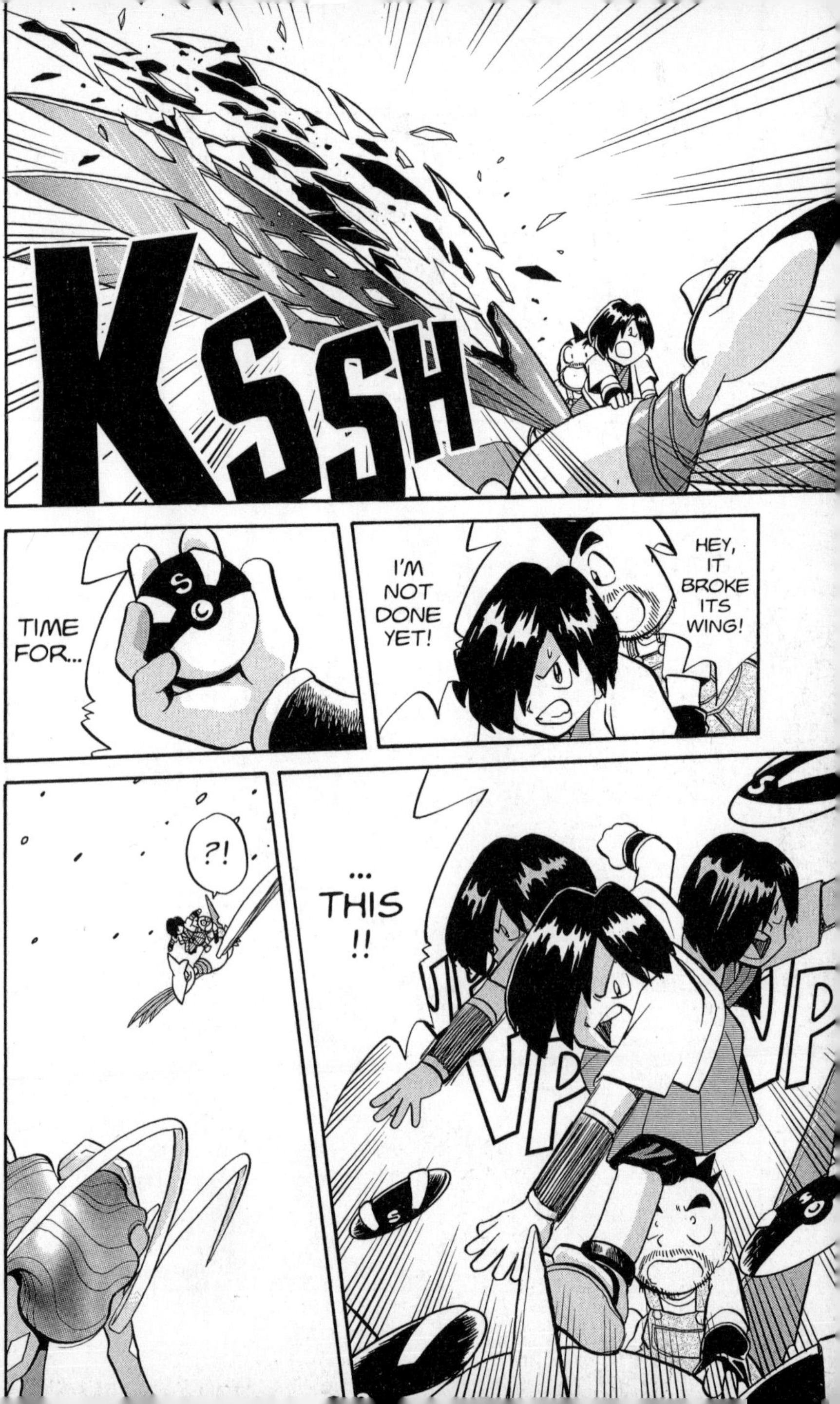
KSSH
HEY, IT BROKE ITS WING!
I'M NOT DONE YET!
TIME FOR...
...THIS!!
?!

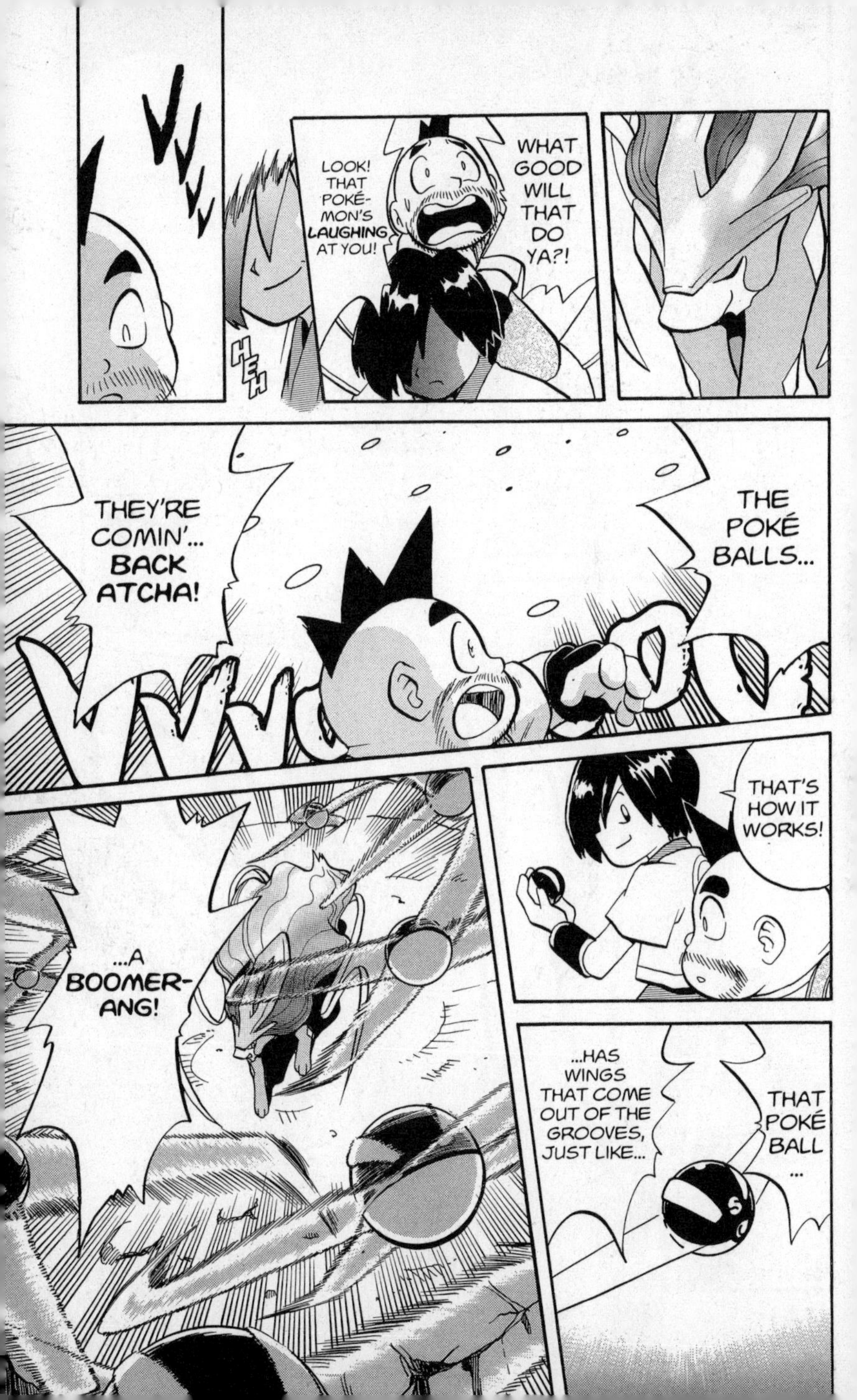
WHAT GOOD WILL THAT DO YA?!
LOOK! THAT POKÉMON'S **LAUGHING** AT YOU!
HEH
THE POKÉ BALLS...
THEY'RE COMIN'... **BACK ATCHA!**
THAT'S HOW IT WORKS!
THAT POKÉ BALL ...
...HAS WINGS THAT COME OUT OF THE GROOVES, JUST LIKE...
...A **BOOMERANG!**

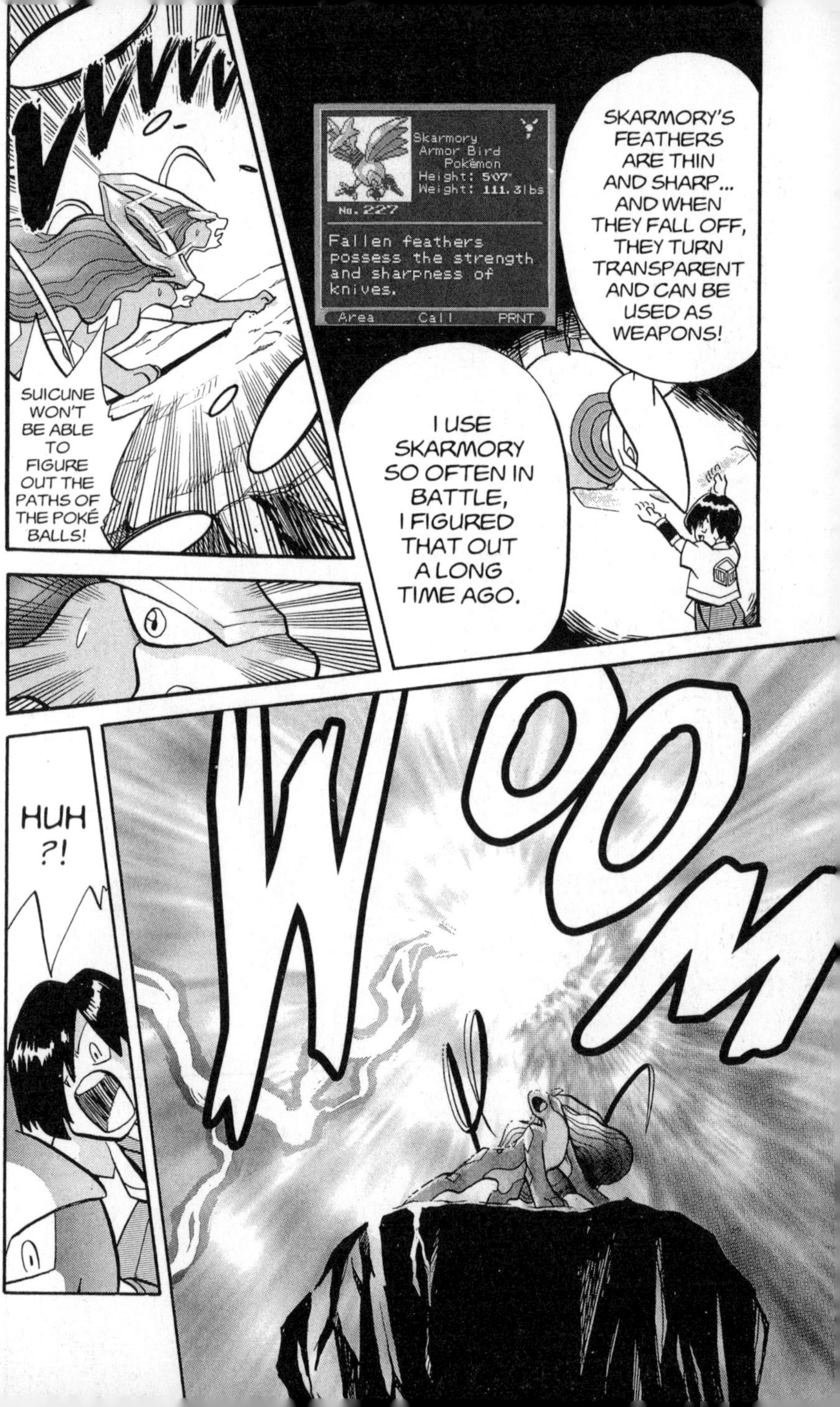
SKARMORY'S FEATHERS ARE THIN AND SHARP... AND WHEN THEY FALL OFF, THEY TURN TRANSPARENT AND CAN BE USED AS WEAPONS!
Skarmory
Armor Bird Pokémon
Height: 5'07"
Weight: 111.3lbs
No. 227
Fallen feathers possess the strength and sharpness of knives.
Area Call PRNT
I USE SKARMORY SO OFTEN IN BATTLE, I FIGURED THAT OUT A LONG TIME AGO.
VVVVV
SUICUNE WON'T BE ABLE TO FIGURE OUT THE PATHS OF THE POKÉ BALLS!
WOOM
HUH ?!

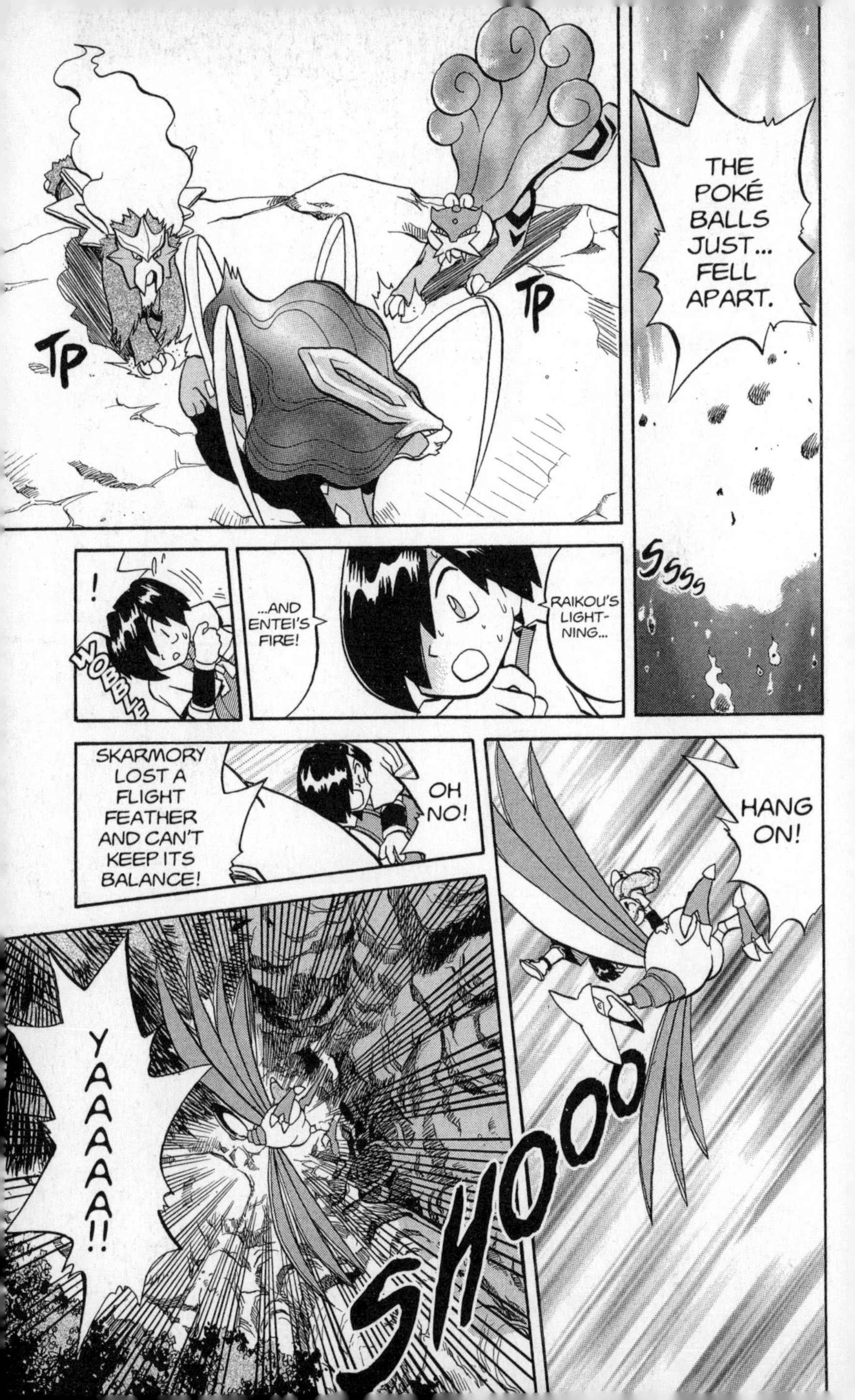
THE POKÉ BALLS JUST... FELL APART.
SSSS
TP
TP
RAIKOU'S LIGHTNING...
...AND ENTEI'S FIRE!
!
WOBBLE
HANG ON!
SHOOOO
OH NO!
SKARMORY LOST A FLIGHT FEATHER AND CAN'T KEEP ITS BALANCE!
YAAAAAA!!

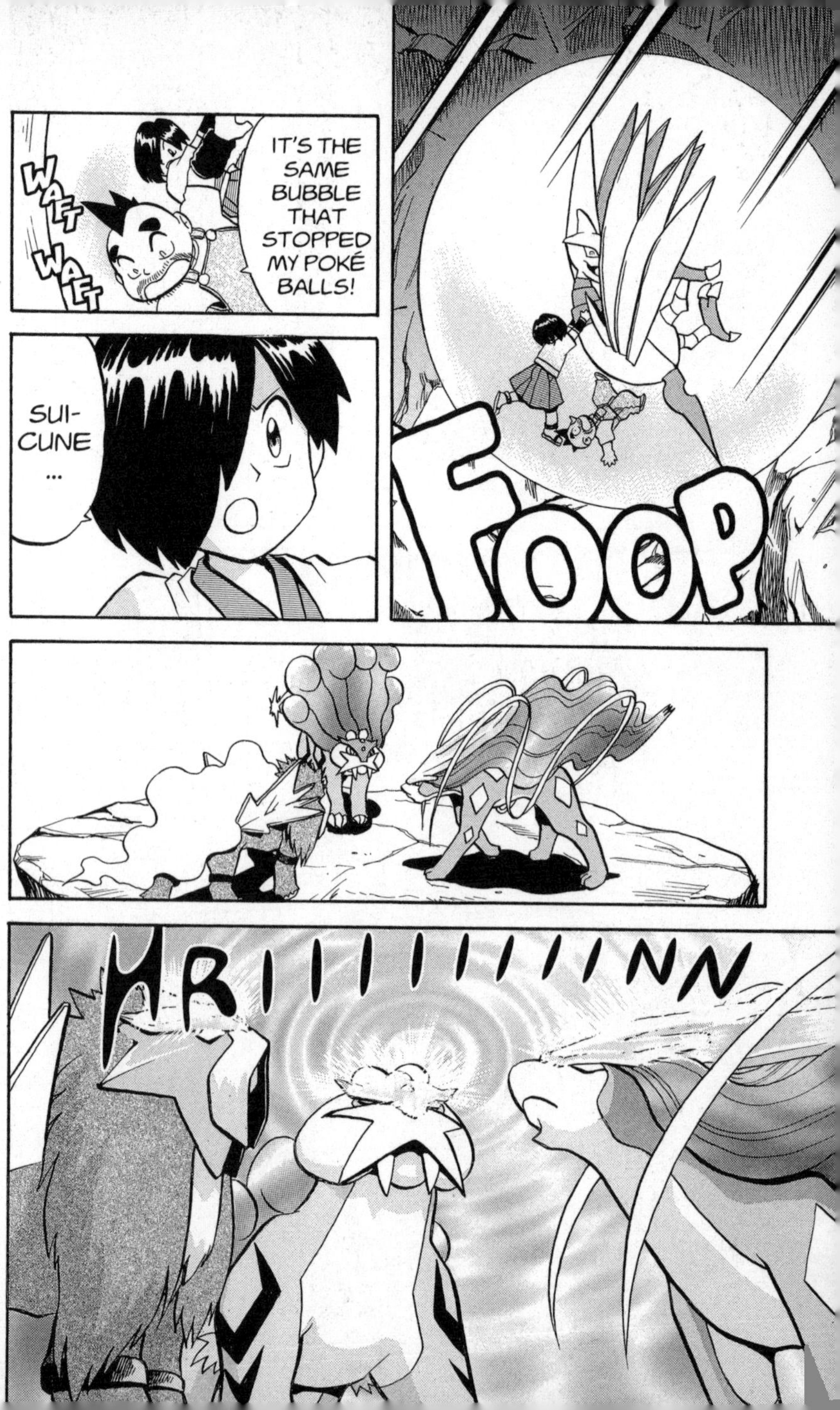
FOOP
IT'S THE SAME BUBBLE THAT STOPPED MY POKÉ BALLS!
WAFT WAFT
SUI-CUNE ...
HRIIIIIINN

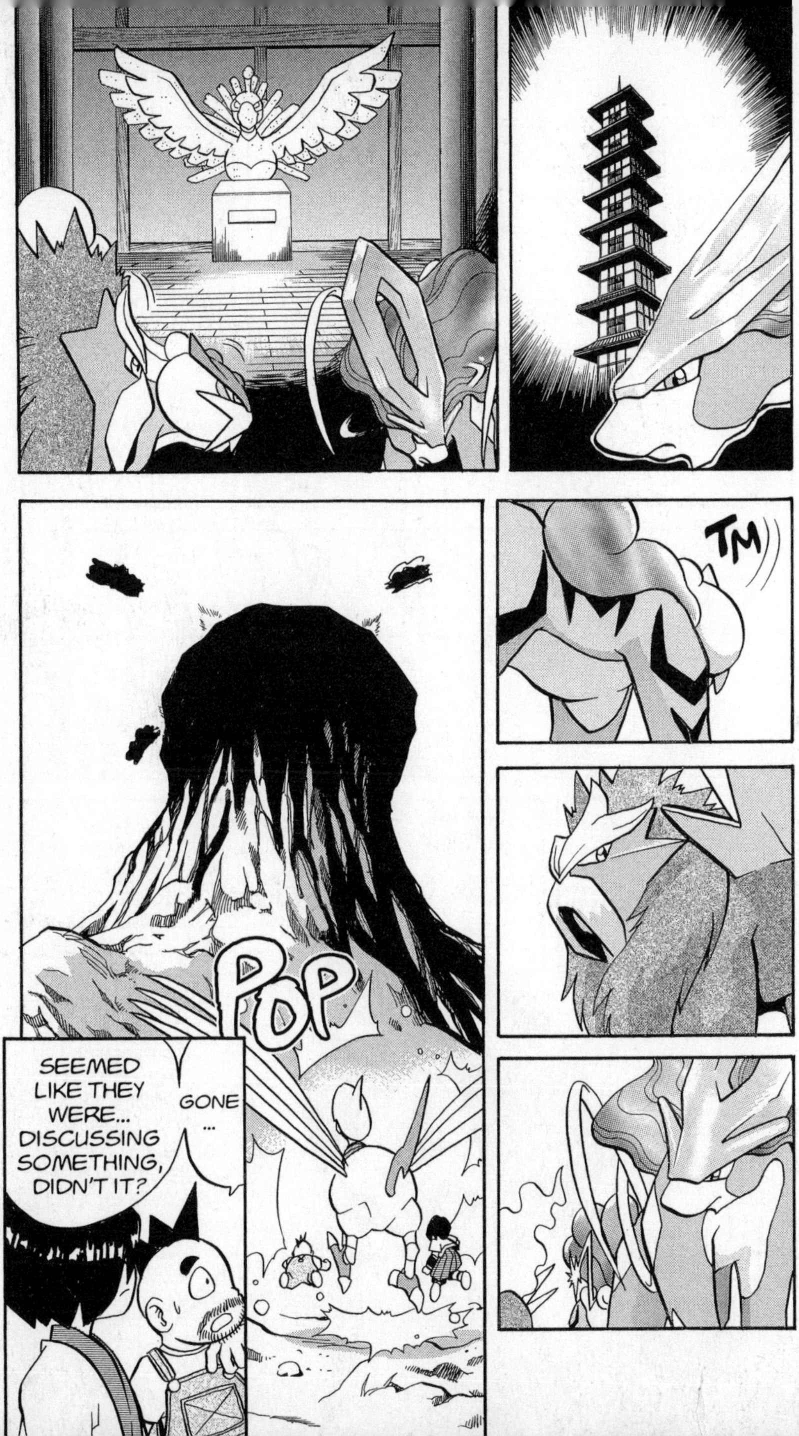
TM
POP
GONE...
SEEMED LIKE THEY WERE... DISCUSSING SOMETHING, DIDN'T IT?

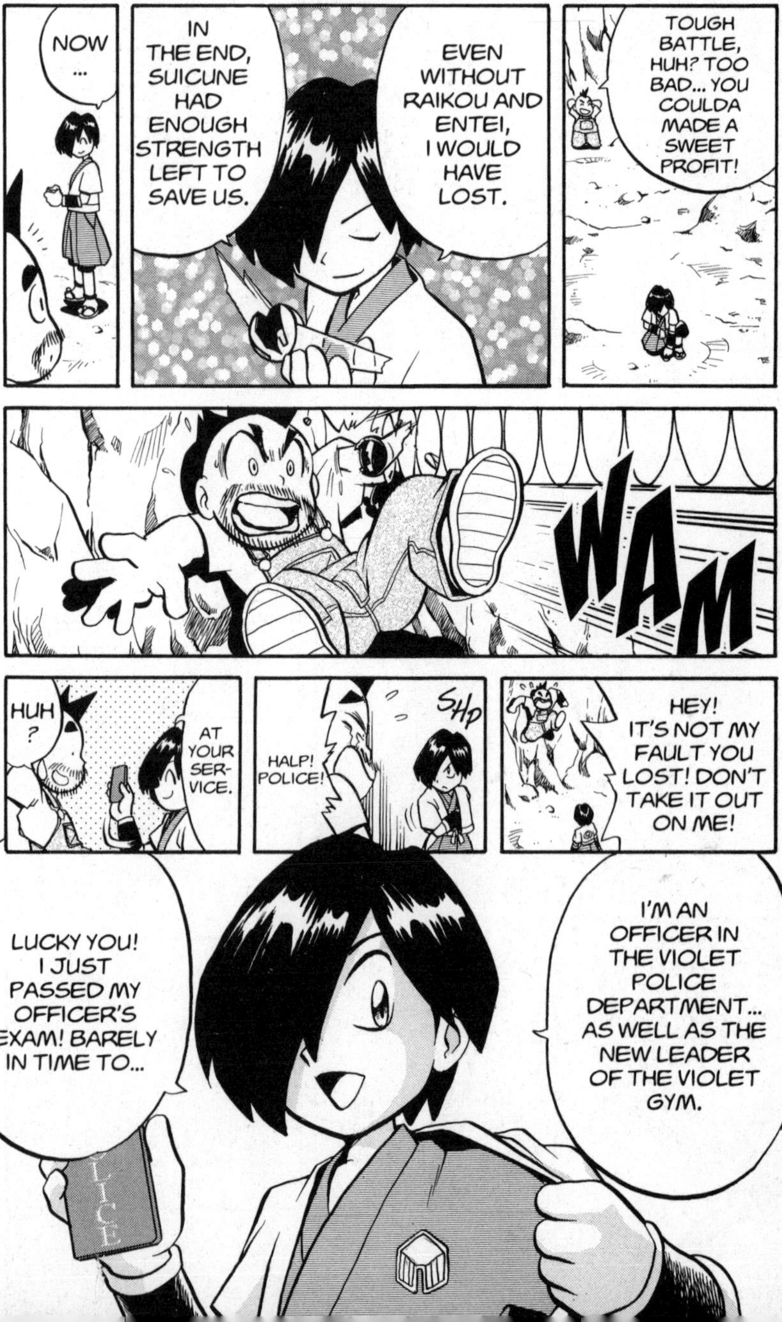
TOUGH BATTLE, HUH? TOO BAD... YOU COULDA MADE A SWEET PROFIT!
EVEN WITHOUT RAIKOU AND ENTEI, I WOULD HAVE LOST.
IN THE END, SUICUNE HAD ENOUGH STRENGTH LEFT TO SAVE US.
NOW ...
WAM
HEY! IT'S NOT MY FAULT YOU LOST! DON'T TAKE IT OUT ON ME!
SHP
HALP! POLICE!
AT YOUR SER-VICE.
HUH ?
I'M AN OFFICER IN THE VIOLET POLICE DEPARTMENT... AS WELL AS THE NEW LEADER OF THE VIOLET GYM.
LUCKY YOU! I JUST PASSED MY OFFICER'S EXAM! BARELY IN TIME TO...

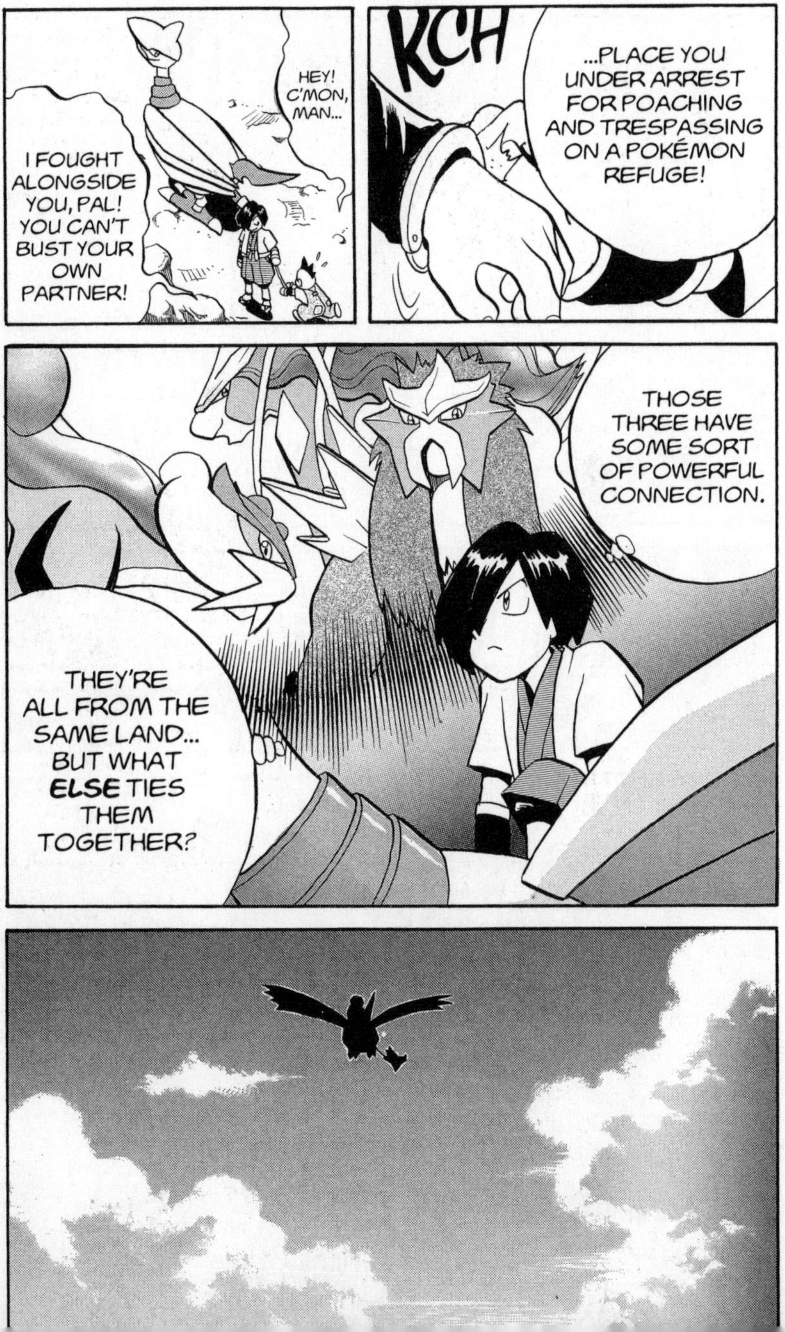
KCH
...PLACE YOU UNDER ARREST FOR POACHING AND TRESPASSING ON A POKÉMON REFUGE!
HEY! C'MON, MAN...
I FOUGHT ALONGSIDE YOU, PAL! YOU CAN'T BUST YOUR OWN PARTNER!
THOSE THREE HAVE SOME SORT OF POWERFUL CONNECTION.
THEY'RE ALL FROM THE SAME LAND... BUT WHAT **ELSE** TIES THEM TOGETHER?

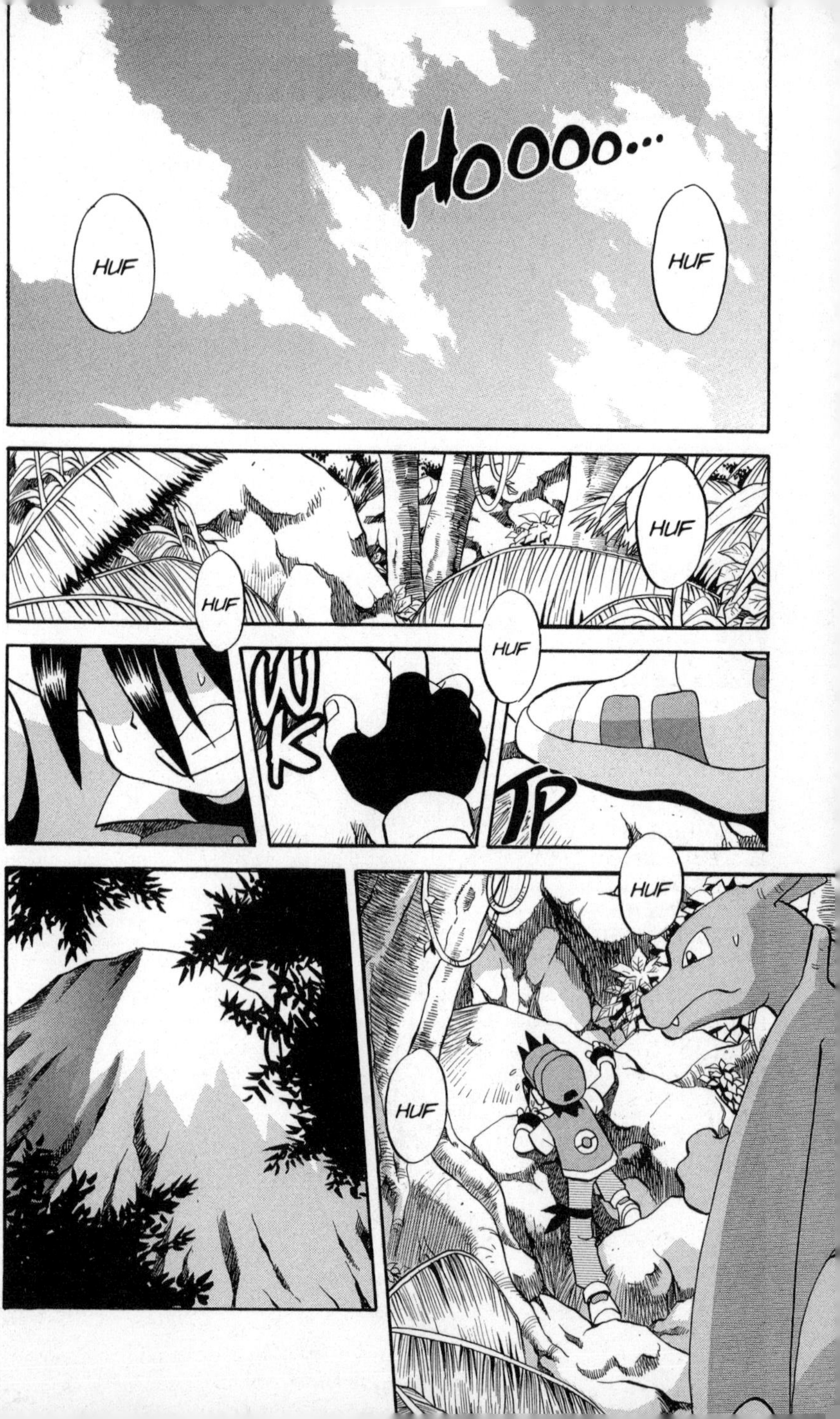
HOOOO...
HUF
HUF
HUF
HUF
HUF
TP
WK
HUF
HUF

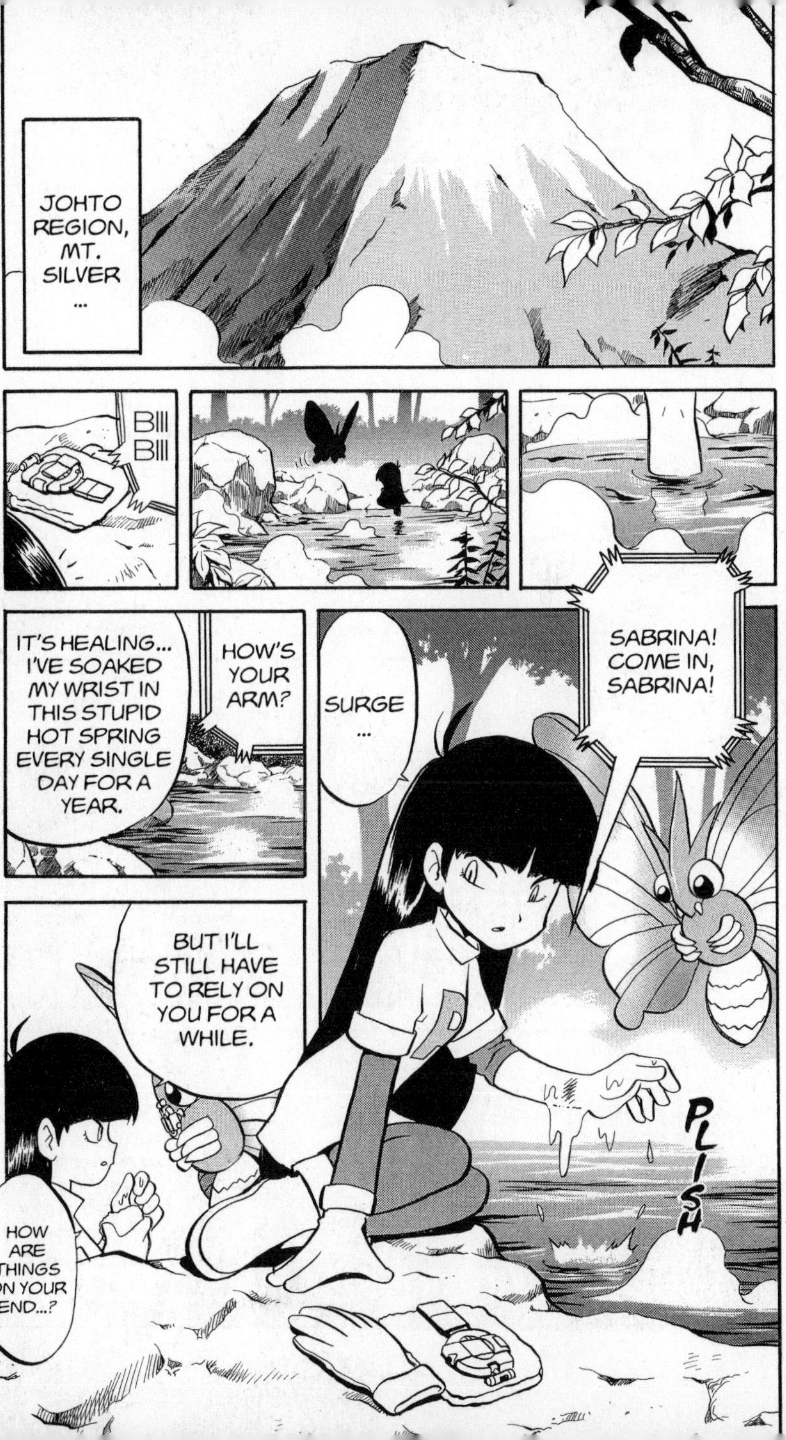
JOHTO REGION, MT. SILVER ...
BIII BIII
SABRINA! COME IN, SABRINA!
SURGE ...
PLISH
HOW'S YOUR ARM?
IT'S HEALING... I'VE SOAKED MY WRIST IN THIS STUPID HOT SPRING EVERY SINGLE DAY FOR A YEAR.
BUT I'LL STILL HAVE TO RELY ON YOU FOR A WHILE.
HOW ARE THINGS ON YOUR END...?

139 Raising Raichu

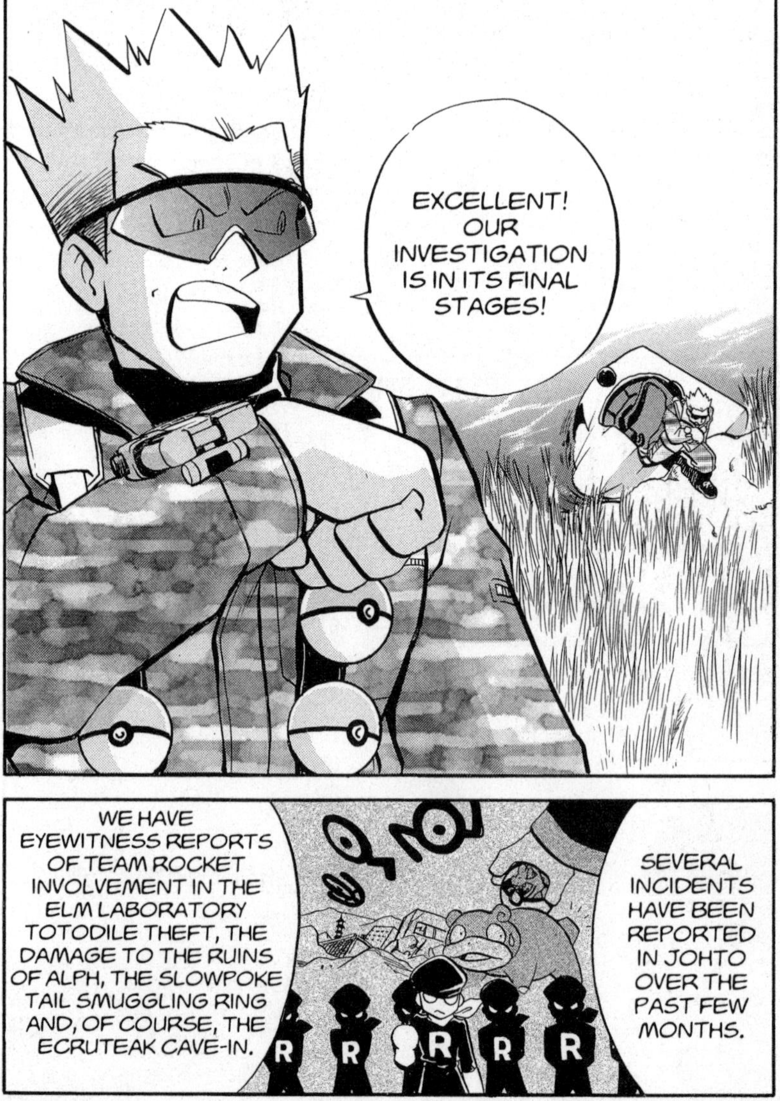

EXCELLENT! OUR INVESTIGATION IS IN ITS FINAL STAGES!
SEVERAL INCIDENTS HAVE BEEN REPORTED IN JOHTO OVER THE PAST FEW MONTHS.
WE HAVE EYEWITNESS REPORTS OF TEAM ROCKET INVOLVEMENT IN THE ELM LABORATORY TOTODILE THEFT, THE DAMAGE TO THE RUINS OF ALPH, THE SLOWPOKE TAIL SMUGGLING RING AND, OF COURSE, THE ECRUTEAK CAVE-IN.

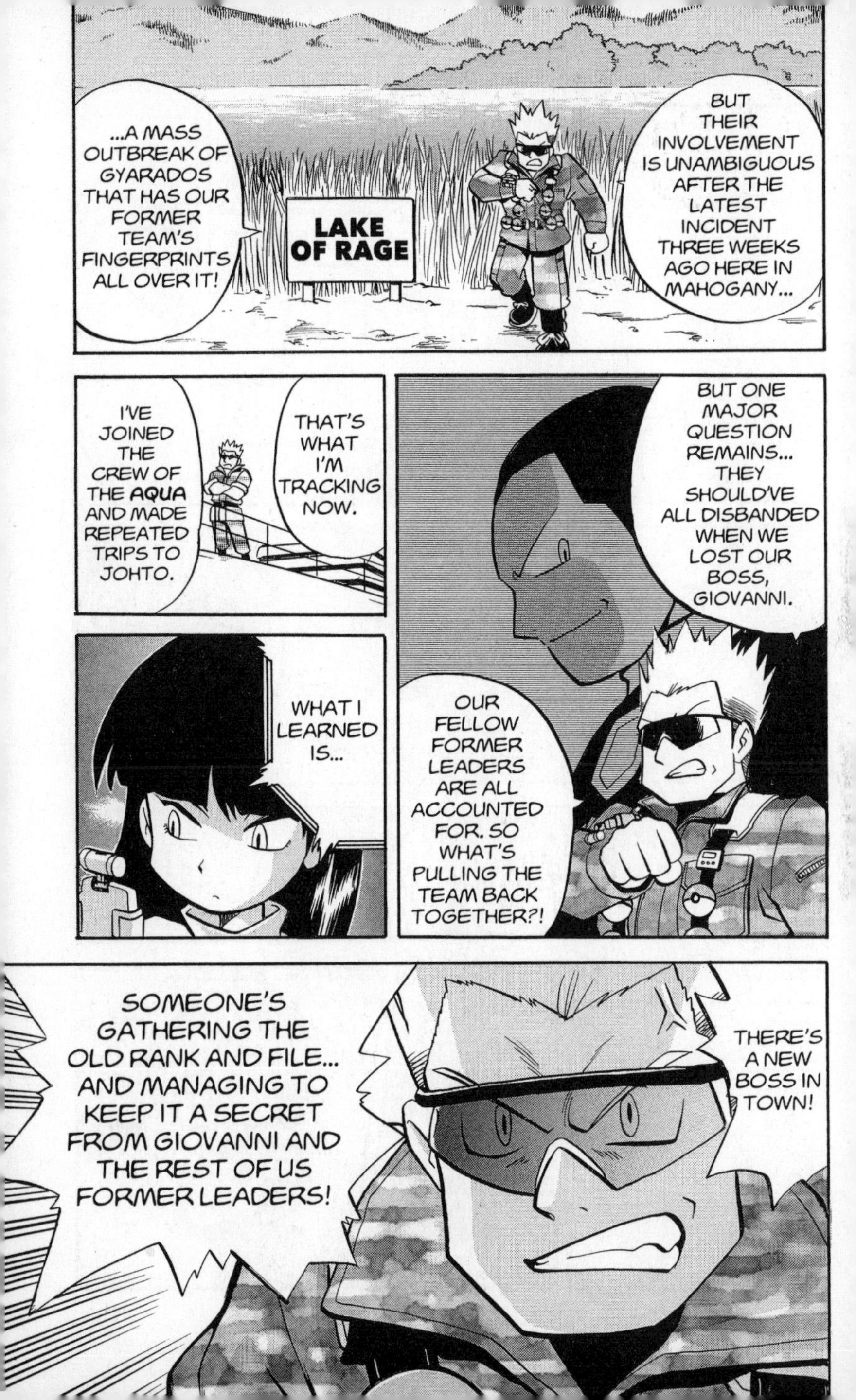
BUT THEIR INVOLVEMENT IS UNAMBIGUOUS AFTER THE LATEST INCIDENT THREE WEEKS AGO HERE IN MAHOGANY...
LAKE OF RAGE
...A MASS OUTBREAK OF GYARADOS THAT HAS OUR FORMER TEAM'S FINGERPRINTS ALL OVER IT!
BUT ONE MAJOR QUESTION REMAINS... THEY SHOULD'VE ALL DISBANDED WHEN WE LOST OUR BOSS, GIOVANNI.
OUR FELLOW FORMER LEADERS ARE ALL ACCOUNTED FOR. SO WHAT'S PULLING THE TEAM BACK TOGETHER?!
THAT'S WHAT I'M TRACKING NOW.
I'VE JOINED THE CREW OF THE AQUA AND MADE REPEATED TRIPS TO JOHTO.
WHAT I LEARNED IS...
THERE'S A NEW BOSS IN TOWN!
SOMEONE'S GATHERING THE OLD RANK AND FILE... AND MANAGING TO KEEP IT A SECRET FROM GIOVANNI AND THE REST OF US FORMER LEADERS!

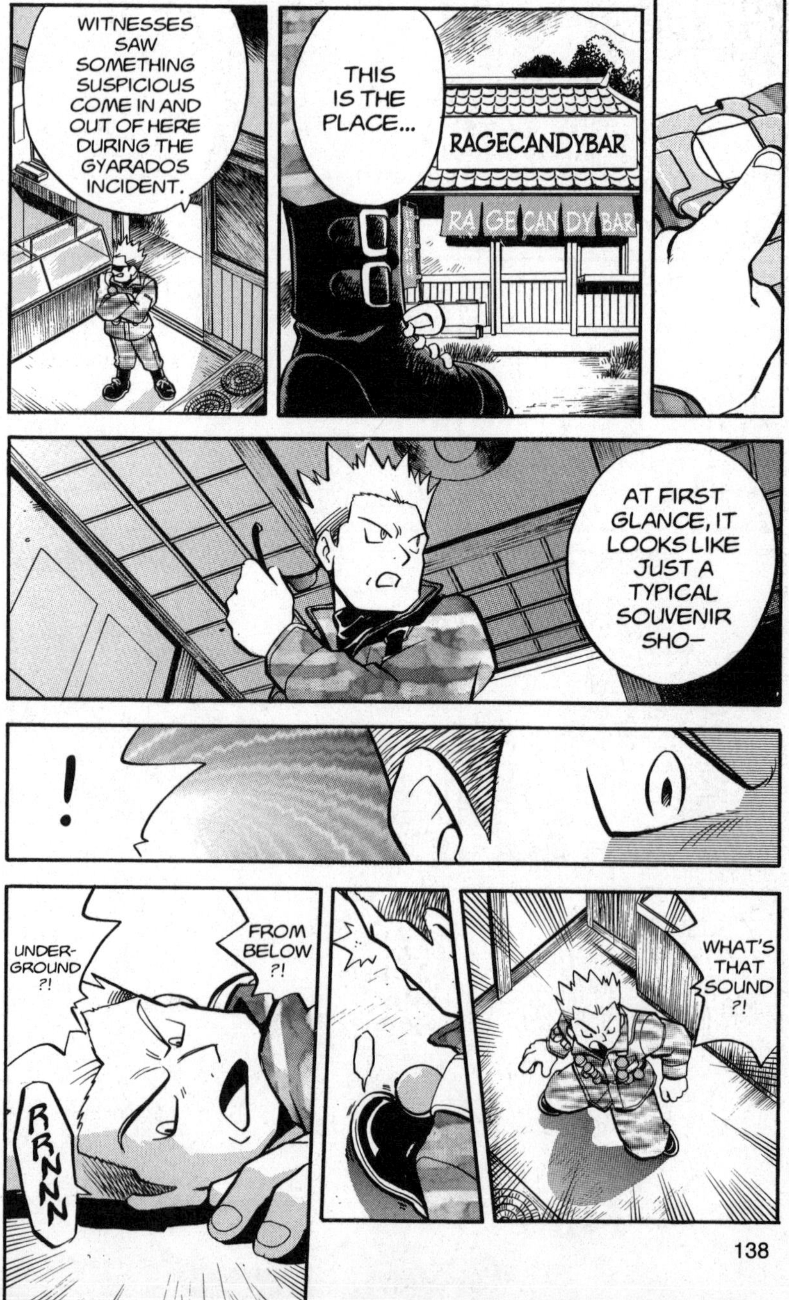
THIS IS THE PLACE...
RAGECANDYBAR
RA GE CAN DY BAR
WITNESSES SAW SOMETHING SUSPICIOUS COME IN AND OUT OF HERE DURING THE GYARADOS INCIDENT.
AT FIRST GLANCE, IT LOOKS LIKE JUST A TYPICAL SOUVENIR SHO-
!
WHAT'S THAT SOUND ?!
!
FROM BELOW ?!
UNDER-GROUND ?!
RRNNN

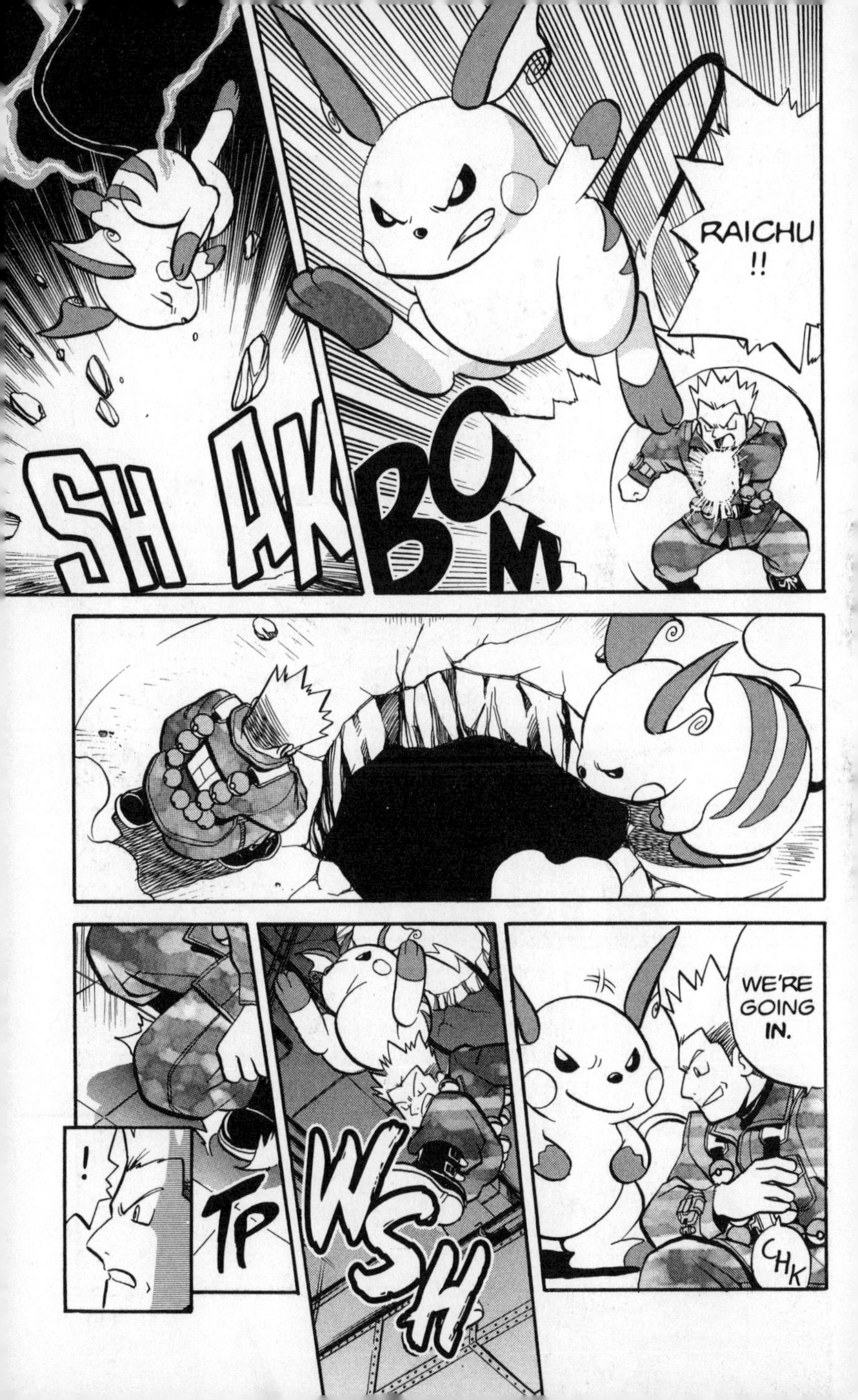
RAICHU !!
BOOM
SHAK
WE'RE GOING IN.
CHK
WSH
TP
!

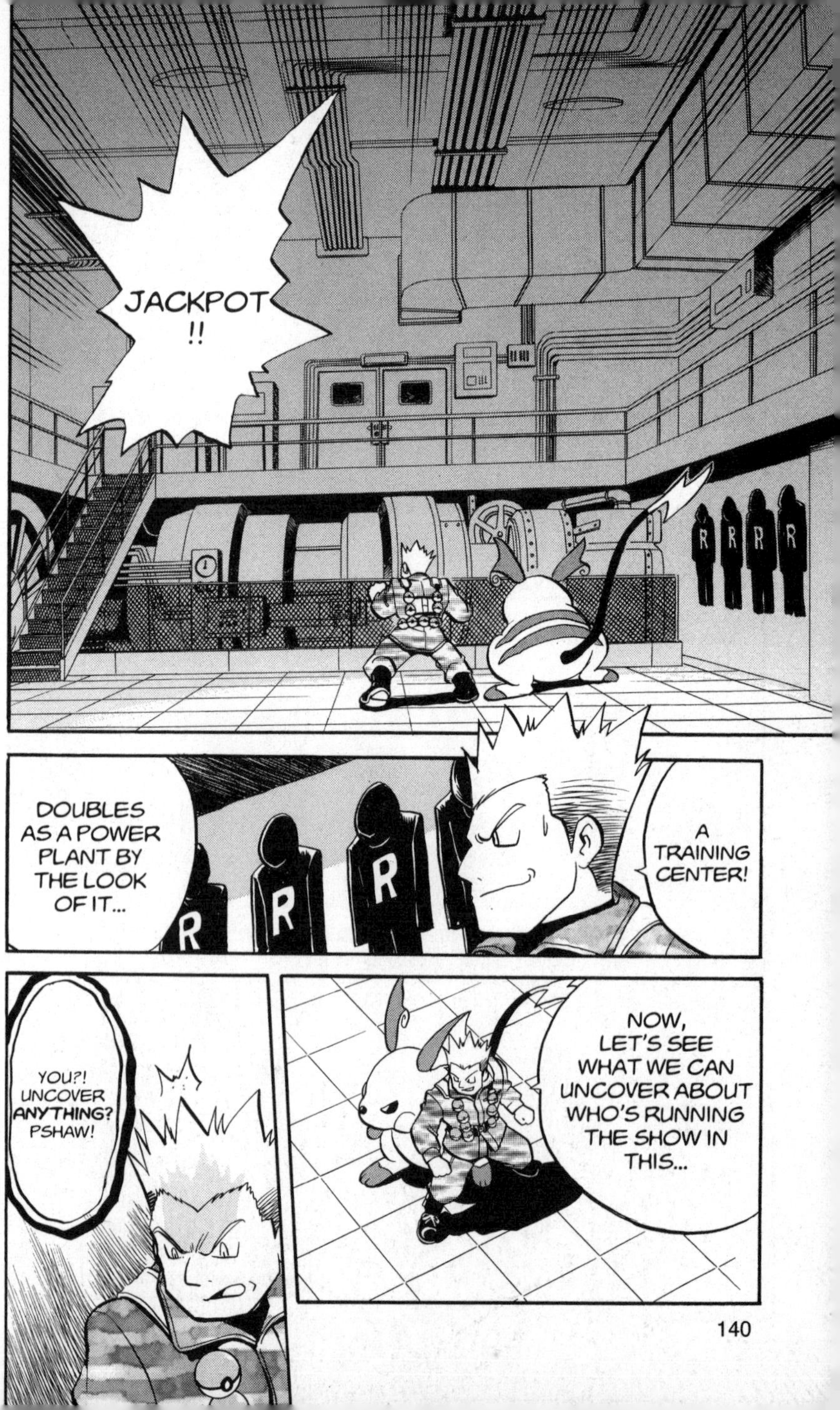
JACKPOT!!
A TRAINING CENTER!
DOUBLES AS A POWER PLANT BY THE LOOK OF IT...
NOW, LET'S SEE WHAT WE CAN UNCOVER ABOUT WHO'S RUNNING THE SHOW IN THIS...
YOU?! UNCOVER ANYTHING? PSHAW!

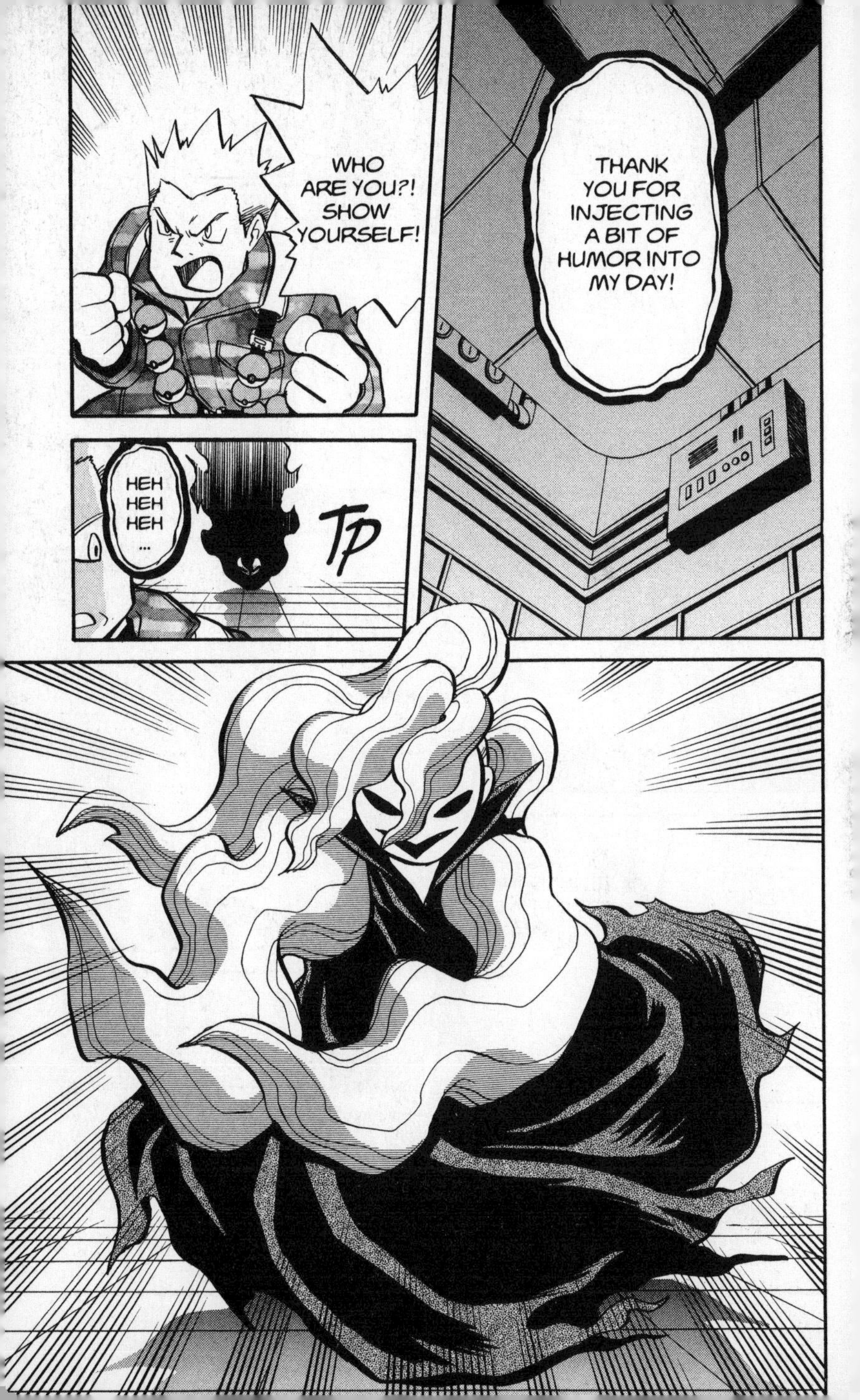
THANK YOU FOR INJECTING A BIT OF HUMOR INTO MY DAY!
WHO ARE YOU?! SHOW YOURSELF!
HEH HEH HEH ...
TP

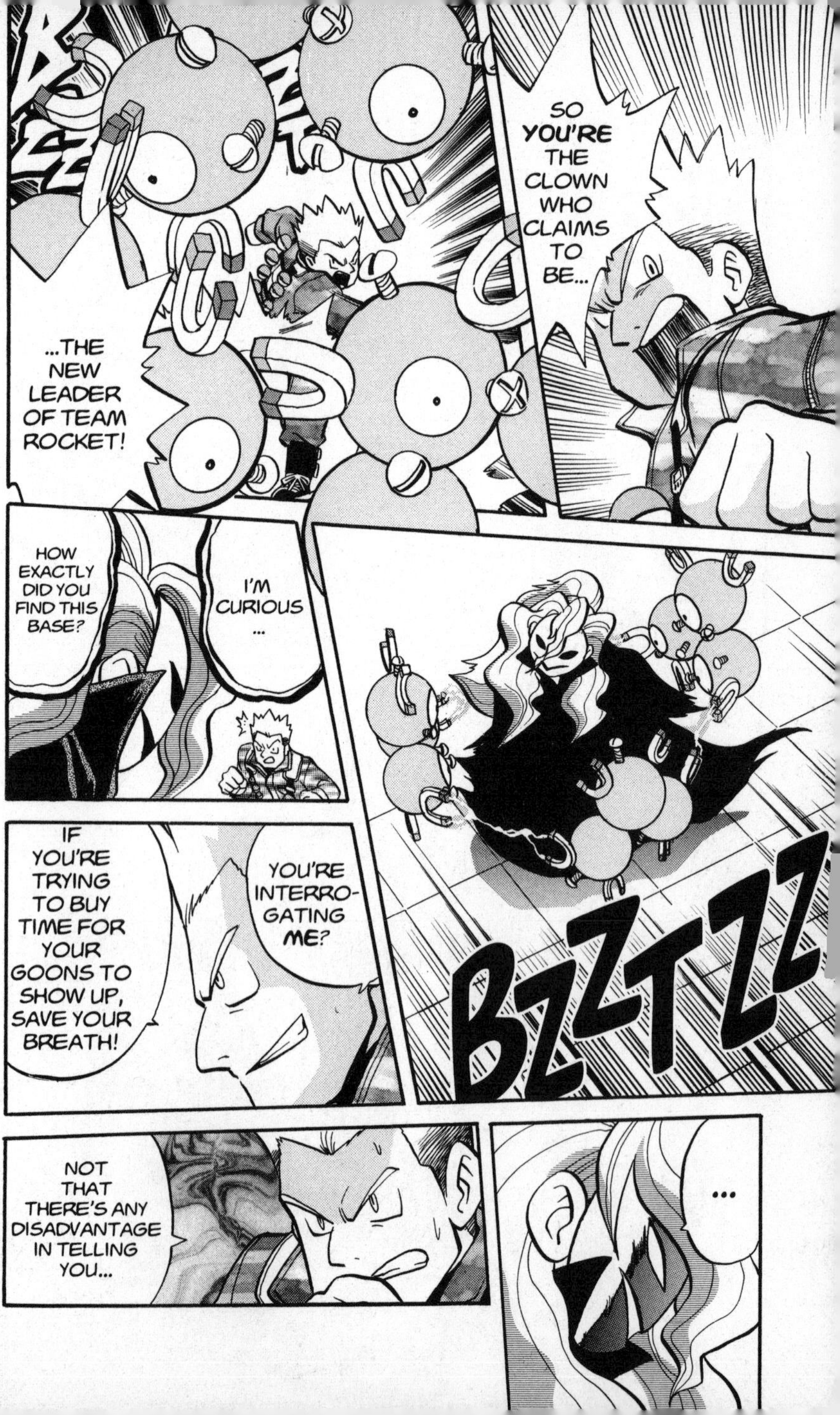
SO YOU'RE THE CLOWN WHO CLAIMS TO BE...
...THE NEW LEADER OF TEAM ROCKET!
BZZTZZ
I'M CURIOUS ...
HOW EXACTLY DID YOU FIND THIS BASE?
YOU'RE INTERROGATING ME?
IF YOU'RE TRYING TO BUY TIME FOR YOUR GOONS TO SHOW UP, SAVE YOUR BREATH!
...
NOT THAT THERE'S ANY DISADVANTAGE IN TELLING YOU...

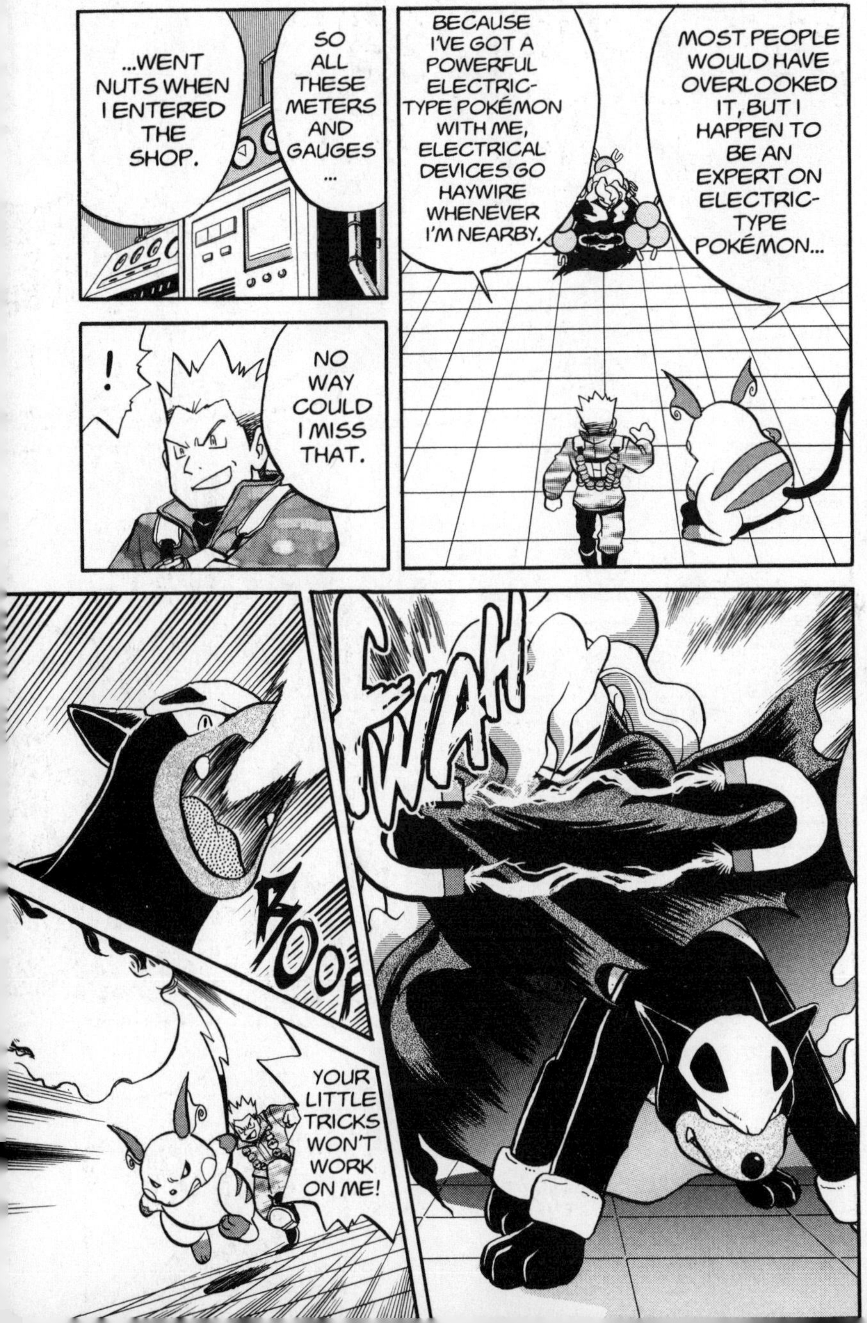
MOST PEOPLE WOULD HAVE OVERLOOKED IT, BUT I HAPPEN TO BE AN EXPERT ON ELECTRIC-TYPE POKÉMON...
BECAUSE I'VE GOT A POWERFUL ELECTRIC-TYPE POKÉMON WITH ME, ELECTRICAL DEVICES GO HAYWIRE WHENEVER I'M NEARBY.
SO ALL THESE METERS AND GAUGES ...
...WENT NUTS WHEN I ENTERED THE SHOP.
NO WAY COULD I MISS THAT.
!
FWAH
BOOO
YOUR LITTLE TRICKS WON'T WORK ON ME!

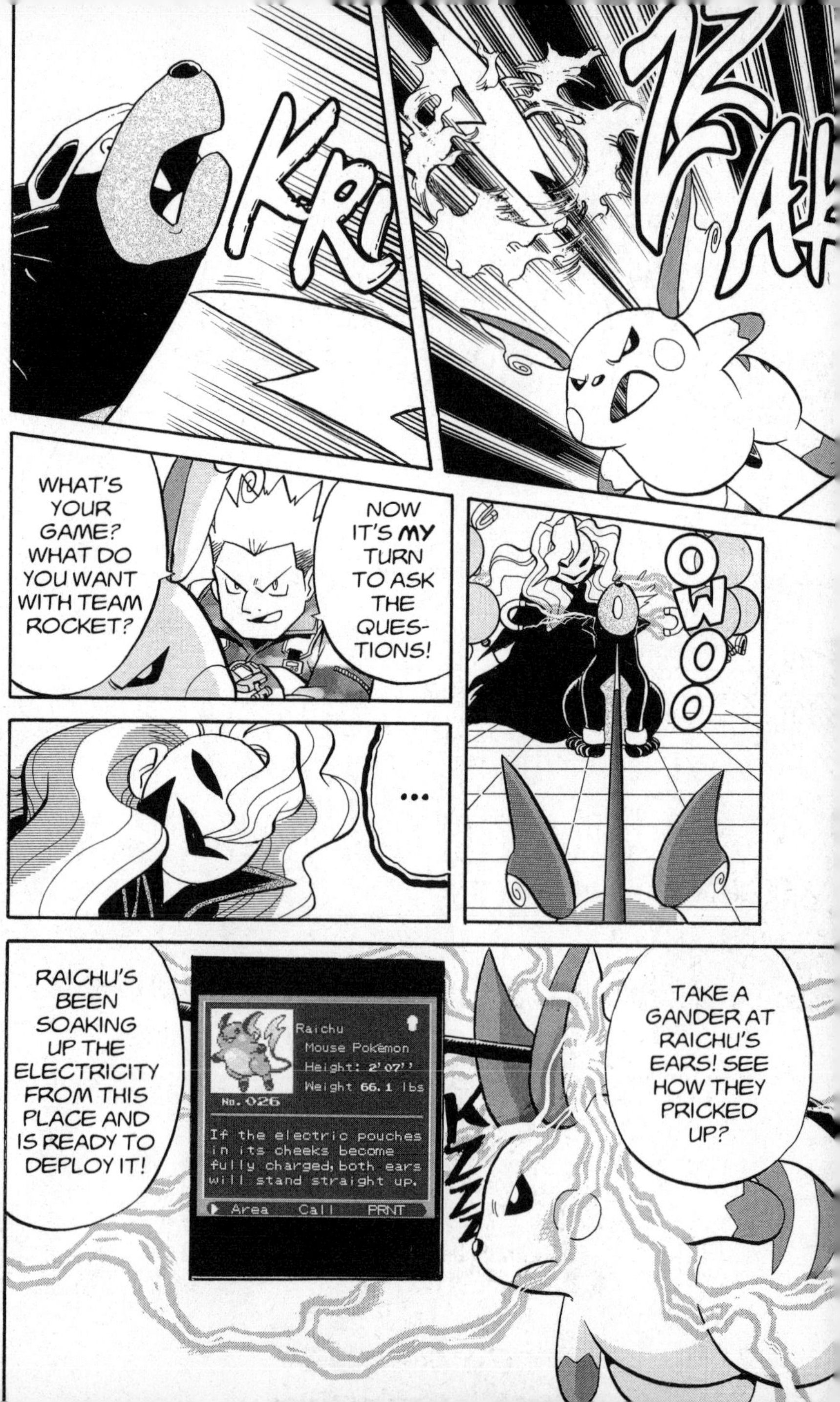
ZZ
ZA
KRO
OWOOO
NOW IT'S MY TURN TO ASK THE QUES-TIONS!
WHAT'S YOUR GAME? WHAT DO YOU WANT WITH TEAM ROCKET?
...
TAKE A GANDER AT RAICHU'S EARS! SEE HOW THEY PRICKED UP?
Raichu
Mouse Pokémon
Height: 2'07''
Weight 66.1 lbs
No. 026
If the electric pouches in its cheeks become fully charged, both ears will stand straight up.
Area Call PRNT
RAICHU'S BEEN SOAKING UP THE ELECTRICITY FROM THIS PLACE AND IS READY TO DEPLOY IT!

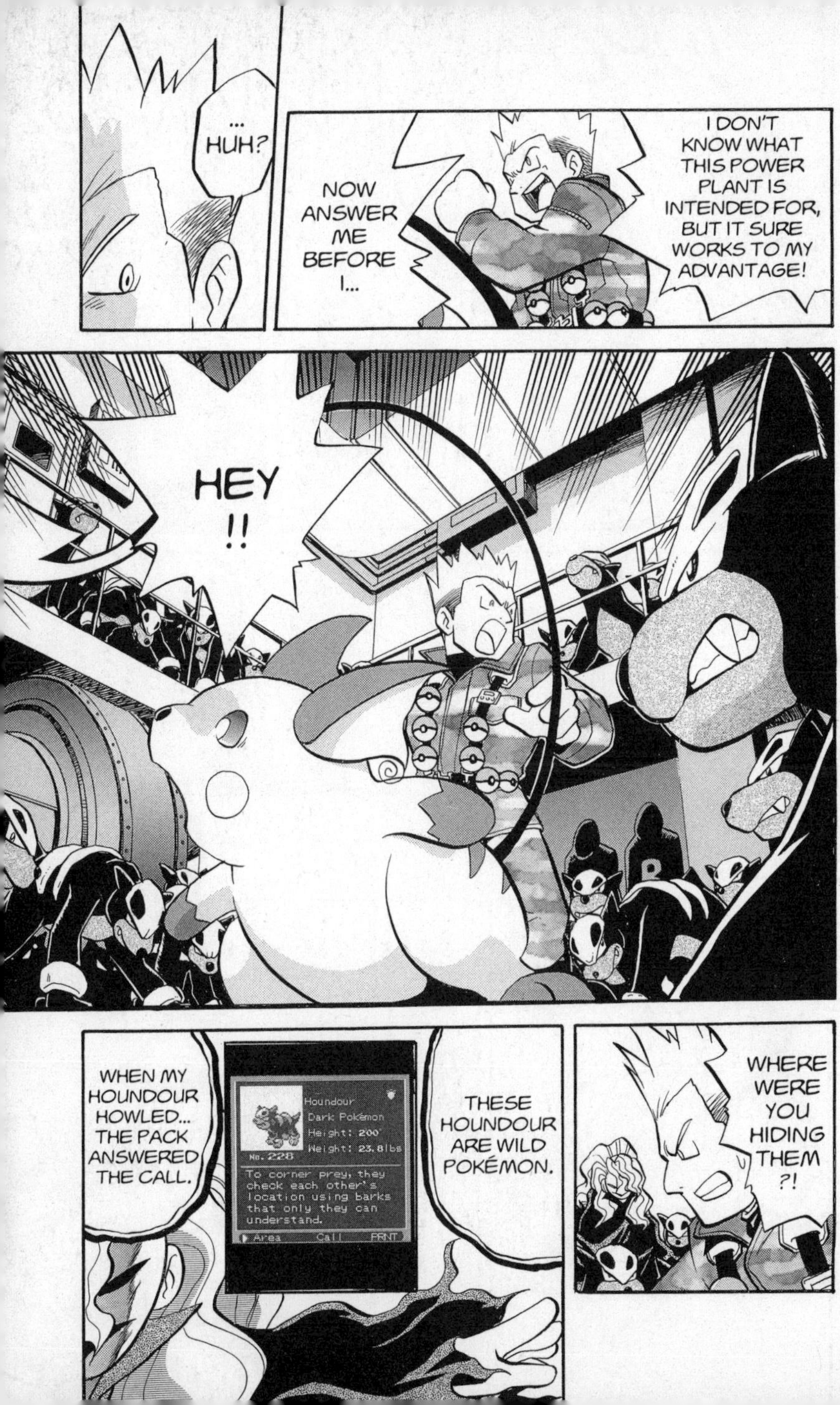
I DON'T KNOW WHAT THIS POWER PLANT IS INTENDED FOR, BUT IT SURE WORKS TO MY ADVANTAGE!
NOW ANSWER ME BEFORE I...
... HUH?
HEY !!
WHERE WERE YOU HIDING THEM ?!
THESE HOUNDOUR ARE WILD POKÉMON.
Houndour
Dark Pokémon
Height: 2'00"
Weight: 23.8lbs
No. 228
To corner prey, they check each other's location using barks that only they can understand.
Area Call PRNT
WHEN MY HOUNDOUR HOWLED... THE PACK ANSWERED THE CALL.

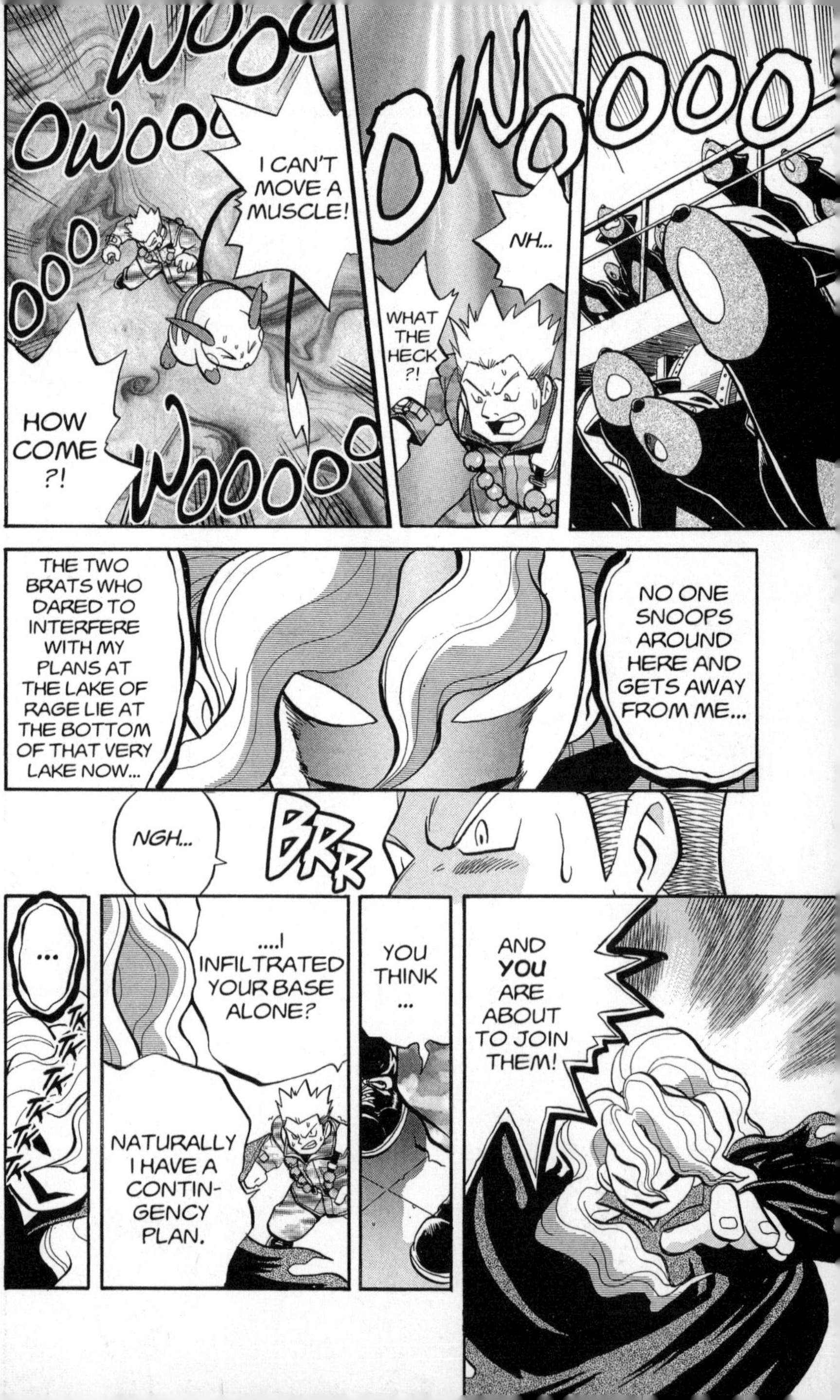

OWOOOO
NH...
WHAT THE HECK ?!
WOOO
OWOO
OOO
I CAN'T MOVE A MUSCLE!
HOW COME ?!
WOOOO
NO ONE SNOOPS AROUND HERE AND GETS AWAY FROM ME...
THE TWO BRATS WHO DARED TO INTERFERE WITH MY PLANS AT THE LAKE OF RAGE LIE AT THE BOTTOM OF THAT VERY LAKE NOW...
BRR
NGH...
AND **YOU** ARE ABOUT TO JOIN THEM!
YOU THINK ...
....I INFILTRATED YOUR BASE ALONE?
NATURALLY I HAVE A CONTIN-GENCY PLAN.
...
TK TK TK TK TK TK

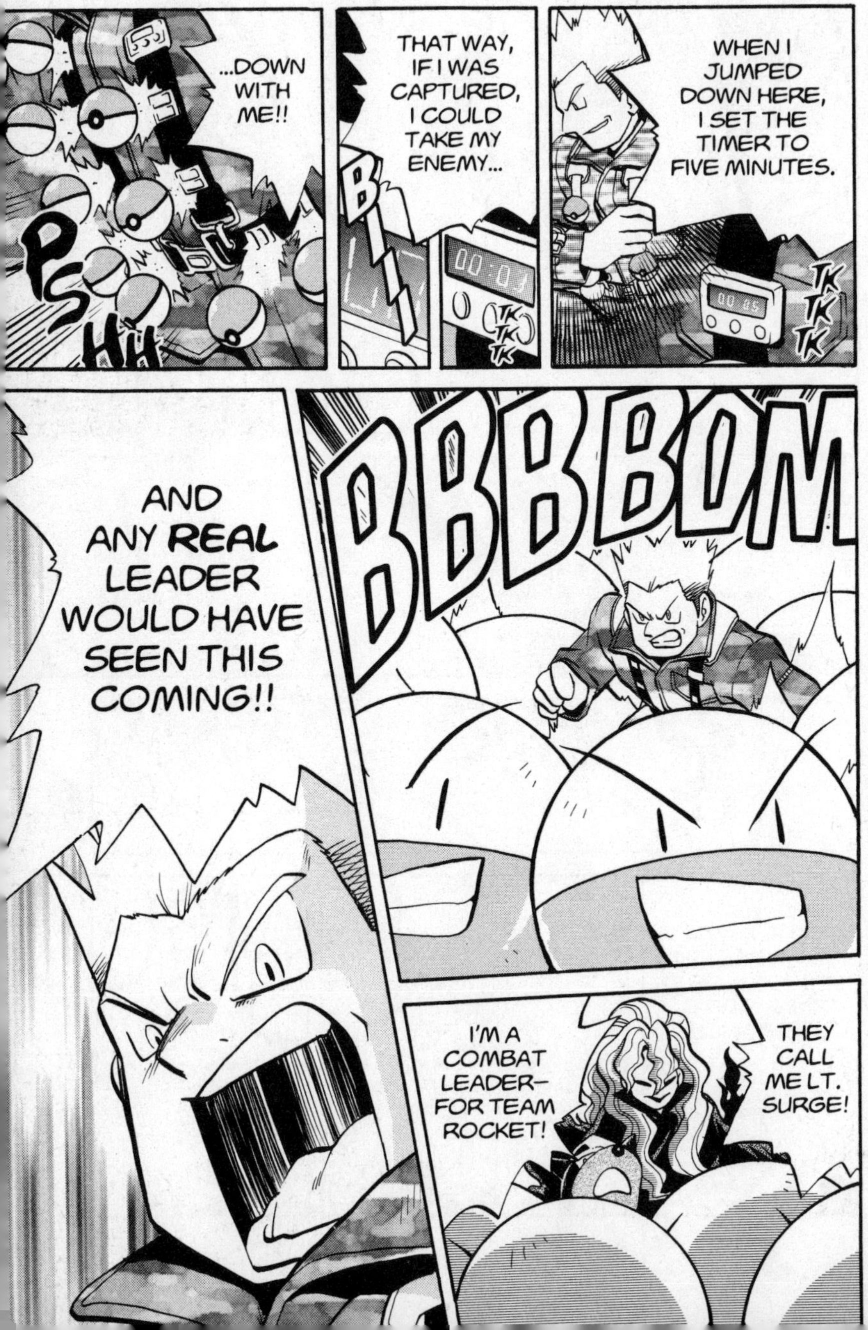
WHEN I JUMPED DOWN HERE, I SET THE TIMER TO FIVE MINUTES.
TK TK TK
THAT WAY, IF I WAS CAPTURED, I COULD TAKE MY ENEMY...
B
TK TK TK
...DOWN WITH ME!!
PSHH
BBBBOM
THEY CALL ME LT. SURGE!
I'M A COMBAT LEADER—FOR TEAM ROCKET!
AND ANY **REAL** LEADER WOULD HAVE SEEN THIS COMING!!

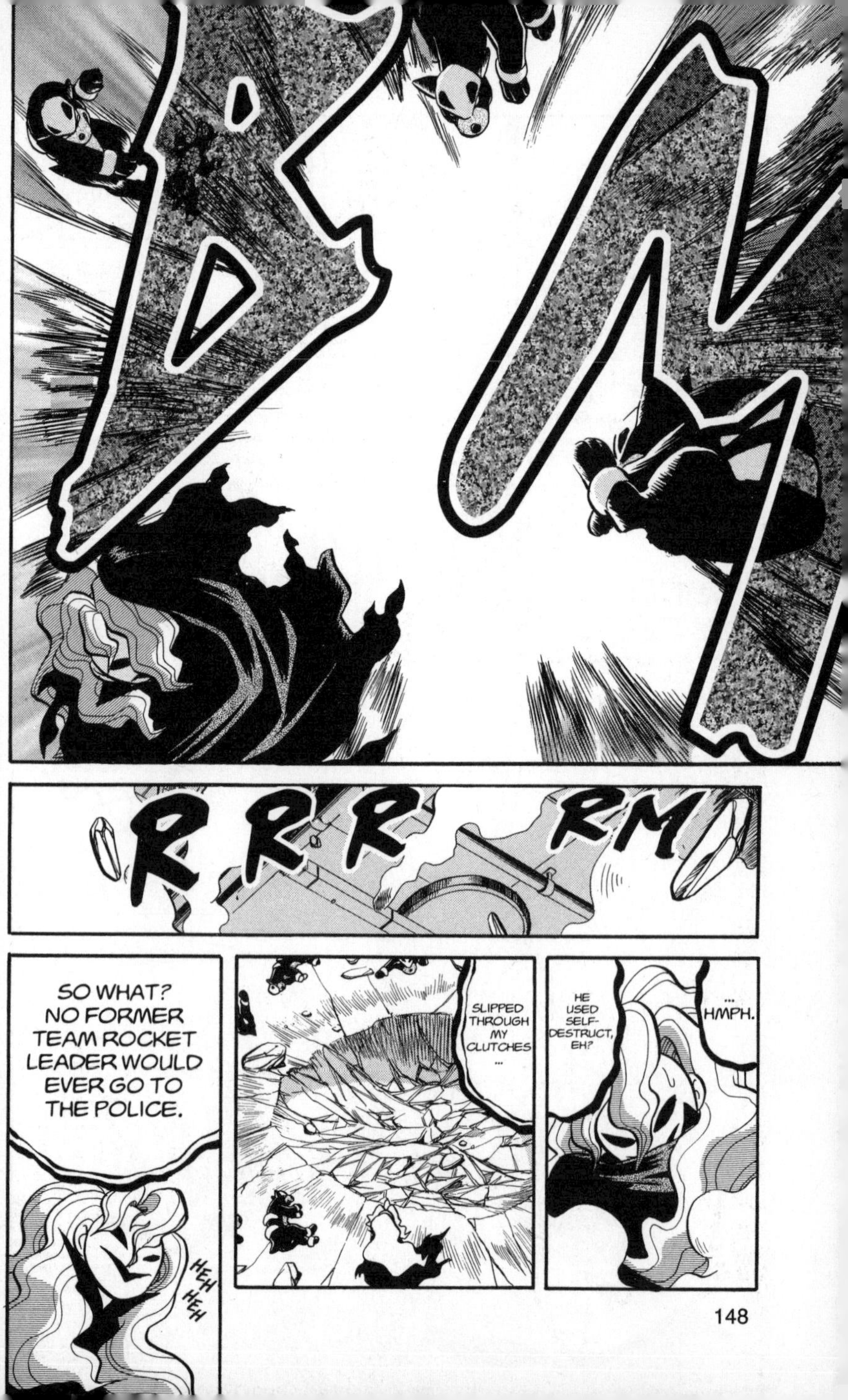
RRR RM
... HMPH.
HE USED SELF-DESTRUCT, EH?
SLIPPED THROUGH MY CLUTCHES ...
SO WHAT? NO FORMER TEAM ROCKET LEADER WOULD EVER GO TO THE POLICE.
HEH HEH

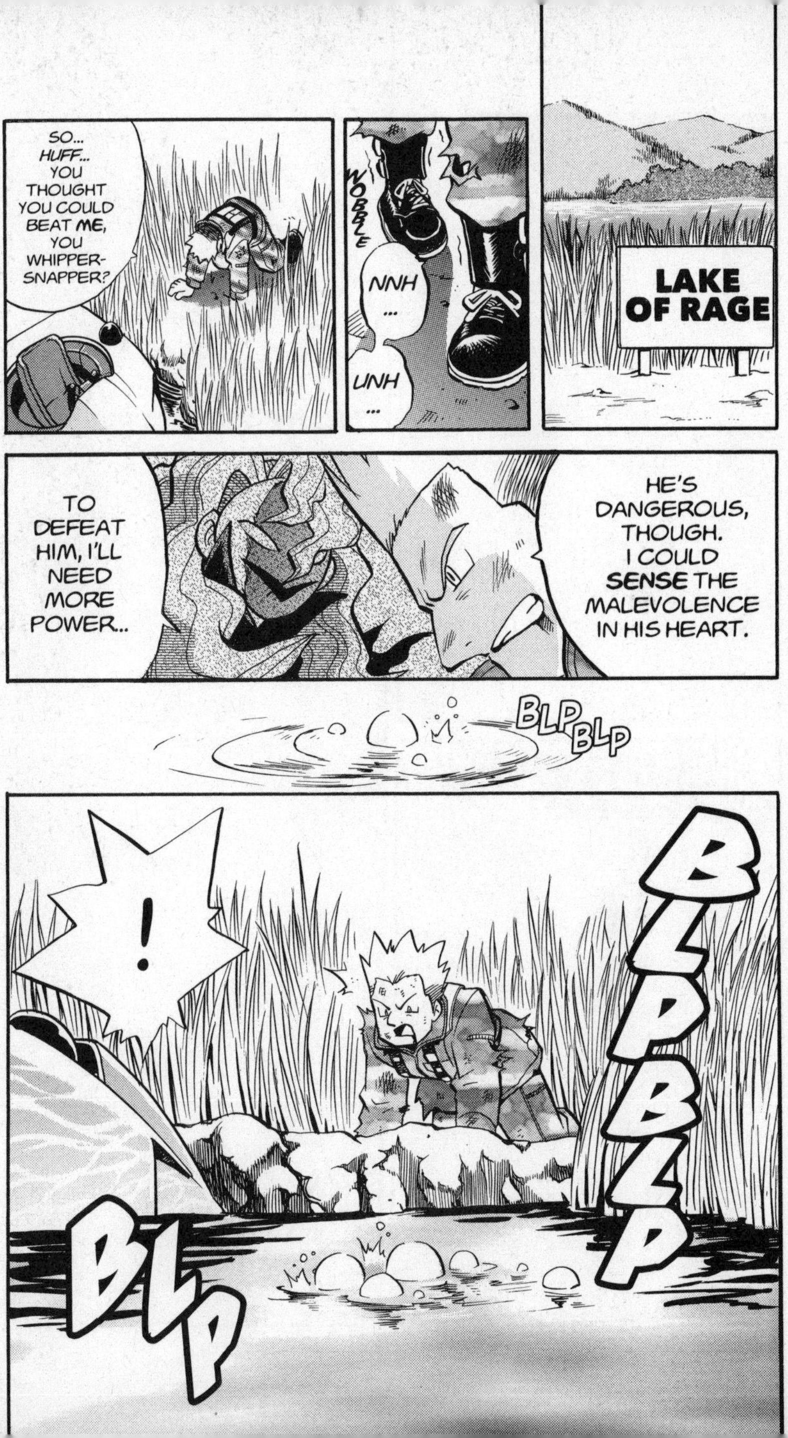
LAKE OF RAGE
WOBBLE
NNH ...
UNH ...
SO... HUFF... YOU THOUGHT YOU COULD BEAT ME, YOU WHIPPER-SNAPPER?
HE'S DANGEROUS, THOUGH. I COULD SENSE THE MALEVOLENCE IN HIS HEART.
TO DEFEAT HIM, I'LL NEED MORE POWER...
BLP BLP
BLPBLP
!
BLP

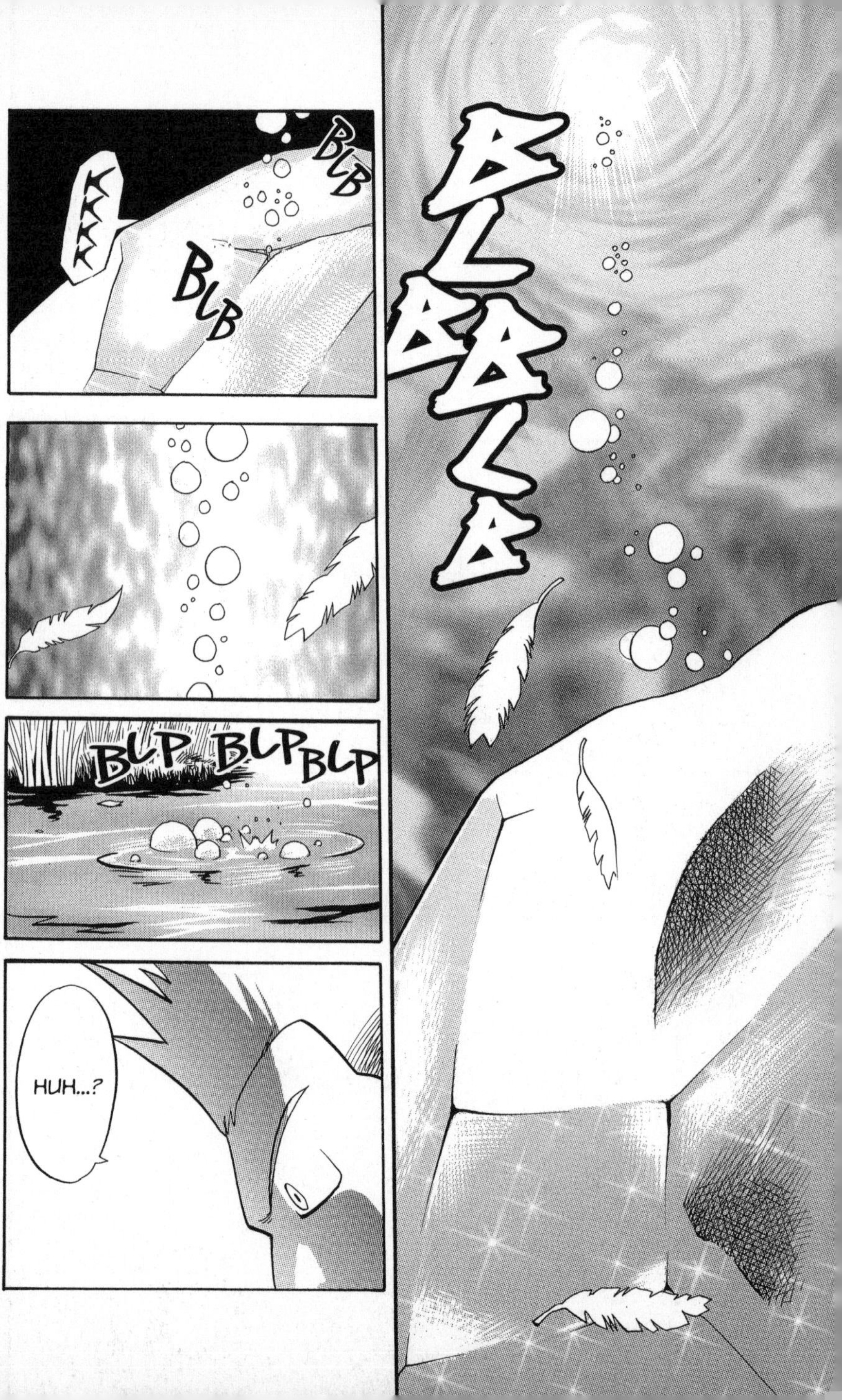
BLBBLB
BLB
BLB
BLP BLP BLP
HUH...?

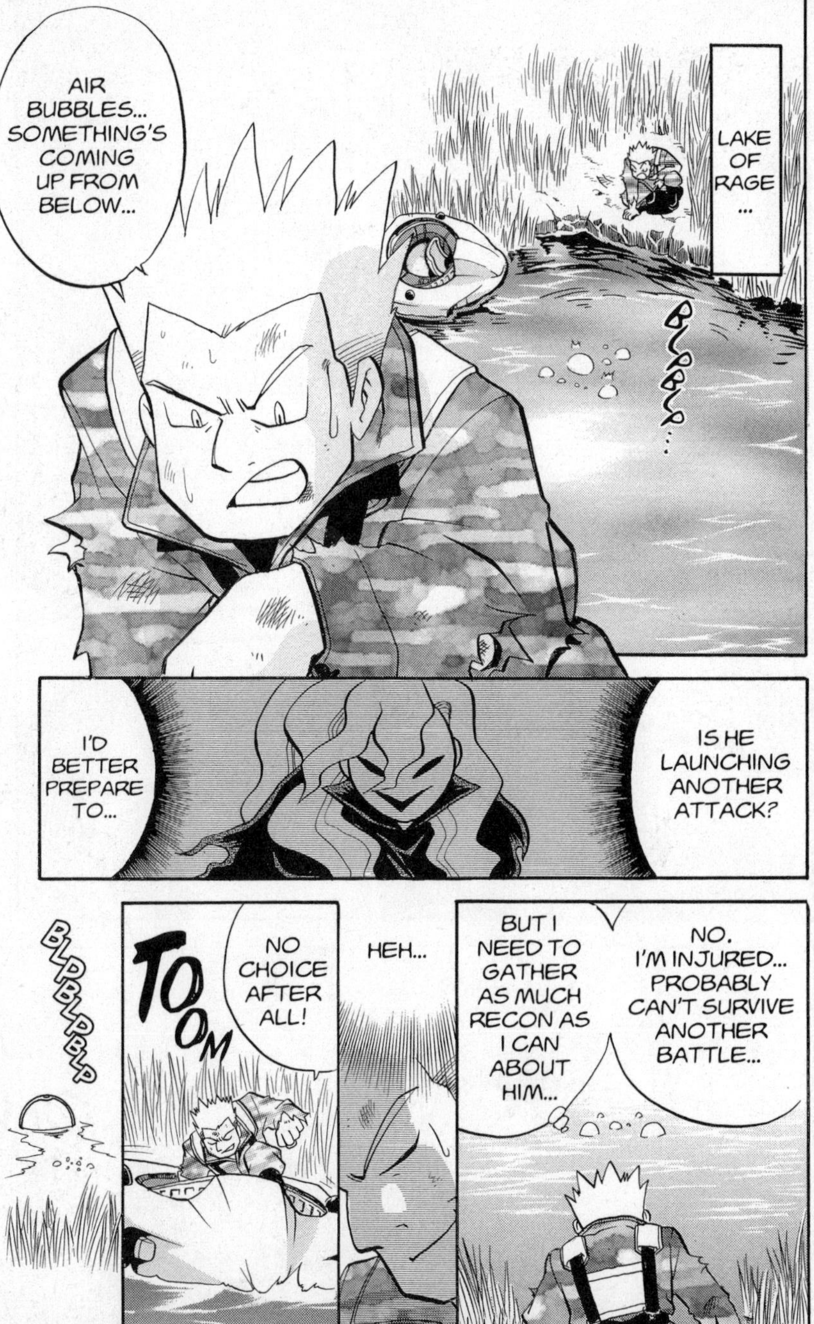
LAKE OF RAGE ...
BLPBLP...
AIR BUBBLES... SOMETHING'S COMING UP FROM BELOW...
IS HE LAUNCHING ANOTHER ATTACK?
I'D BETTER PREPARE TO...
NO. I'M INJURED... PROBABLY CAN'T SURVIVE ANOTHER BATTLE...
BUT I NEED TO GATHER AS MUCH RECON AS I CAN ABOUT HIM...
HEH...
NO CHOICE AFTER ALL!
TOOOM
BLPBLPBLP

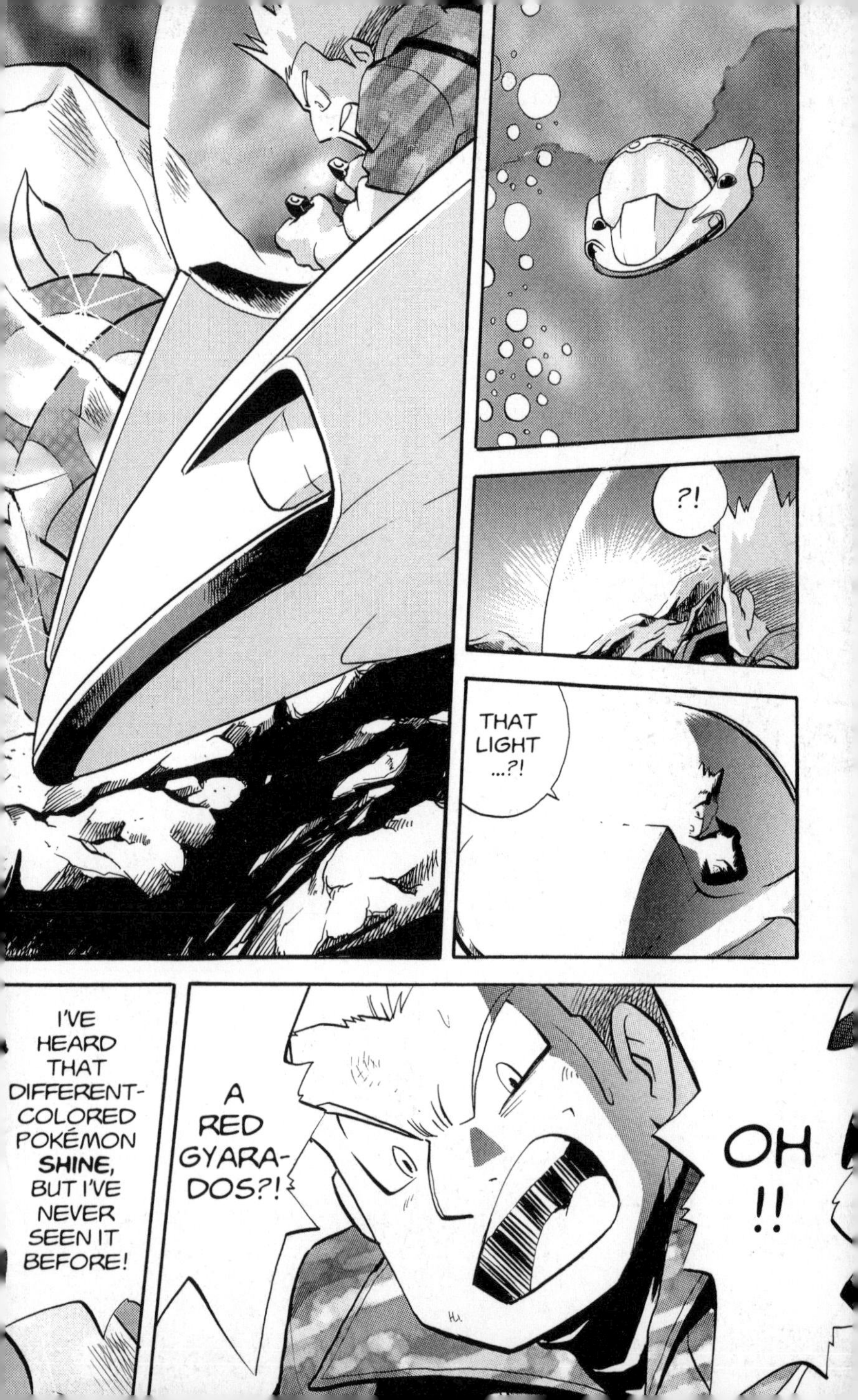
?!
THAT LIGHT ...?!
OH !!
A RED GYARADOS?!
I'VE HEARD THAT DIFFERENT-COLORED POKÉMON **SHINE**, BUT I'VE NEVER SEEN IT BEFORE!

140 Do-Si-Do with Dodrio

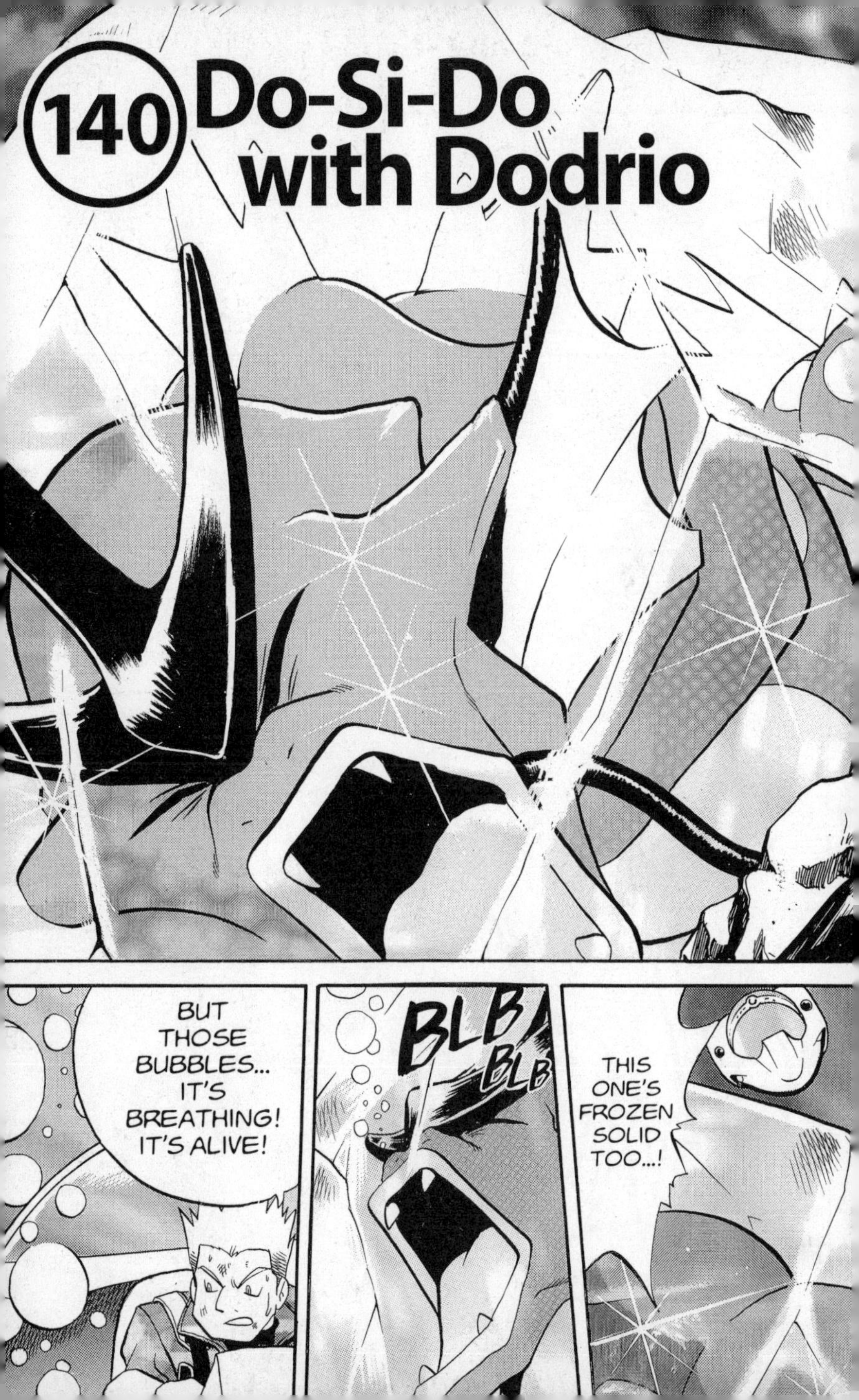
THIS ONE'S FROZEN SOLID TOO...!
BLB BLB
BUT THOSE BUBBLES... IT'S BREATHING! IT'S ALIVE!

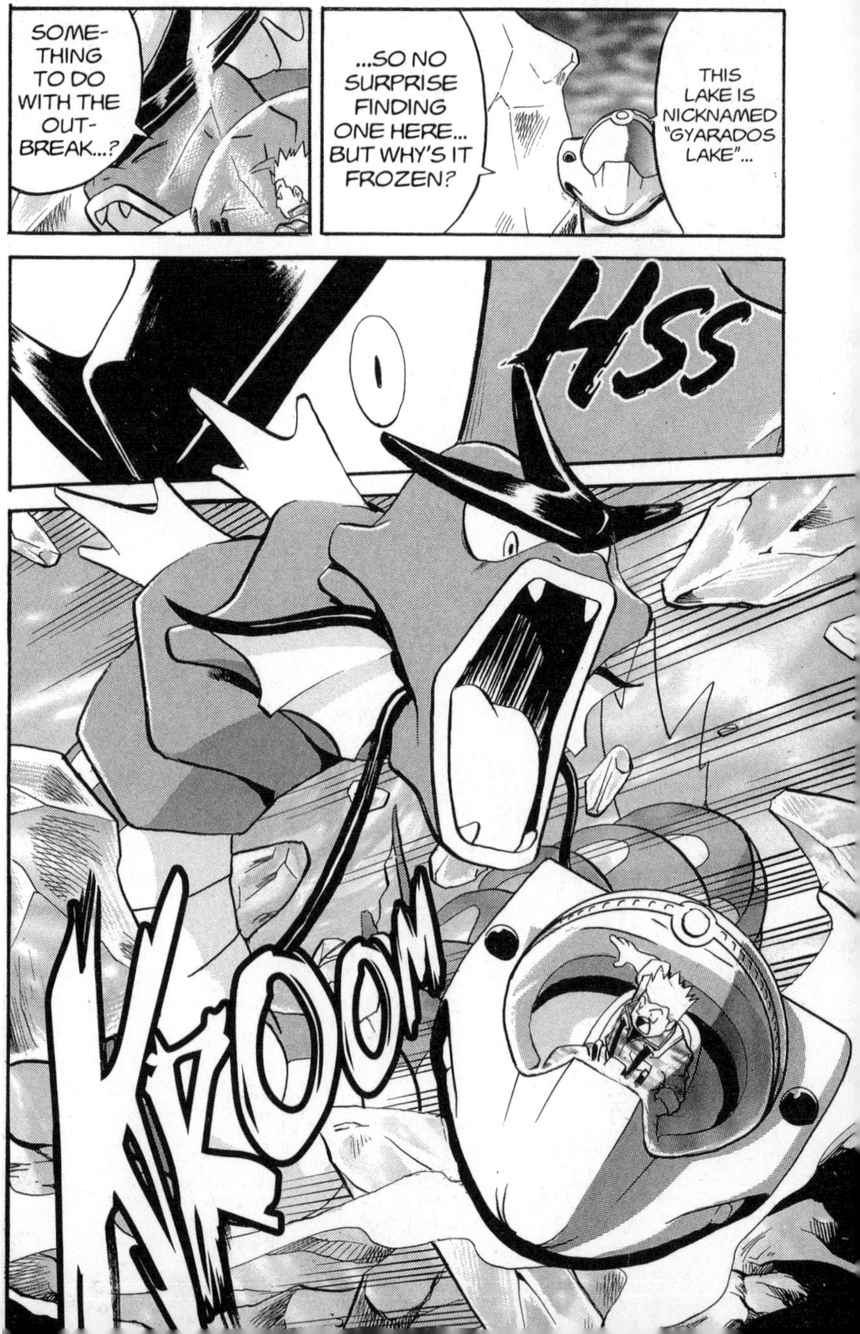
THIS LAKE IS NICKNAMED "GYARADOS LAKE"...
...SO NO SURPRISE FINDING ONE HERE... BUT WHY'S IT FROZEN?
SOME-THING TO DO WITH THE OUT-BREAK...?
HSS
KROOM

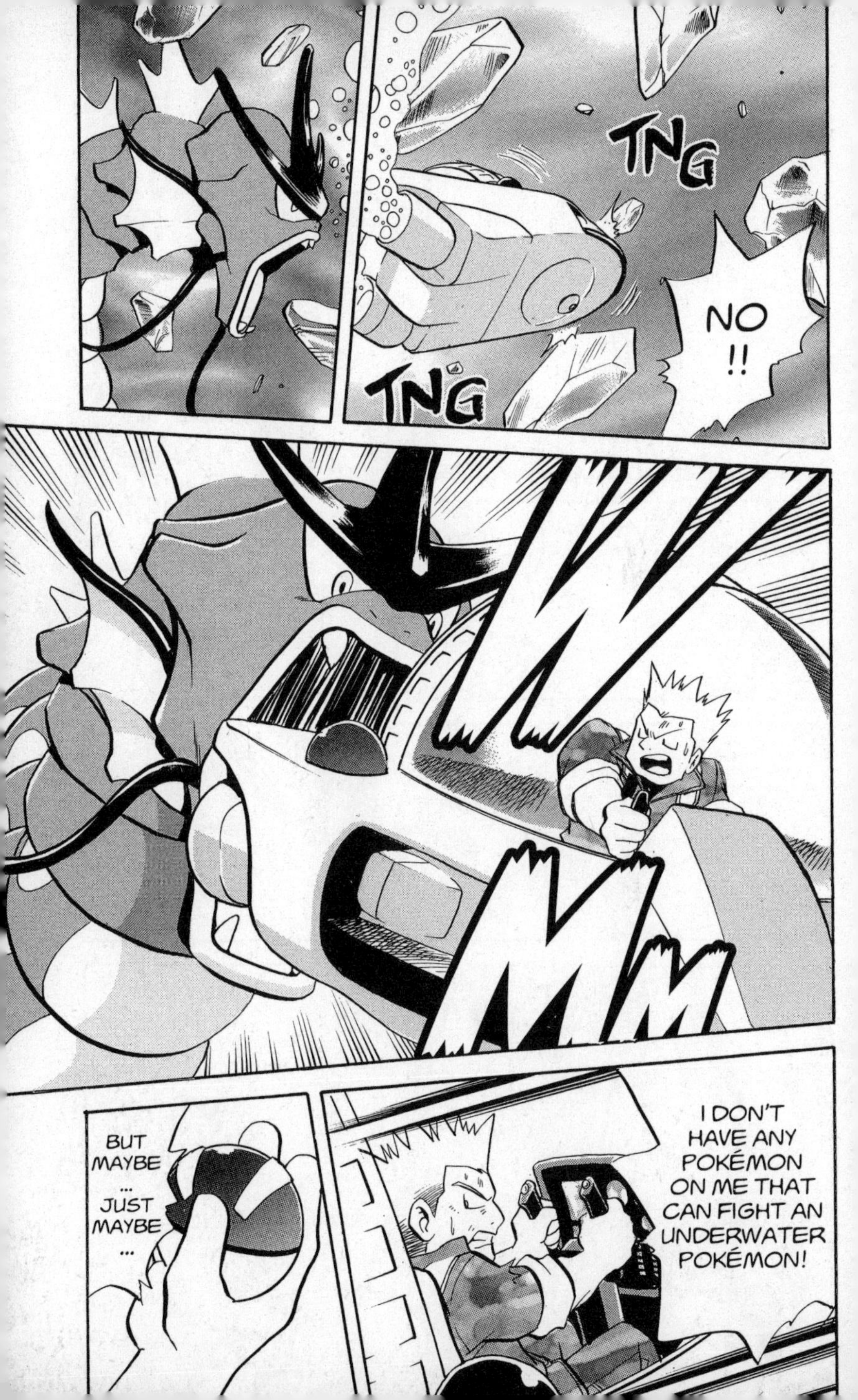
TNG
NO!!
TNG
WMM
I DON'T HAVE ANY POKÉMON ON ME THAT CAN FIGHT AN UNDERWATER POKÉMON!
BUT MAYBE ... JUST MAYBE ...

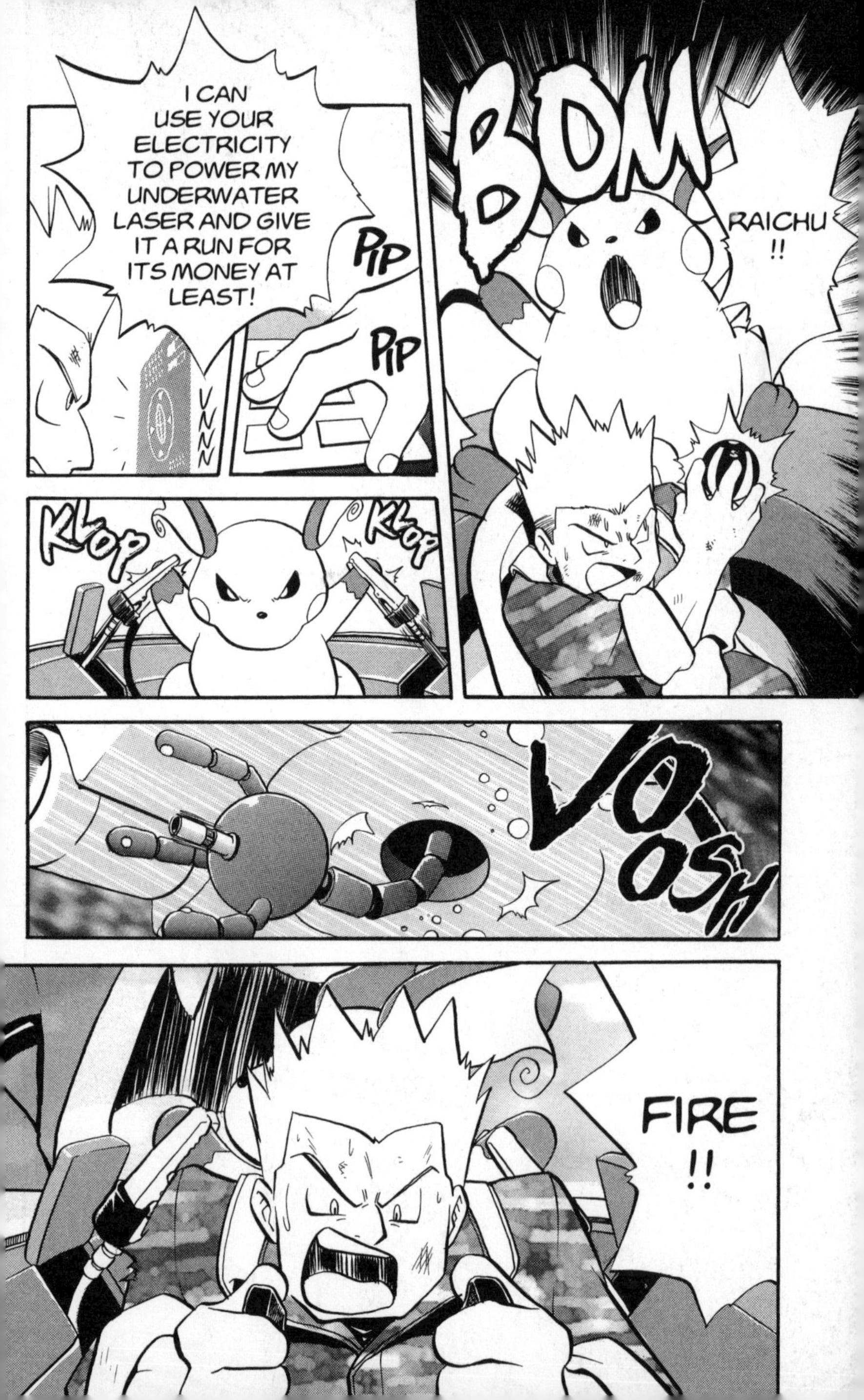
BOM
RAICHU !!
I CAN USE YOUR ELECTRICITY TO POWER MY UNDERWATER LASER AND GIVE IT A RUN FOR ITS MONEY AT LEAST!
PIP
PIP
VNNNN
KLOP
KLOP
VOOSH
FIRE !!

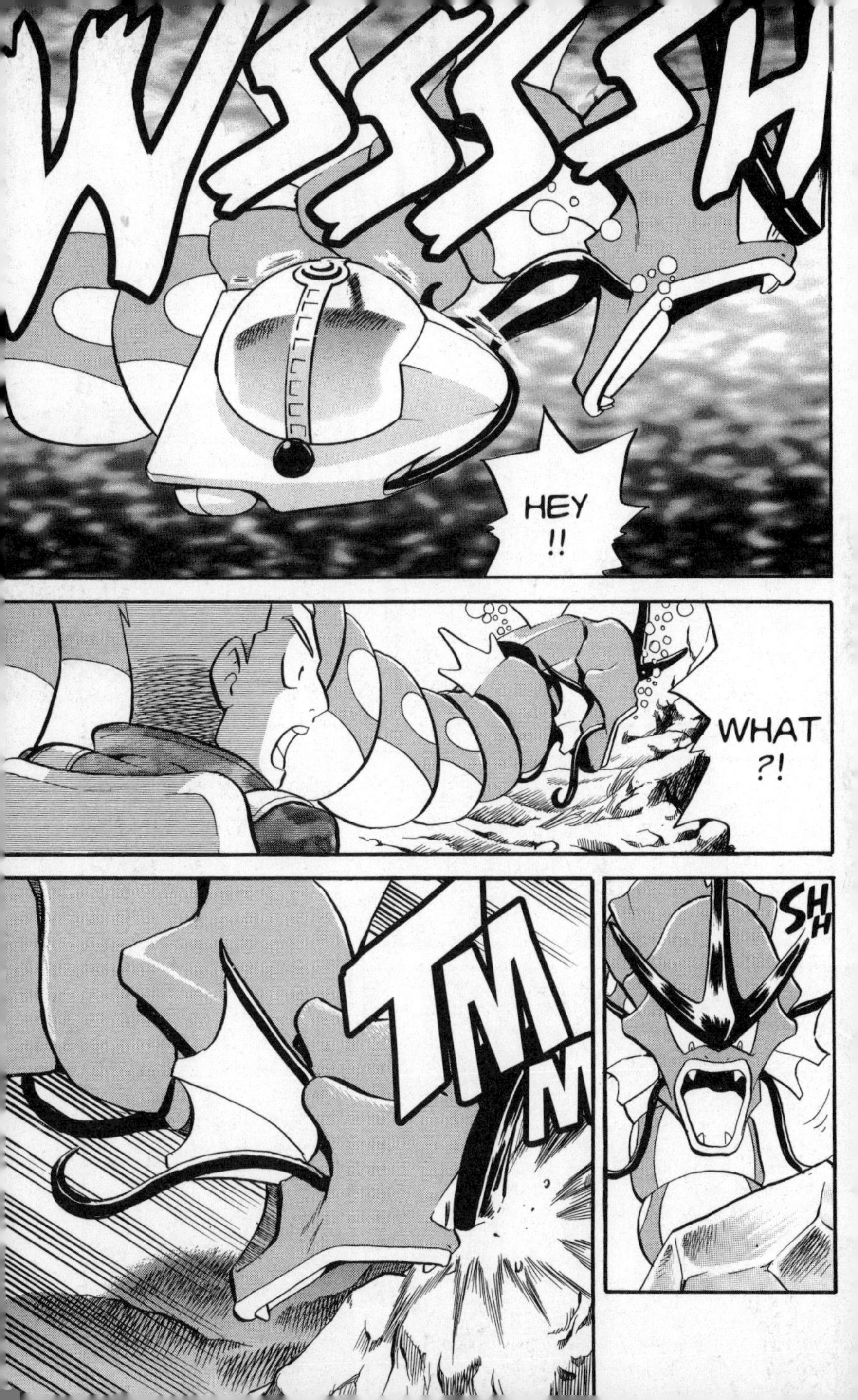
WSSSH
HEY !!
WHAT ?!
SHH
TMM

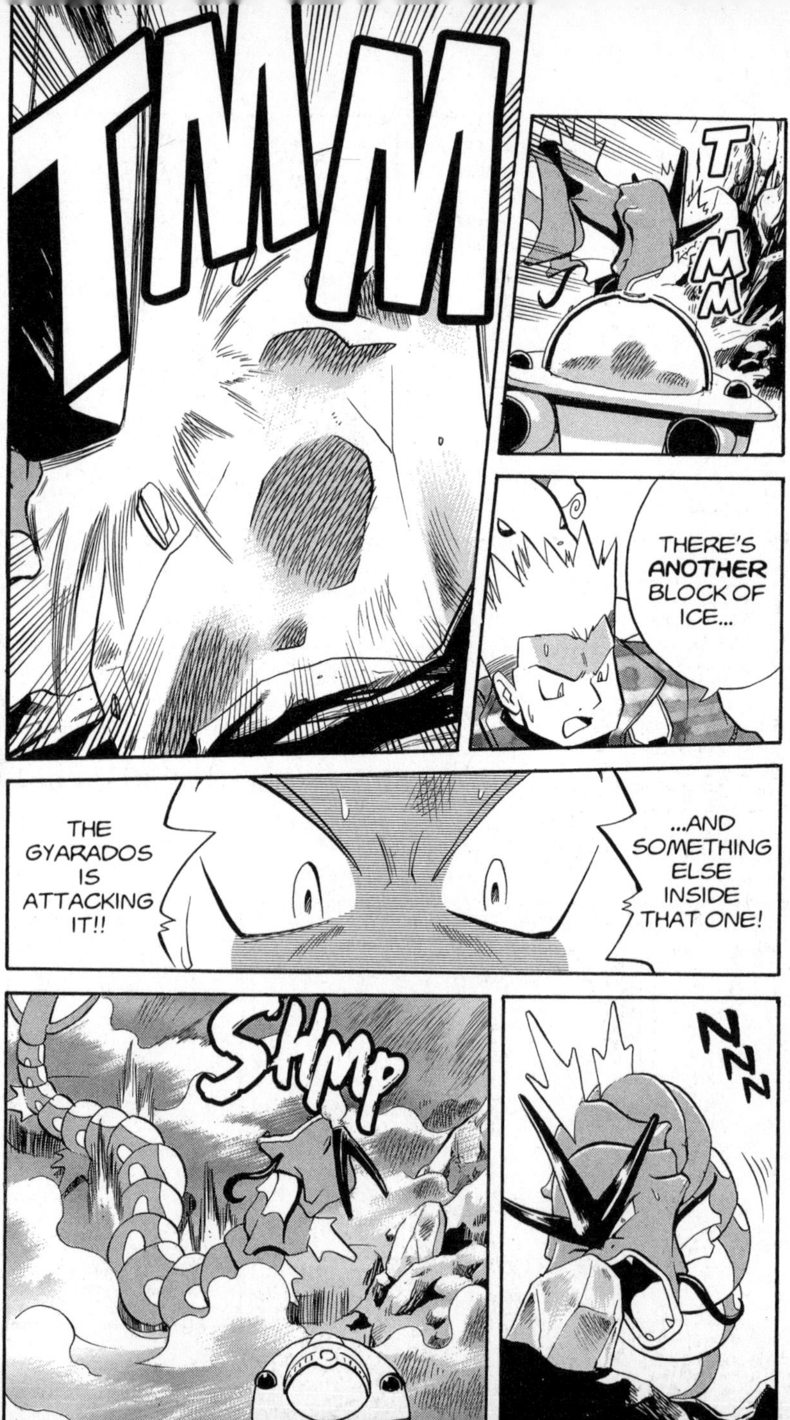
TMMM
THERE'S **ANOTHER** BLOCK OF ICE...
TMM
...AND SOMETHING ELSE INSIDE THAT ONE!
THE GYARADOS IS ATTACKING IT!!
NNN
SHMP

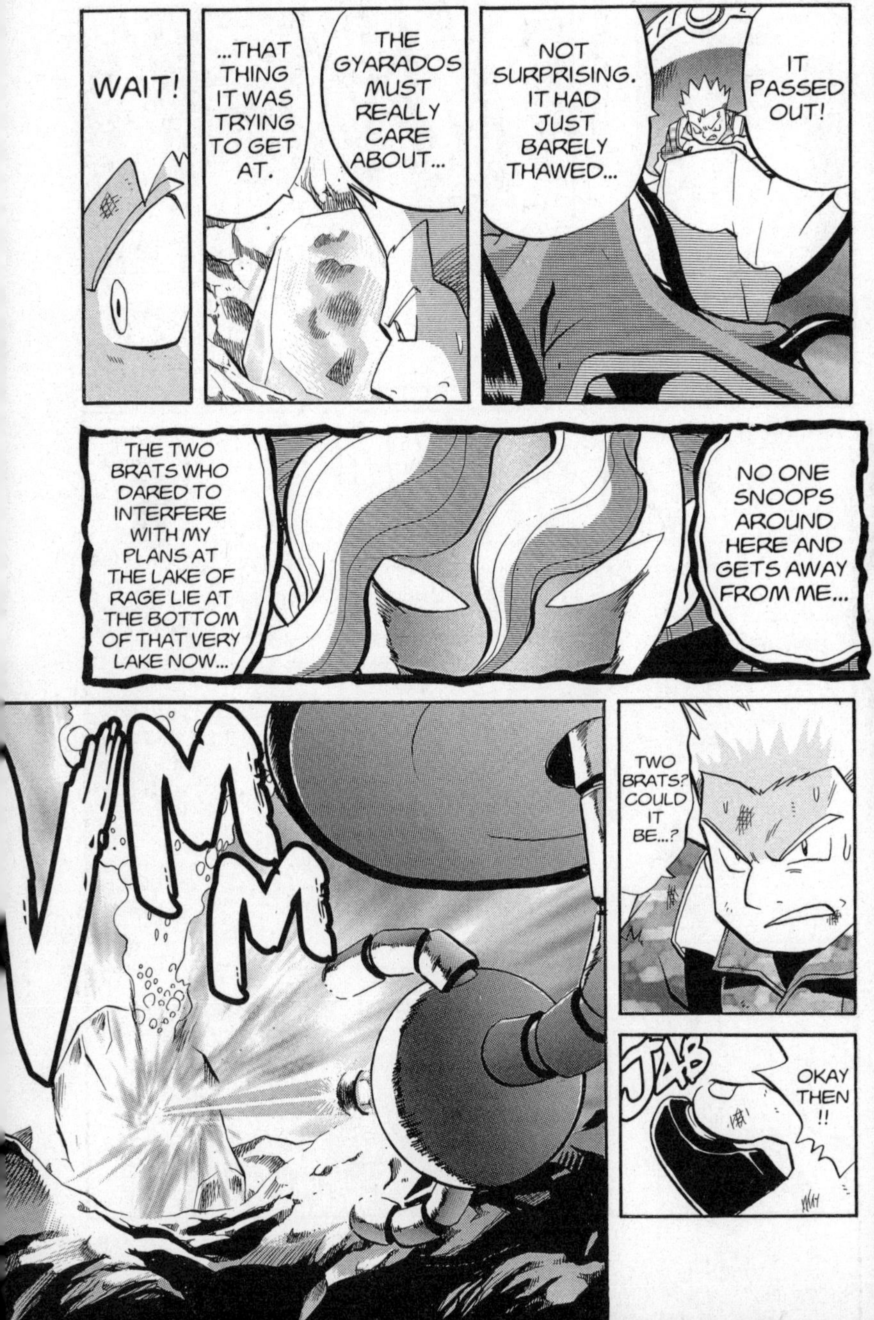
IT PASSED OUT!
NOT SURPRISING. IT HAD JUST BARELY THAWED...
THE GYARADOS MUST REALLY CARE ABOUT...
...THAT THING IT WAS TRYING TO GET AT.
WAIT!
NO ONE SNOOPS AROUND HERE AND GETS AWAY FROM ME...
THE TWO BRATS WHO DARED TO INTERFERE WITH MY PLANS AT THE LAKE OF RAGE LIE AT THE BOTTOM OF THAT VERY LAKE NOW...
TWO BRATS? COULD IT BE...?
JAB
OKAY THEN!!
VMM

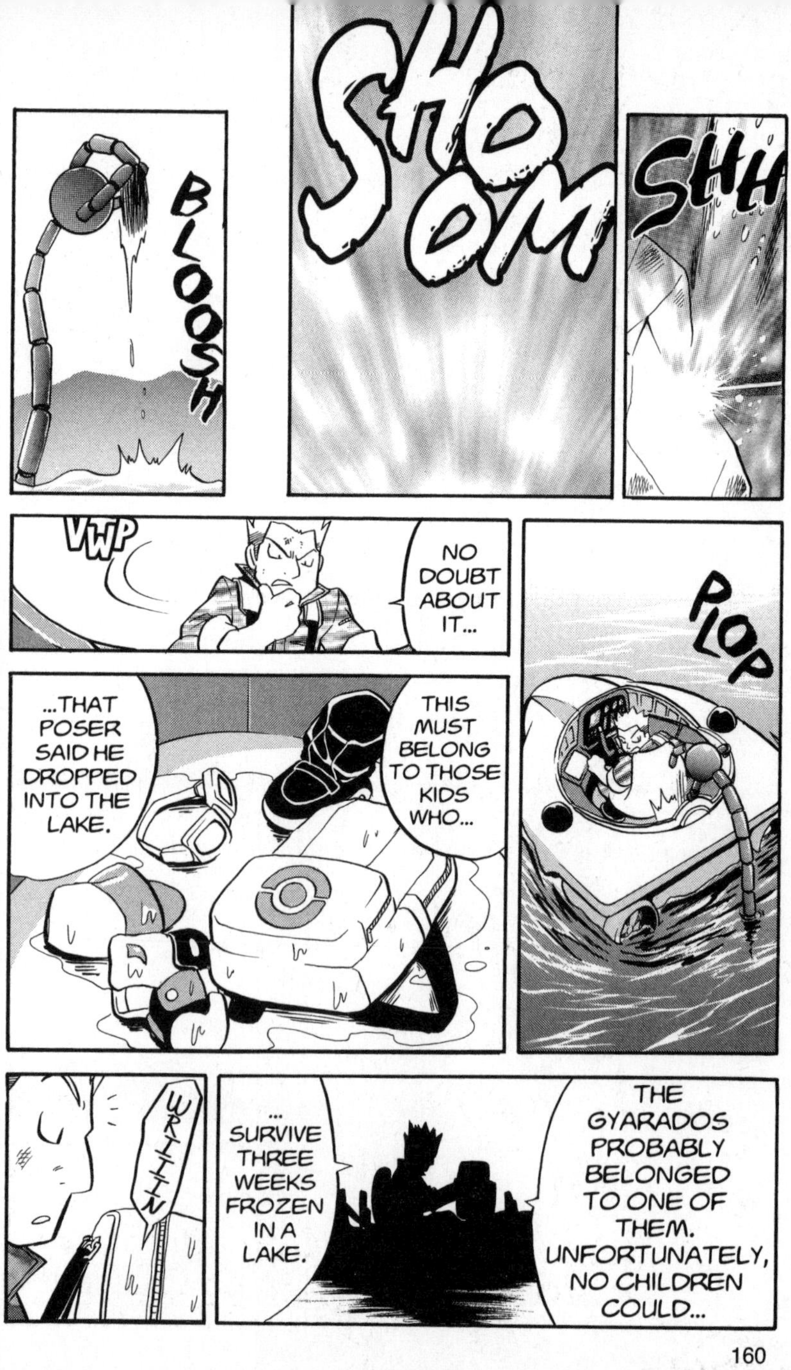
SHH
SHOOM
BLOOSH
PLOP
NO DOUBT ABOUT IT...
VWP
THIS MUST BELONG TO THOSE KIDS WHO...
...THAT POSER SAID HE DROPPED INTO THE LAKE.
THE GYARADOS PROBABLY BELONGED TO ONE OF THEM. UNFORTUNATELY, NO CHILDREN COULD...
... SURVIVE THREE WEEKS FROZEN IN A LAKE.
WRIIIIN

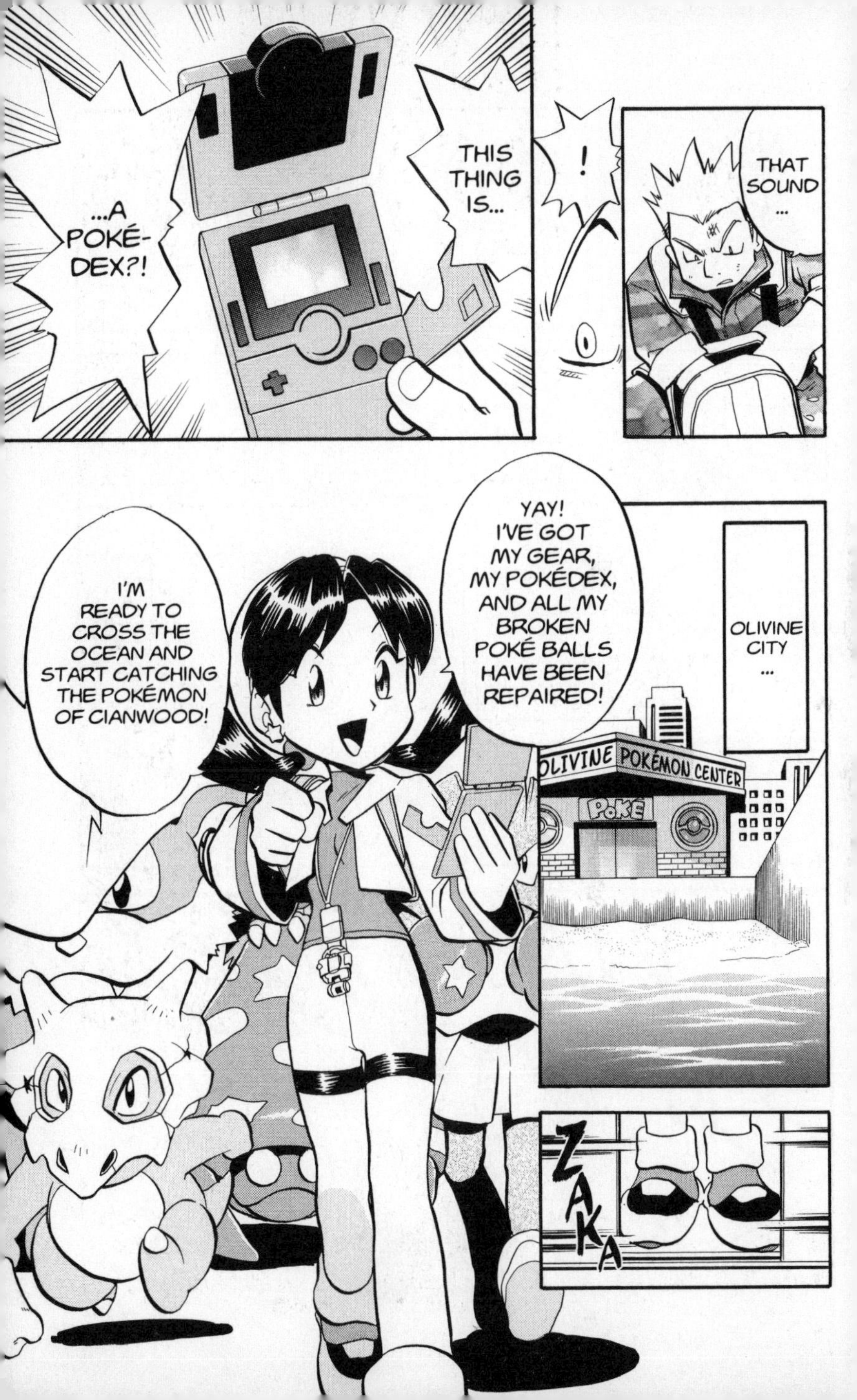
THAT SOUND ...
!
THIS THING IS...
...A POKÉDEX?!
OLIVINE CITY ...
OLIVINE POKÉMON CENTER
POKé
ZAKA
YAY! I'VE GOT MY GEAR, MY POKÉDEX, AND ALL MY BROKEN POKÉ BALLS HAVE BEEN REPAIRED!
I'M READY TO CROSS THE OCEAN AND START CATCHING THE POKÉMON OF CIANWOOD!

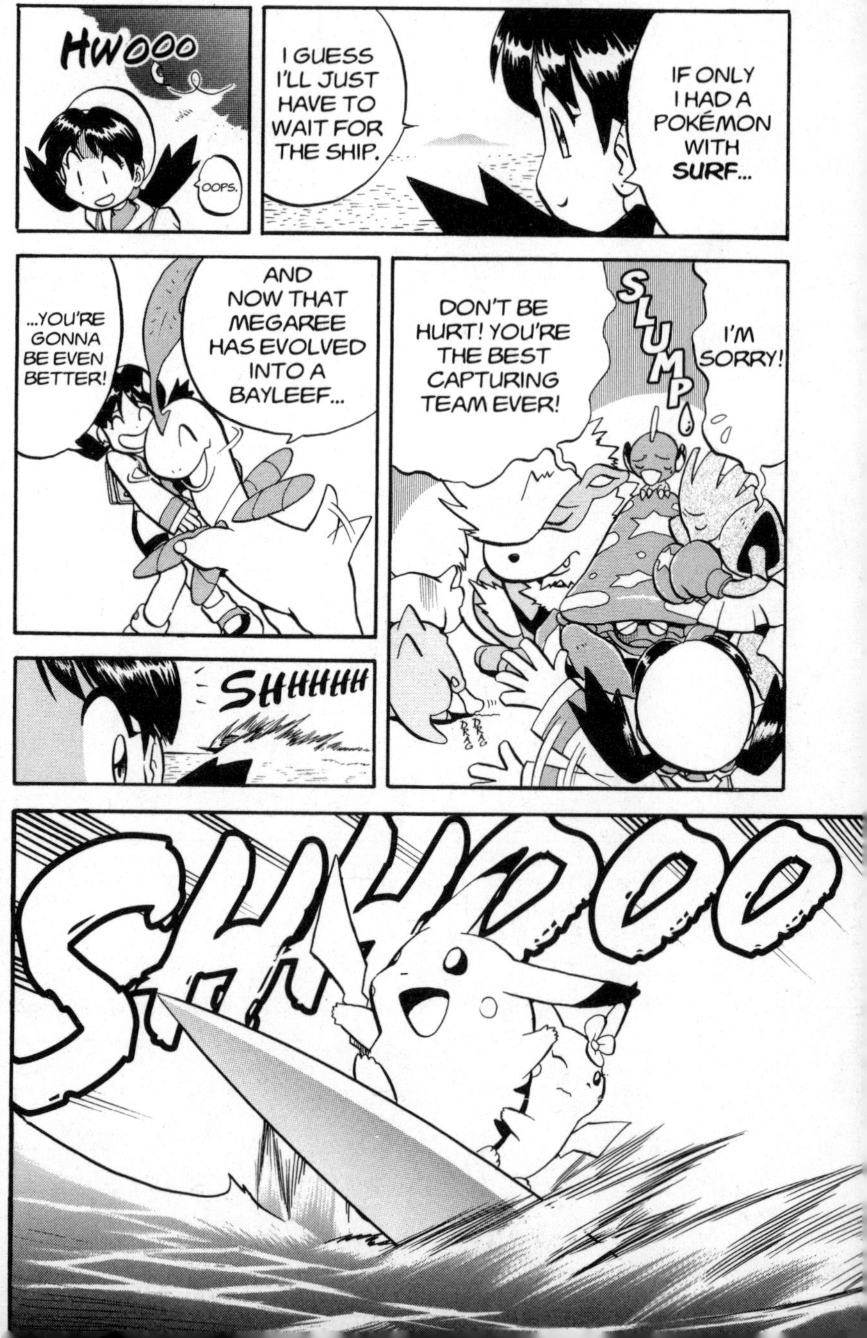
IF ONLY I HAD A POKÉMON WITH SURF...
I GUESS I'LL JUST HAVE TO WAIT FOR THE SHIP.
HWOOO
OOPS.
SLUMP
I'M SORRY!
DON'T BE HURT! YOU'RE THE BEST CAPTURING TEAM EVER!
DRAG DRAG
AND NOW THAT MEGAREE HAS EVOLVED INTO A BAYLEEF...
...YOU'RE GONNA BE EVEN BETTER!
SHHHHH
SHWOOO

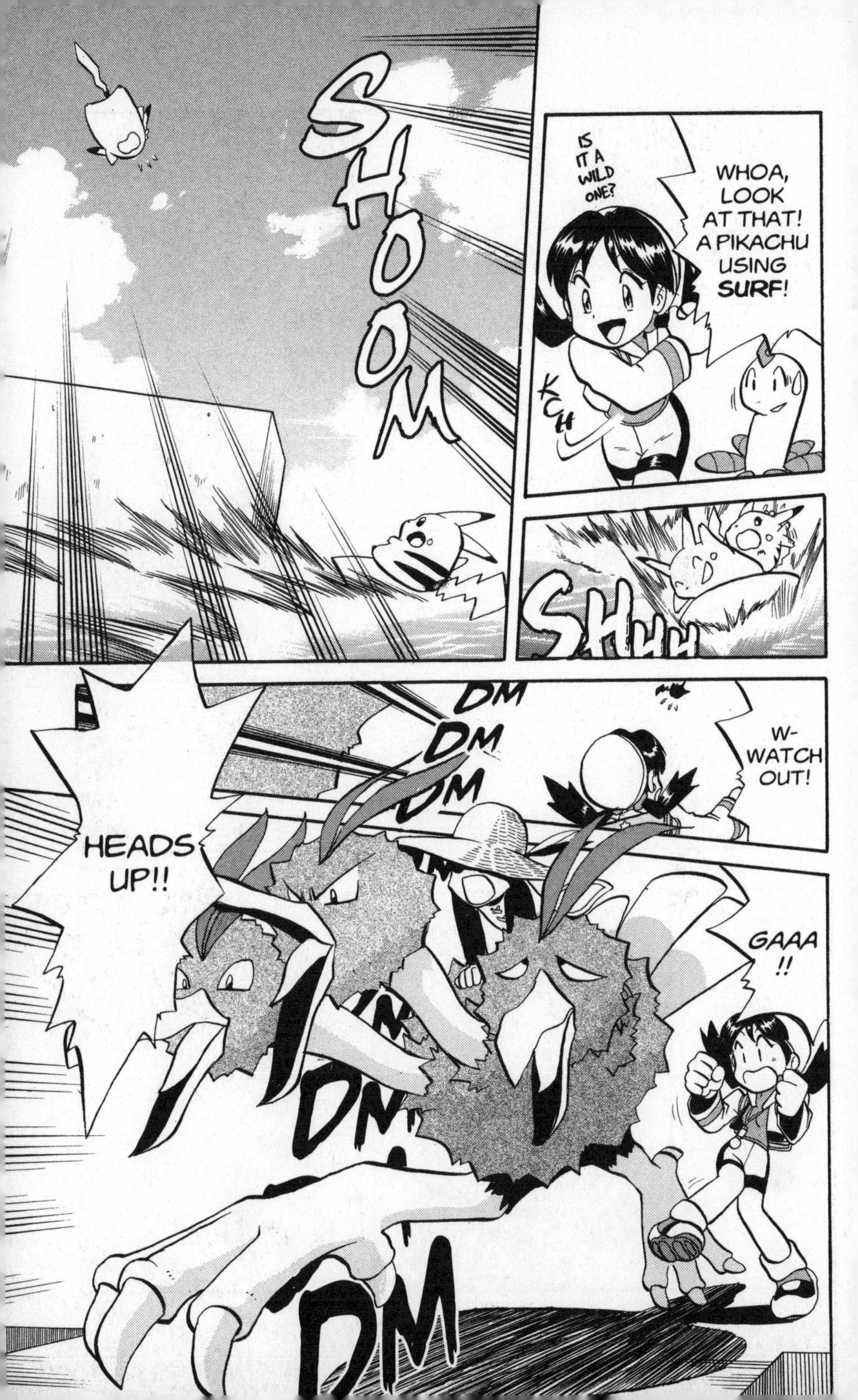
WHOA, LOOK AT THAT! A PIKACHU USING SURF!
IS IT A WILD ONE?
KCH
SHUH
SHOOM
W- WATCH OUT!
DM
DM
DM
GAAA !!
HEADS UP!!
DM
DM

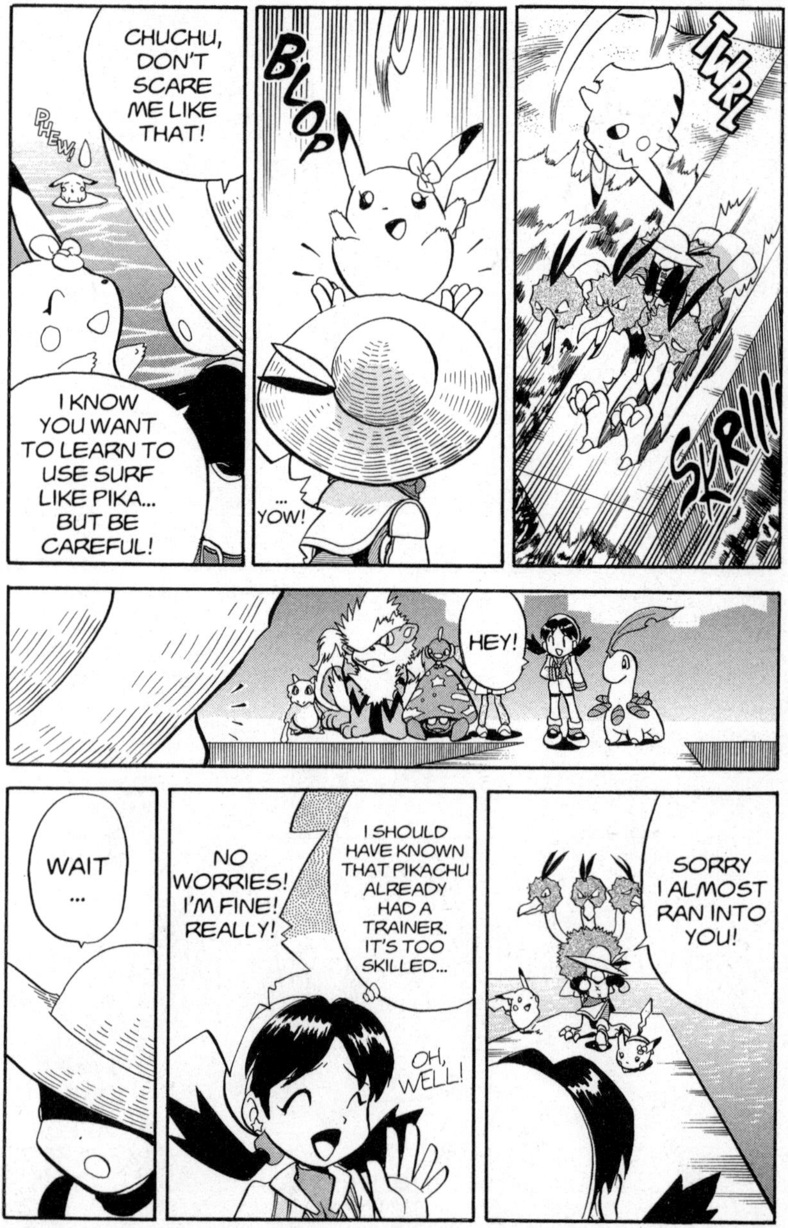
TWRL
SKRIII
BLOP
... YOW!
CHUCHU, DON'T SCARE ME LIKE THAT!
PHEW!
I KNOW YOU WANT TO LEARN TO USE SURF LIKE PIKA... BUT BE CAREFUL!
HEY!
SORRY I ALMOST RAN INTO YOU!
I SHOULD HAVE KNOWN THAT PIKACHU ALREADY HAD A TRAINER. IT'S TOO SKILLED...
NO WORRIES! I'M FINE! REALLY!
OH, WELL!
WAIT ...

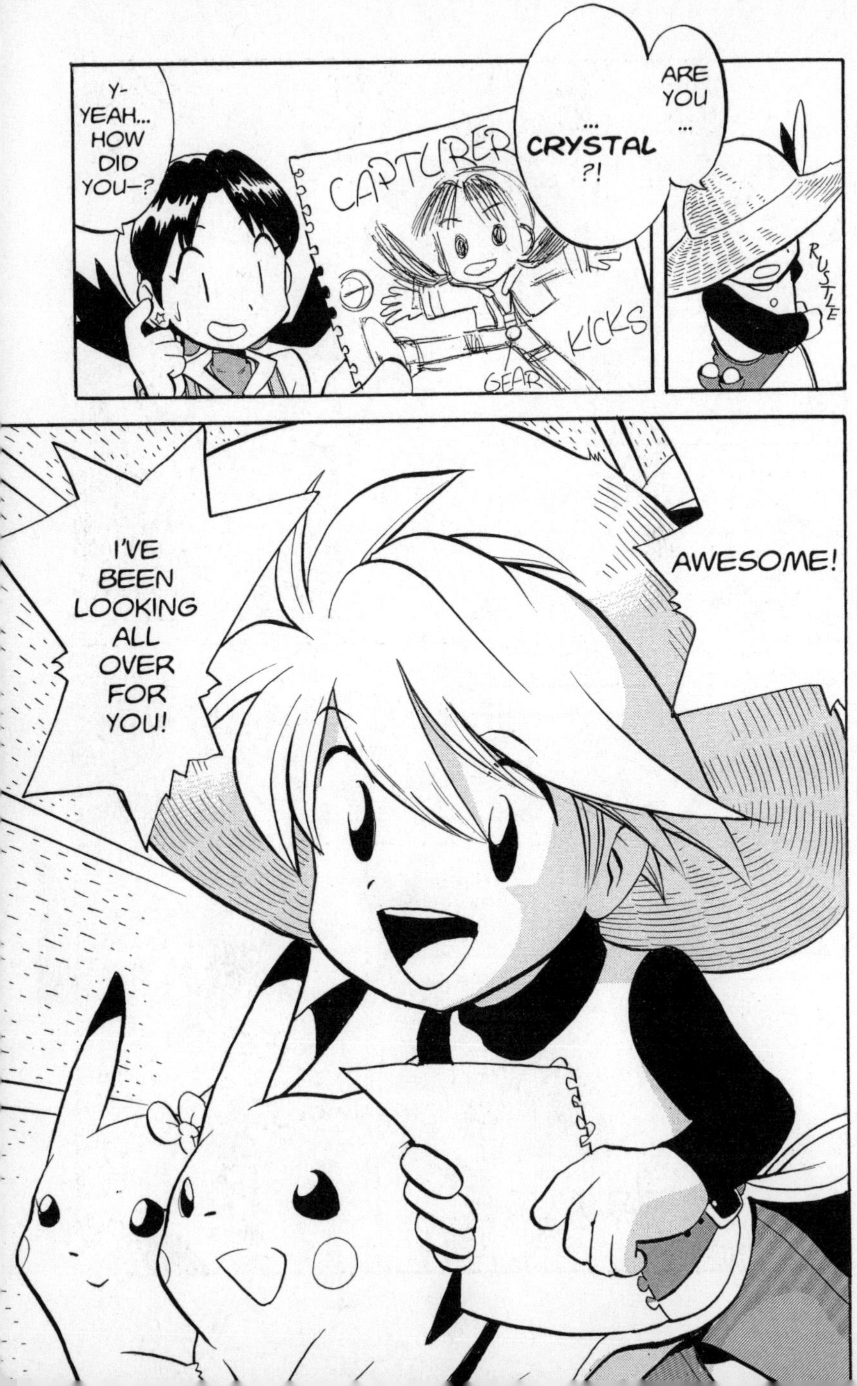
ARE YOU ...
... CRYSTAL ?!
RUSTLE
Y-YEAH... HOW DID YOU-?
CAPTURER
KICKS
GEAR
AWESOME!
I'VE BEEN LOOKING ALL OVER FOR YOU!

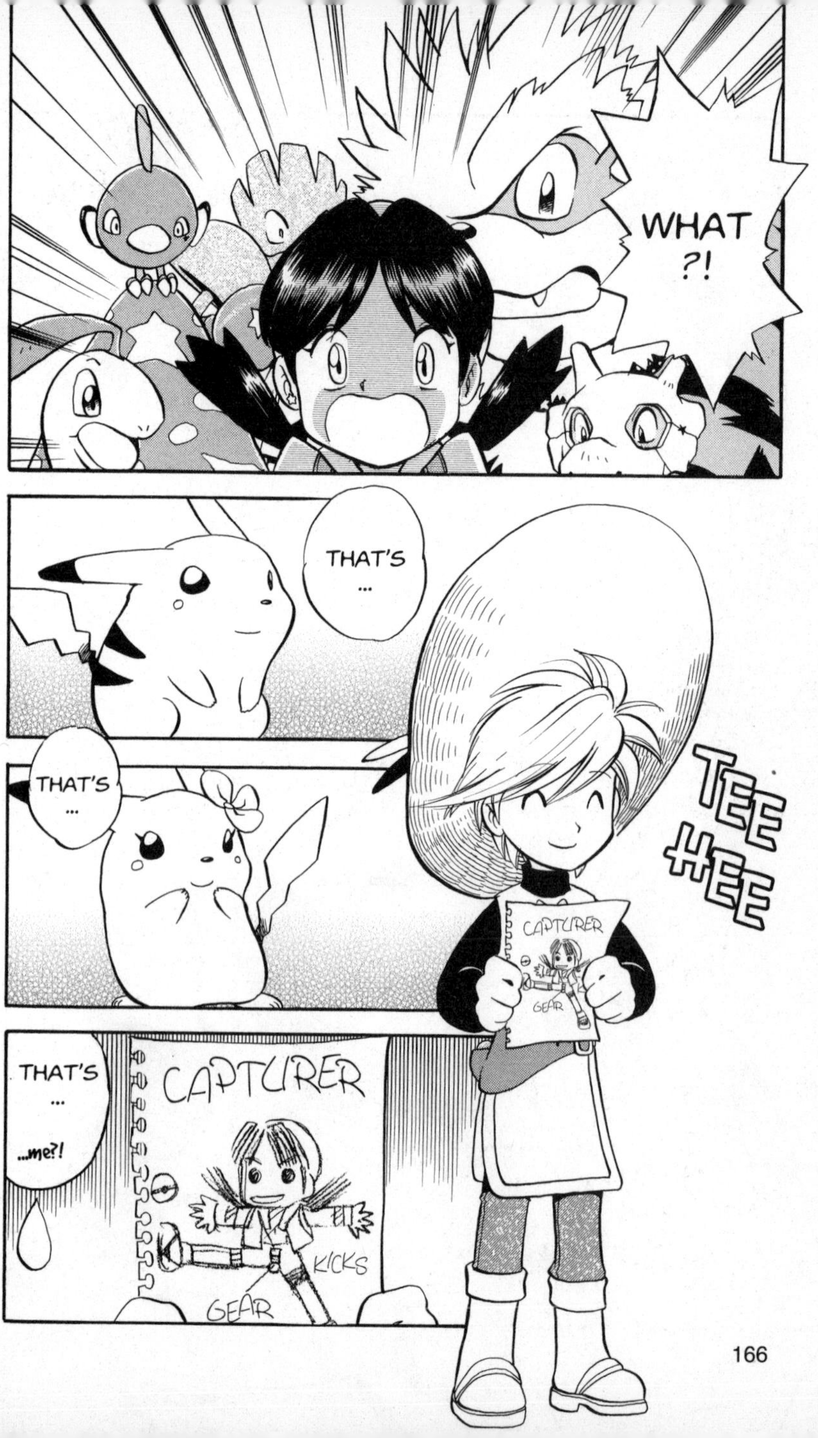
WHAT ?!
THAT'S ...
THAT'S ...
TEE HEE
CAPTURER
GEAR
THAT'S ...
...me?!
CAPTURER
KICKS
GEAR

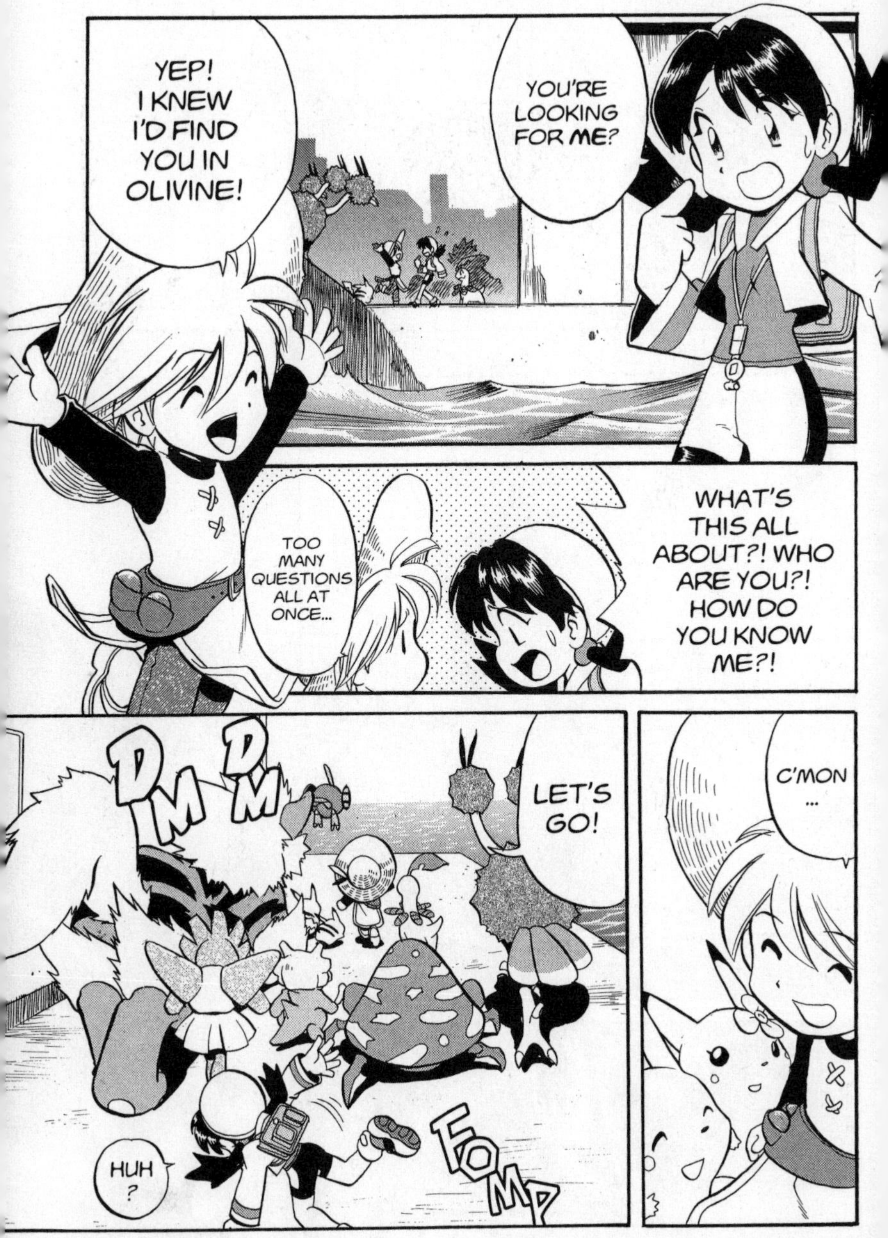
YOU'RE LOOKING FOR ME?
YEP! I KNEW I'D FIND YOU IN OLIVINE!
WHAT'S THIS ALL ABOUT?! WHO ARE YOU?! HOW DO YOU KNOW ME?!
TOO MANY QUESTIONS ALL AT ONCE...
C'MON ...
LET'S GO!
DM DM
HUH ?
FOMP

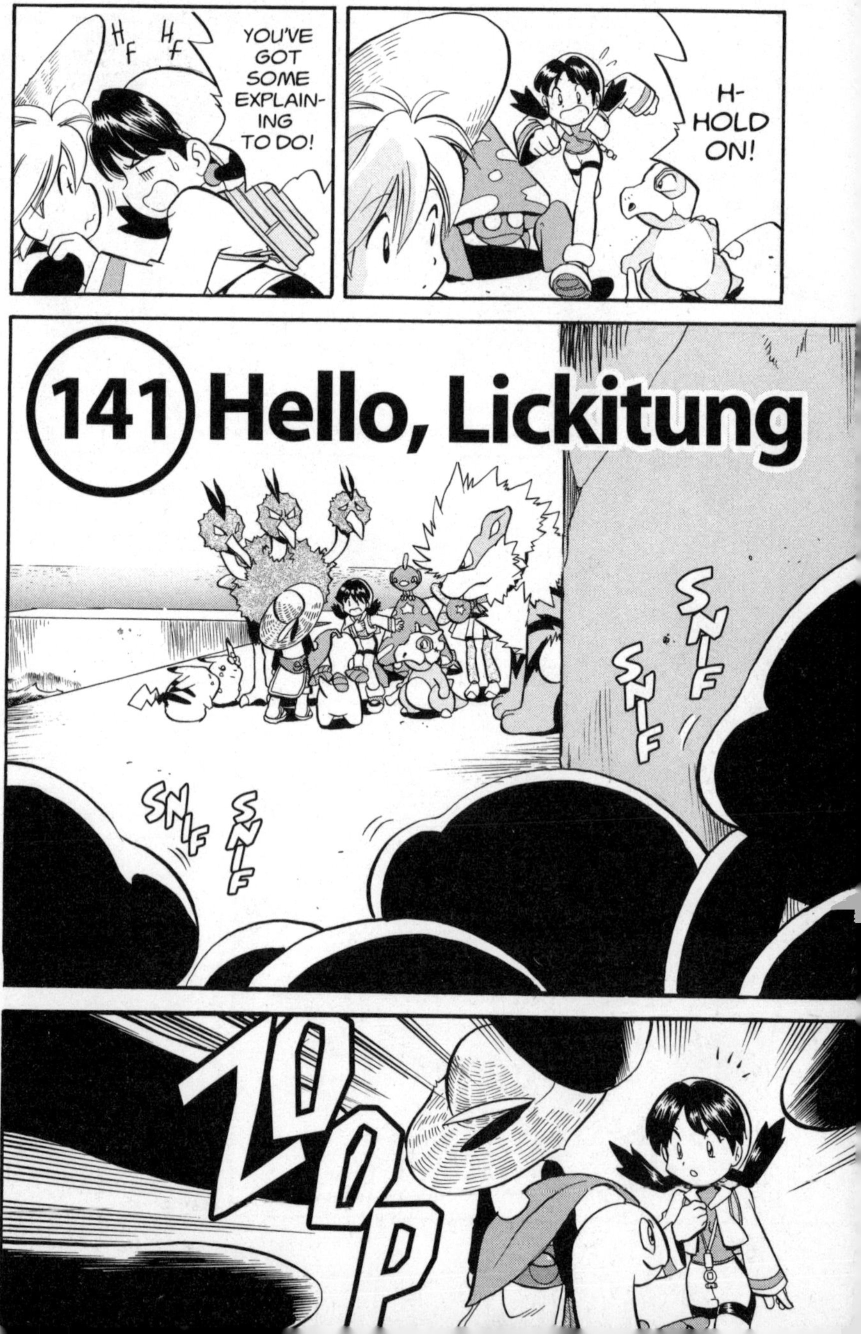
H-HOLD ON!
HF HF
YOU'VE GOT SOME EXPLAINING TO DO!
141 Hello, Lickitung
SNIF SNIF
SNIF SNIF
ZOOP

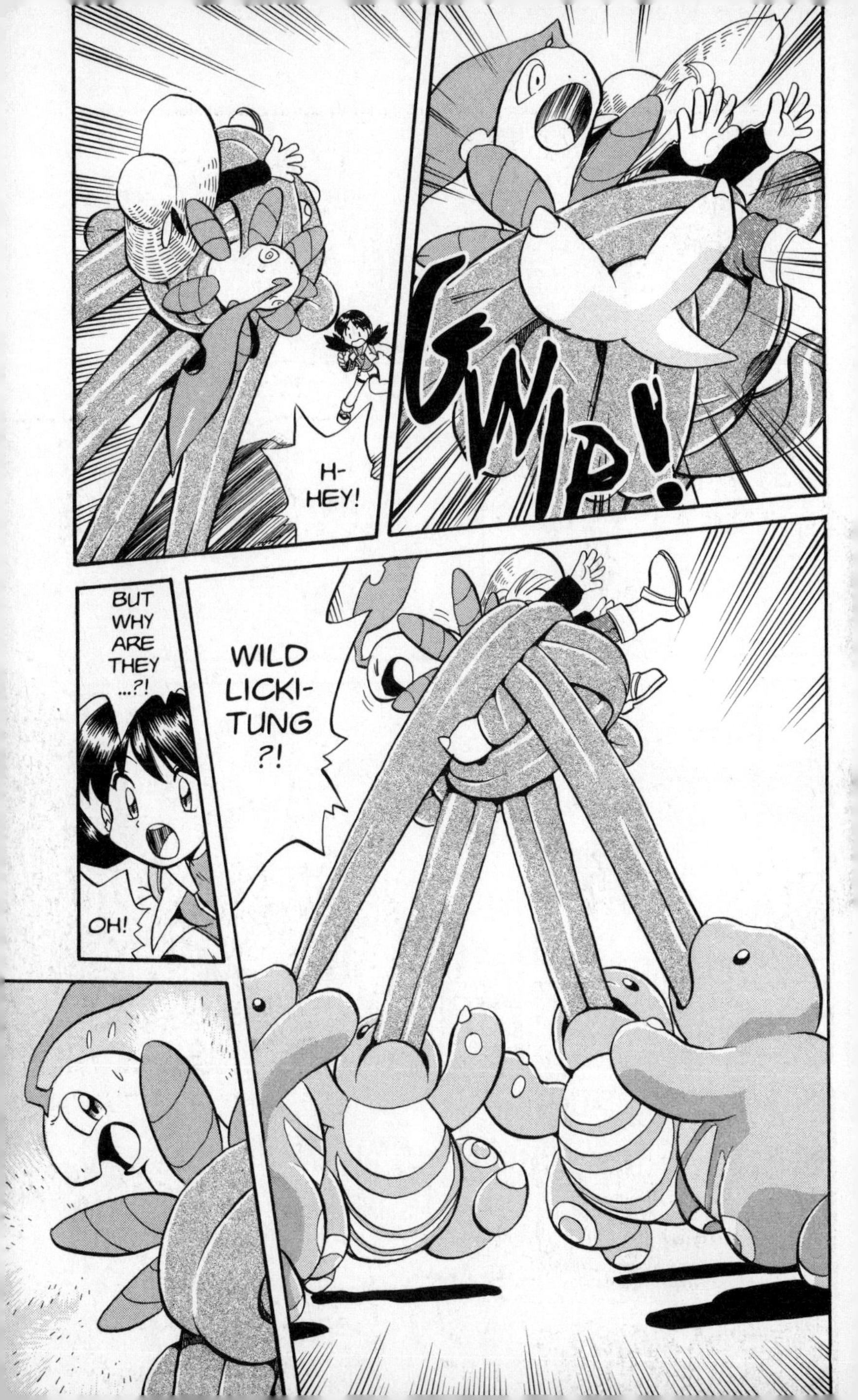
GWIP!
H-HEY!
WILD LICKI-TUNG?!
BUT WHY ARE THEY ...?!
OH!

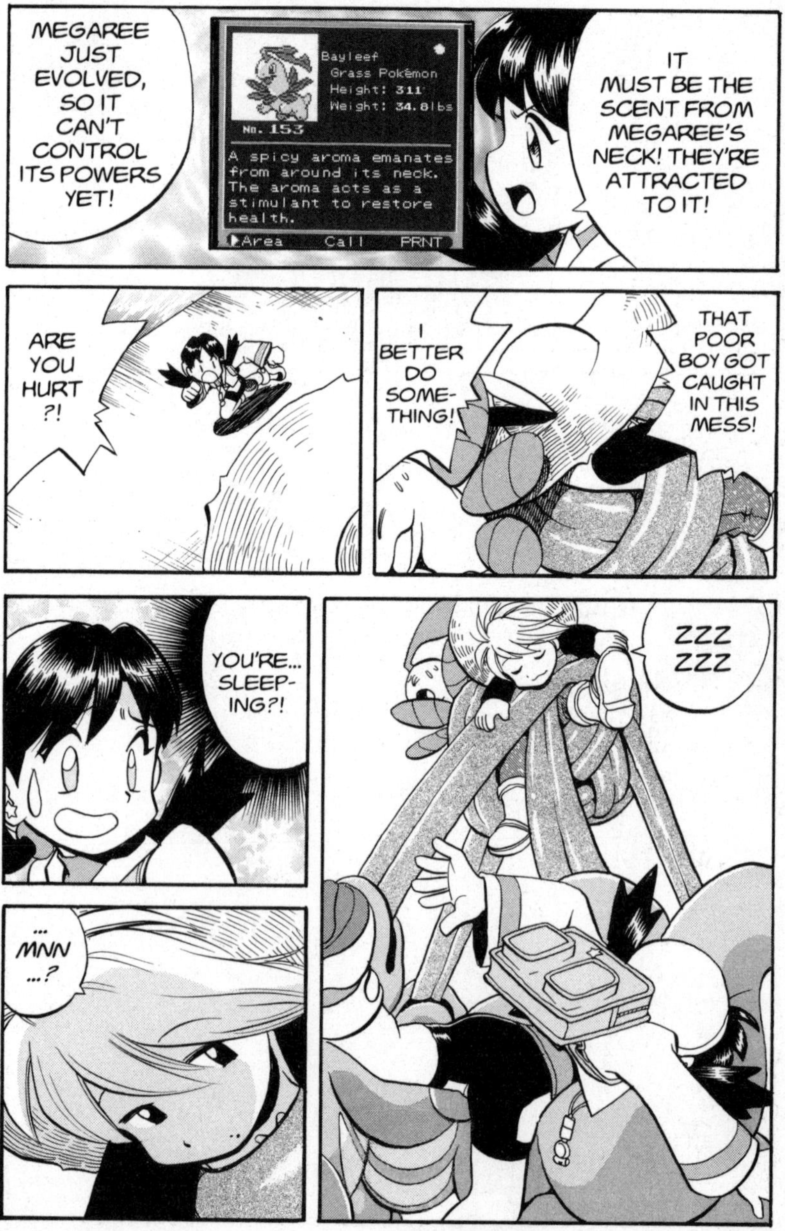
IT MUST BE THE SCENT FROM MEGAREE'S NECK! THEY'RE ATTRACTED TO IT!
Bayleef
Grass Pokémon
Height: 3'11"
Weight: 34.8lbs
No. 153
A spicy aroma emanates from around its neck. The aroma acts as a stimulant to restore health.
Area Call PRNT
MEGAREE JUST EVOLVED, SO IT CAN'T CONTROL ITS POWERS YET!
THAT POOR BOY GOT CAUGHT IN THIS MESS!
I BETTER DO SOME-THING!
ARE YOU HURT ?!
ZZZ ZZZ
YOU'RE... SLEEP-ING?!
... MNN ...?

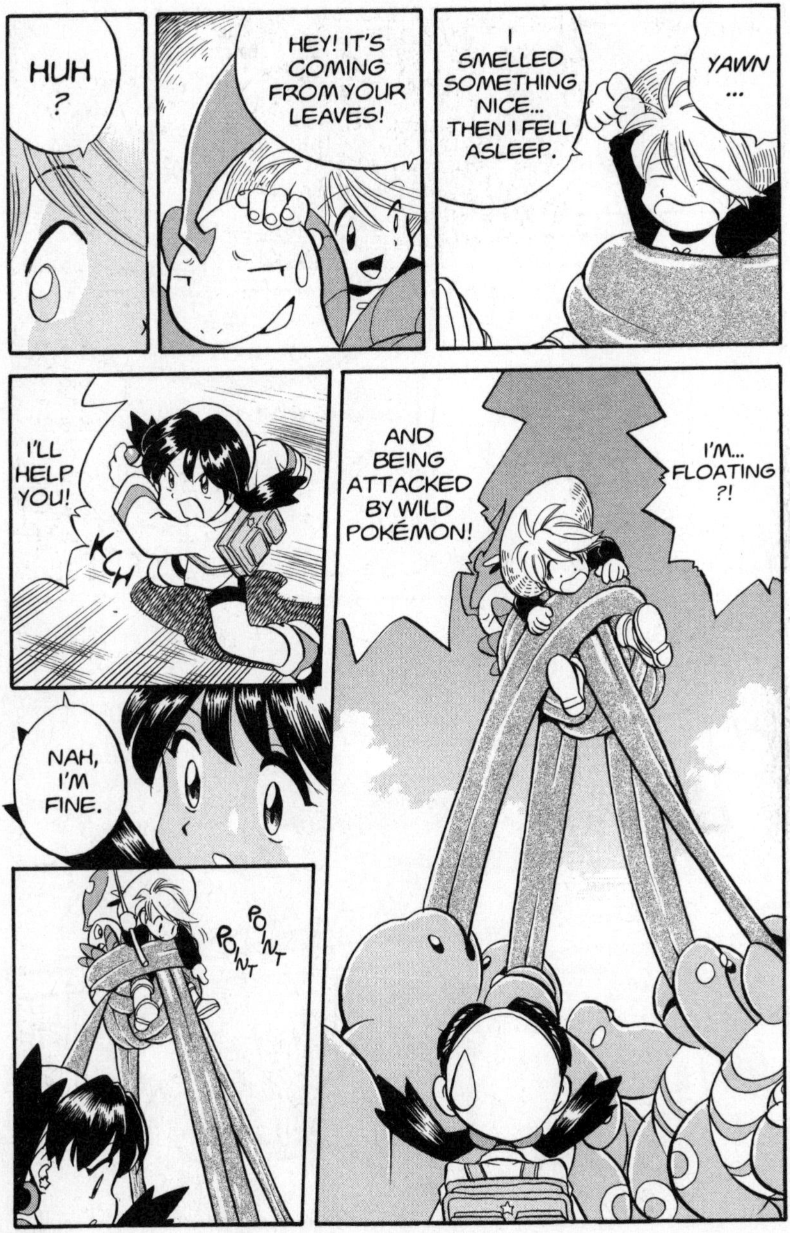
YAWN ...
I SMELLED SOMETHING NICE... THEN I FELL ASLEEP.
HEY! IT'S COMING FROM YOUR LEAVES!
HUH ?
I'M... FLOATING ?!
AND BEING ATTACKED BY WILD POKÉMON!
I'LL HELP YOU!
KCH
NAH, I'M FINE.
POINT
POINT

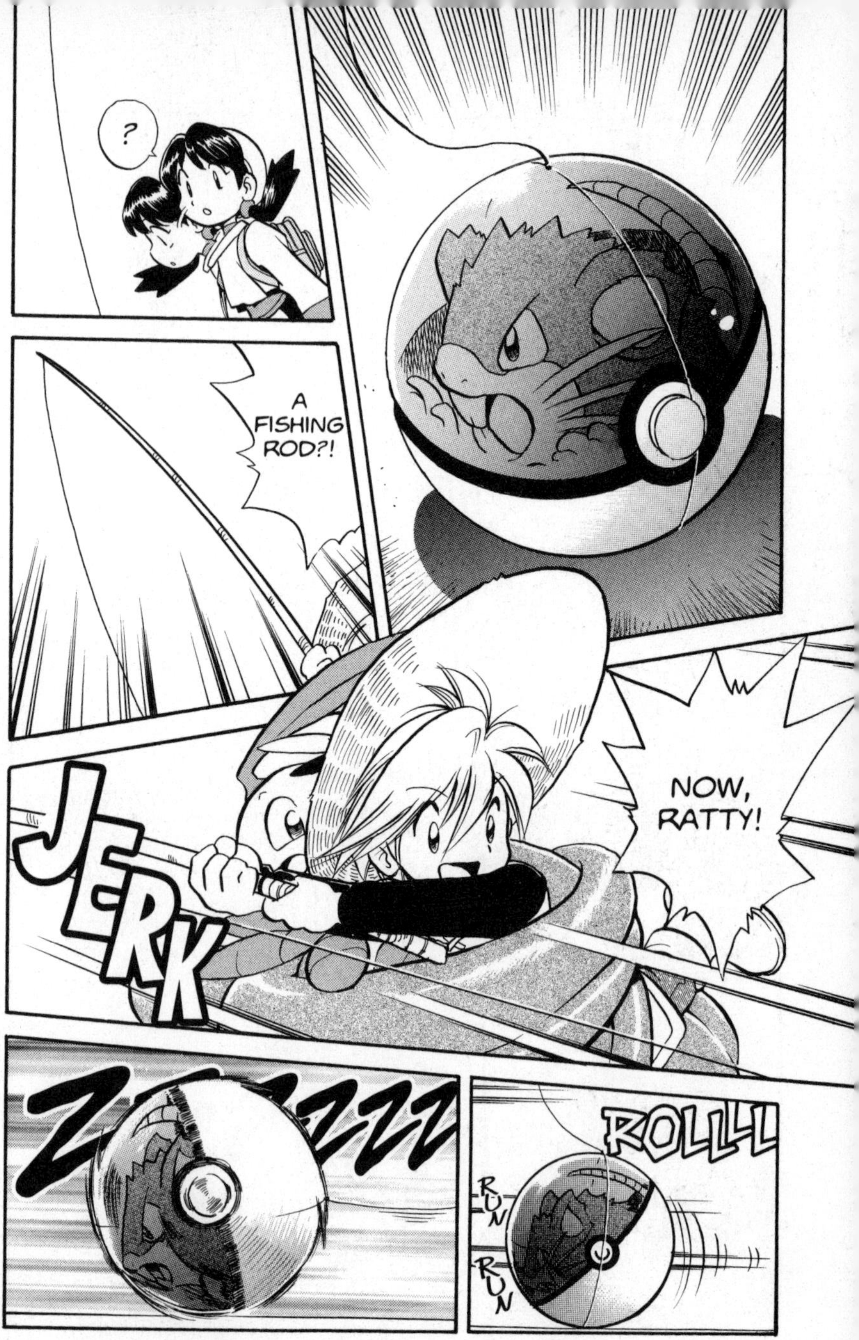
?
A FISHING ROD?!
NOW, RATTY!
JERK
ROLLLL
RUN
RUN

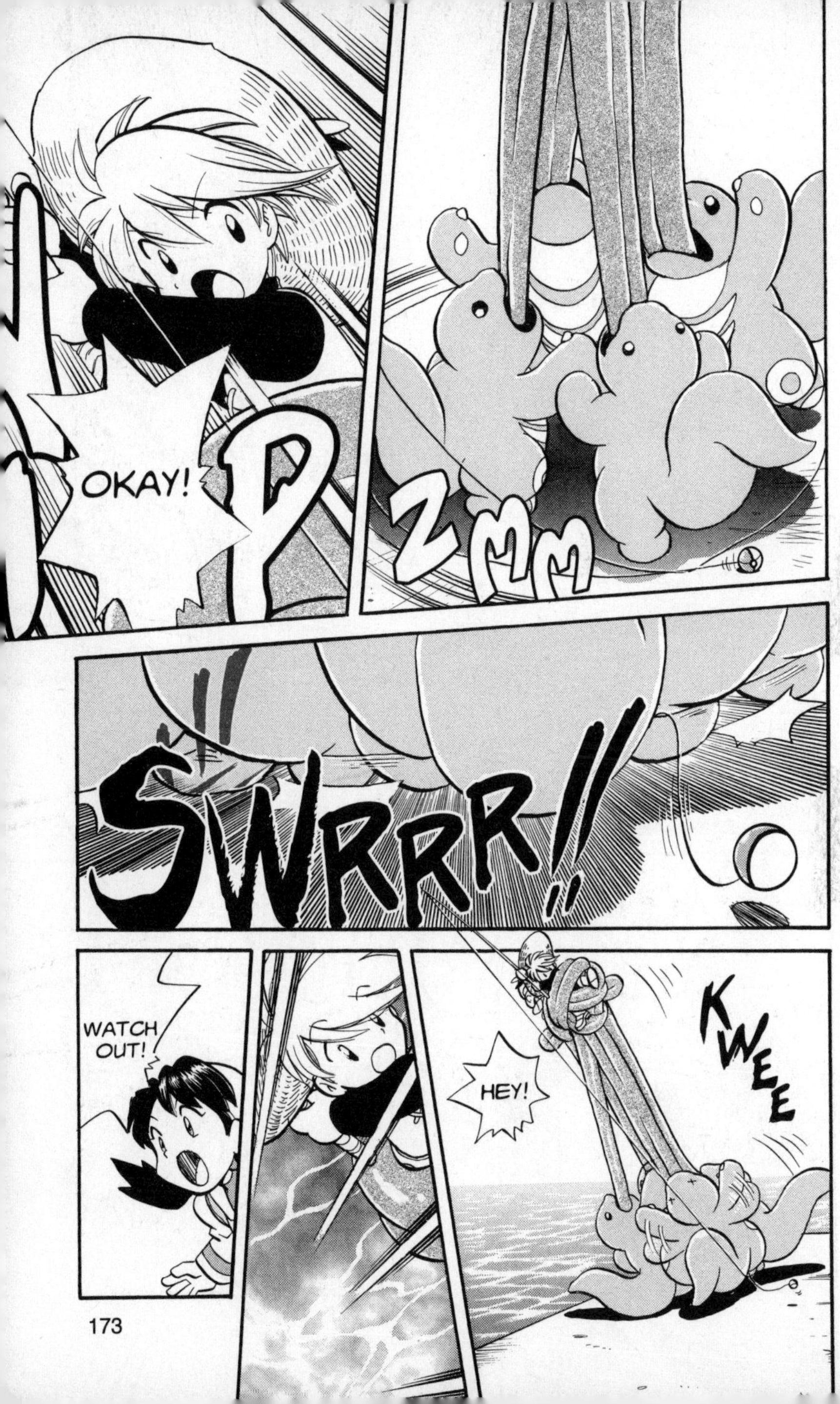
ZMM
OKAY!
P
SWRRR!!
KWEE
HEY!
WATCH OUT!

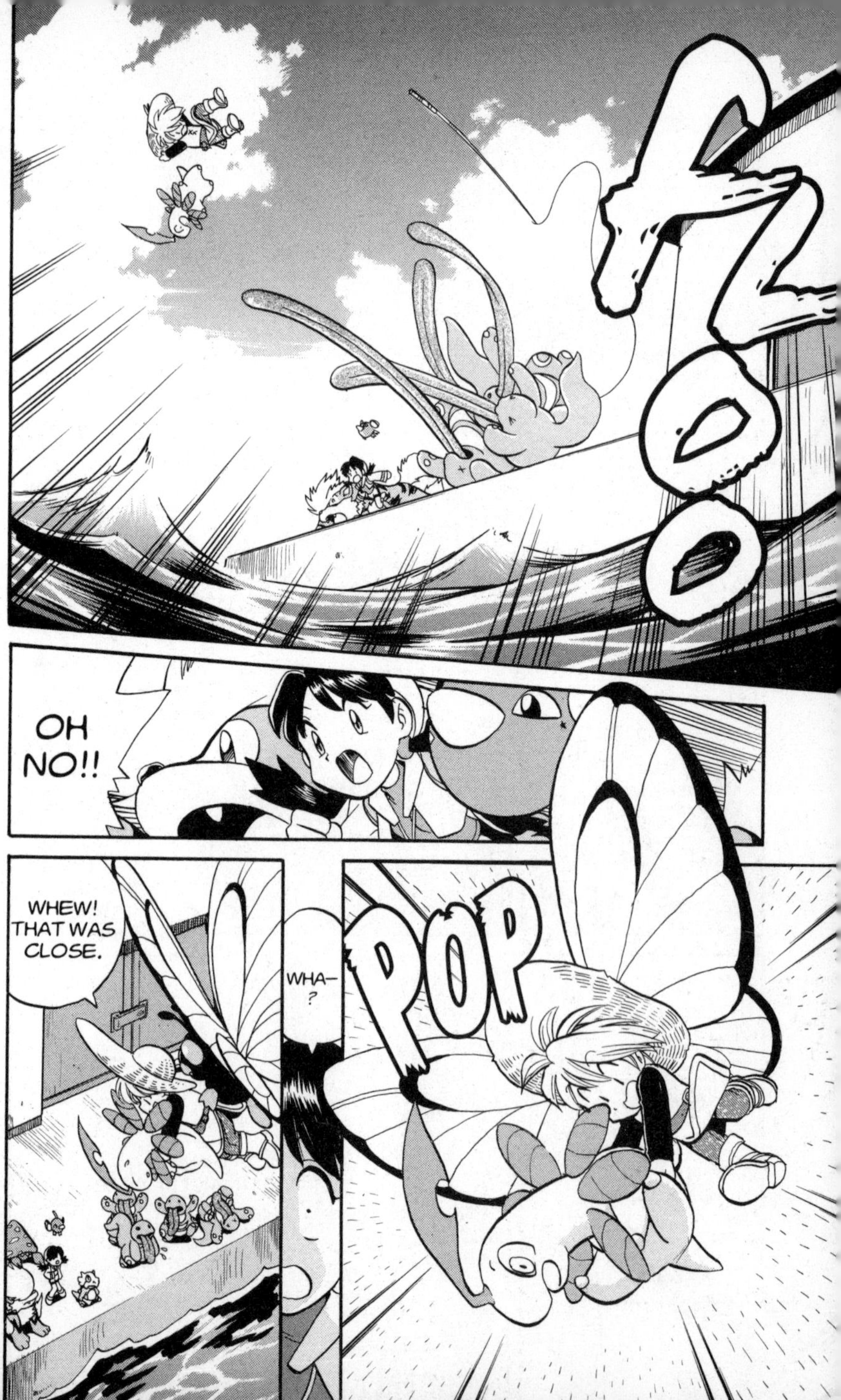
ZOOO
OH NO!!
POP
WHA-?
WHEW! THAT WAS CLOSE.

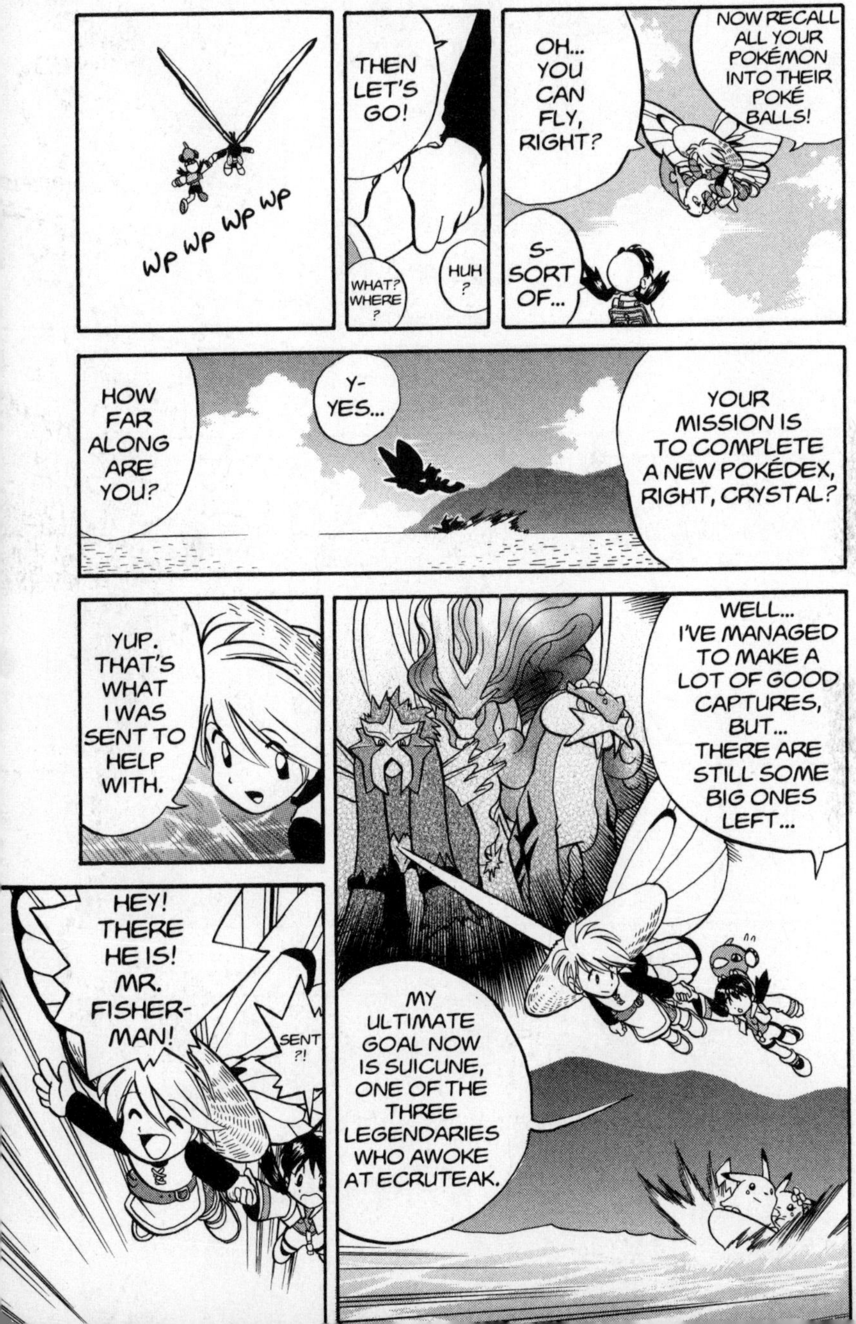
NOW RECALL ALL YOUR POKÉMON INTO THEIR POKÉ BALLS!
OH... YOU CAN FLY, RIGHT?
S-SORT OF...
THEN LET'S GO!
HUH?
WHAT? WHERE?
WP WP WP WP
YOUR MISSION IS TO COMPLETE A NEW POKÉDEX, RIGHT, CRYSTAL?
Y-YES...
HOW FAR ALONG ARE YOU?
WELL... I'VE MANAGED TO MAKE A LOT OF GOOD CAPTURES, BUT... THERE ARE STILL SOME BIG ONES LEFT...
MY ULTIMATE GOAL NOW IS SUICUNE, ONE OF THE THREE LEGENDARIES WHO AWOKE AT ECRUTEAK.
YUP. THAT'S WHAT I WAS SENT TO HELP WITH.
HEY! THERE HE IS! MR. FISHERMAN!
SENT ?!

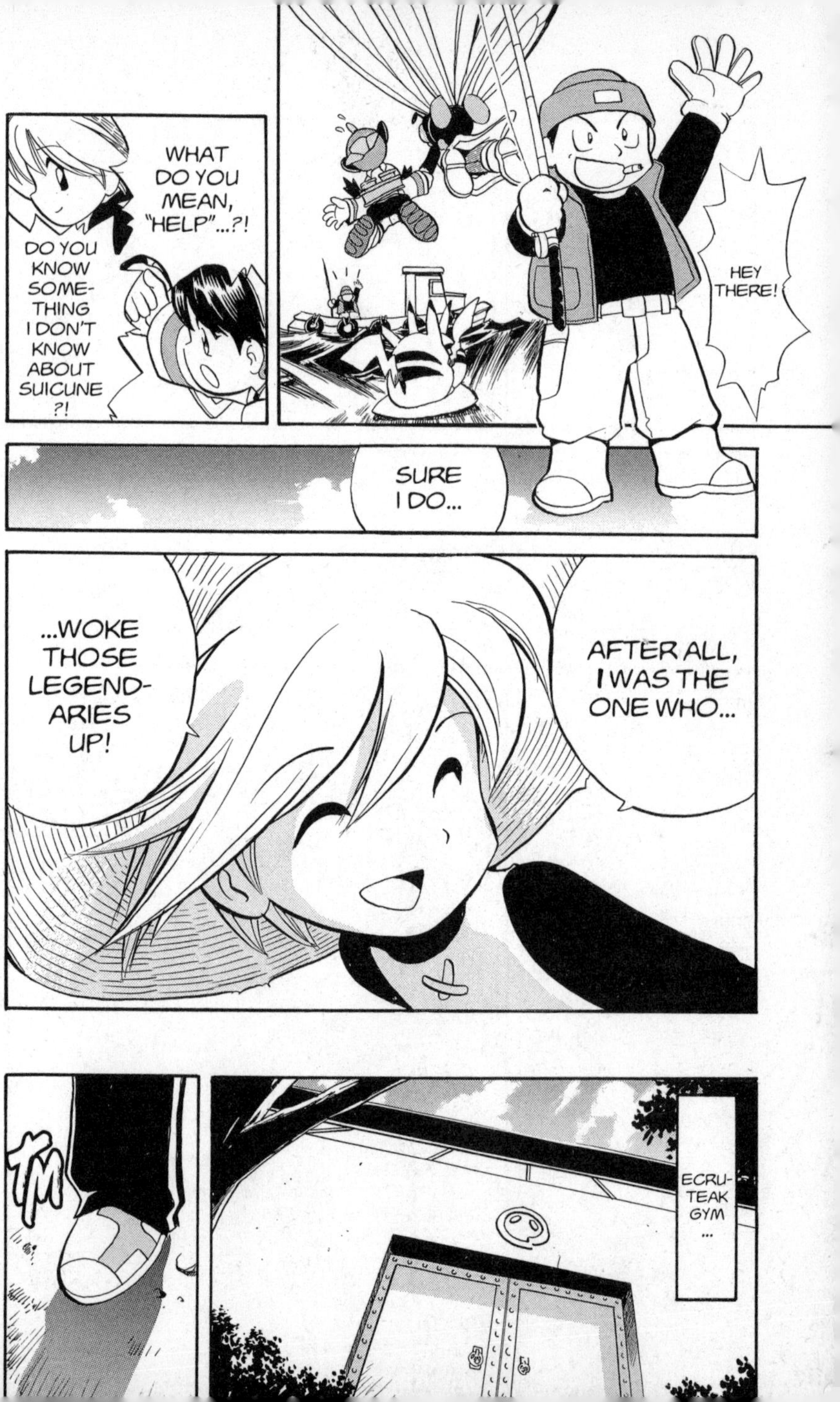
HEY THERE!
WHAT DO YOU MEAN, "HELP"...?!
DO YOU KNOW SOMETHING I DON'T KNOW ABOUT SUICUNE?!
SURE I DO...
AFTER ALL, I WAS THE ONE WHO...
...WOKE THOSE LEGENDARIES UP!
ECRUTEAK GYM ...
TM

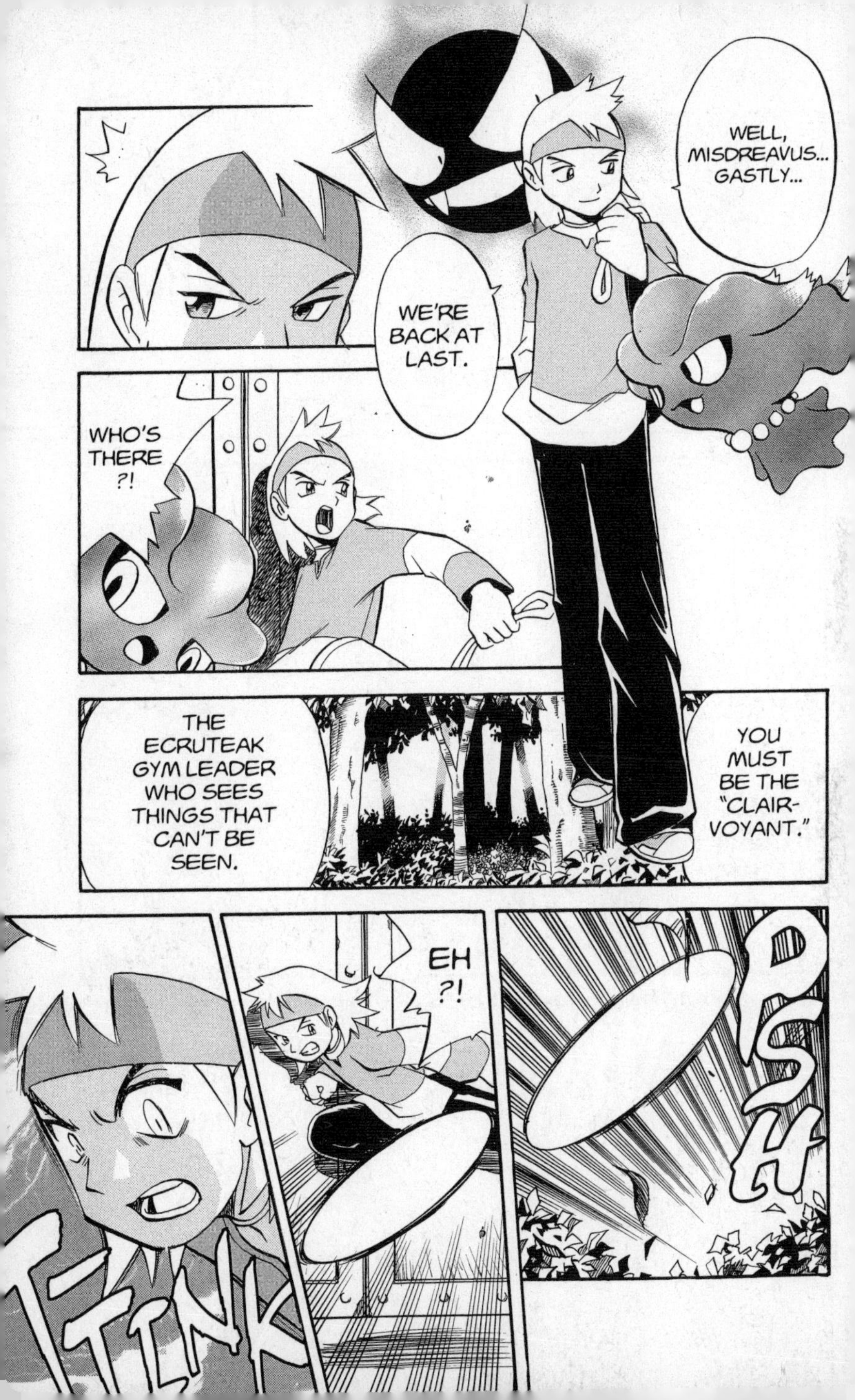
WELL, MISDREAVUS... GASTLY...
WE'RE BACK AT LAST.
WHO'S THERE ?!
YOU MUST BE THE "CLAIR-VOYANT."
THE ECRUTEAK GYM LEADER WHO SEES THINGS THAT CAN'T BE SEEN.
PSH
EH ?!
TINK

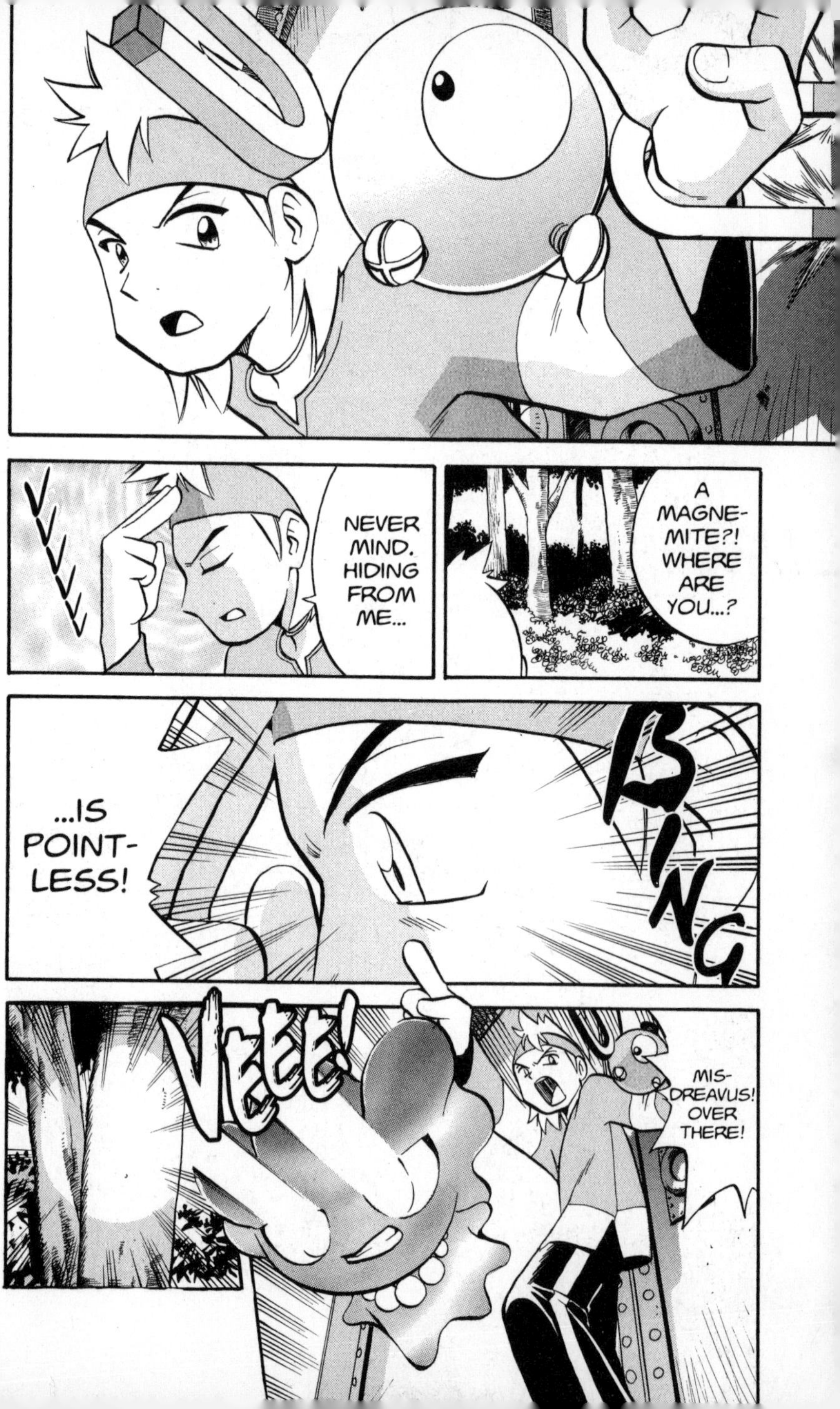
A MAGNEMITE?! WHERE ARE YOU...?
NEVER MIND. HIDING FROM ME...
BING
...IS POINTLESS!
MIS-DREAVUS! OVER THERE!
VEEE!

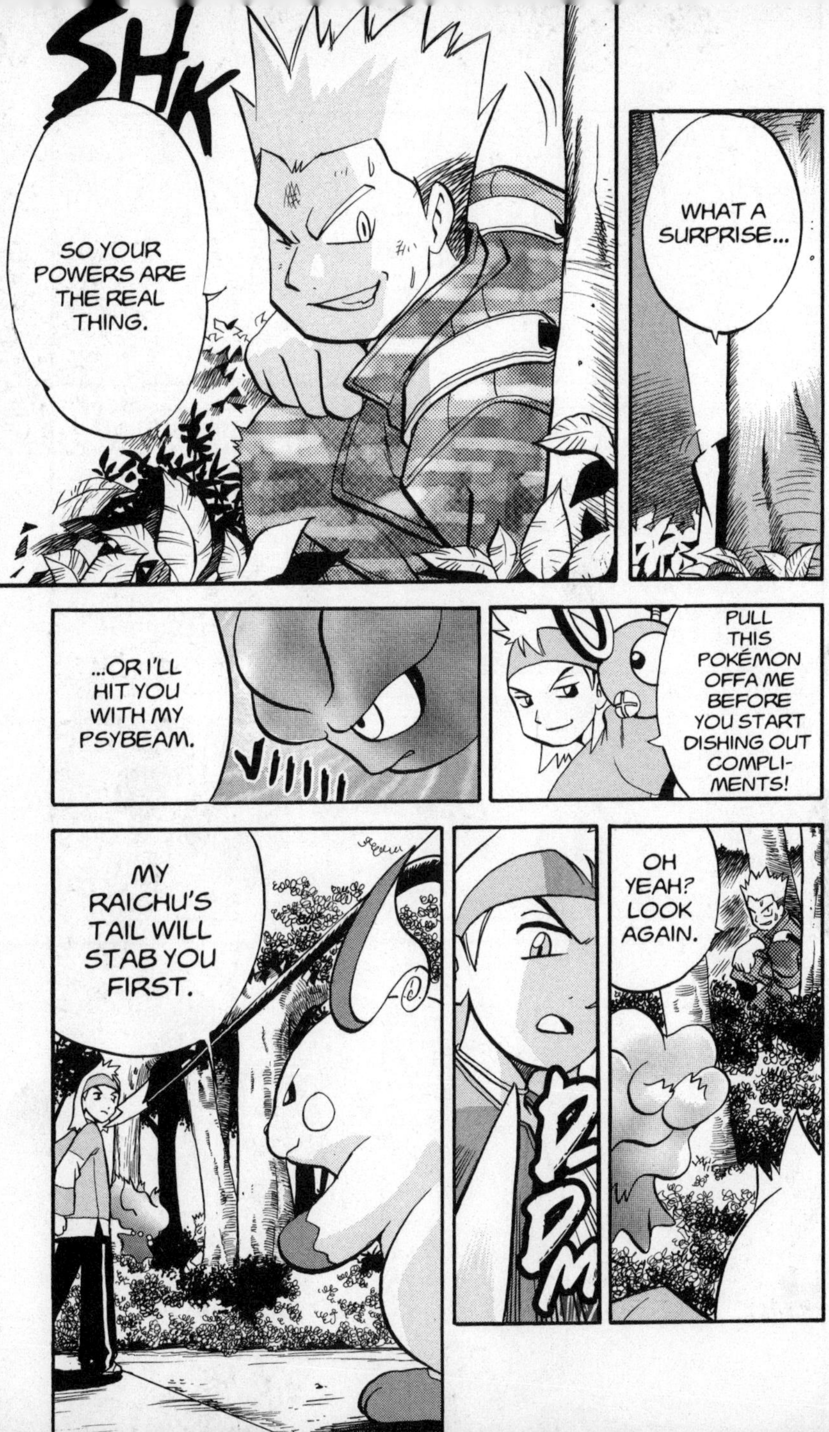
WHAT A SURPRISE...
SHK
SO YOUR POWERS ARE THE REAL THING.
PULL THIS POKÉMON OFFA ME BEFORE YOU START DISHING OUT COMPLI-MENTS!
...OR I'LL HIT YOU WITH MY PSYBEAM.
OH YEAH? LOOK AGAIN.
MY RAICHU'S TAIL WILL STAB YOU FIRST.

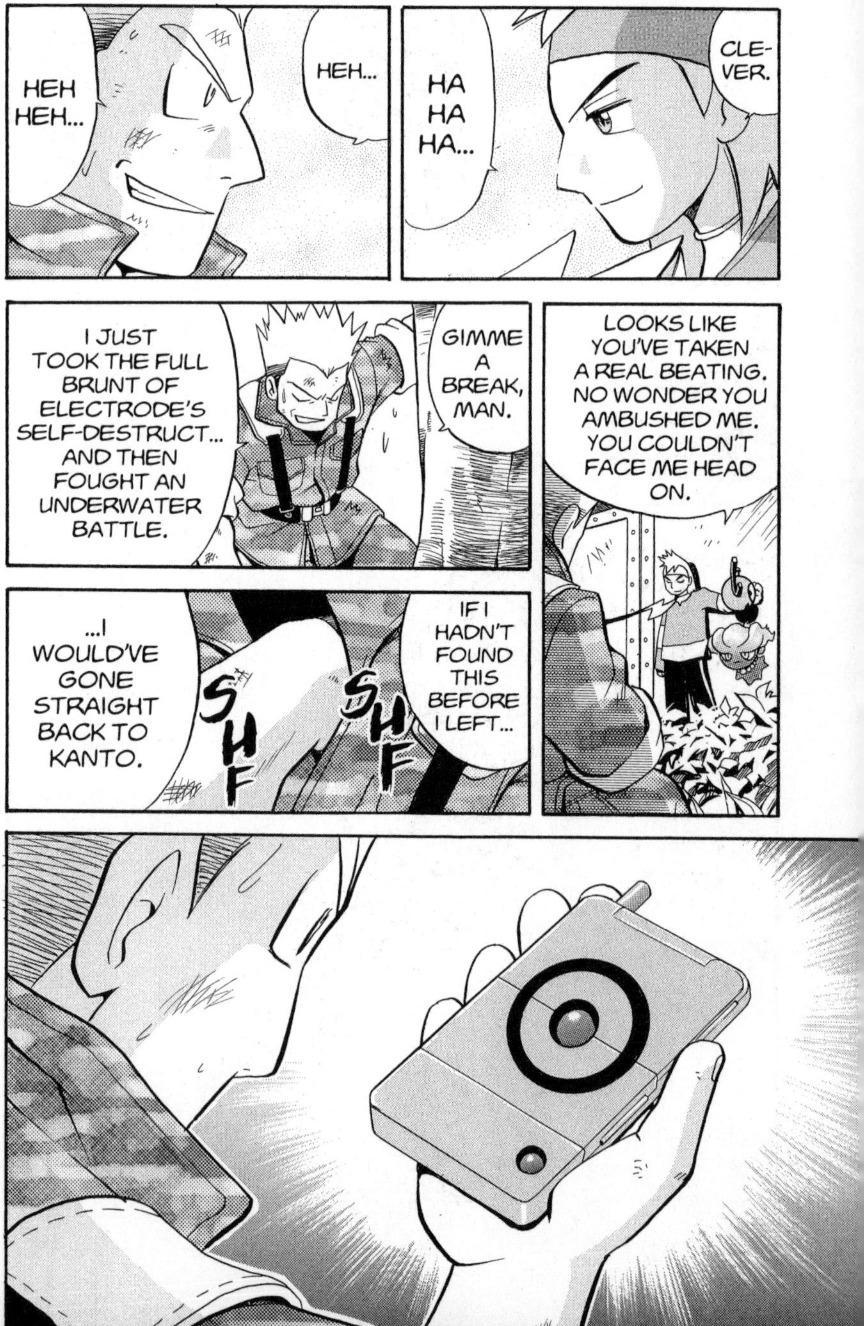
CLE-VER.
HA HA HA...
HEH...
HEH HEH...
LOOKS LIKE YOU'VE TAKEN A REAL BEATING. NO WONDER YOU AMBUSHED ME. YOU COULDN'T FACE ME HEAD ON.
GIMME A BREAK, MAN.
I JUST TOOK THE FULL BRUNT OF ELECTRODE'S SELF-DESTRUCT... AND THEN FOUGHT AN UNDERWATER BATTLE.
IF I HADN'T FOUND THIS BEFORE I LEFT...
SHF
SHF
...I WOULD'VE GONE STRAIGHT BACK TO KANTO.

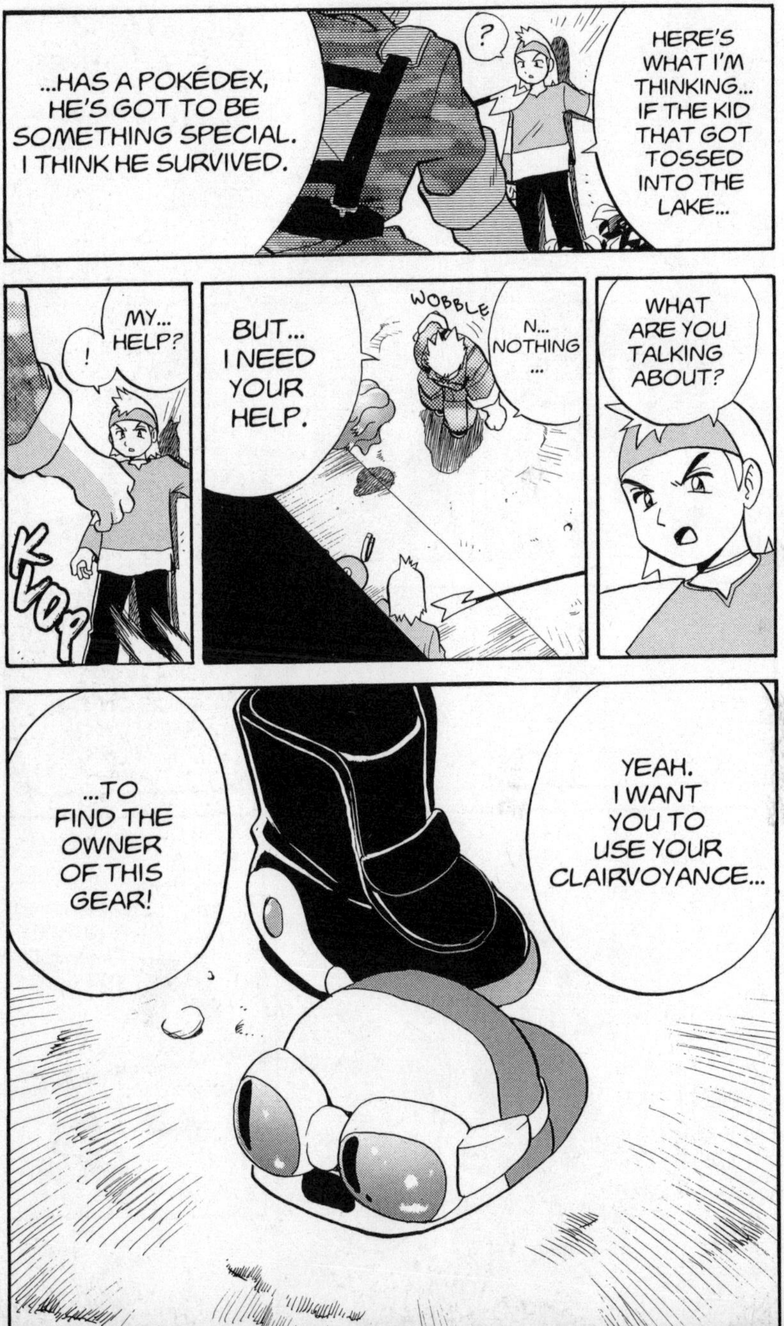
HERE'S WHAT I'M THINKING... IF THE KID THAT GOT TOSSED INTO THE LAKE...
?
...HAS A POKÉDEX, HE'S GOT TO BE SOMETHING SPECIAL. I THINK HE SURVIVED.
WHAT ARE YOU TALKING ABOUT?
N... NOTHING ...
WOBBLE
BUT... I NEED YOUR HELP.
MY... HELP?
!
KVOP
YEAH. I WANT YOU TO USE YOUR CLAIRVOYANCE...
...TO FIND THE OWNER OF THIS GEAR!

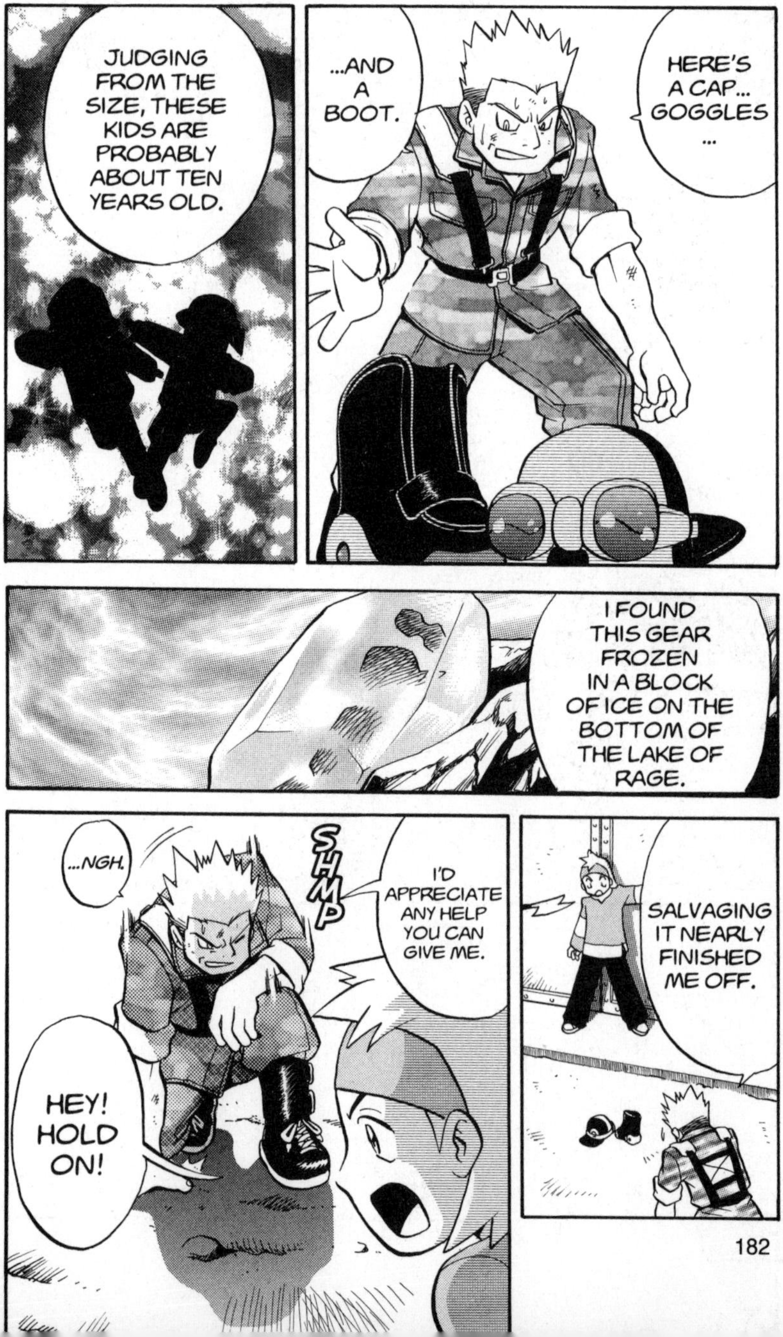
HERE'S A CAP... GOGGLES ...
...AND A BOOT.
JUDGING FROM THE SIZE, THESE KIDS ARE PROBABLY ABOUT TEN YEARS OLD.
I FOUND THIS GEAR FROZEN IN A BLOCK OF ICE ON THE BOTTOM OF THE LAKE OF RAGE.
SALVAGING IT NEARLY FINISHED ME OFF.
SHMP
I'D APPRECIATE ANY HELP YOU CAN GIVE ME.
...NGH.
HEY! HOLD ON!

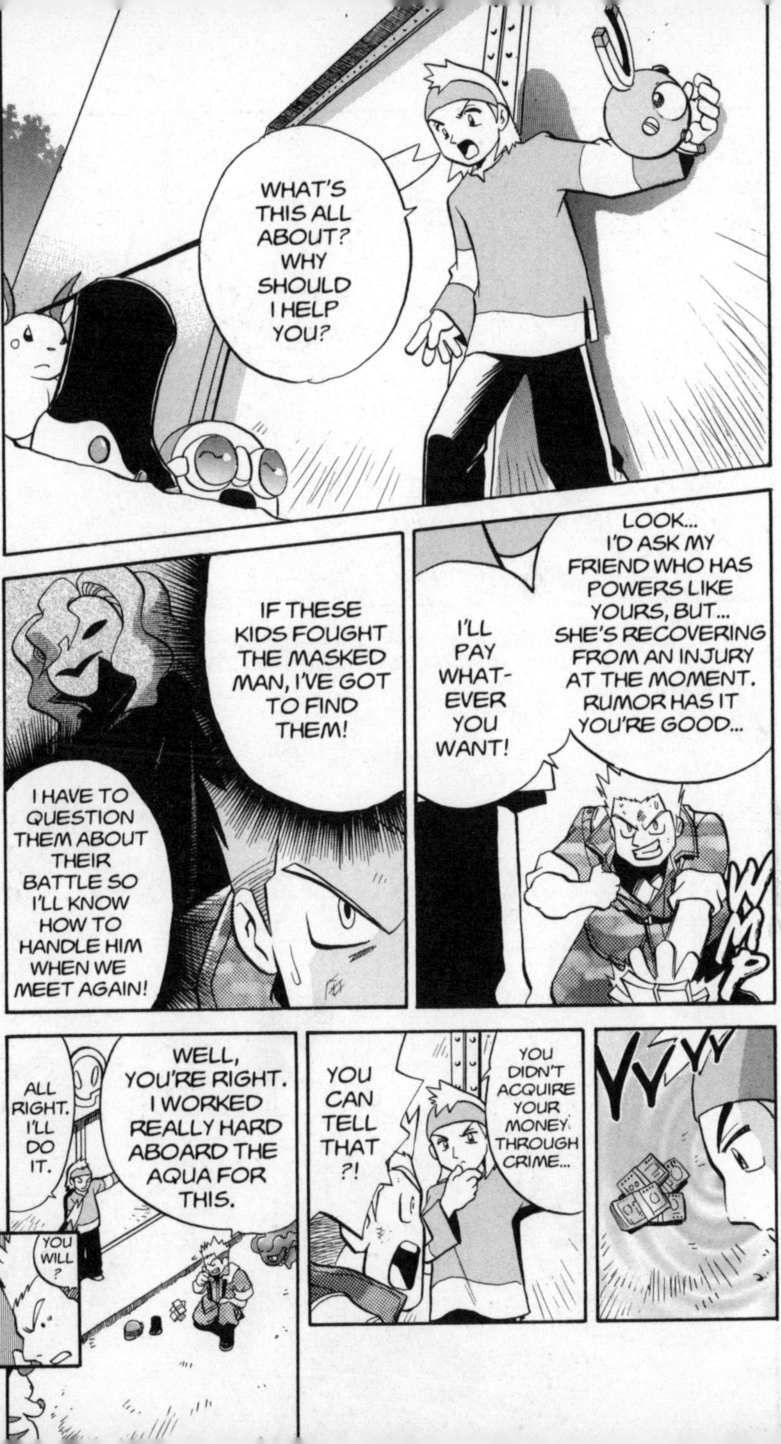
WHAT'S THIS ALL ABOUT? WHY SHOULD I HELP YOU?
LOOK... I'D ASK MY FRIEND WHO HAS POWERS LIKE YOURS, BUT... SHE'S RECOVERING FROM AN INJURY AT THE MOMENT. RUMOR HAS IT YOU'RE GOOD...
I'LL PAY WHAT-EVER YOU WANT!
IF THESE KIDS FOUGHT THE MASKED MAN, I'VE GOT TO FIND THEM!
I HAVE TO QUESTION THEM ABOUT THEIR BATTLE SO I'LL KNOW HOW TO HANDLE HIM WHEN WE MEET AGAIN!
YOU DIDN'T ACQUIRE YOUR MONEY THROUGH CRIME...
YOU CAN TELL THAT?!
WELL, YOU'RE RIGHT. I WORKED REALLY HARD ABOARD THE AQUA FOR THIS.
ALL RIGHT. I'LL DO IT.
YOU WILL?

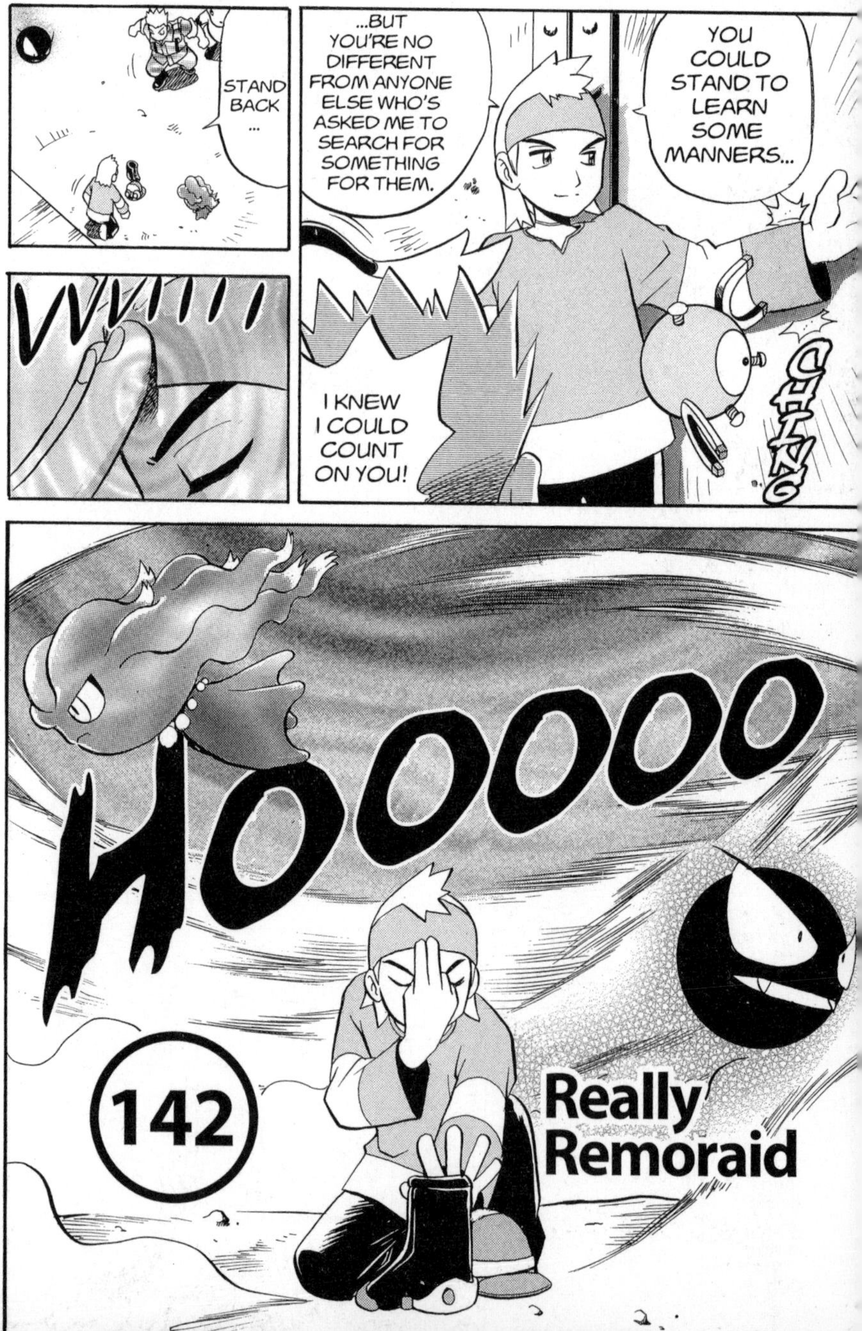
YOU COULD STAND TO LEARN SOME MANNERS...
...BUT YOU'RE NO DIFFERENT FROM ANYONE ELSE WHO'S ASKED ME TO SEARCH FOR SOMETHING FOR THEM.
I KNEW I COULD COUNT ON YOU!
CHING
STAND BACK ...
VVVIIIII
HOOOOOO
142
Really Remoraid

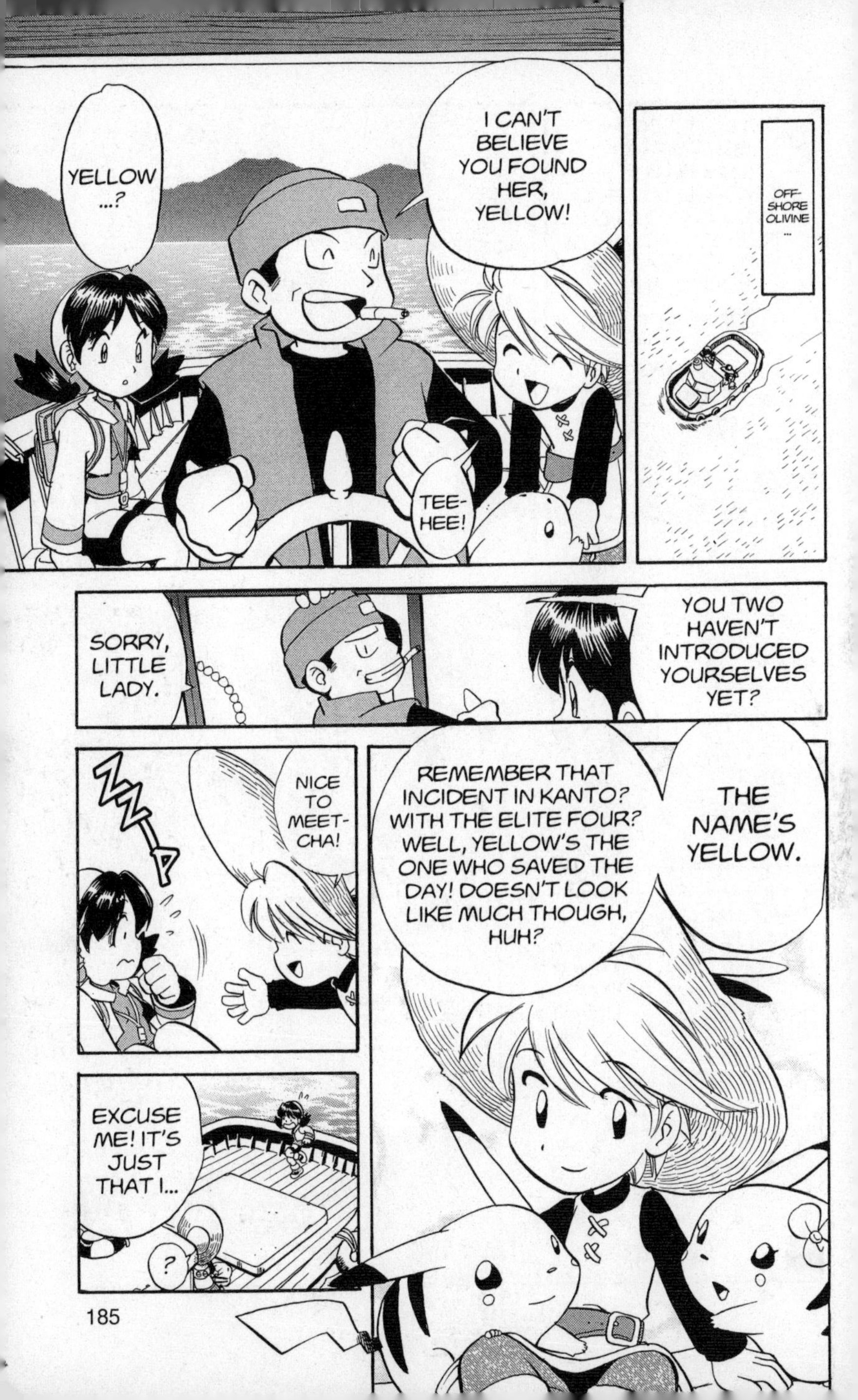
OFF-SHORE OLIVINE...
I CAN'T BELIEVE YOU FOUND HER, YELLOW!
TEE-HEE!
YELLOW...?
YOU TWO HAVEN'T INTRODUCED YOURSELVES YET?
SORRY, LITTLE LADY.
THE NAME'S YELLOW.
REMEMBER THAT INCIDENT IN KANTO? WITH THE ELITE FOUR? WELL, YELLOW'S THE ONE WHO SAVED THE DAY! DOESN'T LOOK LIKE MUCH THOUGH, HUH?
NICE TO MEET-CHA!
ZZAP
EXCUSE ME! IT'S JUST THAT I...
?

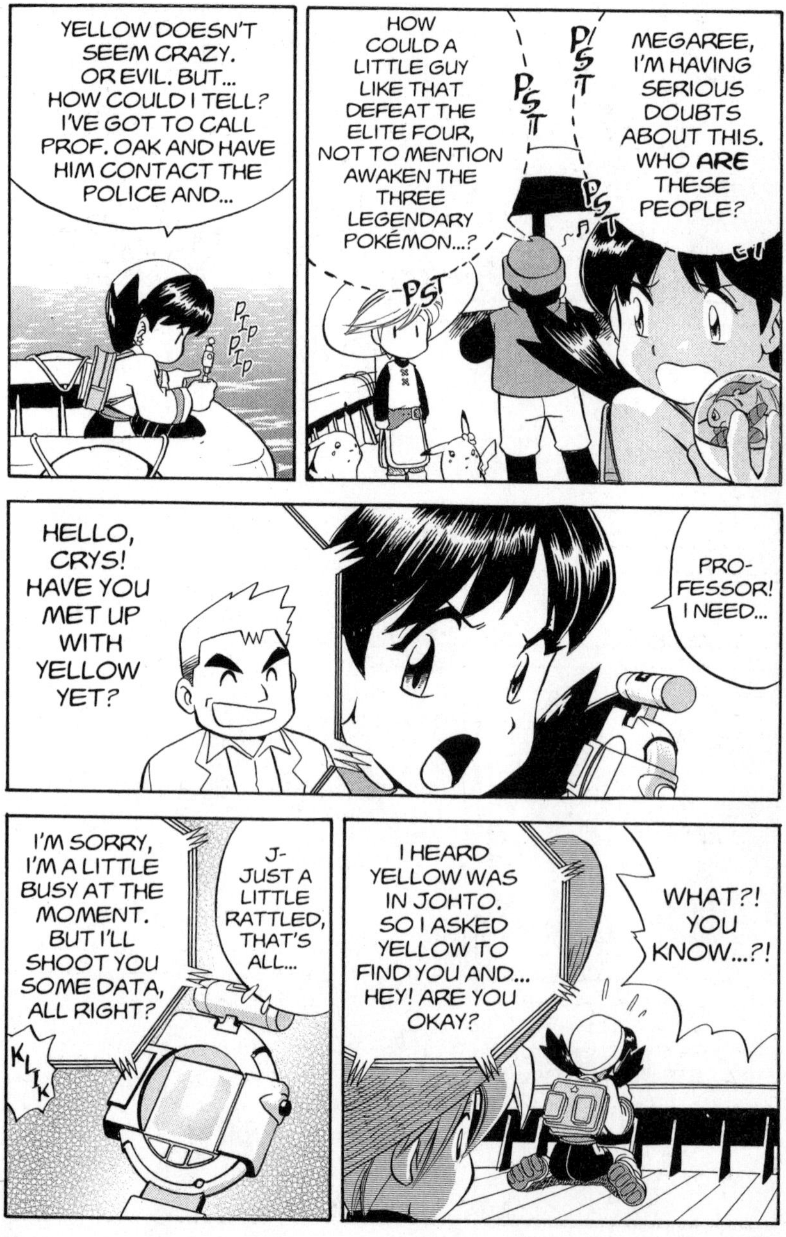
MEGAREE, I'M HAVING SERIOUS DOUBTS ABOUT THIS. WHO **ARE** THESE PEOPLE?
PST PST PST PST
HOW COULD A LITTLE GUY LIKE THAT DEFEAT THE ELITE FOUR, NOT TO MENTION AWAKEN THE THREE LEGENDARY POKÉMON...?
YELLOW DOESN'T SEEM CRAZY. OR EVIL. BUT... HOW COULD I TELL? I'VE GOT TO CALL PROF. OAK AND HAVE HIM CONTACT THE POLICE AND...
PIP PIP PIP
PRO-FESSOR! I NEED...
HELLO, CRYS! HAVE YOU MET UP WITH YELLOW YET?
WHAT?! YOU KNOW...?!
I HEARD YELLOW WAS IN JOHTO. SO I ASKED YELLOW TO FIND YOU AND... HEY! ARE YOU OKAY?
J- JUST A LITTLE RATTLED, THAT'S ALL...
I'M SORRY, I'M A LITTLE BUSY AT THE MOMENT. BUT I'LL SHOOT YOU SOME DATA, ALL RIGHT?
KLIK

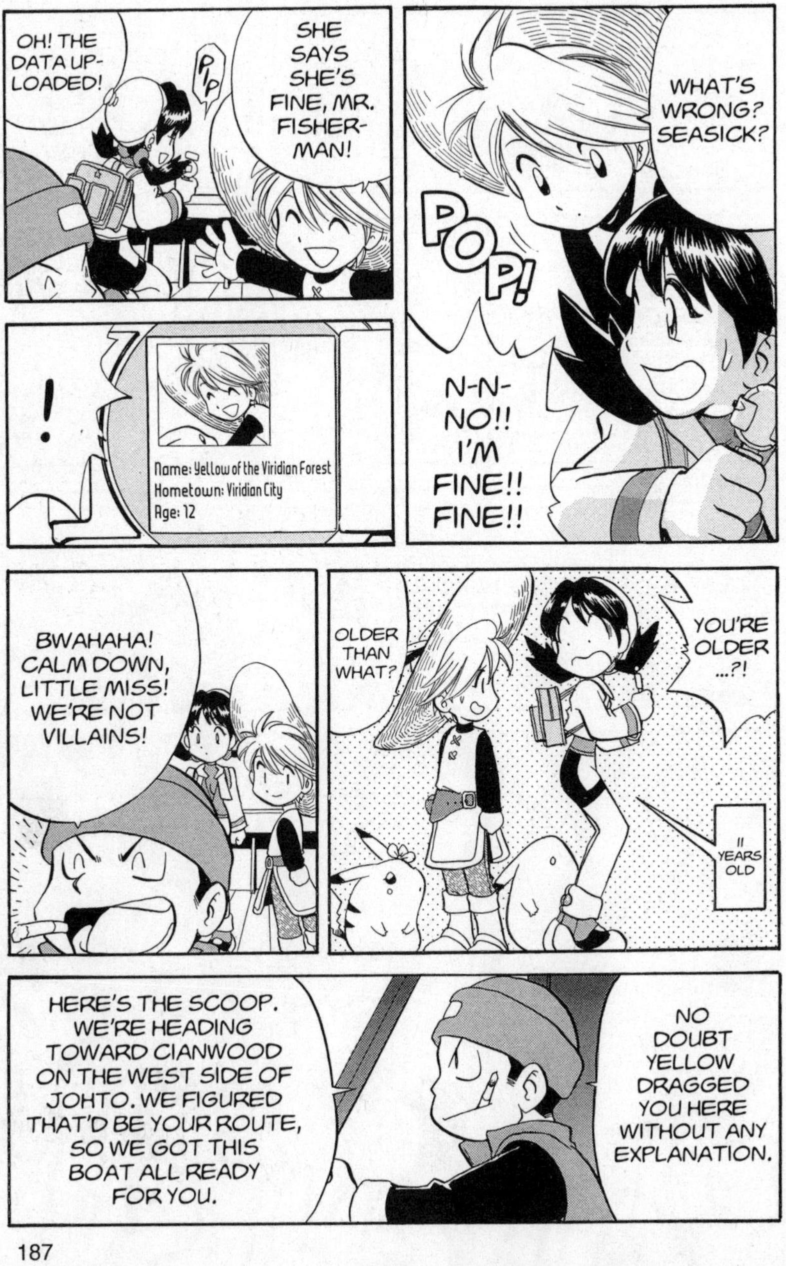
WHAT'S WRONG? SEASICK?
POP!
N-N-NO!! I'M FINE!! FINE!!
SHE SAYS SHE'S FINE, MR. FISHERMAN!
PIP
OH! THE DATA UPLOADED!
Name: Yellow of the Viridian Forest
Hometown: Viridian City
Age: 12
!
YOU'RE OLDER ...?!
11 YEARS OLD
OLDER THAN WHAT?
BWAHAHA! CALM DOWN, LITTLE MISS! WE'RE NOT VILLAINS!
NO DOUBT YELLOW DRAGGED YOU HERE WITHOUT ANY EXPLANATION.
HERE'S THE SCOOP. WE'RE HEADING TOWARD CIANWOOD ON THE WEST SIDE OF JOHTO. WE FIGURED THAT'D BE YOUR ROUTE, SO WE GOT THIS BOAT ALL READY FOR YOU.

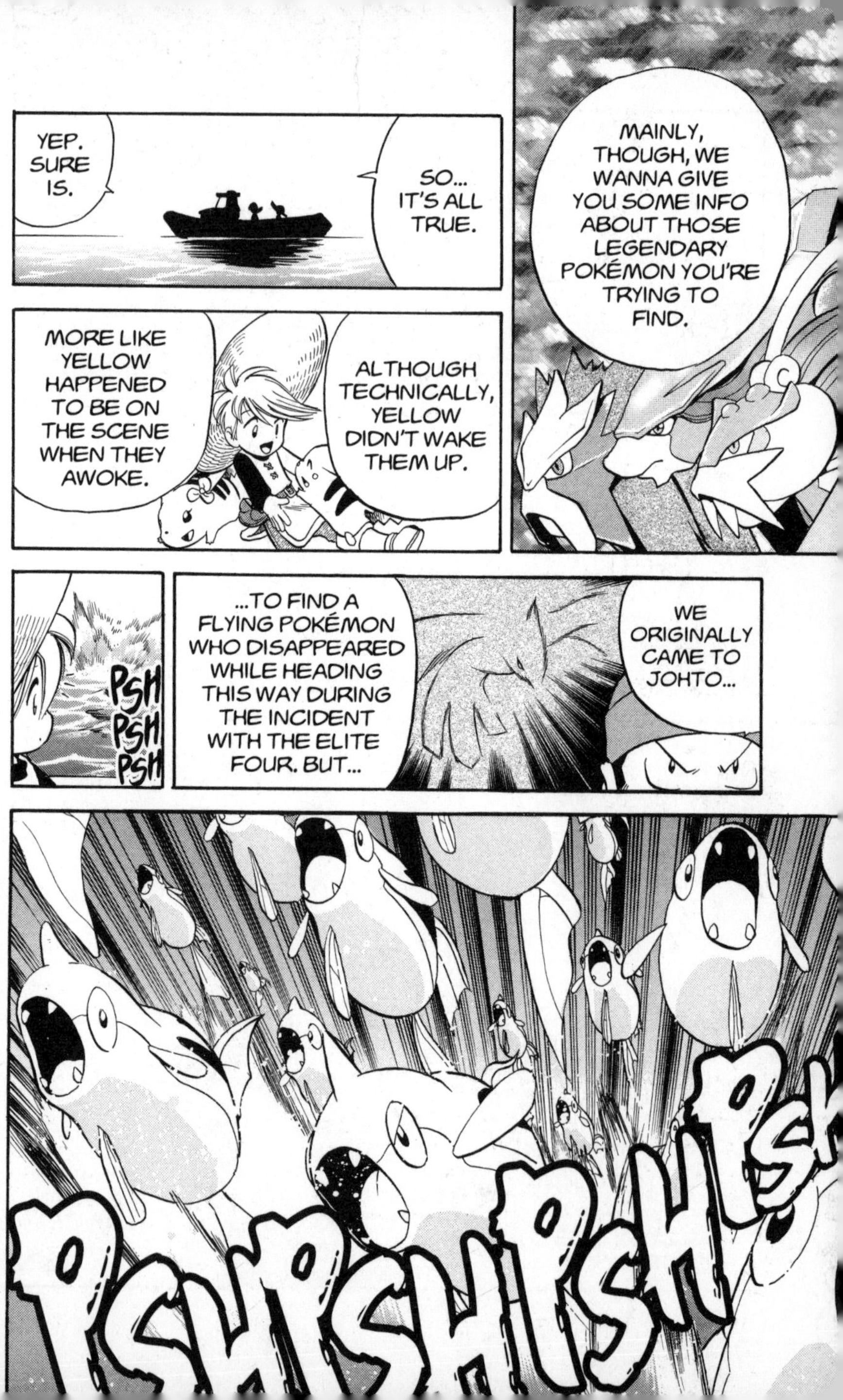
MAINLY, THOUGH, WE WANNA GIVE YOU SOME INFO ABOUT THOSE LEGENDARY POKÉMON YOU'RE TRYING TO FIND.
SO... IT'S ALL TRUE.
YEP. SURE IS.
ALTHOUGH TECHNICALLY, YELLOW DIDN'T WAKE THEM UP.
MORE LIKE YELLOW HAPPENED TO BE ON THE SCENE WHEN THEY AWOKE.
WE ORIGINALLY CAME TO JOHTO...
...TO FIND A FLYING POKÉMON WHO DISAPPEARED WHILE HEADING THIS WAY DURING THE INCIDENT WITH THE ELITE FOUR. BUT...
PSH PSH PSH
PSHPSHPSHPSH

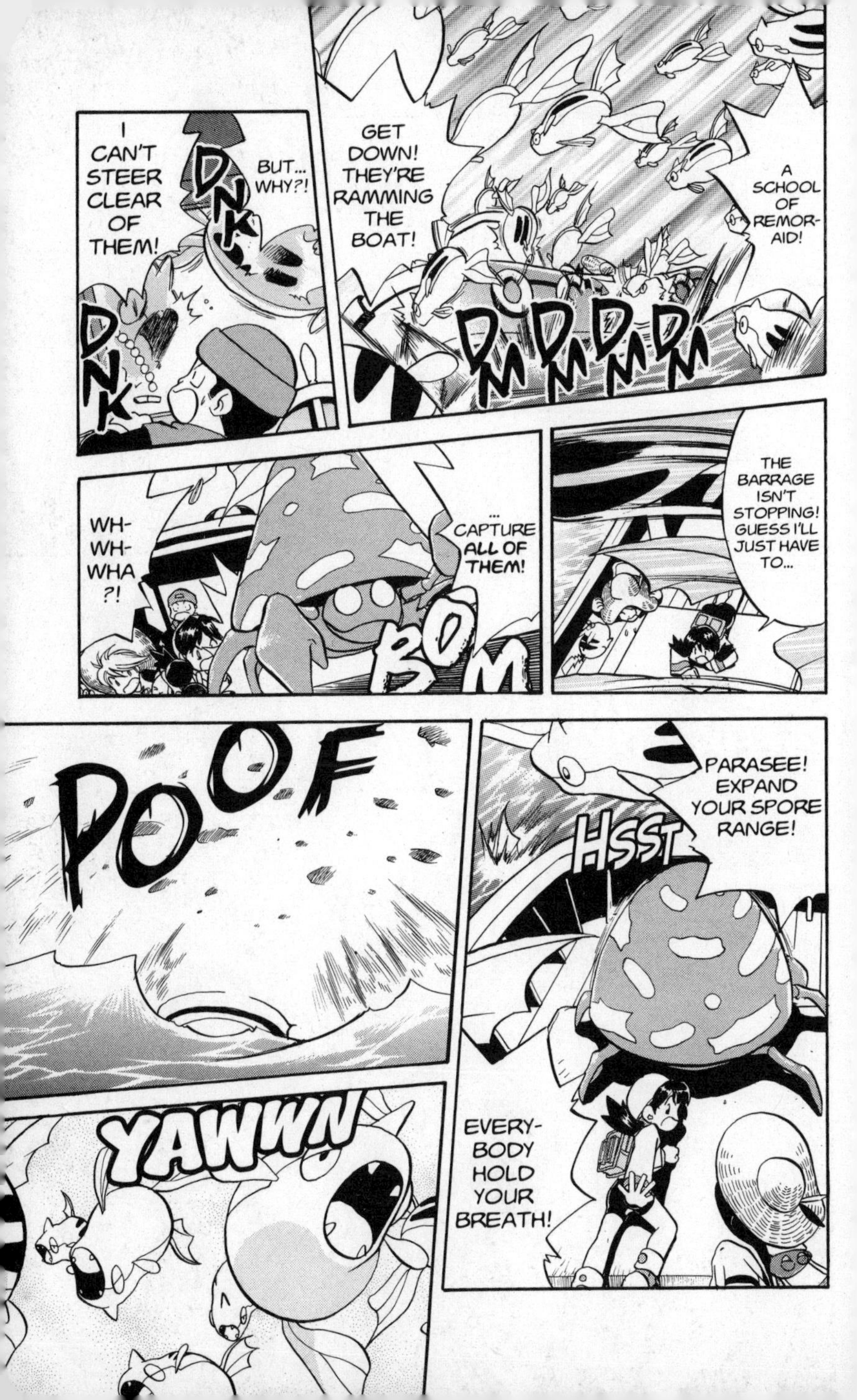
A SCHOOL OF REMOR-AID!
GET DOWN! THEY'RE RAMMING THE BOAT!
DMDMDMDM
BUT... WHY?!
I CAN'T STEER CLEAR OF THEM!
DNK
DNK
THE BARRAGE ISN'T STOPPING! GUESS I'LL JUST HAVE TO...
... CAPTURE ALL OF THEM!
WH-WH-WHA?!
BOOM
PARASEE! EXPAND YOUR SPORE RANGE!
HSST
EVERY-BODY HOLD YOUR BREATH!
POOF
YAWWN

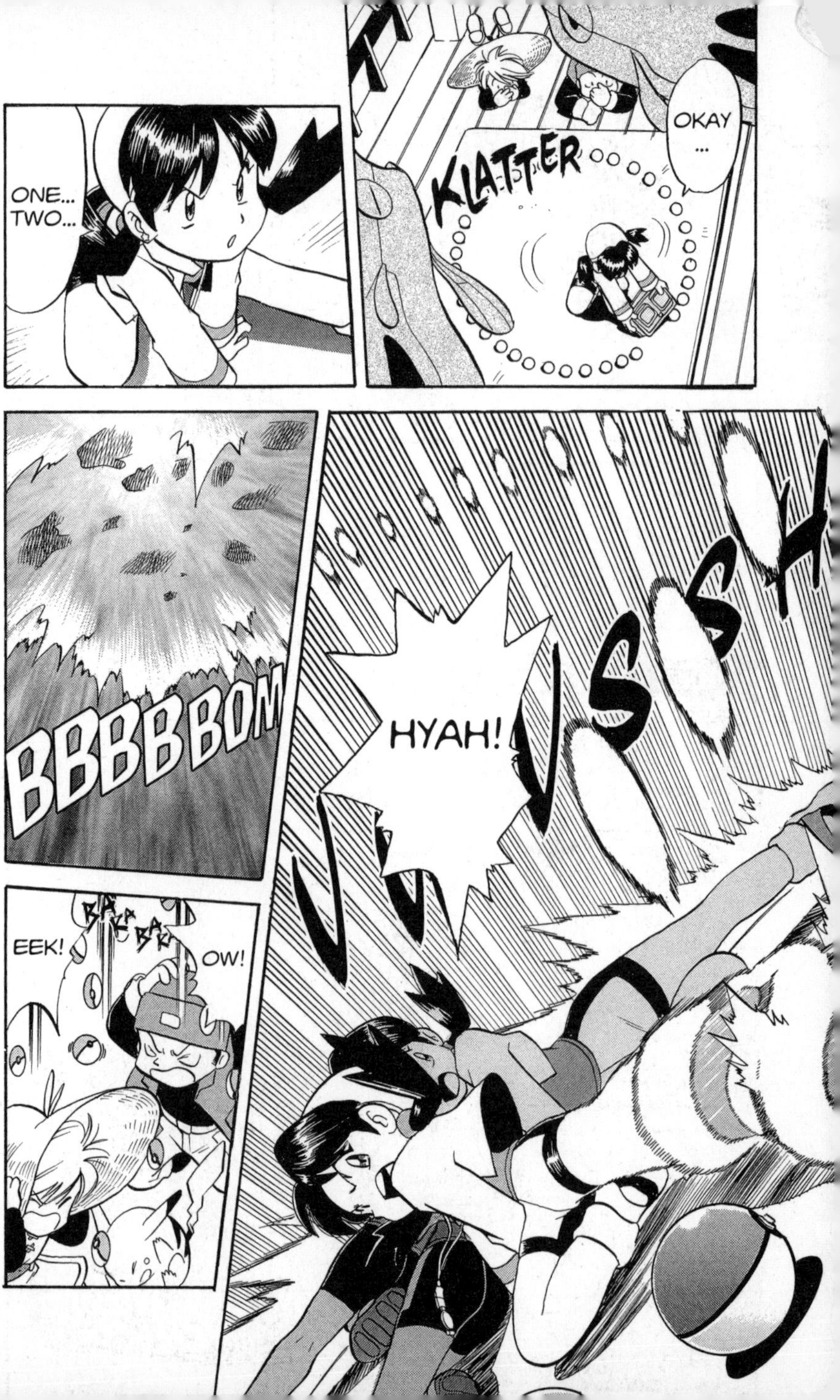
OKAY ...
KLATTER
ONE... TWO...
HYAH!
BBBBBOM
EEK!
OW!

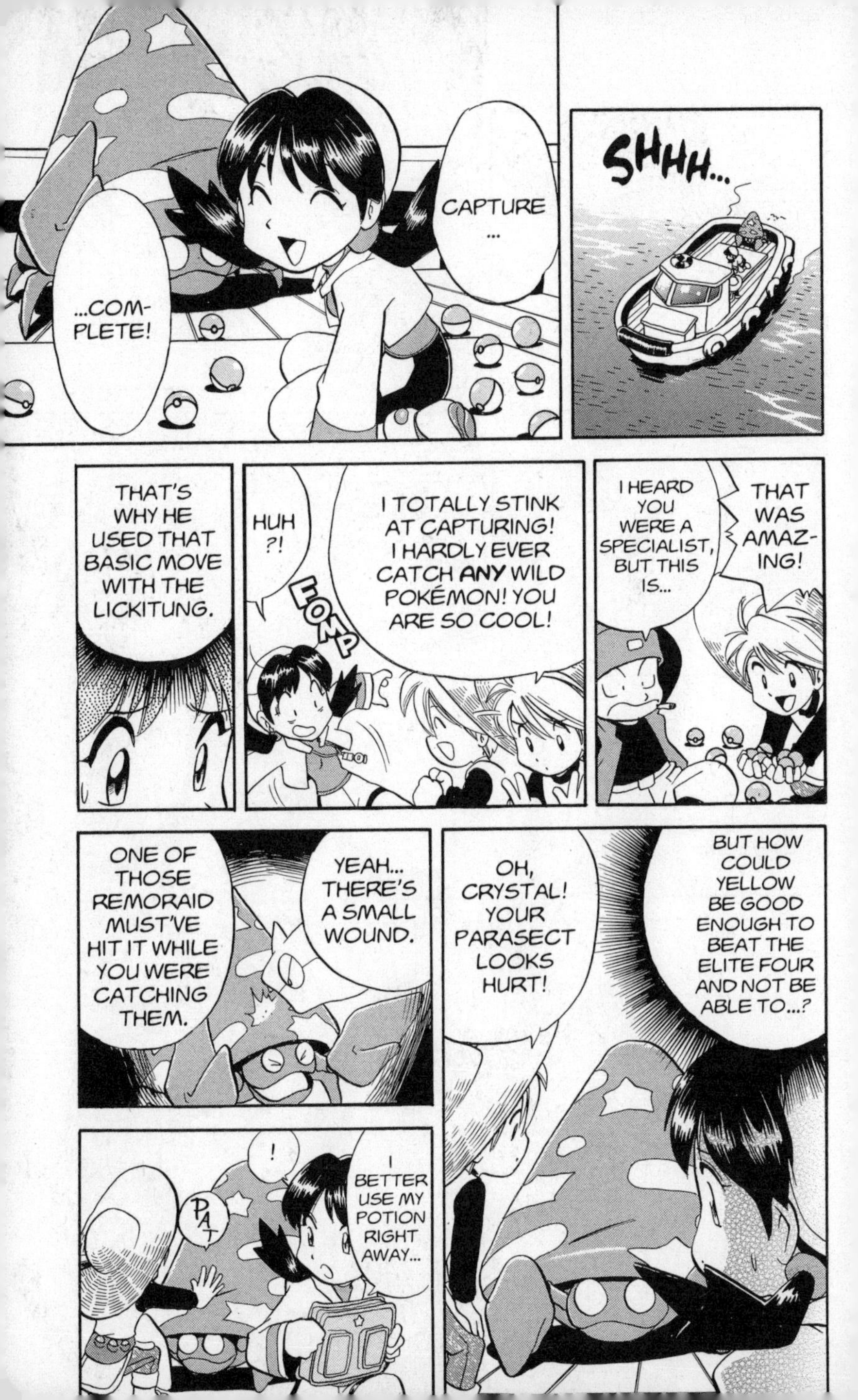
SHHH...
CAPTURE ...
...COMPLETE!
THAT WAS AMAZ-ING!
I HEARD YOU WERE A SPECIALIST, BUT THIS IS...
I TOTALLY STINK AT CAPTURING! I HARDLY EVER CATCH ANY WILD POKÉMON! YOU ARE SO COOL!
HUH ?!
FOMP
THAT'S WHY HE USED THAT BASIC MOVE WITH THE LICKITUNG.
BUT HOW COULD YELLOW BE GOOD ENOUGH TO BEAT THE ELITE FOUR AND NOT BE ABLE TO...?
OH, CRYSTAL! YOUR PARASECT LOOKS HURT!
YEAH... THERE'S A SMALL WOUND.
ONE OF THOSE REMORAID MUST'VE HIT IT WHILE YOU WERE CATCHING THEM.
I BETTER USE MY POTION RIGHT AWAY...
!
PAT

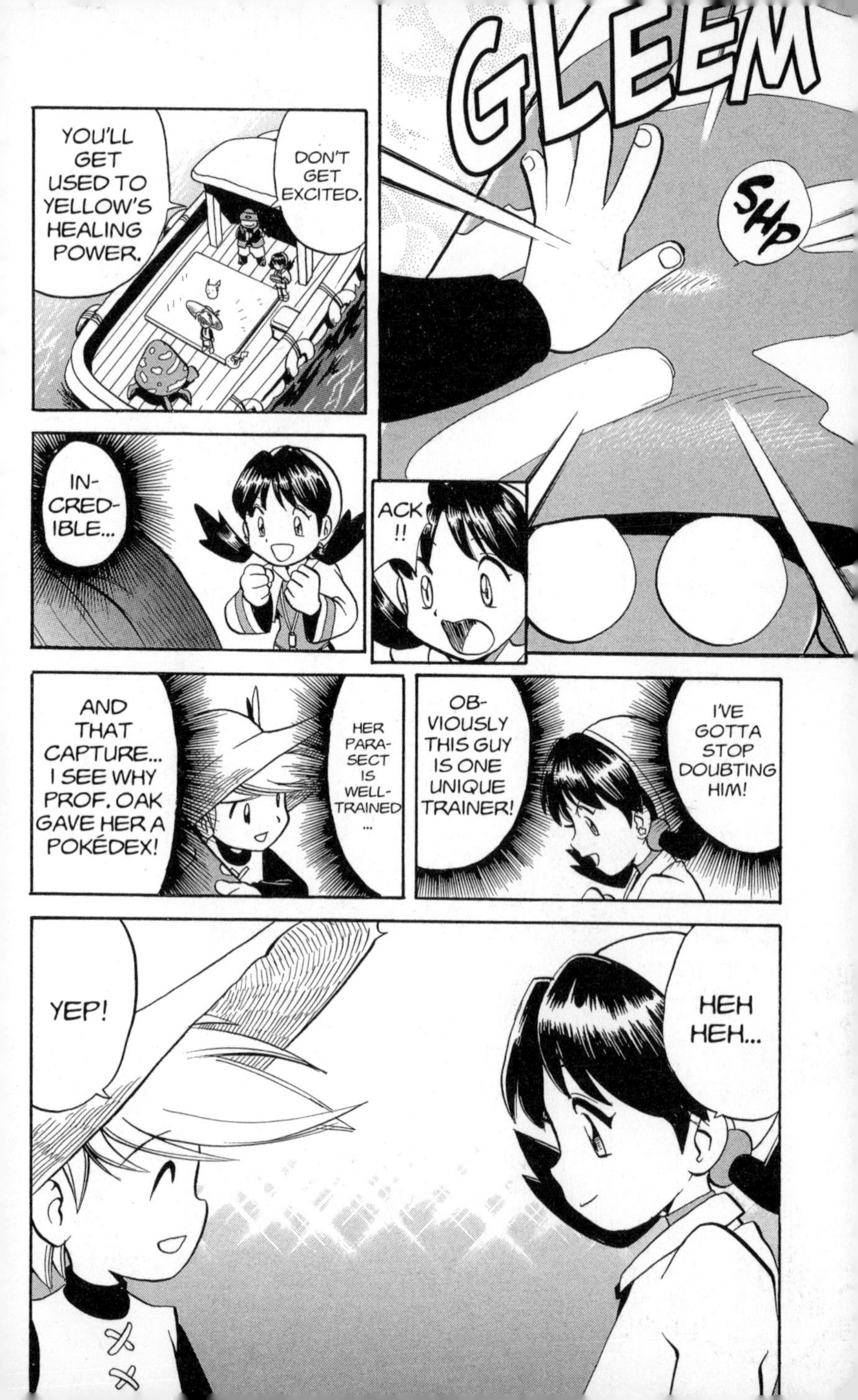
GLEEM
SHP
ACK !!
DON'T GET EXCITED.
YOU'LL GET USED TO YELLOW'S HEALING POWER.
IN-CRED-IBLE...
I'VE GOTTA STOP DOUBTING HIM!
OB-VIOUSLY THIS GUY IS ONE UNIQUE TRAINER!
HER PARA-SECT IS WELL-TRAINED...
AND THAT CAPTURE... I SEE WHY PROF. OAK GAVE HER A POKÉDEX!
HEH HEH...
YEP!

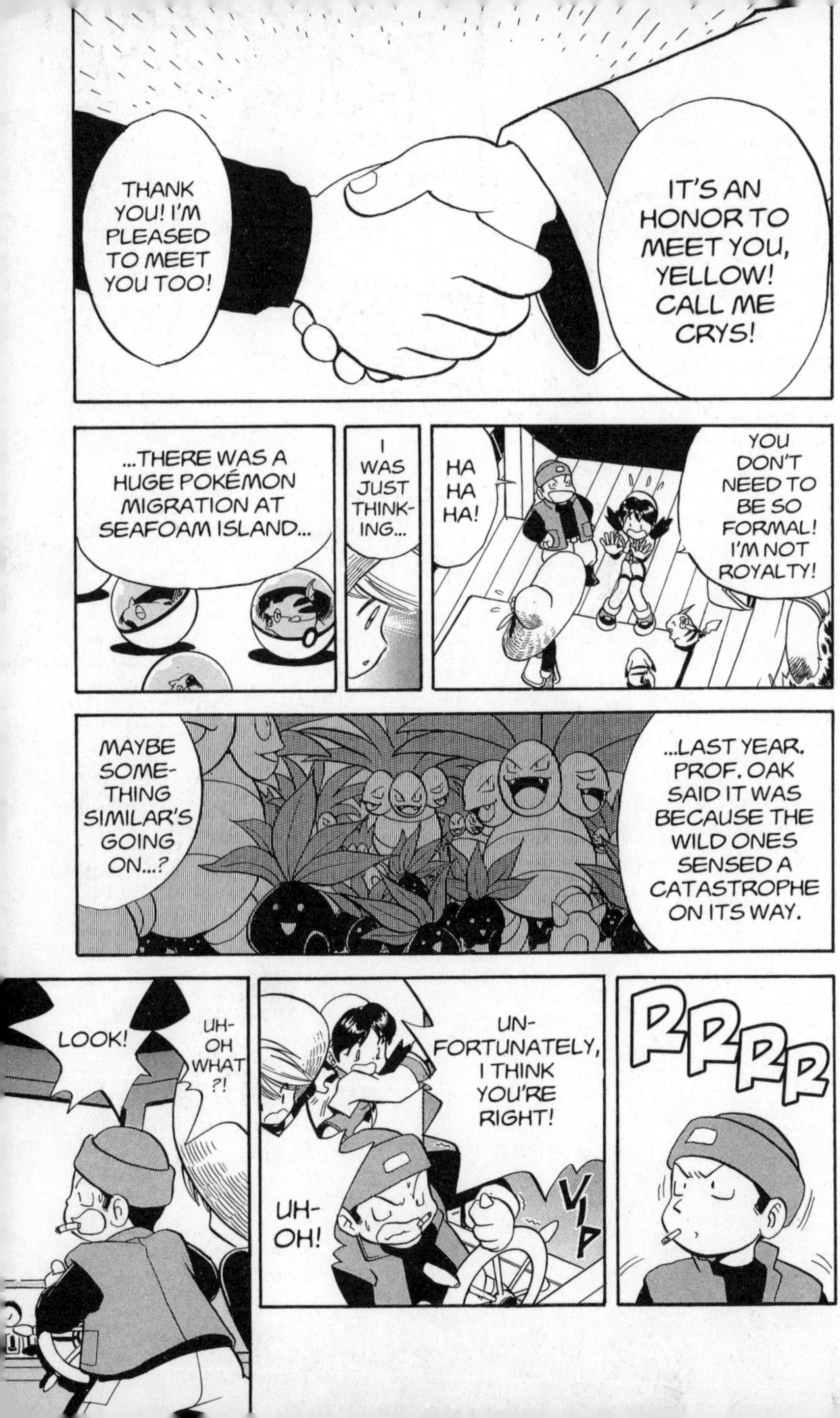
IT'S AN HONOR TO MEET YOU, YELLOW! CALL ME CRYS!
THANK YOU! I'M PLEASED TO MEET YOU TOO!
YOU DON'T NEED TO BE SO FORMAL! I'M NOT ROYALTY!
HA HA HA!
I WAS JUST THINKING...
...THERE WAS A HUGE POKÉMON MIGRATION AT SEAFOAM ISLAND...
...LAST YEAR. PROF. OAK SAID IT WAS BECAUSE THE WILD ONES SENSED A CATASTROPHE ON ITS WAY.
MAYBE SOMETHING SIMILAR'S GOING ON...?
RRRR
UN-FORTUNATELY, I THINK YOU'RE RIGHT!
VIP
UH-OH!
UH-OH WHAT?!
LOOK!

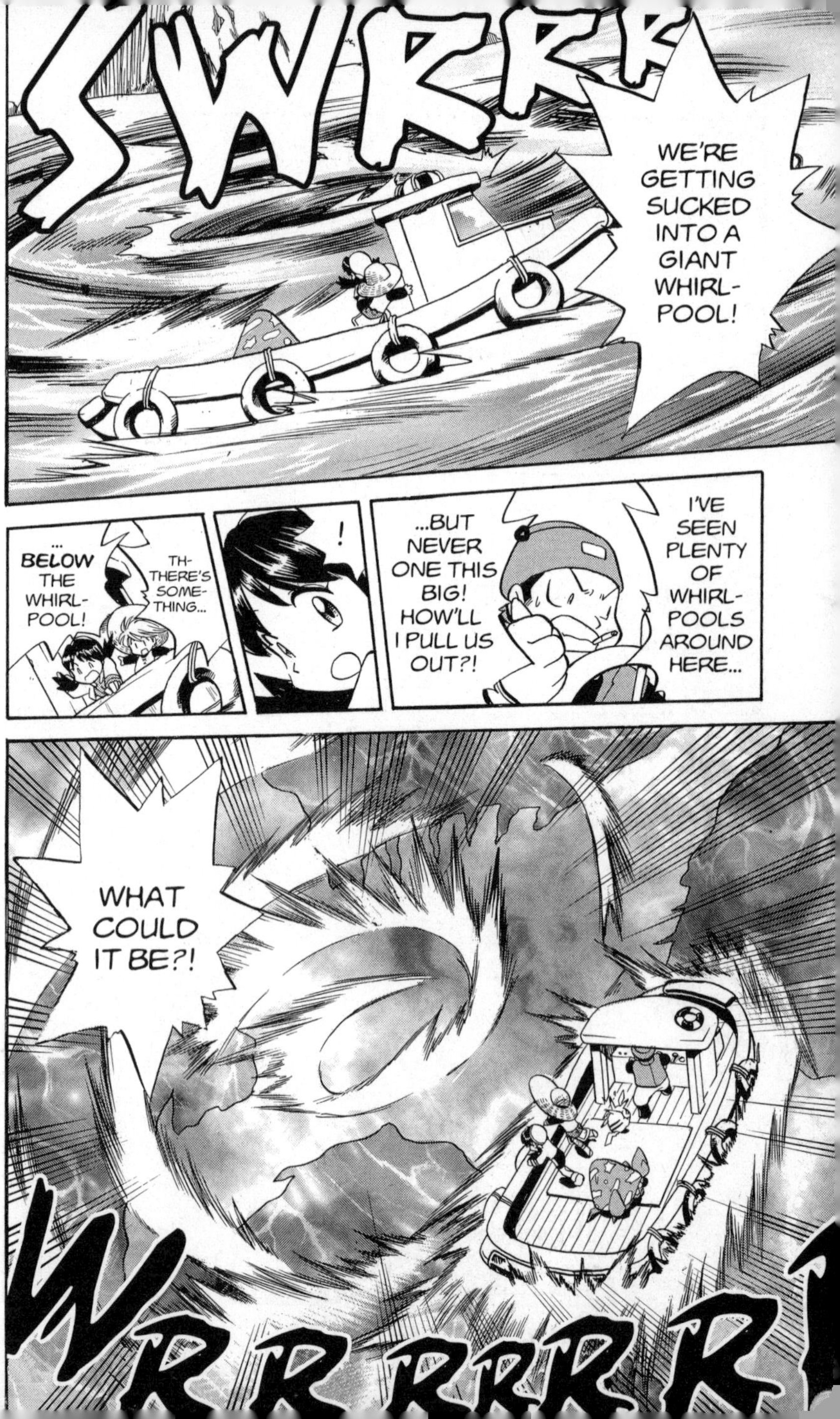
SWRRR
WE'RE GETTING SUCKED INTO A GIANT WHIRL-POOL!
I'VE SEEN PLENTY OF WHIRL-POOLS AROUND HERE...
...BUT NEVER ONE THIS BIG! HOW'LL I PULL US OUT?!
!
TH-THERE'S SOME-THING...
...BELOW THE WHIRL-POOL!
WHAT COULD IT BE?!
WRRRRRR

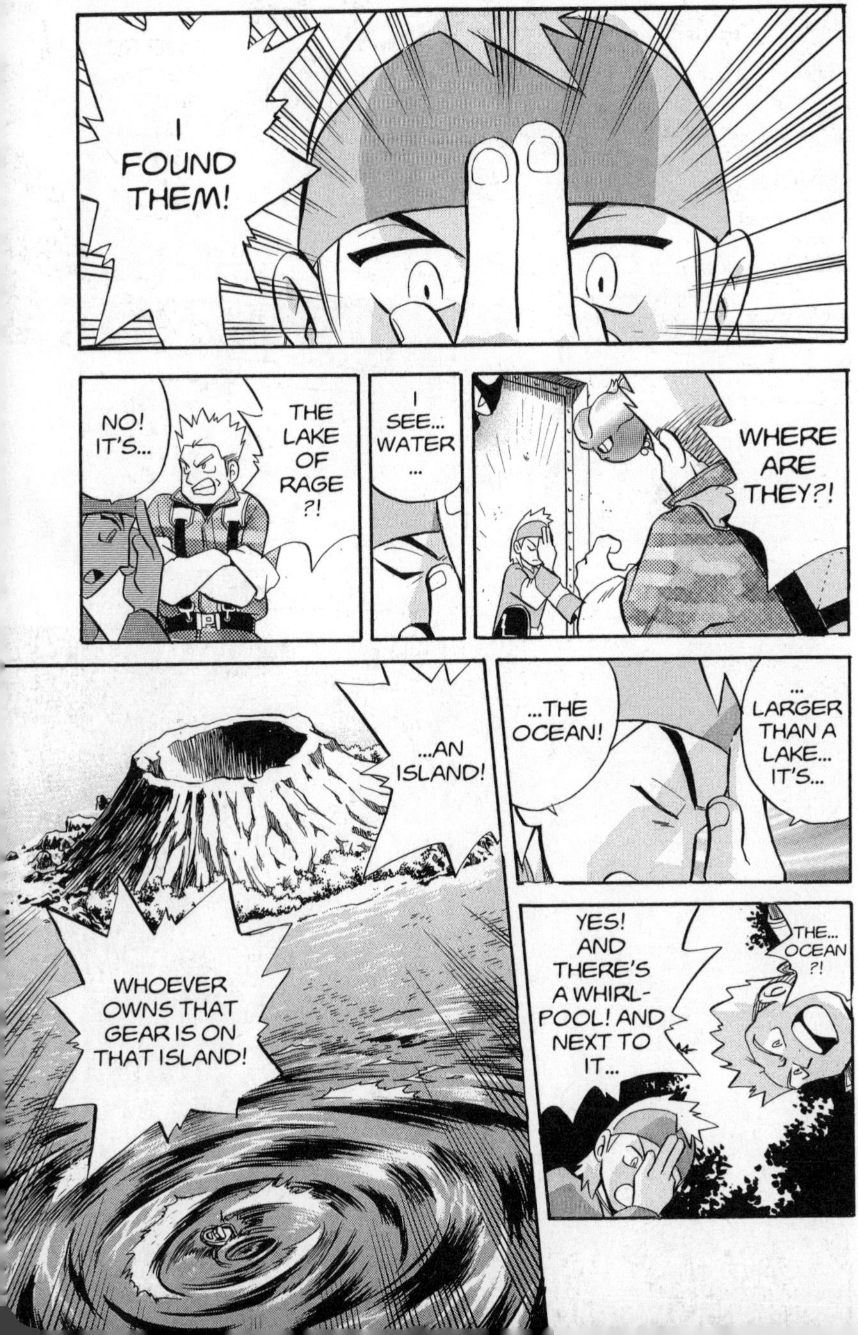
I FOUND THEM!
WHERE ARE THEY?!
I SEE... WATER ...
THE LAKE OF RAGE ?!
NO! IT'S...
... LARGER THAN A LAKE... IT'S...
...THE OCEAN!
THE... OCEAN ?!
YES! AND THERE'S A WHIRL-POOL! AND NEXT TO IT...
...AN ISLAND!
WHOEVER OWNS THAT GEAR IS ON THAT ISLAND!

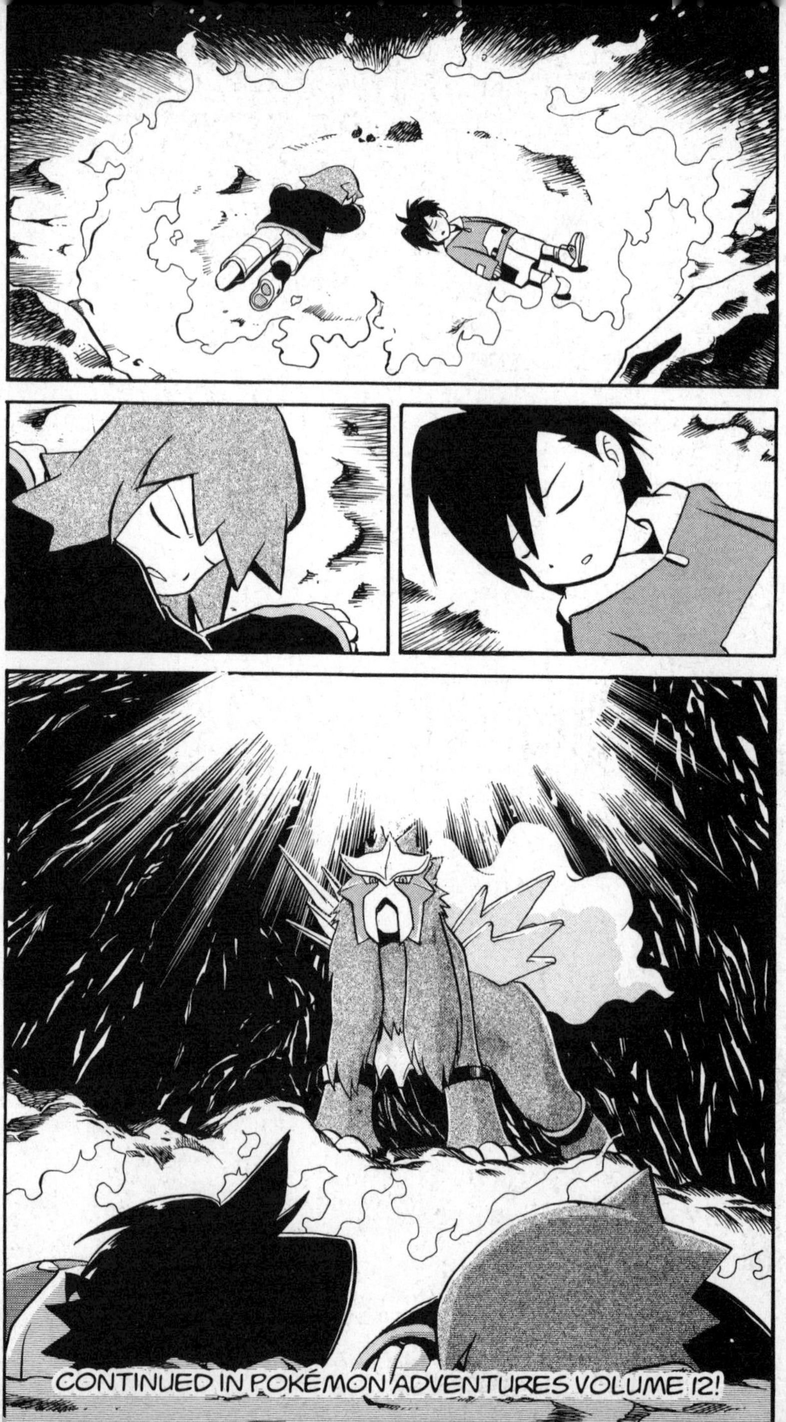
CONTINUED IN POKÉMON ADVENTURES VOLUME 12!

TO BE CONTINUED...

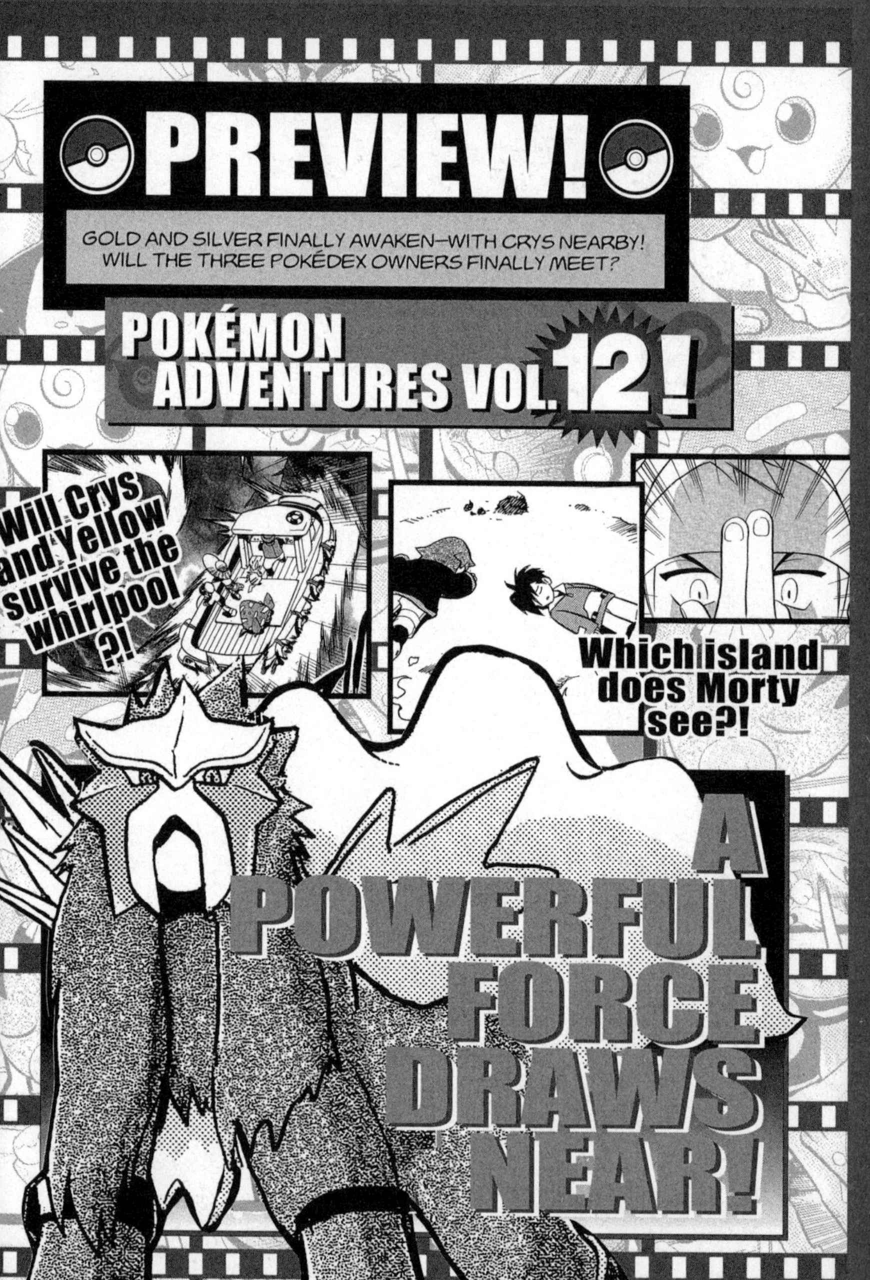
PREVIEW!
GOLD AND SILVER FINALLY AWAKEN—WITH CRYS NEARBY!
WILL THE THREE POKÉDEX OWNERS FINALLY MEET?
POKÉMON ADVENTURES VOL. 12!
Which island does Morty see?!
Will Crys and Yellow survive the whirlpool?!
A POWERFUL FORCE DRAWS NEAR!

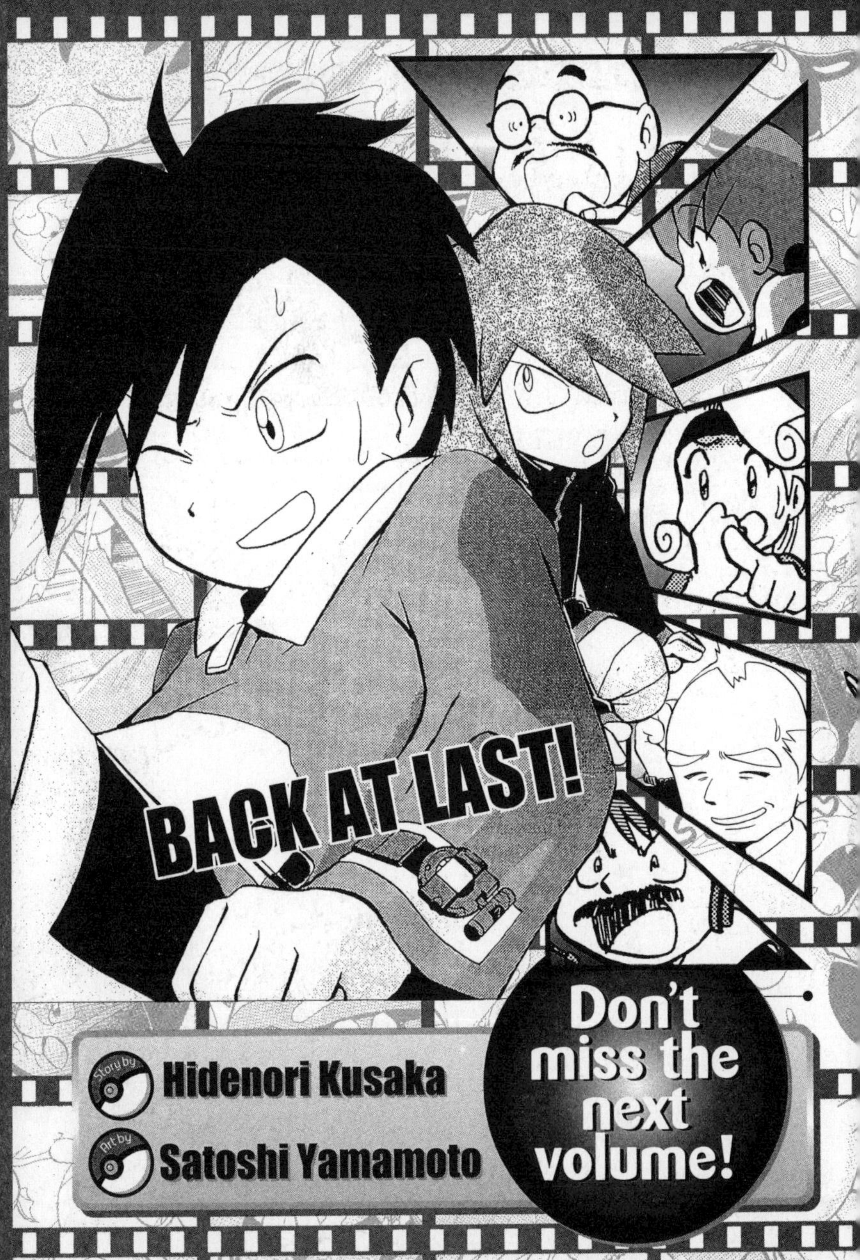
BACK AT LAST!
Don't miss the next volume!
Story by
Hidenori Kusaka
Art by
Satoshi Yamamoto

ADVENTURE ROUTE MAP 11

CRYS'S TRAVELS, INCLUDING HER CAPTURES AND PURSUIT OF SUICUNE.

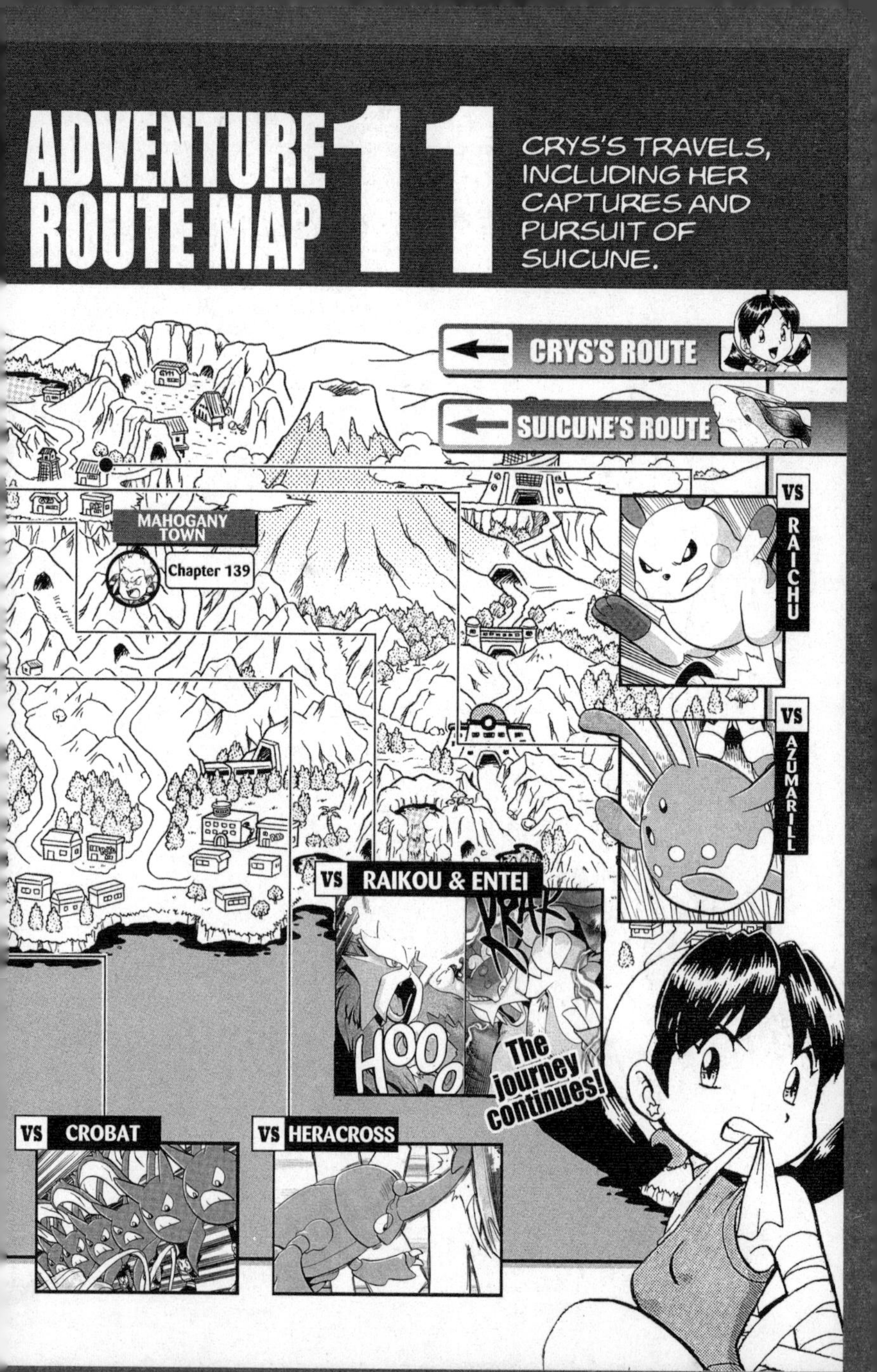

CRYS'S ROUTE
SUICUNE'S ROUTE
VS RAICHU
VS AZUMARILL
MAHOGANY TOWN
Chapter 139
VS RAIKOU & ENTEI
DRAK
HOOO
The journey continues!
VS HERACROSS
VS CROBAT

"GOTTA CATCH 'EM ALL!!"

ADVENTURE ROUTE MAP 11

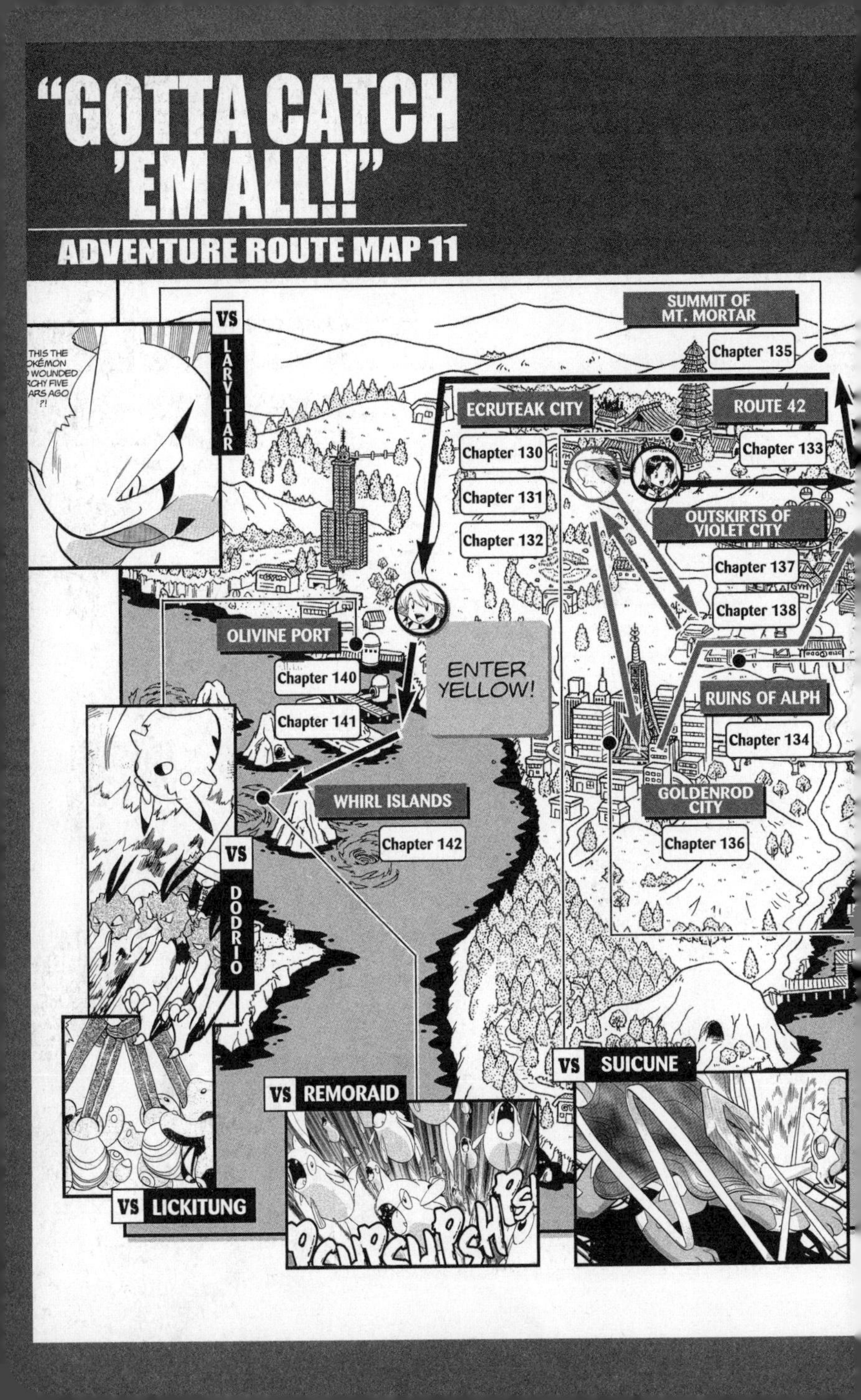

VS LARVITAR
SUMMIT OF MT. MORTAR
Chapter 135
ECRUTEAK CITY
Chapter 130
Chapter 131
Chapter 132
ROUTE 42
Chapter 133
OUTSKIRTS OF VIOLET CITY
Chapter 137
Chapter 138
OLIVINE PORT
Chapter 140
Chapter 141
ENTER YELLOW!
RUINS OF ALPH
Chapter 134
WHIRL ISLANDS
Chapter 142
GOLDENROD CITY
Chapter 136
VS DODRIO
VS SUICUNE
VS REMORAID
VS LICKITUNG

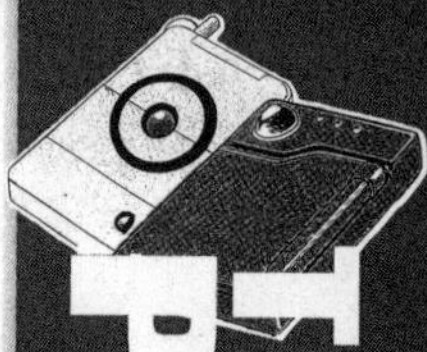

The Pokédex!

POKÉDEX PERFECT DATA

A HI-TECH DEVICE CREATED BY PROF. OAK. THERE ARE TWO TYPES AND THREE OF EACH, MAKING A TOTAL OF SIX. CHECK OUT THE FEATURES AND FUNCTIONS OF EACH TYPE!

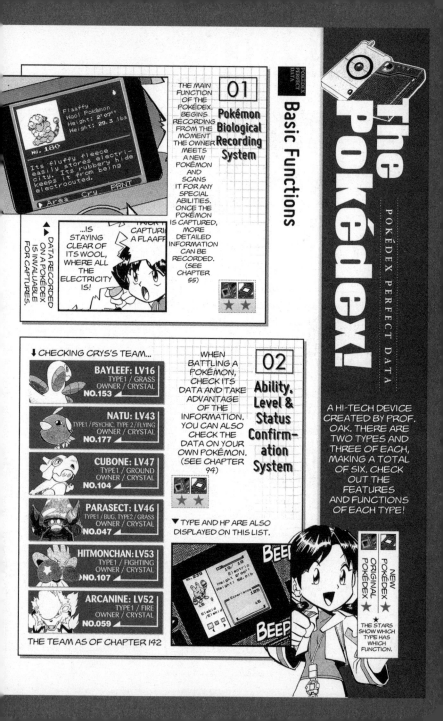

POKÉDEX PERFECT DATA

Basic Functions

01 Pokémon Biological Recording System

THE MAIN FUNCTION OF THE POKÉDEX. BEGINS RECORDING FROM THE MOMENT THE OWNER MEETS A NEW POKÉMON AND SCANS IT FOR ANY SPECIAL ABILITIES. ONCE THE POKÉMON IS CAPTURED, MORE DETAILED INFORMATION CAN BE RECORDED. (SEE CHAPTER 55)

★ ★

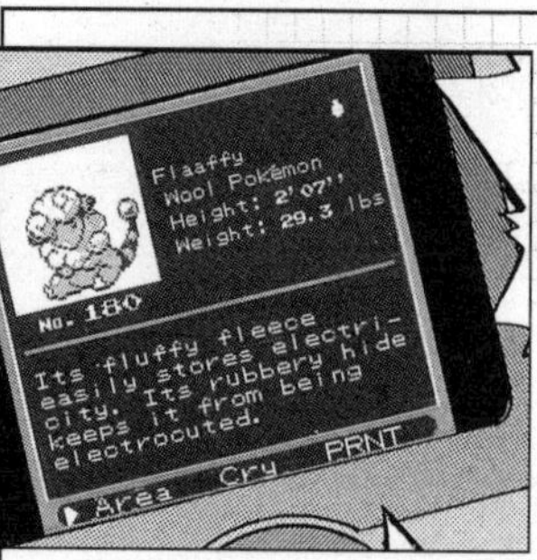

Flaaffy
Wool Pokémon
Height: 2'07''
Weight: 29.3 lbs
No. 180
Its fluffy fleece easily stores electricity. Its rubbery hide keeps it from being electrocuted.
Area
Cry
PRNT

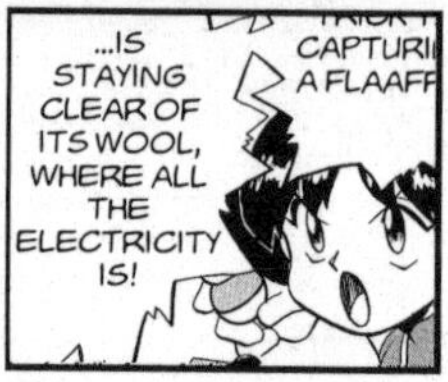

CAPTURI
A FLAAFF
...IS STAYING CLEAR OF ITS WOOL, WHERE ALL THE ELECTRICITY IS!

▲▶ DATA RECORDED ON A POKÉDEX IS INVALUABLE FOR CAPTURES.

02 Ability, Level & Status Confirmation System

WHEN BATTLING A POKÉMON, CHECK ITS DATA AND TAKE ADVANTAGE OF THE INFORMATION. YOU CAN ALSO CHECK THE DATA ON YOUR OWN POKÉMON. (SEE CHAPTER 94)

★ ★

⬇ CHECKING CRYS'S TEAM...

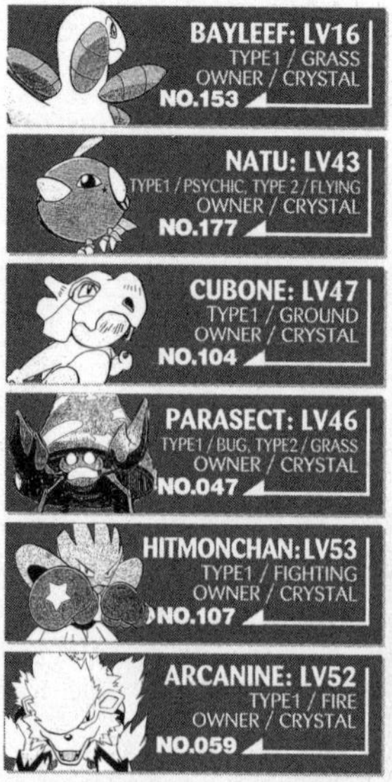

BAYLEEF: LV16
TYPE1 / GRASS
OWNER / CRYSTAL
NO.153
NATU: LV43
TYPE1 / PSYCHIC, TYPE 2 / FLYING
OWNER / CRYSTAL
NO.177
CUBONE: LV47
TYPE1 / GROUND
OWNER / CRYSTAL
NO.104
PARASECT: LV46
TYPE1 / BUG, TYPE2 / GRASS
OWNER / CRYSTAL
NO.047
HITMONCHAN: LV53
TYPE1 / FIGHTING
OWNER / CRYSTAL
NO.107
ARCANINE: LV52
TYPE1 / FIRE
OWNER / CRYSTAL
NO.059

THE TEAM AS OF CHAPTER 142

▼ TYPE AND HP ARE ALSO DISPLAYED ON THIS LIST.

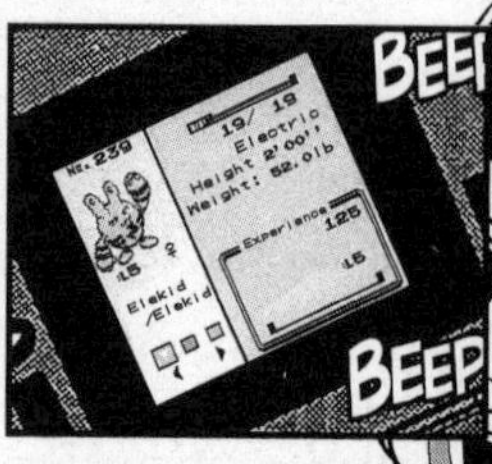

BEEP
No. 239
19/ 19
Electric
Height 2'00''
Weight: 52.0lb
Experience
125
Elekid
/Elekid
BEEP

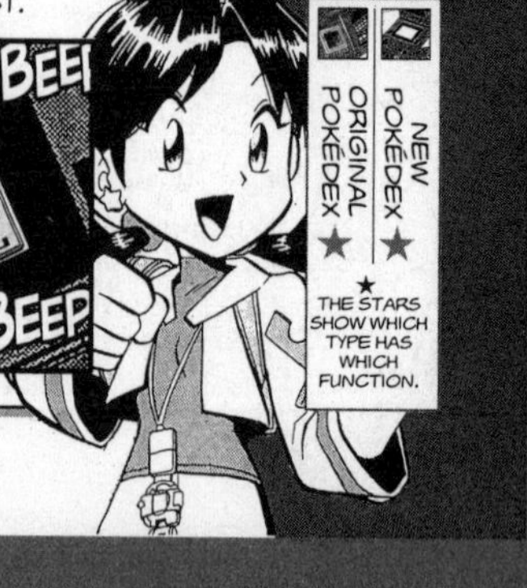

NEW POKÉDEX ★

ORIGINAL POKÉDEX ★

★ THE STARS SHOW WHICH TYPE HAS WHICH FUNCTION.

03 Homing System

ALLOWS YOU TO FIND THE POKÉMON THAT GOT AWAY. EXTREMELY HELPFUL FOR CAPTURING. (SEE CHAPTER 126).

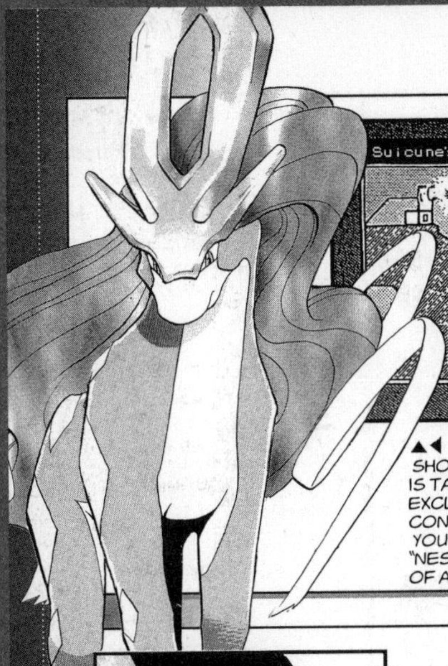

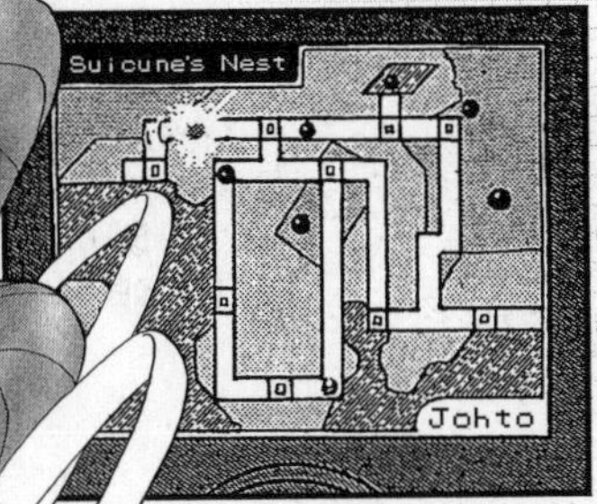
Suicune's Nest
Johto

▲◀ IT READS "NEST" BUT ACTUALLY SHOWS THE ROUTE THE POKÉMON IS TAKING WHILE ON THE MOVE. EXCLUDING POKÉMON WHO ARE CONSTANTLY MOVING (E.G. SUICUNE), YOU WOULD TRACK DOWN THE "NEST" OR DISTRIBUTION OF A POKÉMON.

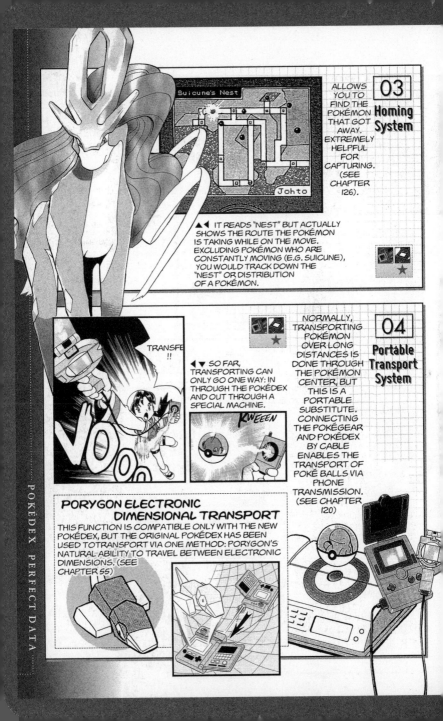

04 Portable Transport System

NORMALLY, TRANSPORTING POKÉMON OVER LONG DISTANCES IS DONE THROUGH THE POKÉMON CENTER, BUT THIS IS A PORTABLE SUBSTITUTE. CONNECTING THE POKÉGEAR AND POKÉDEX BY CABLE ENABLES THE TRANSPORT OF POKÉ BALLS VIA PHONE TRANSMISSION. (SEE CHAPTER 120)

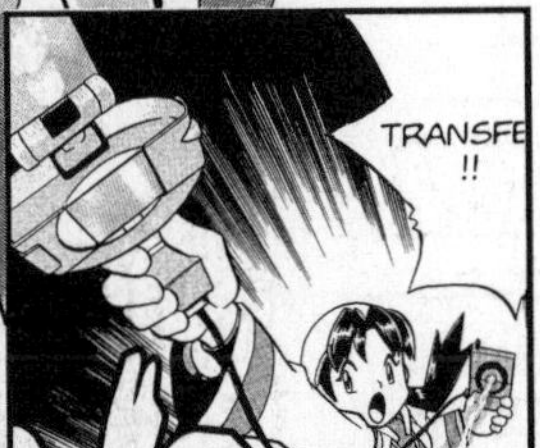
TRANSFE !!
VOOOO

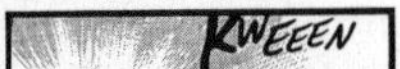
KWEEEN

◀▼ SO FAR, TRANSPORTING CAN ONLY GO ONE WAY: IN THROUGH THE POKÉDEX AND OUT THROUGH A SPECIAL MACHINE.

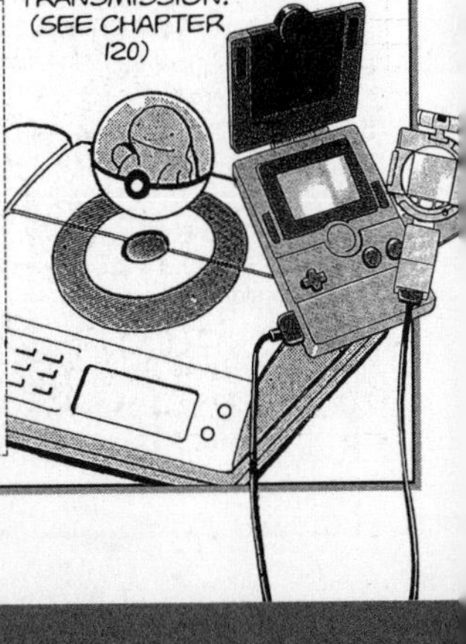

PORYGON ELECTRONIC DIMENSIONAL TRANSPORT

THIS FUNCTION IS COMPATIBLE ONLY WITH THE NEW POKÉDEX, BUT THE ORIGINAL POKÉDEX HAS BEEN USED TOTRANSPORT VIA ONE METHOD: PORYGON'S NATURAL ABILITY TO TRAVEL BETWEEN ELECTRONIC DIMENSIONS. (SEE CHAPTER 55)

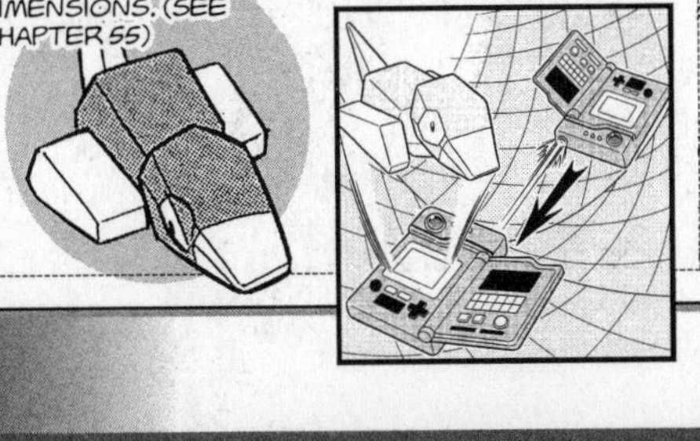

POKÉDEX PERFECT DATA

Special Features

01 Wireless Exchange System

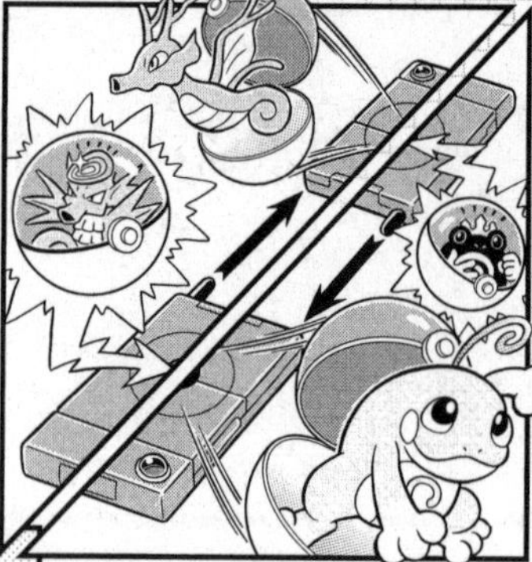

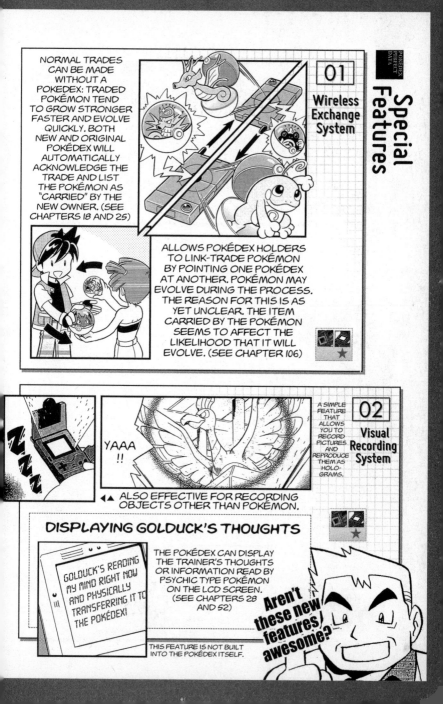

NORMAL TRADES CAN BE MADE WITHOUT A POKEDEX: TRADED POKÉMON TEND TO GROW STRONGER FASTER AND EVOLVE QUICKLY. BOTH NEW AND ORIGINAL POKÉDEX WILL AUTOMATICALLY ACKNOWLEDGE THE TRADE AND LIST THE POKÉMON AS "CARRIED" BY THE NEW OWNER. (SEE CHAPTERS 18 AND 25)

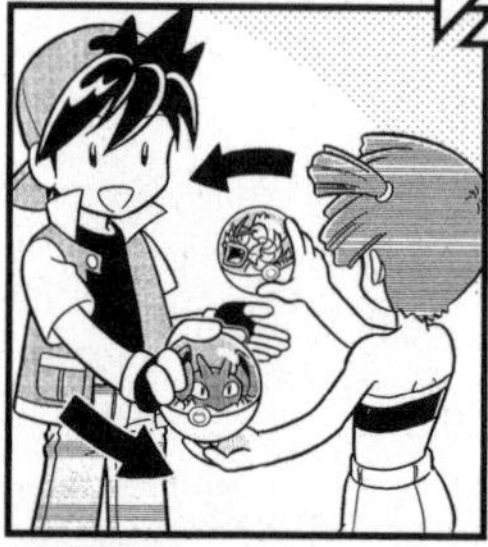

ALLOWS POKÉDEX HOLDERS TO LINK-TRADE POKÉMON BY POINTING ONE POKÉDEX AT ANOTHER. POKÉMON MAY EVOLVE DURING THE PROCESS. THE REASON FOR THIS IS AS YET UNCLEAR. THE ITEM CARRIED BY THE POKÉMON SEEMS TO AFFECT THE LIKELIHOOD THAT IT WILL EVOLVE. (SEE CHAPTER 106)

02 Visual Recording System

A SIMPLE FEATURE THAT ALLOWS YOU TO RECORD PICTURES AND REPRODUCE THEM AS HOLOGRAMS.

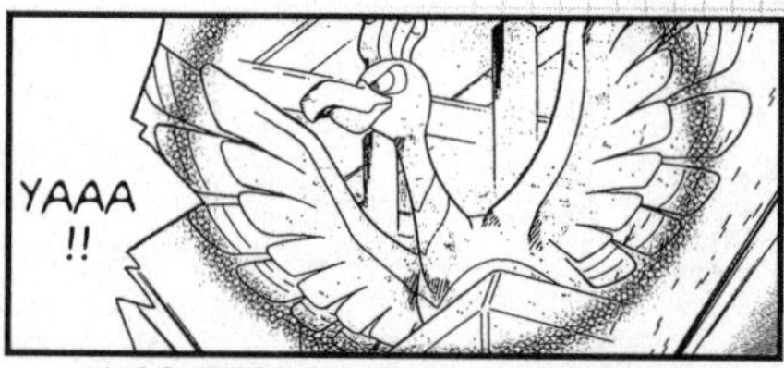
YAAA !!

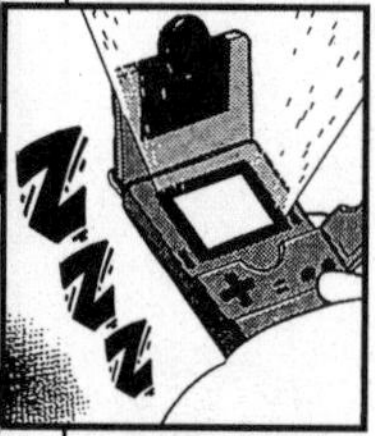
ZZZ

◀▲ ALSO EFFECTIVE FOR RECORDING OBJECTS OTHER THAN POKÉMON.

DISPLAYING GOLDUCK'S THOUGHTS

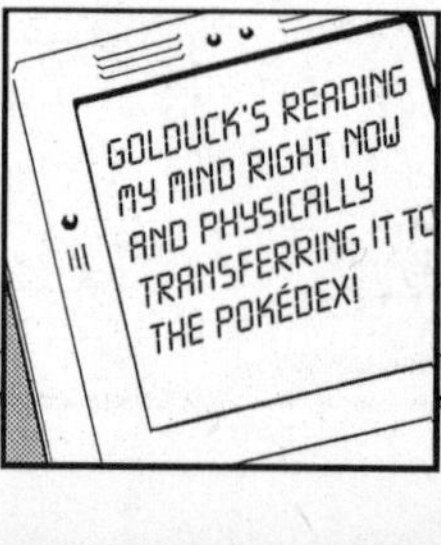
GOLDUCK'S READING MY MIND RIGHT NOW AND PHYSICALLY TRANSFERRING IT TO THE POKÉDEX!

THE POKÉDEX CAN DISPLAY THE TRAINER'S THOUGHTS OR INFORMATION READ BY PSYCHIC TYPE POKÉMON ON THE LCD SCREEN. (SEE CHAPTERS 28 AND 52)

THIS FEATURE IS NOT BUILT INTO THE POKÉDEX ITSELF.

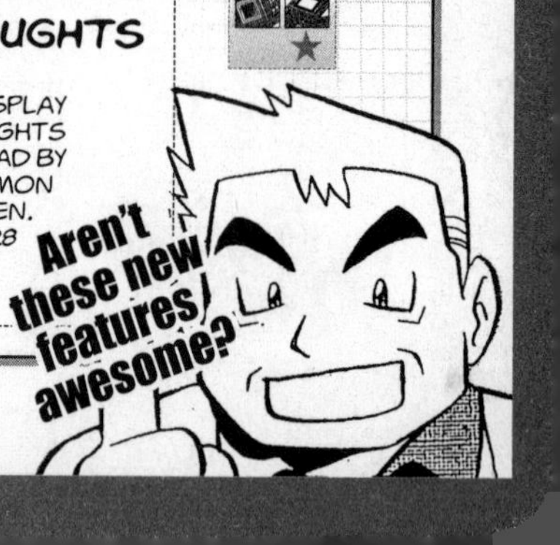
Aren't these new features awesome?

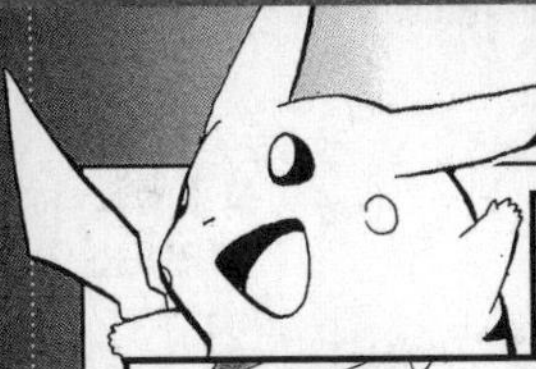

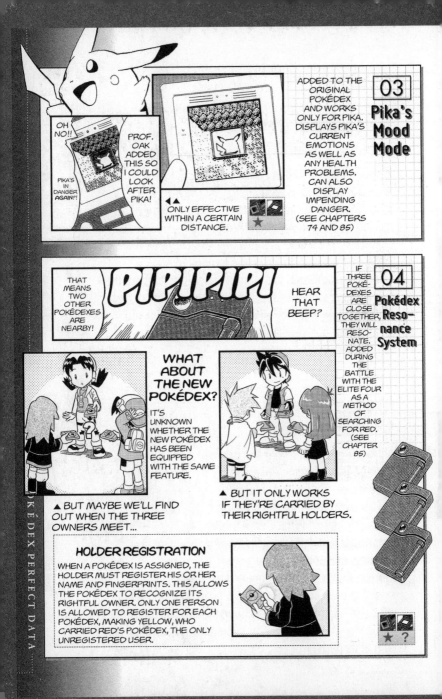

03 Pika's Mood Mode

ADDED TO THE ORIGINAL POKÉDEX AND WORKS ONLY FOR PIKA. DISPLAYS PIKA'S CURRENT EMOTIONS AS WELL AS ANY HEALTH PROBLEMS. CAN ALSO DISPLAY IMPENDING DANGER. (SEE CHAPTERS 74 AND 85)

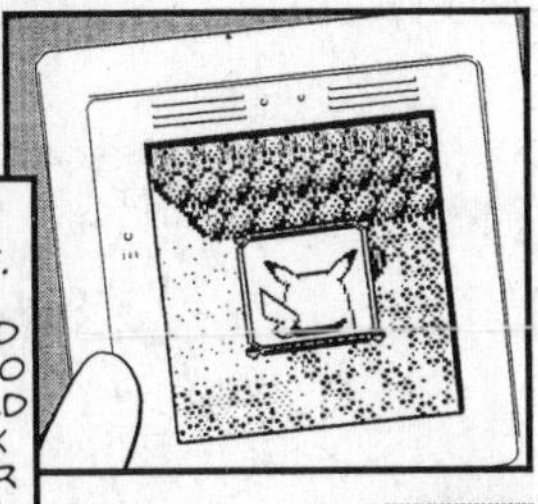

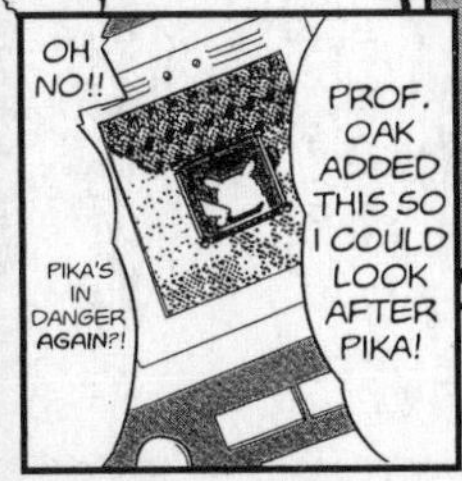
PROF. OAK ADDED THIS SO I COULD LOOK AFTER PIKA!
OH NO!!
PIKA'S IN DANGER AGAIN?!

◀▲ ONLY EFFECTIVE WITHIN A CERTAIN DISTANCE.

04 Pokédex Resonance System

IF THREE POKÉDEXES ARE CLOSE TOGETHER, THEY WILL RESONATE. ADDED DURING THE BATTLE WITH THE ELITE FOUR AS A METHOD OF SEARCHING FOR RED. (SEE CHAPTER 85)

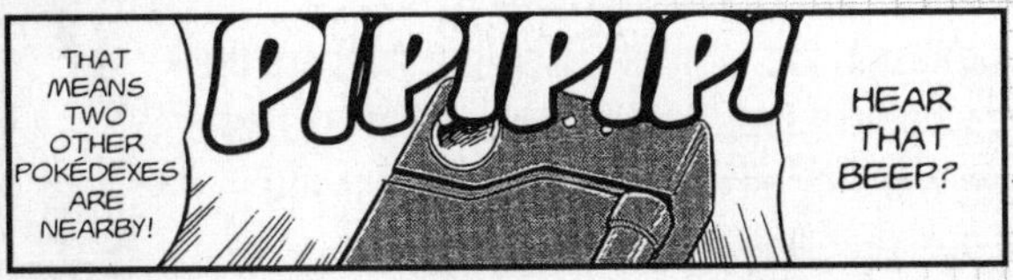
HEAR THAT BEEP?
PIPIPIPI
THAT MEANS TWO OTHER POKÉDEXES ARE NEARBY!

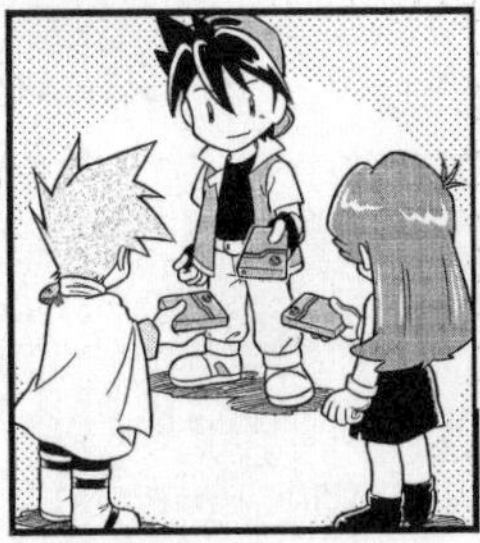

▲ BUT IT ONLY WORKS IF THEY'RE CARRIED BY THEIR RIGHTFUL HOLDERS.

WHAT ABOUT THE NEW POKÉDEX?

IT'S UNKNOWN WHETHER THE NEW POKÉDEX HAS BEEN EQUIPPED WITH THE SAME FEATURE.

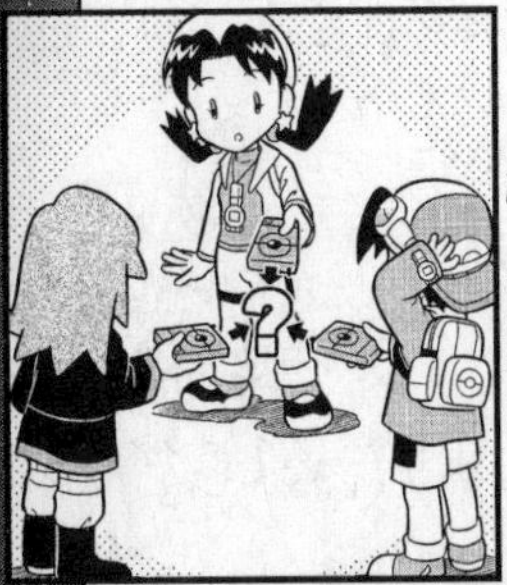

▲ BUT MAYBE WE'LL FIND OUT WHEN THE THREE OWNERS MEET...

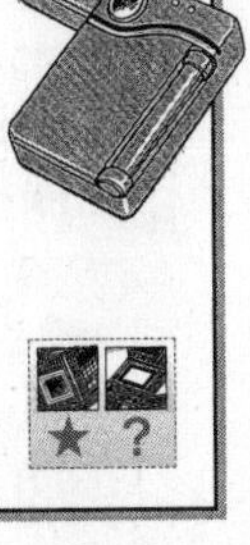

HOLDER REGISTRATION

WHEN A POKÉDEX IS ASSIGNED, THE HOLDER MUST REGISTER HIS OR HER NAME AND FINGERPRINTS. THIS ALLOWS THE POKÉDEX TO RECOGNIZE ITS RIGHTFUL OWNER. ONLY ONE PERSON IS ALLOWED TO REGISTER FOR EACH POKÉDEX, MAKING YELLOW, WHO CARRIED RED'S POKÉDEX, THE ONLY UNREGISTERED USER.

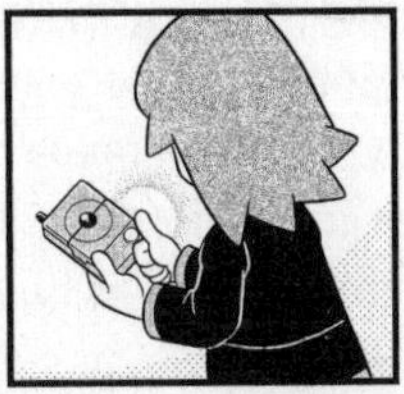

★ ?

Message from
Hidenori Kusaka

It's often been said that *Pokémon Adventures* is a unique manga: it's serialized in three magazines, has lots of story arcs, several lead characters, etc. There are as many main characters as there are Pokémon Game Boy games! In the current series, the stars are the two Trainers who first appeared in volumes 8 and 9, plus Crystal. When will they all meet each other...?! If you want to find out, read volume 11!!

Message from
Satoshi Yamamoto

Although not even a year has passed since I began drawing *Pokémon Adventures*, the second volume has already come out. Isn't that an incredible pace?! What's even more amazing is Kusaka's stories! At every meeting, the stories get more and more complex, which naturally makes me even more excited to draw them. I can't wait to find out what will happen next! I just hope that my art contributes to the story and helps create something greater than the sum of its parts!

More Adventures Coming Soon...

The three Legendary Pokémon Suicune, Raikou, and Entei are each searching for a worthy Trainer. Will they be able to find someone powerful enough to fight by their side?

Meanwhile, Crystal and Yellow have teamed up to find a mysterious flying Pokémon. Watch out for that vortex! That's right, the same one that Gold and Silver fell into...

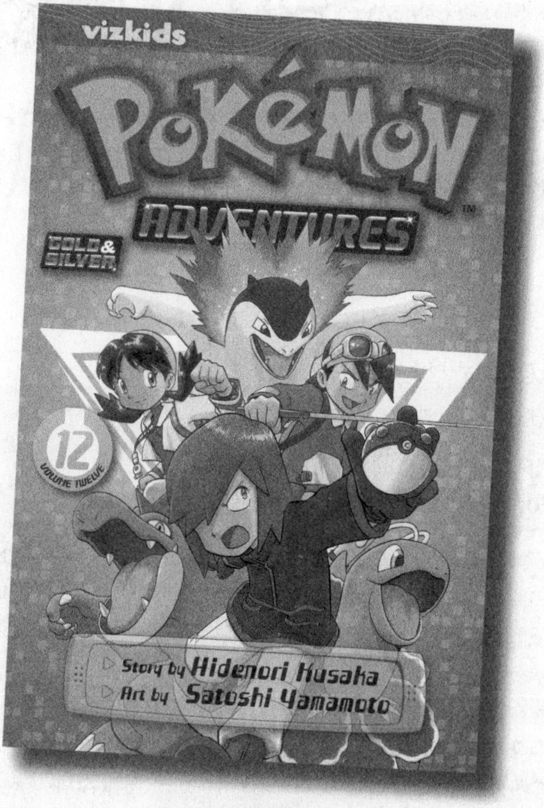
vizkids
POKÉMON
ADVENTURES
GOLD & SILVER
12
VOLUME TWELVE
Story by Hidenori Kusaka
Art by Satoshi Yamamoto

AVAILABLE NOW!

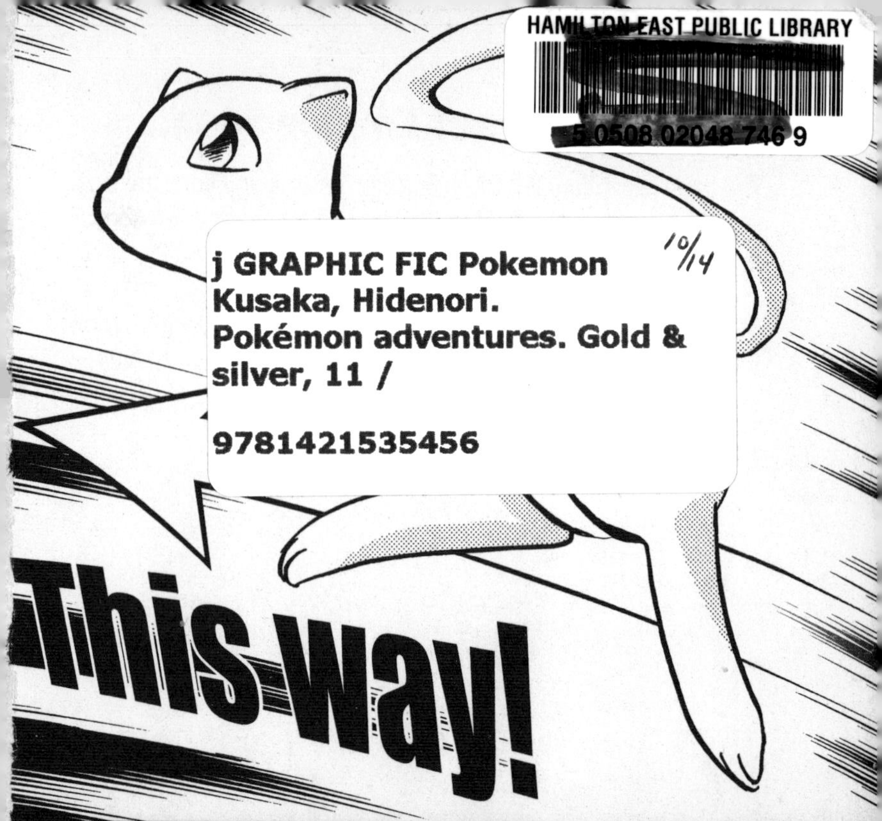
This way!

THIS IS THE END OF THIS GRAPHIC NOVEL!

To properly enjoy this VIZ Media graphic novel, please turn it around and begin reading from right to left.

This book has been printed in the original Japanese format in order to preserve the orientation of the original artwork. Have fun with it!

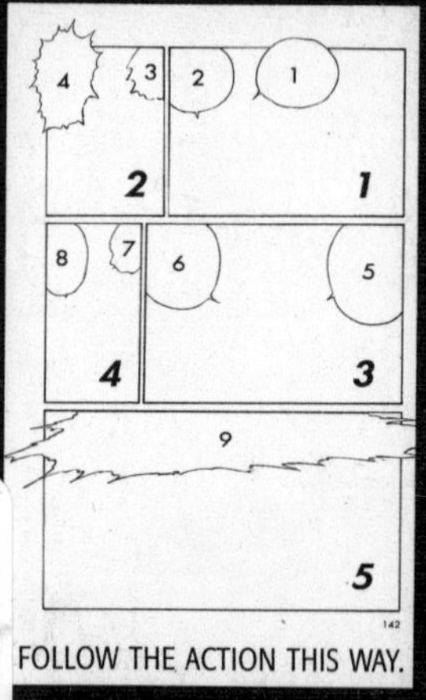
1
2
3
4
5
6
7
8
9
1
2
3
4
5
FOLLOW THE ACTION THIS WAY.